SAVE
HER
SOUL

11/2020

BOOKS BY LISA REGAN

SAVE HER SOUL

LISA REGAN

Bookouture

Published by Bookouture in 2020

An imprint of Storyfire Ltd.
Carmelite House
50 Victoria Embankment
London EC4Y 0DZ

www.bookouture.com

ISBN: 978-1-83888-232-7
eBook ISBN: 978-1-83888-231-0

For Matty and Jane
Without whom this book would never have been written

CHAPTER ONE

Rain lashed against Detective Josie Quinn's face. Strands of her black hair had escaped her ponytail and now stuck to her skin, snaking from beneath the helmet she wore. The Achilles inflatable rescue boat bobbed along in the churning floodwaters, causing a knot of nausea in her stomach. She looked behind her to see her colleague, Detective Gretchen Palmer, holding tightly to one of the ropes affixed to the sides of the boat. Her face had taken on a pale green hue.

"You okay?" Josie asked, hollering to be heard over the motor and the rush of water.

Gretchen nodded and waved a hand in the air to indicate they should keep going. Behind Gretchen sat Mitch Brownlow, a member of the Denton City Emergency Services Department. Mitch was in his sixties, grizzled but spry, and he'd been carrying out water rescues for the last forty years. He didn't spare either of them a glance as he steered the boat further into the flood zone on the east side of Denton.

A large tree branch floated on the water, flying toward them with frightening speed. Josie braced for impact, but Brownlow steered them expertly around it, his determined but calm expression never wavering.

It wasn't normally within the Denton Police Department's purview to assist in flood rescues but the city—and a large portion of the county—had been hit hard by some of the worst flooding in its history in the past few days. Denton was a small city in central Pennsylvania, nestled among several tall mountains. A majority of its residents and businesses were concentrated in the valley, near the banks of a branch of the Susquehanna River. The rest of the city's residents were spread out along the twisty mountain roads. In its entirety, Denton spanned twenty-five square miles, although most of that was mountainous wooded areas. An extremely warm winter, followed by an extended rainy season, had left the land waterlogged and soft. Then came several days of heavy rain and thunderstorms. The Susquehanna and its tributaries had swelled at an alarming rate, swallowing up most of the city proper. Many of the residents had been displaced and were now living in makeshift shelters in the city's high school auditoriums. Just when emergency crews seemed to be getting a handle on the flooding, more rain would dump from the sky, and the flood waters would devour even more areas of the city. Perhaps the only thing Denton had going for it during this disaster was the warm weather. It hadn't fallen below seventy in weeks, and May was nearly over.

Denton's police department was stretched thin trying to assist the city's emergency department. It was an all-hands-on-deck situation. The patrol officers were already working double and triple overtime to try to help the residents, protect evacuated homes, and keep people from entering flood zones. With so many houses and businesses underwater, the flooded areas were filled not just with debris but also with harmful contaminants. Josie and her colleagues on the investigative unit—Detective Gretchen Palmer, Detective Finn Mettner, and Lieutenant Noah Fraley—had also filled in wherever they were needed. With so much of the city underwater, there wasn't much crime to investigate. After the horrific flooding in 2011, Mayor Tara Charleston had spent a good deal of the city's budget on equipment for future flood response. Denton was better prepared than most flood-prone areas of Pennsylvania. A few years earlier, after the Mayor's new budget allocation had been expanded to include flood rescue training for police officers, Josie and Noah had taken a swiftwater rescue course. Mettner was already qualified. For once, Josie agreed with a decision the Mayor had made.

Gretchen had been hired long after that. She was the only one on the team who didn't have water rescue experience, but after disclosing that she did have experience whitewater rafting, Brownlow had insisted she come along. "She can help lift people into the boat, can't she?" he had said. "Besides, she'll be tethered." Someone had found her a dry suit and helmet to wear from the city's stock, and off they went.

Today they were needed to rescue an elderly woman trapped on her porch in northeast Denton. A radio squawked on Josie's shoulder. "Boat two nine two en route to Hempstead Road."

Brownlow answered, "Roger that. Boat three seven one already en route. ETA five minutes."

"Meet you there," the other man's voice chirped back.

Hempstead Road was on the fringe of the city, a block of old houses that sat at the bottom of a small hill. Two blocks to the east was Kettlewell Creek, a small fishing tributary that rarely overflowed its banks. However, that morning, Denton had received several inches of rain in only a few hours, causing flash flooding that extended all the way to the single homes along Hempstead. All but one of the residents had self-evacuated. That resident was an elderly woman by the name of Evelyn Bassett who hadn't been able to make it to safety before the flood. Her frantic call had come in moments ago to 911. A reporter flying overhead in a news helicopter had called in to report her distress as well, advising that she was on her porch, but the water was rising quickly. All the other rescue boats were out on missions elsewhere in the city, which left Brownlow, Josie, and Gretchen to come to Mrs. Bassett's rescue. Evidently, boat 292 had finished up its rescue activity elsewhere just in time to assist them.

"Look out!" Gretchen yelled. She pointed straight ahead where a large clump of debris had gathered in an eddy between two trees.

Pieces of it broke off and sailed away in the current, flashes of red, white, and blue.

"Damn signs!" Brownlow said. "Hard right!"

Josie and Gretchen pitched themselves to the right side of the boat as Brownlow steered hard around the detritus. Josie watched as they narrowly avoided a bunch of *Dutton for Mayor* signs, followed by a series of *Charleston for Mayor* signs. She breathed a sigh of relief when they were out of the way.

With a mayoral primary coming up in two weeks, Denton had been besieged with yard signs from the only two candidates: incumbent Tara Charleston, and her opponent—who was also her neighbor—Kurt Dutton of Dutton Enterprises, a commercial real estate development company. The buzz around the city was that Dutton was dangerously close to ousting Charleston, who had held the position as Mayor for nearly a decade. The issue with the yard signs in flooding was that the signs themselves were attached to galvanized nine-gauge steel stakes which, in swift current, could prove dangerous to inflatable rescue crafts and any person who found themselves in the water.

They followed the sounds of the rotors chopping the air overhead, the boat dropping precipitously as Brownlow steered them onto Hempstead Road. The green and white sign announcing the name of the street was only two feet from being overtaken by the water. More debris rushed past them—tree branches, sticks, household items, and what looked like the roof of a car.

"It's really bad down here," Gretchen said as the last few houses on Hempstead came into view. Beyond them was more rushing water. Josie knew that there had been a wooded area there before. Now only a few treetops reached up from the water, their spindly arms straining toward the gray, swollen sky overhead. Josie blinked moisture from her eyes and stared at the abyss once more. Would there be anything left when the water receded? she wondered.

The rotor wash from the news helicopter above them caused a flattening in the current of the water. Josie felt a sense of heaviness; the air was pressing down on her in the boat. She looked up to see the black helicopter looming, the letters *WYEP* stenciled in bright yellow letters on its side. She motioned with one hand for them to back off and a few seconds later, the helicopter ascended a little.

Gretchen muscled up beside Josie and pointed to their right. "There," she shouted.

The flood had overtaken the front yards and porches of the houses. The last house was a two-story prefab with tan siding, its porch roof held up by thin, square white pillars made of PVC. Several mayoral candidate signs had become stuck on one of the pillars. Evelyn Bassett's scrawny arms were wrapped tightly around another one of them. Her thin face was gray, her white hair pasted to her skull. The water rushed past her, already up to her armpits. Brownlow maneuvered the boat as close to her as he dared, but her arms were already slipping.

"She ain't gonna be able to hold on much longer," he hollered to Josie. "Get the throw bag!"

Josie's hands scrambled to find the heavy red bag on the metal floor of the boat. It was filled with fifty feet of bright yellow floating rescue rope. Quickly, Josie uncinched the bag and pulled out several feet of rope, coiling it in her non-throwing hand. As she worked, Brownlow steered the boat downstream and away from Mrs. Bassett, anticipating that she'd be swept downstream soon. Brownlow was right. Mrs. Bassett's arms tore away from the pillar, and the current rocketed her away. Josie stood, spreading her feet apart for balance, throw bag in her right hand.

"Remember," Brownlow shouted. "To and through. Don't miss."

"To and through," she mumbled to herself. Her heart thundered in her chest as she watched the water practically consume the elderly woman. With an underhanded throw, she tossed the bag toward

Mrs. Bassett, aiming past—or through—her but also directly into her path so she could grab the line as soon as it reached her. The bag landed perfectly, a few feet above her head, the bright yellow line falling across her shoulder. As the current carried her past the boat, one of her hands reached up and grabbed onto the rope. Quickly, Josie wrapped her end of the rope behind her waist.

Brownlow yelled, "Give the end to Palmer! She'll be the anchor."

Handing the end of the line to Gretchen, Josie got on her knees and leaned over the edge of the boat for stability, working to pull Mrs. Bassett toward them.

The woman's head bobbed up and then down, under the water. Gretchen hollered, "She's not going to be able to hold on."

Josie looked at Brownlow and in an instant saw that he agreed with her—the current was going too fast, and Mrs. Bassett was too weak to hold on to the line long enough for them to pull her into the boat. "Get in there, Quinn!" he told her.

Josie checked the line that tethered her to the boat via her life vest and stood, wobbling as the boat rocked beneath her. She dove into the water, paddling after Mrs. Bassett. The woman's arms flailed, the rope gone. Her head tipped back, mouth open, sucking in air.

"He—help me," Mrs. Bassett choked as Josie got within a few feet of her.

Josie swam as fast as she could, grateful to be moving downstream because she didn't have to fight the current. She extended her hand as she got closer. Mrs. Bassett reached for it, fingers closing around Josie's wrist just as a large tree branch shot past them. It knocked into Josie's shoulder and ricocheted off Mrs. Bassett's head. She slipped under the water. Josie lunged forward, fingers searching for anything she could grab onto. This woman was not going to die right in front of her. Something hard and bony brushed against Josie's fingers and she seized it. It was a shoulder, Josie realized, as her own body was slammed against Mrs. Bassett's by the current propelling them both downstream. Working by feel, Josie slipped her arms under Mrs. Bassett's armpits and leaned back, pulling her out of the water. Mrs. Bassett's back rested against Josie's chest, Josie's life jacket keeping them both afloat. She held as tightly to the woman as she could. Relief flooded through Josie when she heard her cough.

"Just relax," Josie told her. "I've got you."

Turning her head, she saw Gretchen pulling her tether back toward the boat. The news helicopter had lowered again, a man hanging out the side in a harness, his camera pointed in their direction. The air was punishing, beating down on them. Josie was vaguely aware of a new sound, a noisier boat motor coming from the opposite direction to where Brownlow had brought them in from—traveling upstream toward them. This boat was metal and much larger than Brownlow's inflatable rescue vessel. It was blue instead of the bright red rescue boats the city of Denton owned, which meant it was owned by one of the surrounding towns in the county. It fought the current, dodging the treetops as it approached. It had to be Boat 292. As it neared, drawing parallel with Brownlow's boat but closer to Josie, a life preserver on a line flew overboard, landing inches from Josie and Mrs. Bassett. Holding Mrs. Bassett with one arm, Josie used the other to hook through the center of the life preserver. A man leaned over the side of the boat and roped them in, hand over hand. Josie didn't recognize him, but he wore a Dalrymple Township Emergency Services uniform with the name 'Hayes' affixed to his left breast.

"Glad to see you," Josie told him as he took hold of Mrs. Bassett's shoulders. He pulled her upper body as Josie pushed her lower body up until she was safely in the boat. Immediately, Hayes turned away from Josie and fitted a life jacket onto Mrs. Bassett while the other man in the boat manned the motor. It squealed as it fought the current to stay in place. Once Mrs. Bassett was secure, the motor revved and the boat took off upstream, back toward the houses. Gretchen pulled Josie's tether until she was close enough to climb back inside the boat. Brownlow made another hard turn and steered his boat back upstream, drawing closer to Hayes's boat until they were side by side. Mrs. Bassett's house came back into view, then those on the rest of the street.

"Nice save," Brownlow yelled to Josie.

She was about to answer when a series of cracks shattered the air. All their heads turned, searching for the source of the sound.

"Was that thunder?" Gretchen asked.

"Don't think so," Brownlow answered.

The sound came again as a new surge of water roared toward them. With a sickening sense of dread, Josie realized the sound was caused by one of the nearby houses shifting and breaking away from its foundation.

"It's one of the houses!" she shouted.

They all watched the row of houses on Hempstead, the porches now fully submerged. More cracks and pops sounded, then Mrs. Bassett's house started to slide, listing toward the left in slow motion. One side of the house slumped. The porch roof splintered.

"It's going," Hayes yelled. He made a circular motion in the air with one of his hands, and both boats began to move away from the house as it slid completely off its foundation. Sagging, it tumbled face down into the water and floated away. It moved strangely slowly, given the force of the current. Hayes looked down at Mrs. Bassett, who was drawn in on herself, arms wrapped around her knees. Josie thought she heard him say, "Sorry about your house, ma'am."

A hysterical laugh bubbled from Mrs. Bassett's diaphragm. Josie couldn't hear it over all the noise around them, but she could tell by the woman's face and the way her shoulders shook, dwarfed by the life vest. They all stared at her, but her laughter continued unabated. Josie recognized it as the kind of strange and inappropriate laughter that erupted occasionally after someone experienced a trauma. Josie had dealt with countless victims of traumatic events. In rare instances, people got so overwhelmed, they laughed instead of breaking down in tears. Finally, Mrs. Bassett stopped. It was difficult to tell if she was crying with the rain pouring from the sky, but she wiped at her eyes. Josie couldn't hear what she said to Hayes.

The boats bobbed violently in the current, still fighting to get upstream. Everyone paused for a somber moment, watching nature's breathtaking savagery all around them.

Where the house had been was now churning brown water swirling with debris, creating a momentary whirlpool as the water rushed into the gap created by the missing house. A large chunk of concrete popped up and floated away, followed by several smaller pieces. Josie spotted what looked like a washer or dryer and pieces of pipes rising from the water and being carried away by the current. As the floodwater rushed past where the house had been and dislodged more of the house's foundation, something bright blue emerged. At first it just looked like a piece of fabric flapping in the current, held in place by something beneath the water. Then another large chunk of concrete sprang up and floated downstream, and the unseen part of the fabric bobbed to the water's surface, revealing that the fabric was part of something larger. Much larger. Human-sized.

"What the hell is that?" Brownlow yelled as the object came into relief, the pounding current cleansing it.

"A body!" Josie and Gretchen both answered loudly.

The blue fabric was a large plastic tarp, wrapped tightly around its contents which Josie estimated to be no longer than six feet and no wider than two feet. Duct tape wound round the tarp in four separate places.

Josie got up onto her knees and met Gretchen's eyes. Gretchen gave her a nod and turned to Brownlow. "Get over there!"

He raised a brow. "You crazy?"

Josie stood, bracing herself on the boat's edge. "We have to get it. It's going to come loose any second."

"What are you doing?" Hayes hollered over the radio. "Let's go!"

Brownlow spoke into his own radio, tucked safely in its water-proof pouch, "She's going after it."

"You can't! It's too dangerous. We have to go!"

Josie tugged on her tether and spoke into her own radio. "I'll grab it and Gretchen can pull me in."

"The kid is right," Brownlow told her. "It's too dangerous."

From the other boat, Hayes watched them.

Brownlow added, "You don't even know that's a body. It's just a tarp, for all you know."

"That's a body," Josie said firmly. "I'm sure of it."

"It could be anything."

Josie thought of all the human remains she'd uncovered in her career. All the murder victims she'd seen, the makeshift graves she'd stood beside.

"No," she said firmly. "It's definitely a body."

Hayes' voice came over the radio again. "This is a rescue operation, not a recovery operation."

"We can't leave it behind," Josie snapped back into her own radio.

She watched as the rolled tarp began to shift. It must have been buried beneath the foundation of the house. Normal people didn't bury their dead in their basements. Whoever was wrapped in the tarp was a murder victim. Josie's instincts rarely failed her. She knew that, given the speed of the current and the unpredictability of the flooding, it could take weeks to find the body if they let it wash away. Not only that, but what if someone besides first responders came upon it before it was found?

"I have to get it," Josie said into her radio.

The tarp was knocked loose by a large branch shooting past it. Josie spread her feet wide to keep her balance. She put one foot on the edge of the boat's side. More mayoral candidate signs rushed by, barely missing the rescue vessel's puffy side.

Brownlow hollered, "Stay in this boat, Quinn!"

Pushing against the side of the boat with her foot, Josie jumped back into the water and began paddling toward the tarp, dimly aware of the shouting behind her and over the radio at her shoulder. The current churned around her, making it difficult for her to stay on course. The rotor wash of the helicopter pressed down again, slowing the current long enough for her to get closer. Every muscle in her body burned with the effort. Her life jacket kept her afloat, but its bulk made swimming more difficult. Finally, she got close enough to grab a handful of blue plastic material. She pulled it closer to her, wrapping both arms around it. A moment later, Hayes' boat bumped against her shoulder, trapping her in place as Brownlow's vessel got closer. Gretchen leaned over, pulling at Josie's tether until only the rolled tarp was between them. Paddling in place, Josie handed it off to her. With great effort, Gretchen pulled it into the boat and came back to help Josie.

Once they were safely in the boat with the body between them, Josie looked around, but the other boat was long gone. Brownlow shook his head at her, and wordlessly, turned the boat and sped away.

CHAPTER TWO

The flooding had forced the city's emergency management department to set up a temporary command post in one of Denton University's parking lots. The campus's elevation and proximity to the hardest hit areas of the city made it the best place from which to dispatch all rescues and supplies. Pop-up tents had been erected and several ambulances and police cruisers filled one corner of the lot, waiting to be called on. The rest of the lot was filled with pickup trucks carrying or towing rescue boats of all shapes and sizes. Some were city-owned and others belonged to volunteers from neighboring towns who had come to aid in the flood response. A mile away was another staging area inside the city park where flood waters had partially submerged the softball field. Rescue crews drove their vessels to the park and launched them into the water from there. When Brownlow guided the boat onto the makeshift ramp, they were the only ones there. Only his truck sat on the other side of the field. Josie and Gretchen hopped out of the boat and helped him drag it onto dry ground. Josie's neoprene boots squished in the mud as she walked.

"That's good," Brownlow told them when the boat was out of the water. "Now, before we go any further, Quinn, I want you to know what you did out there was reckless and irresponsible. You're not getting on my boat again."

Josie put her hands on her hips. "I had—"

He cut her off. "Don't want to hear it. Don't have time to hear it. Don't care. I'll pull my truck over and load her up. What're you going to do with *that*?"

He pointed toward the rolled tarp and both Josie and Gretchen looked at it, nestled inside the bottom of the boat. Face flaming, Josie unhooked the chin strap of her helmet and took it off, shaking water from her hair. Not that it did any good. The rain continued to come down at a moderate rate. "We have to get it to the morgue," she said. "The medical examiner will need to do an autopsy."

"We'll need the Evidence Response Team as well," Gretchen added.

Brownlow raised a skeptical brow. "Evidence response? Your crime scene washed away."

"Not for the scene," Josie told him. "For the tarp and the tape and anything else that's in there with the body."

"Contextual clues," Gretchen told him.

He shook his head. "Hope you ladies are right about this being a body. Else you're gonna feel real silly jumping into floodwaters for it on TV."

They stared at him.

Gretchen said, "What else could it be?"

Brownlow shrugged. "Don't know. A dog or something? Who says it's human?"

Josie said, "I am one hundred percent sure this is human. But I hope we are wrong, and if we are, we'll feel pretty damn good because it will mean we don't have a murder victim on our hands."

Gretchen reached down into the boat. "Let's get this into the truck."

Brownlow put up both hands. "You're not putting that in my truck."

Josie said, "Are you kidding me?"

He didn't reply.

"Just help us get it to the command post. I can put it in my car to get it to the morgue," she said.

"Sorry, ladies," he said. "I told you not to jump in after that thing, and you did it anyway. It's not going in my truck and neither are you two."

As he walked away, Gretchen spat out a few colorful words under her breath.

Josie sighed. "Unbelievable. Help me get the remains out of the boat. You can stay here and guard them while I walk up and get my car."

"Your *new* car?" Gretchen teased as they lifted the tarp out of the boat and found a place away from the water where Gretchen could sit and guard it.

Josie's old vehicle, a Ford Escape, had been totaled in an accident the month before. She had just bought a new one. She sighed, thinking of the pristine gray interior and new car smell that still permeated it. "Yes, my new car."

Gretchen sat on the grass beside the body and pulled her helmet off, running a hand through her short, spiked brown and gray hair. "Get one of the ambulances. They'll take us to the morgue."

"No," Josie said as she stalked off toward the university parking lot. "We need them for the living. I'm not diverting resources right now. Not with these flash floods."

"Good call," Gretchen called after her.

Josie wiped more rain from her face as she passed Brownlow, who was hooking the rescue boat to the back of his pickup truck, and took the long walk to the parking lot where a bright orange sign marked the command post. Immediately she noticed the news vans crowding one of the triage tents. Reporters, garbed in ponchos and raincoats, gathered around Evelyn Bassett where she sat beneath a canopy tent on a gurney, an ice pack held to her head. They held out their phones and shouted questions. Behind them, cameramen pointed large, heavy, plastic-wrapped cameras at her. Next to her was Hayes. As Josie got closer, she saw that he, too, had taken off his helmet. His black hair was in disarray, sticking up everywhere. He looked to be about her age, mid-thirties, with dark stubble along his sharp jaw. He busied himself tucking a blanket around Mrs. Bassett's shoulders.

A reporter said, "Mrs. Bassett, were you scared? Did you think you'd get swept away?"

"Course I was scared," she replied. "I'm seventy-eight! Didn't think I'd get swept away though. You guys know who saved me, right?"

"Detective Quinn," another reporter shouted from the back.

Josie felt unease roil her stomach. Five years earlier, she'd cracked a scandalous missing girls' case in Denton and since then, she'd been instrumental in solving several other high profile cases that had garnered national attention. She'd been on *Dateline* three times—thanks to her sister who was a world-famous television journalist—and had become something of a local hero. Being semi-famous in her hometown didn't really suit her. The cases that had put her on people's radars haunted her. She just wanted to do her job as best she could, but her unwanted celebrity was often unavoidable. Josie put a hand up to adjust her hair as she approached. Mrs. Bassett's voice came again. "There she is! Detective Quinn! My hero. Jumped right in after me, she did."

Josie froze in place. For a split second before the reporters turned and converged on her, she got a glimpse of the frown on Hayes' face. Questions were shouted at her seemingly from every direction though none of them were about her rescue of Mrs. Bassett:

"Detective Quinn, what was inside the tarp?"

"Was that a body that you recovered in the water?"

"Detective, have you confirmed that a body was inside the tarp?"

"Were human remains found inside the tarp?"

Josie held up her hands, silencing the crowd. "I can't comment on that at this time."

More shouts followed, these more enthusiastic. Josie had to talk loudly to quiet them. "When we have more information, we will let you know. Right now, I've got work to do." She leaned past them and caught Mrs. Bassett's eye. "If you don't mind, I'd like to speak to Mrs. Bassett privately."

Reluctantly, the reporters dispersed. Josie walked over to the tent, glad to be out of the rain for a few moments. She waited to make sure all the reporters were out of earshot before she addressed Mrs. Bassett. "How are you feeling?"

Mrs. Bassett winked at her. "Just fine, thanks to you. Now I just need to find a place to live."

Hayes patted her shoulder. "I'll find somewhere suitable. There are options."

Josie said, "Did you have homeowners' insurance? You may be able to rebuild."

Mrs. Bassett shook her head. "That was a rental. It's just the stuff inside I lost."

"I'm sorry that you lost all of your possessions," Josie told her. "We do have a couple of local businesses donating clothing and other things to people who've lost everything in the flooding. You'll be able to get the basics."

"I'll make sure she gets what she needs," Hayes said quickly.

Mrs. Bassett put the ice pack on her lap and grabbed Josie's wrist. "I lost my husband in a fire fifteen years ago. I'd give up everything I ever owned in my lifetime to have him back. Things can be replaced."

Josie was stunned by her optimistic attitude. The last week had been straight out of hell, watching members of her beloved community in dire straits. Some had lost their homes altogether and many others had lost most of their possessions. They'd been lucky so far that no one had died in the flooding, but still, people were displaced and devastated. Josie patted Mrs. Bassett's hand. "I'm sorry about your husband. Do you mind if I ask you a couple of questions?"

Hayes said, "This isn't really the time."

Ignoring him, Josie said to Mrs. Bassett, "How long had you been living in that house?"

"Fifteen years. I moved in right after the fire. I had insurance money to rebuild, but I didn't want to rebuild a home without my husband. But there was the matter of the land, which I still owned. I wasn't sure what to do—I needed time to think. I was homeless—we never had children and I had overstayed my welcome with my sister-in-law—so I looked for a rental while I sorted things out. There was a local attorney looking to rent the house. He was nice enough. We went with a month-to-month lease."

"But you never left," Josie filled in.

Mrs. Bassett relinquished Josie's hand and pulled the blanket tighter around her shoulders. "Things move so fast, don't they? I did sell the land our house had been on and put that money away. I just never got around to buying something else. My heart wasn't in it, to tell the truth. It was easier to stay in the rental. Mr. Plummer—that's the landlord—he always takes care of things. When something breaks, he has it fixed. When an appliance needs replacing, he has one delivered and installed. He takes care of everything, even landscaping and snow removal. He's always been good to me. I just pay rent and utilities. If I bought my own place, who would I call for all those things?"

"Do you know Mr. Plummer's first name?" Josie asked.

"Calvin. Calvin Plummer. His office is in South Denton."

"You said he takes care of things. As long as you've been in the house, has he ever done any work or had anyone do any work on the foundation of the house?"

"No, not that I recall."

"Do you know anything about the item we recovered?"

"Me? No. I didn't know it was there. Basement was concrete. You saw it break apart," Mrs. Bassett answered.

"Speaking of the basement," Josie went on. "Did you ever have any problems down there since you've lived in the house?"

"A burst pipe now and then but that was it. Mr. Plummer just had someone come out and fix everything up."

"Have you lived there by yourself the last fifteen years?"

Mrs. Bassett nodded.

"No relatives stayed with you for any length of time? Room-mates?"

"Just me, Detective Quinn."

"Josie."

Mrs. Bassett smiled, and Josie smiled back. "Do you know who lived there before you?"

"I don't. You'd have to ask Mr. Plummer."

"I will," Josie told her. "I'd give you a business card, but I don't have any on me. All my stuff is in the car. If you need anything, you can call the number for the police station and ask for me."

Josie gave her shoulder a squeeze and walked off toward her car. Rain pelted down on her. Looking to the entrance of the parking lot, she saw reporters converging on Brownlow as he pulled into the lot. Then her view was obscured by the sight of Hayes striding toward her, his blue eyes penetrating. Josie stopped and squared up. Cutting him off at the pass, she said, "Is there a problem?"

"You know damn well there is," he said as he reached her. "You went expressly against your boat operator's orders and jumped out of the boat to retrieve… whatever the hell you retrieved."

"What I retrieved was a dead body, likely a murder victim."

"What you did was dangerous, irresponsible, and reckless. You endangered all of us out there today, recovering that tarp—"

"Body."

He gave a frustrated sigh. "*Tarp*," he emphasized. "You don't actually know that it's a body. My point is that you put yourself in a position where we might have had to rescue you, which would have put the rest of us at risk. The city's resources are already stretched thin."

Josie narrowed her eyes at him. "You don't have to tell me how bad things are, Hayes. When's the last time the emergency department used city detectives to do water rescues?"

He didn't answer.

"Listen, Hayes," she said. "You're an EMS guy, right?"

He folded his arms across his chest. "I'm a paramedic. I'm also certified in swiftwater rescue."

She lifted her chin toward the patch on his dry suit. "You work for Dalrymple Township, is that right?"

He said nothing, glowering at her.

"Dalrymple Township isn't even a part of the city of Denton. You're volunteering here, which we appreciate. But I work for the city police department," she added. "As you know."

"I know exactly who you are," he spat, droplets of rain cascading down his face. "Don't think that your celebrity is going to get you out of this."

Josie took a step toward him and he backed away. "Out of what?"

"You endangered lives today by going after that tarp."

She poked his chest. "Take it up with my Chief, but know this: I don't leave people behind. Dead or alive. Whoever is in that tarp was someone's child. Maybe someone's sibling or parent. Would you want someone you loved wrapped in a tarp and buried under a house?"

Again, he remained silent. His eyes bore down on her, and he pressed his lips into a thin line.

"I didn't think so," Josie said. "Your job is rescuing people, mine is handling dead bodies. How about you stick to your job and let me do mine? Now, if you'll excuse me, I've got to get to the morgue."

CHAPTER THREE

"What an asshole," Josie groused as she and Gretchen drove to the city morgue, the tarp-covered remains in the back hatch of Josie's new Ford Escape. The odor of damp earth filled the car, overpowering the new car smell Josie had enjoyed for the past week. On top of that, her seatback was becoming increasingly soaked with every minute that passed. She and Gretchen had changed out of their dry suits at the park and stowed their gear on the backseat floor. Josie had done her best to dry her hair before getting into the vehicle, but she'd only found one small towel in the backseat. Normally, she used it to wipe the mud from her Boston Terrier, Trout's paws after taking him for a hike in the woods.

"Boss," Gretchen said as she scrolled through her phone. "That guy had a point."

"What?" Josie said.

Gretchen tapped against her phone screen. "I'm going to text Hummel and tell him to get Officer Chan and meet us at the morgue with some equipment. I'll have him call the morgue and make sure Dr. Feist is waiting for us."

Josie stopped for a red light and stared at her colleague. "Gretchen," she said.

Gretchen looked up.

"What do you mean, he had a point?"

Gretchen sighed and put her phone into her pocket. "Don't take this the wrong way—"

Josie cut her off. "Whenever someone says 'don't take this the wrong way,' I know I'm going to take it the 'wrong' way."

Gretchen laughed. "Listen, since last month, since your sister's case, you've been a little off."

Josie felt anger bubble up inside immediately. Defensiveness. She bit back a sharp reply, waiting for Gretchen to elaborate. The light changed and Josie punched the gas, heading up the long hill that was home to Denton Memorial Hospital.

Gretchen said, "You've been a little brash. Quicker to anger. A little more..."

She drifted off and with a sinking feeling, Josie knew the word she was avoiding. "Emotional," she supplied.

Gretchen said nothing.

"I haven't been—" Josie began but stopped herself. Gretchen was right. A month earlier her twin sister, Trinity Payne, had been abducted, and Josie had taken point on the case. It had been especially complicated because of Josie and Trinity's relationship. They hadn't even known they were sisters until a few years earlier. For Trinity, being reunited was a happy occasion, but for Josie, it came with the realization that her entire life had been a lie, and that the trauma she had endured as a child could have been avoided. Trinity's kidnapping had stirred up old feelings of grief, loss, and rage for Josie. She'd thought that after they found Trinity alive, those feelings would go away, but they hadn't. It had helped to have Trinity near, but two weeks earlier she had had to return to New York City to try and salvage her journalism career. Josie missed her terribly. All of it was causing a swell of confusing, difficult emotions. She thought she'd just been tamping them down the way she always did. Apparently not very well.

Gretchen said, "You've been short with the team lately. You snapped on that drunk and disorderly we brought in the other night, and last week, in the bathroom, I heard you crying."

Josie kept her eyes on the road. She couldn't deny any of it, as much as she wanted to. Still, the words came, as if of their own volition. "I wasn't crying in the bathroom. I don't cry, I—"

She stopped. What did she do when she was upset or stressed or anxious? When her demons threatened to overtake her? She used to drink until she blacked out. But she had stopped doing that two years ago because it didn't lead to anything good.

"Right," Gretchen said. "You were trying not to cry, then."

Josie's hands tightened on the steering wheel. "That was the day that drunk driver crashed into a tree. I did the death notification. He had a—a six-year-old daughter."

Still, it wasn't like Josie to break down. She'd given dozens of death notifications in her career. The number of grieving children she'd comforted, as well as the children she'd helped rescue from abusive situations, was in the hundreds. She had always maintained a professional demeanor even when every cell in her body yearned to break down and weep. Compartmentalizing was one of her greatest skills. What was happening to her? Why had that case gotten to her? Why was everything getting to her lately?

"Today," Gretchen went on, "you put the rest of us at risk by going back into the water. Surely you realize that. I just think that under more normal circumstances, you would have thought more clinically about the situation and let that body go."

"I'm sorry," Josie said without looking at Gretchen.

They crested the hill, the large brick edifice coming into view. The city morgue was located in the basement of the hospital. Josie didn't know whether or not the city planners had taken flooding into account when they decided to build the hospital there, but the tall brick building sat high enough over the city that it was well out of the danger zone.

"Boss, I'm always on your side," Gretchen added. "I'm just saying I've noticed a difference in you lately. Hayes got frustrated today. His job is to rescue people. It was tense out there. Everyone's on edge. We're all just trying to save lives."

"I know," Josie said.

"Anyway," Gretchen said. "Forget about that guy, okay? What are the odds you'll have to work with him again—or even see him again after these floods are over? Right now, we've got work to do."

Josie sighed. She swiped a lock of wet hair out of her face. She needed coffee. "Good point," she conceded.

They pulled up to the Emergency entrance and Gretchen went inside to secure a gurney. Ten minutes later, they were pushing their charge down the dank, gray hallways in the bowels of the hospital toward Dr. Anya Feist's large exam room. The doors to the morgue slid open as they approached. Dr. Feist and her assistant, Ramon, stood on either side, ushering them through.

"I just got a call," Dr. Feist said, "Your Evidence Response Team should be here any minute."

"Great," Josie replied.

Ramon moved the gurney into the middle of the room, and he and Dr. Feist transferred the tarp onto one of her stainless-steel exam tables with a movable overhead light. "We'll wait for the ERT so they can take photos," she said. She looked over toward Josie and smiled as she tucked her shoulder-length silver-blonde hair up into a skull cap. "You had quite the morning, didn't you? Exciting stuff. I saw the whole thing on the news. They streamed it live."

"Oh jeez," Josie muttered. Great. Now her humiliation was on video, preserved for the ages. Another thought occurred to her, making her chest feel tight—not only had she jumped back into the water and put the team in danger, but just about anything could have gone wrong on live television.

Gretchen said, "Good thing it was a successful rescue and recovery."

Relief flooded Josie when Officer Hummel and his ERT colleague, Officer Jenny Chan, walked in, stopping the conversation in its tracks. All of them gathered around the table that held the rolled tarp. Hummel and Chan unpacked their equipment.

Gretchen took her notebook and pen out, ready to take notes as they worked. Chan snapped photographs while Hummel took measurements and notes of his own.

Once they were finished, Dr. Feist asked, "How do you want to do this? Should we cut it open?"

Hummel studied the tarp and looked at Chan. Hummel had been the unofficial head of Denton's ERT for the past five years, but Chan had come from a bigger department and had seen a lot more crime scenes. She turned to Josie. "How long was this in the water?"

"A few minutes?"

Gretchen said, "Maybe ten minutes. Once it dislodged, the boss got it and we hauled it into the boat pretty fast."

"There's a slim chance that we could get prints from the tarp and possibly the tape since it wasn't in the water very long," Chan told Hummel. "We'd have to use cyanoacrylate fuming."

From the corner of the room, Ramon asked, "I'm sorry, what?"

Josie said, "It's a way of lifting latent fingerprints by using superglue, basically. Fumes react with the cyanoacrylate to make this sticky white film on surfaces so you can see the prints and photograph them."

"It works on non-porous surfaces, typically," Chan cut in. "But we still might get something from the tarp or tape, or even both."

"Right," Josie agreed. "It would be worth a try."

Gretchen said, "This was buried. We have no idea how long it was under that house. It could be years. You think you could still get prints?"

Chan shrugged. "Like I said, it's a slim chance, but Detective Quinn is right. It's worth trying."

Hummel said, "Then we'll try carefully peeling the tape and unraveling the tarp instead of cutting."

No one protested. Josie and Gretchen stood back and watched while Hummel, Chan, Dr. Feist, and Ramon went to work, trying to keep as much of the tape and tarp intact as they could. Beneath the tarp was a second tarp and more tape. Ramon pushed the gurney flush against the side of the autopsy table as they began removing the next layer. A musty smell tinged with the scent of decay filled the room as they got closer to revealing the body inside the tarps. Finally, after an hour of painstaking work, the tape and tarps were carefully bagged and marked, and Dr. Feist and Ramon arranged the body on the autopsy table.

Josie and Gretchen stepped forward to take a closer look. Josie's breath caught in her throat, and her heart did a little flutter. Hummel took out his camera and started snapping photos.

Gretchen said, "Is she—is she mummified?"

"Yes," Dr. Feist answered softly, surveying the body.

Josie's gaze panned the tableau from top to bottom. She had expected skeletal remains given how deeply the body had been buried beneath the foundation of Mrs. Bassett's house. While much of the skeleton was evident, its bones were held together by taut blackened vestiges of skin and sinew. Long brown hair tangled near the scalp, the skin slippage having kinked it to the side. Blackened bony fingers curled from the sleeves of a jacket, still intact, now brown and faded where it had once been blue and gold, showing the Denton East High School mascot—a blue jay—on its left breast, and the letters 'D' and 'E' embroidered on the right breast. Denim jeans clothed the legs and the shriveled feet were still encased in a pair of silver ballet flats. Both the jeans and the flats had turned brown from decomposition. A wave of sadness crashed over Josie.

Dr. Feist said, "Wrapped as thoroughly and tightly as she was in plastic immediately after death, then buried beneath a house, she wouldn't have been exposed to oxygen. The conditions would not have allowed for insects and bacteria to use the body as a host. The normal decomp process would have been stunted."

Gretchen stopped taking notes and pointed the cap of her pen to the jacket. "It looks like she might be a teenage girl."

"Yes," Josie breathed. "Looks like she went to the same high school as me."

"Is there a year number?" Gretchen asked.

Hummel continued to take photos as Chan used gloved hands to probe the sleeves of the jacket. "Here's a patch for state baseball champions for…" She brushed some dirt away from the patch. "The year was 2004."

Josie felt as though something was crawling up her neck into her hair. She brushed a palm down over her scalp.

Gretchen looked at Josie. "Was that the year you graduated?"

"No, I graduated in 2005; 2004 would have been my junior year."

Chan came over to Josie's side and probed at that sleeve. "There's a number here. Twenty-seven."

The crawling sensation continued, working its way all over her skull. She clamped both hands over her head.

"Boss," Gretchen said. "You okay?"

"Yeah, I'm fine," Josie said. "What else do you see, Chan?"

Chan leaned in. "It's another patch. A baseball with flames behind it."

Now Josie felt as though someone had poured cold water over her head. She tried not to flinch. She remembered the baseball state championship during her junior year. She'd been there when they won. Cheered them on. She remembered the blue and gold jackets the team received that year. Each jacket had the player's number on one sleeve and the championship patch on the other. Only one player had had the patch with the flaming baseball. He had died in Josie's arms five years ago during the missing girls' case. It couldn't be his jacket, could it? But how? How had it gotten there? And who was the girl who had been buried in it?

Dr. Feist said, "I'll confirm her age range once I do a full autopsy. The first order of business will be to get these clothes off her and take some x-rays."

Gretchen turned to Josie. "Did any girls you went to high school with go missing?"

"No," Josie said. "And the missing girls' case turned up all the girls who had been missing in the town—the county—going back decades."

Gretchen frowned.

Josie felt lightheaded. "Can we—can we get back to the station? Maybe we can run down some information while Dr. Feist does the autopsy."

Gretchen didn't question her. She put her notebook and pen away and thanked Dr. Feist and Ramon. "Good idea, boss. We'll talk to the owner of the house, and maybe we can get some yearbooks from Denton East."

Hummel said, "Chan and I will stay and get the clothing and anything else relevant tagged and bagged."

"Great," Josie said. "Hummel, can you upload the photos of the clothing to the file as soon as possible?"

"You got it, boss."

high school, including junior year. That year Ray was a pitcher for the baseball team."

Gretchen said, "The very team that won the state championship."

"Yes," Josie said. "He was very good. He was being scouted. He actually went to college on a baseball scholarship. He was scouted there as well, but he only ever wanted to be a police officer, so he never pursued it."

"He was on the team. They had letter jackets, and when they won the station championship that year, they were given special championship patches," Gretchen said. "And his number was twenty-seven, wasn't it?"

Josie nodded. Below them, she counted three rescue boats buzzing through the submerged streets of the city.

"The blazing baseball patch?"

"Ray got into a fight—over me—he was defending me. It was something stupid. He was a hothead. Hell, so was I. He tore his jacket. He'd just gotten the championship patch put on. He was pretty upset. Those jackets were expensive to have replaced completely. But his mom said it was no problem for her to sew it up. She did but it looked terrible, so she found the blazing baseball patch to sew over top of the tear. She said—"

Unexpectedly, Josie felt tears sting the backs of her eyes remembering the look on Ray's face when his mother gave him the jacket and said the words to him: *I'm so proud of you.* Their childhoods had been so full of trauma, abuse, guilt, and shame. Something as simple as hearing those words from his mother had been like winning the lottery for Ray.

Josie swallowed her emotion and continued, "She told him she was very proud of him."

"Ray would have been the only one on the team that year to have that patch on that sleeve, then," Gretchen said.

"Yes."

"But the body in the morgue right now does not belong to Ray."

CHAPTER FOUR

Josie flinched at the pungent, earthy odor that lingered inside her vehicle as she climbed into the driver's seat. She couldn't wait to get home and take a hot shower even though it would be her second one before lunch time. Before she could turn the keys in the ignition, Gretchen placed a hand on her arm.

"You want to tell me what's going on?"

Josie's shoulders slumped. She looked at Gretchen and opened her mouth to speak and then closed it. Confusion clouded her mind. How could she explain the jacket? Was it the same one? It had to be. There was no other explanation. Her mind reached back to high school, sifting through memories.

"Boss," Gretchen said. "You look like you saw a ghost."

I did, she wanted to say, but the words wouldn't come.

Gretchen said, "Start with the facts. With what you know."

Josie gave Gretchen a pained smile. That made it easier. "You remember Ray? Well, I know you never met him, but you do remember who he is, right?"

"Your late husband," Gretchen answered easily. "Of course."

Josie nodded. She looked out the windshield at the valley below the hospital. Where once the lovely brick buildings of the city's main street had stood tall, now they were mired in murky brown water. "We were high school sweethearts," she said. "We met when we were nine. I lived in a trailer park, and he lived in the development behind the trailer park. We used to meet in the woods between the park and the back of his house. Our freshman year, the friendship turned into more. We were together all of

"No," Josie said, her voice coming out huskier than intended. "I buried him five years ago. I don't know how his jacket ended up on the body of a girl buried under a house on Hempstead. It doesn't make any sense."

"There's no chance that one of the other pitchers on the team saw Ray's awesome blazing baseball patch and got one for himself?"

Josie looked at Gretchen. "And changed their number to Ray's?"

"Okay, then what happened to the jacket? Do you remember him losing it? It getting stolen?"

Josie closed her eyes, trying to think back, but her memories from high school seemed light years away now, like someone else's life. "I don't know. I don't remember. It was summertime right after they got the jackets—I remember that, because it was so hot. He wore his anyway for awhile. I guess I didn't ask questions when he stopped wearing it because I just assumed he put it away for the summer because of the heat."

"Do you have his old things?" Gretchen asked.

"Some of them. His mother also took some and Misty has some stuff too."

Misty was the woman Ray had been seeing after his and Josie's marriage fell apart.

Gretchen took out her phone and started typing in a text. "The fastest way to verify if that jacket belongs to Ray would just be to have Hummel turn the sleeve inside out and check for the tear you mentioned, don't you think?"

"Yes," Josie said. "But I already know that jacket belonged to Ray."

Gretchen hit send on her text to Hummel and said, "Then we just have to figure out who that girl is and how she got Ray's jacket. Maybe that will help us find out what happened to her. We can check yearbooks and also look into the history of owners and renters of the house she was under. But first, we both need a shower and change of clothes."

*

The Denton Police headquarters was a three-story stone building with ornate molding over its many double-casement arched windows and a bell tower on one end. Thus far, it had narrowly avoided the flooding. As the water level had risen over the last few days, emergency workers and volunteers had packed sandbags and built a wall of them near the front entrance of the building, holding the water back. A portable tube barrier, which required far less work to set up, had been allocated for the front of the police building but when members of the Emergency Services Department went into their supply building to get it, they found it was missing.

The sandbags worked well enough, but no one could get in or out through the front lobby. Luckily, the water hadn't yet reached the ground floor of the building where their holding cells were. Josie pulled into the municipal parking lot at the rear of the building and let Gretchen out, promising to return with her high school yearbook.

Josie counted herself lucky that her house, where she lived with her boyfriend and colleague, Lieutenant Noah Fraley, was in one of the neighborhoods outside of the flood zone. She knew Noah wasn't home as he had been dispatched to South Denton to work with emergency crews there. Misty Derossi's vehicle, however, was parked in the driveway. Misty owned a large, beautiful Victorian home in the historic district of the city which had been under water for days. Josie had invited Misty, her four-year-old son, Harris, and their chi-weiner dog, Pepper, to stay with her and Noah until the flooding passed. As Josie turned her key in the door, she heard the click of dog paws on her foyer floor and then Pepper's high-pitched bark mingled with Trout's deeper bark. As she opened the door, both dogs jumped on her legs. Their tongues lolled as they huffed, trying to get her attention. Trout, who was normally very friendly toward Pepper, snapped at her as she tried to get Josie's attention.

Josie scolded him and knelt to pet both of them, rubbing their sides and reminding them both that they were good dogs.

"JoJo!" Little Harris Quinn came barreling toward her from the kitchen, his arms open.

The dogs made way as he leapt into her arms. She laughed and stood up, twirling him around and planting a kiss on his blond scalp. "What's going on?"

"Your hair is all messed up," he observed.

"I'm in here!" Misty called from the kitchen.

Harris gave Josie a serious look. "Mommy is stress-baking."

Josie laughed as she carried him into the kitchen. The dogs followed. "Stress-baking?"

Misty turned away from the open oven and smiled at Josie, then gave a little eye-roll. "His grandmother said it and now he won't stop telling everyone that's what I'm doing."

Josie looked around the kitchen. Two pies cooled on the counter. On the kitchen table were two loaves of bread swaddled in dish towels. From the oven, Misty pulled a tray of cookies. She deposited it onto the only open space on the kitchen counter and pulled off her oven mitts.

Josie raised a brow. "Well, it is just the four of us here. I'm not sure we'll finish all this."

Misty shook her head. "Don't be silly. This is for the first responders. I'm going to make baskets and drop them off at the command post."

Both dogs sniffed the kitchen floor from one end of the room to the other, looking for any scraps Misty might have dropped. But Misty was one of the cleanest, neatest people Josie had ever known. It wasn't the first time she and Harris had stayed with Josie. They'd formed an unusual friendship over the years. After Josie and Ray separated, Ray had begun frequenting the local strip club with his buddies where Misty was a dancer. They started dating. Josie had despised her at first, letting petty jealousy get the best of her and projecting blame for the disintegration of her marriage onto Misty. Over time, she realized that Misty had had nothing at all to do with the end of their marriage. She'd grown to accept that Ray had fallen in love with Misty before his death. After he died, Misty gave birth to Ray's son. Josie had thought it would be difficult to even lay eyes on Ray's child. When she and Ray were married, they had made a conscious decision not to have children of their own. Their childhoods had been so traumatic that they were terrified of bringing a child into the world together. They couldn't escape the fear that they might make terrible parents. But the moment she saw Harris and held him in her arms, she felt a surge of love and protectiveness she had never experienced before. She had known in that moment that she would take a bullet for this child, and she'd vowed to do whatever she could to help Misty raise and care for him. Misty had moved on from dancing to working as an intake counselor at the local women's center. She worked long hours and had no family nearby. Along with Ray's mother, Josie was one of Harris's primary babysitters.

"Why is your hair all yucky?" Harris asked, pulling at one of her stringy locks. "You didn't brush it today?"

Josie set him on the floor. "I got soaked in the rain," she told him. "I didn't have a chance to comb it out yet."

Harris, apparently accepting her answer, asked his mother if he could play a game on her tablet. Misty said, "For a half hour but that's it. Go ahead; I left it in the living room." Once he was out of the room, Misty said, "I saw you on the news. That scared the hell out of me. I thought you were going to stop doing crazy dangerous stuff."

Josie laughed. "I never said that."

Misty's face turned serious. "Was it a body?"

Josie nodded.

"I'm sorry," Misty said. "That's terrible."

"Misty," Josie said. "When Ray was alive—"

She saw Misty's shoulders tense. Even after all these years, the topic of Ray was difficult for Misty. Josie understood why. For Josie, Ray had been her best friend, high school sweetheart, and then her husband. He had been her lifeline. Misty hadn't known him nearly as long as Josie, but she'd fallen hard for him. Before his death, Ray had done some morally questionable things, and Josie knew that Misty struggled just as much as she did reconciling the love she had felt for him with the man he'd turned out to be. Any discussion of him always stirred up those conflicting feelings.

Misty leaned her narrow hip against the counter and folded her arms over her chest. "It's okay," she said. "Ask me."

Josie pushed a mess of tangled hair behind one of her ears. "When Ray was alive, did he ever talk about high school?"

"No, not really. You two were together in high school, so it wasn't something we talked about much. He really couldn't talk about it without your name coming up. It was kind of awkward at the time."

Josie gave a pained smile. Misty was right. Josie couldn't talk about high school without talking about Ray either. So why didn't she remember what happened to his letter jacket? "Did he ever talk about baseball?"

Misty nodded. "Oh, well, yeah. He was the starting pitcher for the state championship game in his junior year. I had to hear that story about a million times, especially after he'd had a few drinks. So almost nightly."

Josie laughed drily. "Right. What kinds of things did he say about that time?"

Misty narrowed her eyes. "Josie, I know enough about your job by now to know that whatever it is you're working on—whether it's that body you found today or something else—you can't tell me details. At least not now." She lowered her voice and did an impression of every police officer Josie had ever seen on the news. "We can't comment on an ongoing investigation." Then she smiled. "So just ask me what you need to ask me."

Josie said, "But you can't ask any follow-up questions. You can, but I can't answer them."

"I know that too."

"Did Ray ever talk about his letter jacket?"

Misty rolled her eyes, but the smile on her face was full of love and longing. "His prized letter jacket that his mom sewed up after he tore the sleeve? The one with the special patch on it? The baseball on fire? For a smoking fast pitcher?"

Josie felt a lump in her throat. She still felt uncomfortable hearing stories from Misty that had been intimately shared between herself and Ray or that she had witnessed firsthand. Misty had only known him a couple of years and yet Ray had told her things that Josie had spent a lifetime experiencing alongside him. "Yes," she croaked. "That jacket."

"Well, the first few times I heard the story, he said he lost it."

"Lost it?" Josie said. "Where?"

Misty raised a hand in the air. "I didn't believe that. The way he talked about that team and that season and that last game? That jacket meant something to him. No way would he have lost it. I asked him a few times what really happened to it."

"What did he tell you?"

Misty shook her head. "About a half dozen different things. He gave it to you. He left it in the locker room at school and it was stolen. He lent it to someone and never got it back. He put it in storage in his mom's attic, and when he went looking for it as an adult, it was gone. He lost it in a move. You took it when you two broke up."

Josie's mind worked through these possibilities. Four of them she could immediately dismiss. He never would have packed it away in his mother's attic. He would have wanted to wear it again as soon as the weather got cool. But he hadn't, Josie realized. She hadn't seen him wearing the jacket after junior year. He hadn't given it to Josie nor had she taken it when they broke up. It hadn't been lost in a move. They had moved several times after they got married, living in a series of shitty apartments before finding a house together. But Josie had never seen the jacket during any of their moves. That left the possibilities that it had been stolen or that he had loaned it to someone who hadn't returned it. But if it had been stolen, why wouldn't he just say that? Why make up a bunch of other excuses for what happened to the jacket? Josie had known Ray better than anyone. Or she thought she had. He had done silly things and lied about them for no other reason than because he thought Josie would be upset or disapprove.

"I take it you don't have the jacket," Misty said, interrupting Josie's thoughts.

"No, I don't have it."

If it hadn't been stolen, that meant Ray had loaned it to someone. But he'd still lied to Misty about the whole thing. Why? A feeling like icy fingertips trailing up her spine gave Josie a shiver. Because the person he'd loaned it to hadn't given it back to him? Because she'd been wearing it when she died?

Misty was staring at her intently. "But you saw the jacket," she said. "Today. After you were in the flood."

Josie said nothing.

Misty turned and picked up a spatula, probing the cookies on the tray. One by one, she slid the spatula beneath them and transferred them into a Tupperware container.

Josie said, "I just have to get something from the garage before I get in the shower."

She turned to walk out of the room. From behind her, came Misty's voice. "Ray was a lot of things—good and bad. He disappointed us. People got hurt because of what he did. Because of what he didn't do, really. He was weak. But Josie—"

Josie looked over her shoulder. They locked eyes. Misty said, "Ray would never kill anyone."

CHAPTER FIVE

2004

Josie pulled her jacket tighter around herself. Cold seeped from the stone beneath her. The blanket Ray had brought did nothing to make their perch warmer or more comfortable. Then again, there was nowhere particularly comfortable to sit at the Stacks. That didn't stop teenagers from Denton East High from congregating there, though. Hidden in the woods behind the high school, it was the perfect spot for them to get away from adults. Students drank, smoked, and did other things adults wouldn't approve of at the Stacks. The place had gotten its name from the large slabs of rock that had fallen from the mountainside, forming literal stacks of flat stone. The Stacks were more crowded than Josie had ever seen them, but that was because the Denton East Blue Jays were only one win away from the Pennsylvania state baseball championship.

"We should have gotten closer to the fire," Josie said to Ray. "I'm freezing."

He put down his beer can and pulled his jacket off. He wrapped it around her, tugging at the lapels and drawing her closer. After planting a soft kiss on her lips, he said, "There. That better?"

Josie smiled, resting her forehead against his. "Your letter jacket? Really?"

He pulled his head back so she could see his smile. "I want it back."

"Of course. You'll need it back when you get your state championship patch."

He kissed her again. "We have one more game to go."

Josie checked her watch. "Speaking of that, it's getting late, Ray. How many beers have you had?"

He tucked a strand of hair behind her ear. "Not many," he answered. "But you're right. It is getting late. We'll get going soon, okay?" He picked up his beer and slugged down what was left of it. "One more, okay?"

Josie huddled inside his jacket, grateful for its warmth. "Just one though, okay?"

"Chill, Jo," he said.

He hopped down from the rock where they sat and sauntered over to a group of guys from the baseball team. They gathered in a knot next to the campfire, all in their letter jackets, all laughing and carrying on, some accompanied by their girlfriends. "Quinn!" one of them said as Ray approached. He handed Ray a beer. "Let's get messed up! What do you say?"

Ray took the beer and smiled. "Can't. We've got school and practice tomorrow. I don't want to be hungover."

A collective groan went up around the group. "Live a little, Quinn," another boy said. His name was Harley. He was the catcher.

"Yeah," said a third boy, Carter, one of the relief pitchers. "You don't have to do everything your *mommy* says."

Carter said the word mommy with sarcastic emphasis and a pointed look at Josie.

"Dude," said Harley. "Don't talk about his girl. He'll kick your ass."

Josie was already striding over to the group. "Ray," she said. "Let's go." In the firelight, she saw a muscle in his jaw tic. "It's not worth it," she told him in a tone only he could hear.

"Go ahead, Quinn. Go home with your mommy," teased Carter.

Josie turned to him. "Ever wonder why you're so far down on the lineup, Carter? Why you're not a starting pitcher?"

All conversation stopped. Josie felt everyone's eyes on her. Carter glared at her, his dark eyes glittering in the flickering light. Josie leaned into him. "It's your bad attitude," she told him.

He shook his head. "Shut up, bi—"

"Watch it," Ray said, pushing Carter's shoulder, hard.

Harley stepped between them, both of his hands up. "Come on, guys. Chill out."

Ray pushed the unopened can of beer into Harley's chest. "I'm leaving," he said. "I'll see you assholes at practice tomorrow."

He laced his fingers through Josie's and pulled her along to the school parking lot. As they reached her grandmother's car, Josie said, "You know, Ray, you don't have to fight everyone who acts like a jerk."

He smiled at her. "I do if they disrespect you."

She peeled off his jacket and handed it to him.

"Keep it," he said. "Won't you be cold?"

"Not in the car," she said. "Take it."

He shrugged it on before sliding into the passenger's seat.

Josie got in and started the car. "I'm just saying, Ray. You don't have to pick a fight every single time. You could have let that one slide."

He reached over and put a warm hand on her thigh. "I don't give a rat's ass about Carter, or any of those guys. I don't give a shit about anyone else on this entire planet except you, Jo. Only you."

Josie felt a flush rise in her cheeks as she turned out of the Denton East parking lot and onto a rural road bathed in night. To her left was forest, trees reaching out from the darkness with their thin branches. To her right was a wide-open field. With the moon hidden behind thick clouds, the night was blanketed in darkness. There were no streetlights or even residences with lights on inside. As they crested a small hill, blue and red police lights spun in the distance. Ahead, a Denton PD cruiser had pulled someone over.

"What's this?" Josie wondered out loud. She slowed the vehicle as they approached.

"I recognize that car," Ray said. "It's some girl in our class. Oh, what the hell is her name?"

As they passed, they saw a Denton police officer standing beside the small blue sedan he'd pulled over. He opened the driver's side door, and Josie saw a flash of blonde hair. The officer motioned for the girl to get out. His head swiveled toward them as they rolled slowly past.

"Shit," Josie said. "That's Frisk."

"Go back," Ray said, turning his head to look behind them. "Quick."

Frisk was the nickname the kids had for Officer James Lampson. He was known for pulling over teenage girls for simple violations—or sometimes no violation at all—and making them get out of their cars so he could frisk them. Only the rumors were that the frisking was a little too familiar.

Josie pulled up on the opposite side of the road beneath a canopy of trees, stopping parallel to Frisk and the sedan. Ray said, "Lana, that's her name."

Josie eyed Frisk as she unbuckled her seatbelt. Both he and his prey were well-illuminated by the headlights of his cruiser. Lana stood beside him, facing away from Josie. Her legs were spread far apart, both hands up against the car. Frisk stared back at Josie. "Stay here," she said.

Ray grabbed her wrist. "Are you kidding me? No. You stay here. I'll go."

"You think I can't handle Frisk?"

"Jo, I know you can handle anyone. That's not the issue. Frisk is a pig. He'll take it better if I go over."

"Ray, you're drunk. One whiff of your breath and Frisk can take you in. He'll ruin everything for you. No baseball. No scholarships. No college. Stay here."

Before he could reply, Josie got out of the car. The night seemed to close in on her as she strode over to Frisk. He folded his arms across his chest, leering at her. "Well, well, what have we got here? You lost, young lady?"

Josie glanced behind him where Lana stood against her car. A barely detectable tremor shook her body. "I was supposed to be following Lana home," Josie lied. "We've got a project due tomorrow. We're supposed to be at her house right now finishing it up. But I got lost."

"Did you now?" Frisk asked. He licked his lips and smiled, a carnivore showing its teeth. "It's awfully late to be working on a school project, isn't it?"

Josie stepped closer. "True," she acknowledged. "That's why we really need to get going." She gestured toward Lana. Neither Frisk nor Lana moved.

Josie's heart did a double tap. Her hands felt cold. She hadn't thought this through. She didn't have a plan. She just knew she didn't want Frisk's hands on a teenage girl, but how exactly was she supposed to accomplish that? She had no authority over him. She wasn't even a legal adult. Absconding with Lana wasn't really an option. What the hell could she do?

"Officer," Josie tried, "if we promise to drive carefully, would you mind if we went home?"

"I pulled this young lady over for a busted taillight," he told Josie. "You think I should just let her go?"

"A busted taillight?" Josie blurted. "You need to frisk her for a busted taillight?"

The instant the words were out of her mouth, she regretted them. Frisk's eyes narrowed. He motioned toward the space next to Lana. "Truth be told, we've had a lot of kids from Denton East getting caught with illegal drugs. Your friend here seemed like she might be on something. In fact, I'm thinking you might be on something too. So if you don't mind, step up and I'll pat both of you down."

Josie's body began to tremble. She wished she could hide it. Hugging herself, she glared at him. "No," she said.

Shadows warped his face as he tipped his chin back and laughed. Josie glanced up and down the road, wishing someone else would drive by, another adult, another cop, maybe. But they wouldn't stop, would they? All they'd see was a police officer dealing with some sort of traffic violation. Nothing to see here.

Frisk said, "I'm sorry, what's that? Did you say no to an officer of the law?"

Before Josie could respond, a car door slammed, and Ray jogged across the road. He smiled at Frisk. "Officer Lampson, is everything okay over here?"

Frisk studied him. "I'm not sure that's any of your business, son."

"Oh, sure," Ray said. "I meant no disrespect, sir. In fact, we don't mean to trouble you at all. We were just looking for our friend, Lana. Here she is. Thought we'd lost her. You saved us a lot of searching by pulling her over, actually. Right, Jo?"

He looked at Josie, his eyes imploring her to go along. All she could manage was a nod. Her mouth was full of saliva. Frisk stared at Ray, taking in his easy smile and then his jacket.

"Hey," Frisk said. "You're that pitcher, aren't you? Denton East Blue Jays."

Ray held out a hand for Frisk to shake. "Yes, sir, Ray Quinn."

Frisk took his hand, holding onto it a moment longer than necessary. "You boys are gonna win the championship," he said.

"Hope so," Ray agreed as Frisk relinquished his hand. "Sir, if you wouldn't mind, I really need to get these ladies home."

There was a long, silent moment. Crickets chirped in the darkness beyond the vehicles. A moth fluttered in front of Frisk's cruiser, causing a strange, momentary strobe effect. Frisk looked from Ray to Josie, then to Lana and back to Ray, as if he were trying to decide something. Finally, he said, "You ladies shouldn't keep our star pitcher out so late." He waved them toward Ray. "Get out of here, and go right home."

"Thank you, sir," Ray said, maneuvering himself between the two girls and Frisk.

Josie grasped Lana's upper arm and dragged her toward her grandmother's car. Opening the back door, Josie pushed her inside. "Get in."

Ray got into the passenger's seat. Josie's hands shook as she put the car in drive. Ray said, "Go, go, go."

Lana said, "My car."

"I'll bring you back for it tomorrow," Ray told her. "Right now, we need to get out of here before that shithead changes his mind and decides to screw with all three of us."

Once Frisk's car receded from view and they were back in town, Josie let out a sigh of relief. From the backseat, Lana said, "Thank you."

Ray said, "No problem."

"How did you know?" Lana asked. "About him?"

Josie answered, "I have a list."

Ray laughed.

"A list of what?" Lana asked.

"Pervy guys to avoid," Ray supplied.

"Like Mr. Rand?" Lana asked.

"Eighth period chemistry?" Josie said. "Yeah. Exactly. Anyway, that guy back there? He's on the list. We call him Frisk."

In the rearview, Josie watched Lana's eyes widen. "That's Frisk? I've heard of him but didn't know what he looked like." She reached forward and tapped Ray's shoulder. "Thanks for getting involved. You took a big risk."

Josie glanced at Ray. "She's right. You did. He could have taken you in for underage drinking. Really, he could have made up anything and taken you in. Bye-bye championship game. Hello criminal charges. You think your mom could afford a lawyer right now?"

Ray looked behind them but there were no flashing police lights pursuing them. "We got lucky."

"Lucky you were there," Lana said. "We'll put you on the list of good guys."

CHAPTER SIX

A half hour later, after a shower, change of clothes, and a quick lunch, Josie pulled into the parking lot at police headquarters. The rain still poured down steadily, but that hadn't stopped a handful of reporters from gathering at the entrance to the building. They wore raincoats and huddled beneath umbrellas. A lone cameraman sagged beneath the weight of a large camera wrapped in clear plastic. The last several days they'd been out and about in town, trying to capture footage of the destructive flooding and the water rescues. If they were waiting here in the rain, that meant they were still trying to get information about the body Josie had recovered on Hempstead. With a sigh, she reached across to the passenger's seat and grabbed up her high school yearbook—which she had retrieved from her garage—as well as the basket of baked goods Misty had given her to distribute to her colleagues. She'd paged through the yearbook in her bedroom before taking a shower, but no one had caught her eye or jarred anything loose in her memory. She would have remembered if someone had gone missing from Denton East while she was a student there. Even if she hadn't, all missing-persons cases in the county had been reopened and reevaluated five years ago during the vanishing girls case.

She emerged from her vehicle and hurried toward the door, keeping her gaze focused straight ahead as the reporters converged on her, shouting the same questions they'd lobbed at her at the command post. She barked out a few "no comments" and then she was safely inside. Trudging up the stairs to the second floor, Josie entered the great room. It was a large, open area filled with desks and filing cabinets. A television was affixed to one wall. Today it streamed coverage of the flooding. Josie ignored it and walked over to the four desks pushed together in the center of the room. They were reserved for the detectives on the force: herself, Detective Gretchen Palmer, Lieutenant Noah Fraley, and Detective Finn Mettner.

Josie and Noah had started their careers in Denton, moving up the ranks to the investigative team after several years on patrol. Gretchen had come to them from Philadelphia where she had worked for fifteen years on their homicide squad. In fact, Josie had been the one to hire her when Josie was serving as interim chief of police. Eventually, that position was filled by their current chief, Bob Chitwood. He had promoted Finn Mettner from patrol to detective from within the department. Mettner was the youngest of the four of them, but he was dedicated and thorough and had already worked as the lead on some major cases in his new position.

Josie set the basket in the center of the desks and looked around. The room was empty save for one patrol officer doing paperwork at one of the shared desks. Bob Chitwood's voice boomed from behind his closed office door. Josie wasn't surprised. As the detectives liked to joke, Chitwood had two volumes: loud and louder. Josie took a few steps toward his office, catching some of his words: "… I don't give a rat's ass if the Mayor lives in that development. Or you, Dutton. You're just a candidate. That doesn't mean anything to me. City council? I don't care if you're on the damn UN. I don't care if the goddamn queen of England and the pope have houses in Quail Hollow. You can't divert public resources away from areas that need them…"

Josie rolled her eyes. The "Quail Hollow Estates Scandal", as a local reporter had dubbed it, had been the bane of the Chief's existence since the flooding began. Quail Hollow was a section of the city where more wealthy residents lived, including the Mayor, Tara Charleston, and her surgeon husband as well as her mayoral opponent, Kurt Dutton, and his wife. In the last few years, Dutton had built the area up, adding more luxury homes for the city's rich to flock to and a small creek around the development. The Quail Hollow Estates' surrounding neighbors called it "the moat" even though Quail Hollow's residents took great pride in it. It was lovely, Josie supposed, and its banks were beautifully landscaped. What the builders had not foreseen was the issue of flooding. One particular section of the moat had been badly affected by the recent rainstorms, spilling over into the yard of an unfinished luxury home at the back of the development. City engineers had deemed that the lot was too dangerous to continue work on in its present condition. There was also concern about a possible landslide, which would be catastrophic to the Quail Hollow residents not to mention the neighborhood adjacent to Quail Hollow.

It had recently come to the authorities' attention that the residents of Quail Hollow had been stealing resources from the city stores such as barriers, portable pumps, and other equipment. When one of the WYEP reporters exposed what they were doing, the Mayor had stepped in. She had changed the word stealing to "diverting," as if that were any better. The rest of the city's residents were enraged, but that hadn't stopped Quail Hollow residents from "diverting" more and more resources to keep their homes from being flooded.

Chief Chitwood's voice blared even louder from behind his door. "Those are public resources! They're not for you rich assholes to take at your discretion. That's right. They do belong to the city, and the city gets to say where they go and when. Who? The head of Emergency Services, that's who. Oversight? I'm giving you the oversight right now. I'm telling you to return those barriers and the pumps and the rest of the supplies by the end of this week or I'm going to drag my people out of rescue boats to come and arrest the lot of you!"

There was a moment of silence. Then Chitwood hollered, "Don't threaten me, son. I've been doing this job since you were in diapers. You can't intimidate me. I've got a job to do!"

She heard his receiver slam down, and she scurried over to her desk. Gretchen had appeared, sitting at her own desk, riffling through the baked goods. "Chief's at it again, is he? With the Quail Hollow folks?"

"Yeah," Josie said. "I think that was Dutton. He broke out his 'I've been doing this since you were in diapers' line on him."

Both women laughed. It was one of Chief Chitwood's signature lines, one he used when he was most incensed. He was in his sixties, past retirement age, and well past caring about the politics that went with his job. Josie hadn't agreed with his heavy-handed approach at first but now that she and her team had earned his respect, he backed them up consistently and they'd grown to accept him.

Josie handed Gretchen the yearbook. "I've been through this. Nothing jumped out at me. No missing girls."

Gretchen popped a cookie in her mouth and paged through the book until she found Ray's photo. "What about anyone Ray was friends with during that time?"

"You mean other girls? He wasn't friends with many girls at that time. The two of us had a few friends, and I can flag them for you in the yearbook, but as far as I know, they're all still alive and accounted for."

Gretchen said, "Okay, we can do that. I think we should also look at the previous residents of the house. See if there's anything there."

Josie booted up her computer and brought up the database for property searches in the county. A few minutes later, she had a history of the house on Hempstead. "Looks like Calvin Plummer has owned this for decades." She pulled up the search feature again and this time searched by his name. "He's got six rental properties in Denton, plus his office and what looks like his permanent residence, which is—get this—in Quail Hollow Estates."

Gretchen leaned back in her seat and raised a brow. "No kidding."

Josie pulled up the house on Google maps and clicked on street view. "Yeah, but his is one of the original homes, not the newer ones. He was living there long before they turned it into Quail Hollow."

"Wonder if he's going to represent Quail Hollow Estates when Chitwood arrests them all," Gretchen remarked.

Josie pulled up Plummer's website. "I don't think so. Looks like he does tax law."

"Excuse me?" came an unfamiliar female voice from the stairwell.

Josie and Gretchen swiveled in their seats to see a young woman with long, auburn hair and pale skin standing in the doorway. She was dressed in a form-fitting skirt that rose high above her waistline; a white blouse tucked into it, accentuating her figure. The top few buttons of the blouse were open, revealing an expanse of pale skin. A long necklace sporting an amber-colored stone hung from her neck. In one hand, she carried a briefcase. She took a few tentative steps toward them, heels clicking on the tile, and looked at Josie. She smiled, and up close, Josie saw that she was strikingly beautiful, her eyes a blue so vivid they almost looked turquoise.

"You're Josie Quinn," she said.

Josie offered her a smile. "Can I help you?"

She offered her hand. Josie shook it. "Amber Watts," she said. "I'm the new press liaison."

Josie looked at Gretchen. For a moment, both of them went blank. Then Gretchen said, "Press liaison?"

"Yes," Amber answered. "I'm here to facilitate and maintain communication between the police department and the public. I'll also be working to enhance communication between the police department and the Mayor's office."

Gretchen said, "You give press conferences so we don't have to."

Amber gave a small laugh. "Yeah, pretty much."

"Who hired you?" Josie said.

Innocently, Amber said, "Mayor Charleston."

Josie suppressed a groan. Gretchen mumbled, "The Chief's gonna love this."

"What was that?" Amber asked, her expression uncertain.

"Nothing, nothing," Josie said. "We just had no idea that a press liaison was being hired. You really need to talk to the Chief. Come on, I'll show you to his office."

Before Josie could lead her over, Bob Chitwood's door swung open. He stepped out into the great room, wisps of his white hair floating over his scalp. His brown eyes darted around, taking in the three women.

"Quinn, Palmer. We need to talk about— Who the hell is this?"

Amber strode over to him and extended a hand. "Amber Watts," she said. "The Mayor sent me over. I'm the police department's new press liaison."

For a long, pregnant moment, Chitwood stared at her. His face grew more ruddy by the second. Finally, he said, "Horseshit. We don't need a press liaison. You're a spy, is what you are. Go back to the Mayor and tell her she can pound sand."

To her credit, Amber didn't miss a beat. She gave him a megawatt smile, as if they were in on some joke together and said, "Chief, I know how this looks."

He folded his arms over his chest and looked down his nose at her. "Do you?"

"I do," she said easily. "With the Quail Hollow Scandal in the news and the conflict over city resources putting you and the Mayor at odds, it must seem as though she's planting me here to keep an eye on you. I can assure you that's not the case."

"Can you? How is that?"

"I answered the job listing for a press liaison months ago. I interviewed for this position before the flooding even started," she answered.

He pointed a finger at her. "More horseshit. The Mayor can't hire people without telling me."

"Well, sir, I'm afraid that's something you'd have to take up with her. My job is not only to manage press briefings and other matters here in-house but also to coordinate between the police department and the Mayor's office to be sure that both city departments are sending the same message to the public."

Josie said, "What you really mean is that you're here to make sure that we stay on message."

Chitwood, who normally would have rebuffed Josie for speaking up, remained silent, staring hard at Amber, waiting for her response.

Amber turned to Josie, her smile never faltering. "No, that's not my job. I'm not the Mayor's lackey."

"She's here to spin things," Gretchen said.

Amber said, "I'm sorry. We haven't been introduced. You are?"

"Detective Gretchen Palmer."

"Oh yes. Well, Detective Palmer, if I recall, you were personally involved in a case a couple of years back that was heavily covered in the media."

"That's none of your business," Josie snapped.

Gretchen reached over and touched Josie's arm. "It's okay, boss."

Amber's smile slipped. "I'm not here to make enemies. Far from it. I know it doesn't seem like it, especially since the Mayor hired me, but I am on your side. The only reason I brought up your history, Detective Palmer, is to make the point that this city has been the home of several high-profile criminal cases over the last five years. Cases that have captured national interest. You really should have had someone like me in place a long time ago. My job is not to get in your way or to make your job harder. In fact, my job is to make yours easier. I deal with the press so that all of you can carry on with your investigative work. Just this morning, Detective Quinn was captured on the news recovering what looked like a dead body from a flood zone. The press are camped outside, and their numbers are growing by the minute. I can help you deal with them. That's what I do."

The three of them regarded her warily. When none of them spoke, Amber said, "I can see that the Mayor didn't exactly pave the way for my arrival. I don't want us to get off on the wrong foot." She turned to the Chief. "How about if I set up a meeting with the Mayor? The three of us can discuss this in private. Would that put your mind at ease?"

Chitwood raised a brow. "What would put my mind at ease is if the damn Mayor would stay the hell out of my way and stop screwing around with Emergency Services!"

From inside her briefcase, Amber produced a cell phone. "We can definitely put your concern on the agenda. I'll give her a call right now."

Josie and Gretchen stared at Chitwood, braced for an explosion. He had one of the foulest tempers Josie had ever seen on the job. Most people were intimidated by him—or at least annoyed—but Amber was unfazed. They all listened as she spoke with the Mayor, never once breaking from her professional demeanor. She was smooth, Josie would give her that. Unflappable. She pulled the phone away from her ear for a second and asked the Chief, "Today at two? At the restaurant just past the university campus? I think neutral territory would be best."

The Chief's pitted cheeks flamed. Haltingly, he said, "Uh, sure, yeah."

Amber confirmed with the Mayor and ended the call. "Lovely," she said. She graced them all with another smile and said, "I can see you've all got work to do so I won't make myself a nuisance. Chief, I'll see you later today."

He didn't answer. Amber tilted her head, her voice softening. "The awkwardness of my arrival aside, I really do look forward to working with all of you. Detective Quinn, I've been an admirer of yours for some time."

Josie managed a weak "thank you," and they watched Amber disappear back into the stairwell. Chitwood patted down the stray hairs on his scalp, letting loose a stream of muttered expletives before addressing Josie. "Quinn, I want you to find that job listing for me, you got that?"

"Of course," Josie answered, grateful that Amber's arrival had overshadowed her actions from this morning. She fully expected to be dressed down by the Chief, but he was more worried about the Mayor's machinations.

"I'm not going into this meeting unprepared," he said. "I will not be intimidated by this woman. I don't care if she's my boss."

Josie remembered her own experience with the Mayor back when she had served as interim chief of police. They'd had a case where an infant had been abducted, his mother beaten. The Mayor's husband had briefly been a person of interest. The Mayor had personally and privately requested that Josie brush his connection to the case under the carpet. Josie hadn't agreed to it, and her relationship with the Mayor had been strained ever since. "I'll dig up whatever I can," she assured Chitwood.

He nodded. "Also, Palmer brought me up to speed on today's events. I expect Dr. Feist's autopsy will show we have a murder victim on our hands. Palmer and Quinn will take the lead on the case."

Josie waited for him to mention her dive into the river after the tarp, but he said nothing.

"We're headed over to see the owner of the house now," Josie told him. "Calvin Plummer."

Chitwood gave a pinched expression. "He's one of those Quail Hollow Estate assholes. Not the worst of them, though. Good luck. Keep me up to speed. I've got to get out to the command post and assess the shitshow for the day before I see the Mayor."

CHAPTER SEVEN

Calvin Plummer's office was located in South Denton, which was primarily a commercial district. Squat, flat-roofed buildings sat along the main route, housing strip malls, a car rental agency, and a storage facility among other things. The residences left over had long been converted into businesses as well. Josie drove along back roads to avoid the flooding but when she went to turn onto the main road, there was water flowing across it for as far as the eye could see. Two patrol cars sat at the intersection, lights flashing. Uniformed officers in bright yellow raincoats walked up and down the road, waving cars out of the now flooded area.

"The south branch of the river must have overflowed," Josie said. "There are a bunch of creeks down here that flow into it." About a quarter mile down the road to the right, she could see the two-story colonial home with the sign hanging from its porch that announced: *Calvin Plummer, Attorney-at-Law*.

"It's moving fast," Gretchen said.

"You bring your waders?" Josie asked her, putting the car into park.

Gretchen smiled. "You kidding me? After this week? They're in the back."

They rushed out into the rain, and Josie popped open her hatch. They pulled on their waders and raincoats and set off toward Plummer's office. The uniformed officers nodded at them as they moved through the ankle-height water. The strip of grass between the road and Plummer's front door hadn't yet been overrun with water, but the ground was soft beneath their feet. Just inside the open door was a small sitting area with a couch, two overstuffed chairs, and a coffee table in the center of them. A small cherry reception desk stood empty. Across from the front entrance were two doors, both open, and to the far left, a flight of stairs. A man emerged from one of the doors carrying a cardboard file box in his hands. Josie knew from the website that they were looking at Calvin Plummer. He was short and stocky with thinning gray hair and a chubby face. He wore a suit with no jacket.

"I'm sorry," he said. "This really isn't the time. The police are evacuating us."

Gretchen flashed her credentials at him as she and Josie approached. "We are the police."

"Oh," Calvin said, glancing at Gretchen's ID. He raised a brow. "Detective? I assume this is about my property on Hempstead."

"Yes," Josie said, offering him her credentials as well.

He took a cursory look at her ID and shifted the box in his hands. "I'm happy to talk to you, but right now I've got to get these files up to the second floor before we get out of here."

Josie looked around. The sound of a metal drawer slamming sounded from the room Calvin had just emerged from. "My secretary," he explained. "Tammy. Now, if you don't mind."

He muscled past them and started up the steps.

Josie said, "We'll help."

Gretchen gave her a brief glare but then nodded at Plummer.

"Fine," he said. His head bobbed in the direction of the file room. "In there. Tammy will give you some boxes."

From outside came a hammering sound on the porch roof, as the rain picked up. The long, low howl of the South Denton fire company's emergency alarm began. "Hurry," Plummer told them.

Tammy was in her early twenties with long, dark hair that swished across her back as she unloaded file folders from the metal cabinets lining the room and tucked them into letter boxes. She was shorter than Josie and much curvier, her tight black dress and six-inch heels oozing more sexual energy than professionalism. She was going to have a hell of a time carrying letter boxes up and down the steps quickly in those shoes.

They introduced themselves, and Tammy handed them each a box. Plummer joined them, taking a third box. Josie and Gretchen followed him up the steps as he talked. "I've had that house on Hempstead for years," he said. "A damn shame. Is Mrs. Bassett okay?"

"Yes," Josie said. "A small bump on the head but otherwise fine. Happy to be alive."

"She lost everything though," Calvin muttered. At the top of the steps, they followed him left and down a long hall. On the second floor, the insistent drum of the rain was nearly a roar. "Do you know where I can reach her? I can at least return her security deposit. I definitely don't need it now. She was always a great tenant. Do you have any idea how hard it is to find good tenants?"

Gretchen started with his first question. "We're not sure where she'll be placed but as soon as we know, we can pass that along."

"Speaking of tenants," Josie said as they came to a doorway. "We were wondering if you could tell us about the tenants who lived in the house before Mrs. Bassett."

Calvin walked into a large room which was empty, save for a stack of file boxes along one wall. He motioned for them to place their boxes on top of the pile. "This is to do with that thing you jumped into the water for, isn't it? On the news, reporters are speculating that it was a body. Is that the case?"

"Yes," Josie answered, setting her box down. "It is a body. It's with the medical examiner now."

Calvin hung his head. "You're telling me there was a body buried under one of my houses?"

Gretchen put her box on top of Josie's. "Yes. Do you have any idea how it might have gotten there?"

Calvin laughed as he headed back down to the file room. "If I knew anything about a dead body underneath one of my properties, you'd be having this conversation with *my* attorney. Of course I don't know anything about it. Listen, that property has always been a rental. Like I said, I've had it for decades. Before Mrs. Bassett, there were a bunch of tenants; not the most savory types, if you take my meaning. Any one of them could have been doing illegal things there. In fact, it wouldn't surprise me at all if they had been. I was lucky to find Mrs. Bassett. I'm sad to see her go. Sad to see the house go. Insurance will cover it, I imagine."

"About those former tenants," Josie said, trying to keep him on track as they took more boxes from Tammy and followed Calvin upstairs again. "Do you have records? A list? Something we can use to track them down?"

Over his shoulder, he said, "I'm only required to keep records for seven years, but I suppose I can check and see what I've got. Actually, Tammy probably knows where those records are better than me."

Back in the file room, he addressed his young secretary.

"Tammy," he said. "I need you to find all the records we have on the Hempstead property, if you can find them quickly." He looked out of the file room toward the front door. Beyond, the murky brown water began to cover the grass.

With a sigh, Tammy turned away from them, walking sideways through a narrow passage between two piles of letter boxes and then navigating her way to a file cabinet in the corner of the room, blocked by a rolling cart with computer equipment on it. "I think those are in this one," she said, pushing the cart aside. They watched as she bent at the waist to open the bottom drawer. As she riffled through it, Josie looked over to see Plummer's gaze glued to his secretary's rear, eyes hungry. Gretchen's elbow jabbed at Josie's side, an indication for Josie not to stare. Josie tore her eyes from the attorney and stepped forward, searching for an empty file box. A moment later, she and Tammy were loading file folders marked "Hempstead" into it.

Plummer said, "I trust you'll return them to me when you're finished? We don't really have time to make copies right now."

Outside, the mournful wail of the emergency fire siren went on. Gretchen said, "We don't need copies. We can bring them back as soon as we've finished with them."

"Perfect," Plummer said. He gestured to the rest of the files in the room. "You mind helping us with these?"

CHAPTER EIGHT

"I feel dirty," Gretchen joked once they were back in the car. She shifted the letter box that Plummer had given them on her lap. "And not just because I'm sweating. From now on, check with me before you volunteer us for hard labor."

Josie laughed. "What do you think the age difference is between Plummer and Tammy?"

"It's gross," Gretchen answered. "However many years gross comes out to."

Josie laughed harder and started the car, turning her windshield wipers up as fast as they'd go. Two more patrol cars pulled up, maneuvering around her vehicle to block off the road. The water had been up to their calves by the time they left Plummer's office. Josie turned her vehicle around, driving away from the flooded area. "Some people say age is just a number," she teased.

Gretchen shook her head. "To be fair, I was twelve years younger than my husband, but I'm thinking there's a lot more years than that between Plummer and Tammy."

They returned to the police station, pushing through the soaking wet throng of reporters still staked out at the back door, and took the file up to their desks. Once they got out of their raincoats and waders and felt sufficiently dry, they spread the paperwork out across Josie's desk and pored over it. Josie said, "This guy saved a copy of every check Evelyn Bassett ever sent him."

"That's a lot of checks," Gretchen said. "Here we go. This is the tenant before her."

She pulled out a thin manila file from the box. Josie gathered up the documents from Mrs. Bassett and made room for the new file. Gretchen opened it and began placing various documents side by side. The lease, copies of checks, letters, and what looked like legal documents. Josie picked one up and skimmed over it. The top of it was marked with the Denton City Municipal Court seal. "This is an eviction action," she said. "Calvin Plummer versus Vera Urban, April 9, 2004."

Something in the shadows at the back of Josie's mind fought to burst forth.

Gretchen picked up more documents. "Looks like Vera lived there for about seven years before Plummer filed that. Did it go through?"

Josie flipped through the pages but found no evidence that Vera had actually been evicted. She moved on to the rest of the legal documents until she found a Petition to Withdraw. "They must have worked it out," Josie said. "Because he withdrew the action June 18, 2004."

"So what happened?" Gretchen asked.

Josie paged through the copies of Vera's rent checks, then she went back to Evelyn Bassett's checks. "There's a year-long gap here between Vera Urban's last rent check and Evelyn Bassett's first one."

"So the house on Hempstead was vacant for a year?"

"It appears that way. From the eviction proceedings, it looks like Vera hadn't paid her rent for two months when Plummer filed against her. Then he withdrew the action, but I don't see that she ever squared up with him or that he ever returned her security deposit," Josie said.

"Maybe she took off, and he kept the security deposit," Gretchen suggested.

"We'll have to ask him. In the meantime, let's see what we can find out about Vera Urban."

Gretchen paged through the rest of the stuff in the letter box while Josie pulled up the TLO database. She took a few minutes to search through it. "This is strange," she said.

Gretchen leaned over her shoulder to look at the screen.

Josie said, "She's had no property purchases, no utilities, not even a phone for the last sixteen years."

Gretchen slid her reading glasses on and leaned in closer. Josie moved her chair out of the way a bit to make room for her. "This can't be right," Gretchen mumbled.

Josie reached over and clicked through a few more tabs in the database. "She was born in 1962. Here we've got high school graduation from Denton West in 1980. No criminal record. A couple of speeding tickets. She was arrested once for a bad check but not charged. Here are utilities at various addresses including Hempstead but that's it."

"Pull up her driver's license," Gretchen said. "She would have to have kept that up to date."

Josie looked it up, but the last license on file was sixteen years old as well. A sinking feeling began in her stomach. Gretchen nudged Josie out of the way and went through all the searches and information that Josie had just been through. She said, "Vera Urban stopped existing after 2004. She could be the body we found."

Josie said, "It's possible, but why would she be wearing a high school jacket?" *Why would she be wearing* Ray's *high school jacket*, she added silently. Vera would have been old enough to be his mother.

"I don't know," Gretchen said. "We'll know more about the age of the body after Dr. Feist's autopsy."

"Wait a minute," Josie said. She sprung up from her chair and went around to Gretchen's desk to get her yearbook. Paging through it, she found the photos of students in their junior year. In high school, her last name had been Matson. She found her own photo easily, cringing at her lank hair and acne. Then came Ray Quinn, looking less attractive in his school photo than Josie's memories of him dictated. In her mind, he would always have the glow of feverish, passionate first love. But in his photo, he looked kind of dorky; his blond hair combed to one side and stiff with gel, his smile toothy. He hadn't yet grown into his looks. She flipped a few more pages, toward the end of the alphabet.

"Oh my God," she breathed.

"What is it?" asked Gretchen.

Josie came around and showed her the photo. "Beverly Urban," she said. "She was in mine and Ray's class. I think she was Vera's daughter."

Josie set the yearbook down and searched the database, looking for anyone associated with Vera Urban. Sure enough, Beverly's name was listed under "close relative." Wanting more confirmation of their relationship, Josie looked through Plummer's records again until she found the lease originally signed by Vera. There was a section where she had to disclose the name, age, and relationship of everyone who intended to live with her on Hempstead. She had written Beverly's name there, along with her age, and under the "relationship" question, she had written: "daughter."

Josie tapped a finger against the yearbook page. "I was right. She's Vera's daughter. Well, she *was* Vera's daughter."

Josie studied the photo. Beverly had been taller and curvier than Josie. Among the girls in their class, she'd been the first to get breasts, the first to get her period, and, rumor had it, the first to have sex. Whereas Josie didn't fully fill out until the end of junior year, Beverly had arrived on the first day of eighth grade looking like a college-aged woman. Josie remembered how gangly and unattractive she and many of the other girls in their class had felt when Beverly seemed to go through puberty overnight. She remembered how the boys leered at her and vied for her attention.

"She's pretty," Gretchen said.

The yearbook photo only showed her from the shoulders up, but Gretchen was right. Beverly had a wide smile; clear, pale skin;

and long, curly brown hair. Her brown eyes held just a hint of mischievousness. If you didn't know her, you might find it intriguing. But Josie knew that the look hid her malicious side.

"She is very pretty," Josie said. "But she wasn't very nice."

Gretchen looked up. "Why do you say that?"

Josie laughed. "She was the school bully."

Gretchen raised a brow. "Somehow, boss, I can't imagine you getting bullied by anyone, even in high school."

Josie leaned a hip against her desk. "I wasn't bullied. But that didn't stop Beverly from trying."

Gretchen took her phone out and snapped a picture of Beverly's yearbook photo. "What kinds of things are we talking about?"

Josie sighed. "Everything from spreading rumors about other kids to getting into fist fights. She could be very domineering. You know how when you're a kid they tell you that some people make other people feel badly so they feel better about themselves? I think that was Beverly."

"Did she ever spread rumors about you?"

"Sometimes, but she was mostly fixated on Ray."

The memory came back fast and hard, like a stone landing on her chest. For a few seconds, it felt difficult to breathe.

"Boss?" Gretchen coaxed.

"She had a crush on Ray," Josie said. "Or at least, I think so. I'm not sure if it was that she had a crush on him or that she hated me, but she started spreading rumors in our junior year that Ray was cheating on me with her."

"You didn't believe them?"

"Of course not. Ray and I—" Josie broke off. How could she explain it? The bond she and Ray had formed, especially in those early years, had been sacred. They'd both been abused by the people who were supposed to love and protect them. They both bore the deep scars of shame. As children, and then teenagers, they'd only had one another. The trust between them had been unbreakable.

Josie had believed that in her soul. At the time, rumors of Ray sleeping with Beverly had been laughable. She would have bet her life on them being untrue. But now, sixteen years had passed. They'd broken up before college, gotten back together, gotten married, separated, and then Ray had betrayed her, not just in their marriage, but because he had turned out not to be the man she knew at all. Was it possible that the rumors had been true?

A sick feeling rolled in her stomach. She pulled her chair over and sunk into it.

Gretchen set the yearbook aside and logged into another database. "What about Beverly's father?"

"Not in the picture," Josie said. "I never knew that much about her family situation, but everyone knew that it was just her and her mom." She handed Gretchen the lease between Vera and Plummer. "Vera didn't list any other occupants besides herself and Beverly."

Gretchen studied it and then set it aside, returning to her computer. With a few clicks, she pulled up Beverly Urban's birth certificate. "No father listed here," she noted. "Born in 1987 at Geisinger. That's about an hour from here, right?"

"Yeah," Josie said. "It must have been a difficult birth if they sent Vera to Geisinger to deliver. They have much more specialized services there."

Gretchen said, "What happened to Beverly?"

Josie said, "I don't know, but now I'm beginning to wonder if someone killed her and buried her under the house on Hempstead."

"She didn't graduate with you?"

Josie shook her head. "No. There were rumors toward the end of junior year that she was going to have to move because her mom couldn't afford their house. Summer came and then senior year started, and she wasn't there. Everyone just assumed she and her mom had moved away."

"Obviously they didn't," Gretchen said. "According to public records, Vera disappeared off the face of the earth and it's safe to assume Beverly did as well. I think you're correct in assuming that the body we found yesterday belongs to one of them."

"Check the TLO database," Josie told her. "See if there's any evidence of Beverly existing after 2004. Renewed driver's licenses, utilities, credit cards, loans, home purchase, anything."

Gretchen turned her attention back to the computer. Josie watched as each search Gretchen attempted came up empty. The database didn't provide much information on minors. It relied on information pulled from cell phone data, utility companies, and the like. Beverly would have had to reach adulthood to begin engaging the kinds of services that would leave a record. If Beverly had gone on to graduate high school and live her life as normal people did, there would be some record of her activities even if it was just utilities in her name. But there was nothing.

"Okay," Gretchen said. "Looks like they both disappeared off the face of the earth in 2004. I didn't see any other bodies when the house washed away, did you?"

"No," Josie said.

"Who do you think we recovered from the flood today?"

"Beverly," Josie said. "Because of the jacket."

"You think Ray gave it to her? Maybe she stole it from him? If she had a crush on him, she might have. Or if she wanted to get at you, she might have stolen it to make it look like he gave it to her."

"I don't know," Josie admitted. She thought back to what Misty had said and what she knew about Ray. "I think he gave it to her, but I don't know why."

"You don't think—"

Josie squeezed the bridge of her nose with her thumb and forefinger. "Oh my God," she said. "That Ray really was having a relationship with her? That he gave her the jacket? That he… killed her? I realize that one of the first people we look at in murder cases are the deceased's significant others, but Ray wouldn't do that. He couldn't have killed someone, especially a woman."

"Boss, I don't want to sound disrespectful, but I think your judgment might be clouded in this instance."

Josie opened her mouth to protest, but then the memory of the night her marriage with Ray had ended came flying back at her in all its horror. Ray had gotten blackout drunk and hit her. It was a sin she could not forgive. If he had been capable of hitting Josie, his childhood best friend, his high school sweetheart, his wife, then surely it wasn't outside the realm of possibility that he could have killed someone else. Could he have killed Beverly to cover up the relationship?

"But if the body is Beverly's and he killed her, what happened to Vera?"

"I don't know," Gretchen said. "But before we speculate anymore, we really need to confirm that the body belongs to Beverly Urban."

Josie said, "Let's start calling around to see if any local dentists have her records. DNA could take weeks or months."

Gretchen moved around to her desk. "I'm also wondering how the body ended up under the concrete floor of the basement."

"We should see if Plummer has records of work done on the home," Josie agreed. "And check with the City Codes office to see what kinds of permits they've got on record for the place."

They spent the next half hour calling local dentists until they found the one that had treated Beverly Urban in high school. Josie held her breath while the receptionist checked to make sure they had records that far back. Luckily, they did.

"They're films though," the woman told Josie. "That was before we went digital."

"If I come there with a warrant in the next hour, can I pick them up?"

"Sure," said the woman. "But hurry because I think we're about to be evacuated. The creeks are overflowing."

"I know," Josie said. "We'll be there as soon as we can."

She hung up, ready to relay the news to Gretchen, but her desk phone rang. It was Dr. Feist. "The autopsy is finished," she told Josie. "Meet me in the morgue, would you? You'll want to see this."

CHAPTER NINE

Dr. Feist was at her desk, typing away at her desktop computer, when Josie and Gretchen entered her office. It was a far cry from the sterile exam room next door where she carried out countless examinations of dead and decomposed bodies. The walls were painted blue cinderblock, and Dr. Feist had done her best to make the room feel cheery and warm. Lamps gave off softer lighting than the typical overhead fluorescent glare in the rest of the hospital. Abstract paintings in soothing pastel tones hung from the walls. Since Josie had last been there, she had added a large potted plant beside her desk.

"Detectives," she greeted them with a grim smile. "You've got a homicide victim on your hands."

"Not surprising," Gretchen said. "Given where she was found."

Dr. Feist stood up. From the back of her chair, she pulled an old nubby white sweater and put it on over her blue scrubs. She pointed to the large envelope beneath Josie's arm. "What have you brought me?"

"Dental x-rays," Josie answered. "We think we know the identity of the victim."

She handed the envelope to Dr. Feist, and they followed the doctor into the large exam room. Josie's eyes were immediately drawn to the nearest exam table, but it had been covered with a sheet. Dr. Feist strode across the room, taking the x-ray films out of the envelope and snapping one of them up onto the old, wall-mounted x-ray film viewer. "Can one of you grab my laptop?" she asked over her shoulder.

Gretchen picked it up from the counter near the exam table and brought it over. Dr. Feist opened it, the camera picking up on her face immediately and taking her to the home screen. She moved her elegant fingers across the mousepad, bringing up x-rays she'd taken during the autopsy. The two detectives stood behind her as she compared the two sets of images. A few moments later, she turned to them, open laptop in her hands and said, "This is a match."

Gretchen and Josie looked at one another. Josie felt a weight settle on her shoulders. She and Beverly had been arch enemies at school, but Josie would never have wished death on the girl. Nothing that may have happened between Beverly and Ray would change that. No one deserved Beverly's fate: murdered, buried, and forgotten.

Dr. Feist walked past them and back to the counter, setting her laptop down and regarding them. "What do we know?"

Josie said, "Her name is Beverly Urban. From what we can tell so far with the limited information we have, she was likely killed sixteen years ago. She had just finished her junior year at Denton East High School."

Gretchen pulled out her notebook and paged through it. Putting her reading glasses on, she said, "She had just turned seventeen. We'll have to investigate further, but based on what Detective Quinn has said, she did finish her junior year but did not return senior year, so it is possible that she was killed sometime during the summer of 2004." Gretchen took out her phone and showed Dr. Feist the yearbook photo of Beverly.

"But we really need to talk to her friends and any relatives out there to confirm the last time anyone saw or spoke to her," Josie added.

Dr. Feist said, "Well, I'll leave the detective work to you. My findings on exam are consistent with a five-foot-six, seventeen-year-old Caucasian girl based on the shape of her skull and the cranial sutures that are still open, as well as the size of her mastoid process, the condition of her growth plates, and, of course, her pelvic bones.

I won't bore you with the scientific stuff which you two are already well acquainted with. You'll have a copy of my report. What is probably of most interest to you right now is this."

She turned back to her laptop and pulled up more digital x-rays. Clicking through them, she came to several x-rays of the skull. "Here, you can see, at the back of her head? It looks almost like a starburst, with the hole in the center and all these fractures webbing outward. It's consistent with a bullet hole. I was able to retrieve the bullet from inside her cranium."

She moved past them to another part of the counter where a small stainless-steel basin rested. Inside, Josie saw the partially flattened nub of a bullet, darkened with age. Josie took a pair of latex gloves from her jacket pocket. "May I?"

"Yes," Dr. Feist said, holding the basin out to her. "I already checked with Hummel. He said he couldn't get prints from this."

Josie took the bullet and held it up. Gretchen leaned in closer, peering at it through her reading glasses. "Nine millimeter," she said. "Don't you think?"

"Yes," Josie said. "Definitely. A pistol. This has to go to the state police lab for ballistics analysis."

"Of course," Dr. Feist said.

Josie put the bullet back into the basin and snapped off her gloves, disposing of them in a nearby trash bin. A shiver ran down her spine. "Beverly was shot in the back of the head."

"Yes," Dr. Feist said with a frown. "Given the measurements I took from her body, and the appearance of the wound, I can extrapolate that the person who shot her was most likely around six feet tall, give or take a couple of inches. It's difficult to say with any degree of accuracy just how close range the shot was—not without some ballistics testing—but I would say whoever shot her was standing within three feet of her."

"You think she was standing up when she was shot," Gretchen said.

"Yes. If she had been kneeling or sitting, I'd expect the shot to have been closer to the top of her head instead of the back. If she were kneeling or sitting, any shot taken at this angle would have been very awkward."

"But still," Josie said. "Shooting a seventeen-year-old girl in the back of the head—it's like an execution."

Dr. Feist nodded. "I don't typically see these kinds of gunshot wounds unless they are the result of gang activity—or drug deals gone wrong."

Gretchen turned to Josie. "Was Beverly into drugs?"

"I really didn't know her that well," Josie answered. "It's hard to say, but it's definitely an angle we can investigate."

"That's not all," said Dr. Feist.

From the set of her shoulders, Josie could tell that whatever Dr. Feist was about to show them would not be good. She walked over to the exam table and gently peeled back the sheet to reveal Beverly's remains. Dr. Feist stowed the sheet and moved to the bottom of the exam table. "Here," she said softly, pointing. "I removed these remains from Beverly's pelvic region. I imagine you'll want to have them tested for any DNA that might still be there."

Josie took a step closer, feeling her heart stutter. The bones were tiny and delicate, almost birdlike. She was amazed something so fragile had survived sixteen years buried beneath the earth. She, Gretchen, and Dr. Feist stood around the autopsy table, staring at the bones that Dr. Feist had removed from the larger body, and bowed their heads in an unspoken moment of silence for the life that had been cut short before it had even begun.

Gretchen cleared her throat. "How far along was she?"

Dr. Feist said, "I believe she was five months pregnant when she was killed."

Josie said, "My God."

CHAPTER TEN

2004

A bead of sweat rolled down Josie's face. She shifted uncomfortably in her desk chair, not hearing a word her teacher was saying about chemistry. The air around her smelled of body odor, and the haze of perfume some of the other girls had used to mask said body odor. The air conditioning in Denton East High had broken on the hottest day of the year so far. Even the open windows offered no breeze. Glancing at the clock, Josie was relieved to see there were only five minutes until the final bell of the day. She needed a shower. Something hit her shoulder from behind. A square of paper landed beside her desk. Giggles erupted from behind her.

"Is there a problem?" asked Mr. Rand.

Behind her, Josie thought she heard a girl hiss, "You guys, stop!" It sounded like Lana.

One of the other girls said, "No, no problem. Josie dropped something."

He stared at her until she reached down and picked up the folded piece of loose-leaf paper. Squeezing it in her palm, she smiled stiffly at Mr. Rand.

"Ms. Matson," he said. "Is that something I should be concerned about?"

The other students in her grade had been taunting her all day, but she would be damned if she ratted them out. Attention was what they wanted, her grandmother always said, so don't dare give it to them. Besides, she'd look like a wuss and a tattle if she dimed them out. No one did that. Josie liked to handle things on her own. "No," she told him as she tucked the paper into the back of her chemistry textbook.

He took a step toward her, his eyes lingering on her chest. Josie suddenly wished she hadn't stripped down to her tank top. Before he could speak again, the bell rang. Bodies sprang from their seats and rushed toward the door. Ignoring the ongoing commentary behind her, Josie let herself get caught in the surge of students trying to get out of the door and into the hallway where it was only marginally cooler. The crowd carried her down the hall to her locker.

"Better start looking for a new prom date," a voice said behind her back. Josie didn't turn around. She focused on making her fingers open her locker.

Another voice answered the last, "Yeah right. Good luck with that. No one is gonna want to date that."

Rage bubbled in her stomach as she flung open her locker door. It clanged against the locker beside it. Taking a deep breath, Josie started methodically switching out her textbooks, trying to keep her mind on which ones she would need to take home with her that night. Placing her chemistry book into the locker, her hand froze.

Don't look at it, said a voice in her head. *It's all lies anyway. Rumors.*

"None of it is true," she muttered to herself. But it was the third time this year that this particular rumor had circulated through Denton East.

Her fingers extricated the square of paper. As she unfolded it, a hand-drawn heart came into view. Black ink. An arrow punched through it. Inside were the names Ray and Beverly. The page made a crinkling sound as she squeezed it in her hand. She slammed her locker closed, hoisted her bookbag onto her back and found the nearest trash can, happy that most of the students were gone for the day.

Bracing herself for the sweltering stairwell, Josie pushed through the door only to run directly into Beverly Urban.

"Watch it," Beverly said, her voice high-pitched.

Josie felt a flutter in her chest. "You watch it," she snapped back.

"Don't tell me what to do, you loser," Beverly responded.

Josie pushed past her, toward the steps. Over her shoulder she said, "Oh, I'm the loser? I'm not the one who has to make up rumors about other people's boyfriends just so it looks like someone wants to be with me. Get your own damn boyfriend."

Beverly let out a loud breath and then Josie felt something push hard against the bookbag on her back. The steps rushed at her. She threw her hands up, searching for something to grab onto, but it was too late. She toppled down the steps, only her packed bag slowing the fall, coming to rest face-down on the landing. Pushing herself to standing, she glared up the steps toward Beverly even as her mind did a mental inventory of her body. Her left knee hurt, and so did both her hands and wrists. Her right shoulder also felt funny. But she didn't think anything was broken. Her hands searched her face and head but there was no blood. Above her, Beverly watched, chest heaving, a strange look on her face. Triumph? Pleasure?

"What is your problem?" Josie shouted. "You could have killed me!"

Beverly descended the stairs slowly, almost regally, like a queen looking down on a royal subject. When she reached the landing, she brushed against Josie and gave her a withering look. "Too bad I didn't. Ray deserves better."

Josie's fist shot out, making contact with Beverly's left eye socket. Beverly let out a shriek, hands flying to her face. That was going to leave a mark, Josie thought. Instantly, she regretted it. She was already in hot water with the principal and with her gram. "You need to learn to control these impulses," they both said to her every time she was forced into a meeting with the two of them. The only thing that kept the principal from suspending her was Lisette's constant reminders to him of the abuse Josie had suffered at her mother's hands before Lisette took custody of her. Josie hated that Lisette had to bring that up all the time, but it did keep her in school. Besides, Josie didn't normally have behavioral problems. The meetings were almost always as a result of altercations involving Beverly. Although before today, Beverly had never been so overtly violent toward Josie, and while Josie had wanted to on many occasions, she hadn't ever punched Beverly before now.

Beverly's hands came away from her face. To Josie's shock, tears streamed down her cheeks. "How could you?" she gasped. "You—you hit me. You could have—I—"

The sentence was swallowed up by a sob. The reaction was so out of character for Beverly, Josie was rendered speechless. Beverly was the queen of taunts, known school-wide for her cruelty. She had never once cried, not in front of anyone. While she wept, Josie stared at her, dumbfounded. Pain from her fall down the steps began to course through various body parts. She was suddenly aware of the sweat pouring down her face.

The door at the top of the steps swung open, and Mr. Rand appeared above them. "You girls," he said, shaking his head. "To the principal's office. Now."

An hour later, Josie sat on a bench outside the main office. Her clothes stuck to her, glued to her skin from hours of sweat. Her left knee throbbed. Inside, her grandmother was still trying to convince the principal not to suspend her.

"Jo, there you are." Ray appeared before her. She smiled weakly.

He knelt in front of her and touched her face. "Don't," she said. "I'm so sweaty. I know I smell."

He smiled. "The whole school smells. I heard what happened. Are you okay?"

Josie looked away from him. "You're not worried whether or not your girlfriend is okay?"

"I just asked you if you were."

She met his eyes, glaring. "You know what I mean. The whole school thinks you're sleeping with Beverly behind my back. That you're taking her to the prom. The first couple of times these rumors started, it was funny. But now I'm starting to wonder, Ray. You know that saying? Where there's smoke, there's fire?"

He rolled his eyes. Sitting beside her, he put an arm around her and pulled her close to him. The shirt of his baseball uniform was scratchy against her cheek. In spite of herself, she leaned into him, feeling a rush of relief.

"There's no fire. You don't believe those rumors, Jo. Tell me you don't," he said.

"I don't know what to believe."

Using a finger, he tipped her chin up toward his face. "Believe me," he told her. "Believe us. I've never even had a conversation with Beverly Urban in my life. I don't care about her. I don't care about anyone but you. I love you, Jo. You know that."

Josie stared into his eyes. He brushed a droplet of sweat from her forehead. "It's you and me, Jo. No one else matters. You know what's between us. I know you feel it too. What you and I went through with your mom and my dad… no one else could ever fill your shoes, Jo. Those are just rumors. This is real."

She thought about Ray and Beverly, tried to picture them meeting, kissing, embracing. She couldn't. Besides that, she and Ray spent so much of their free time together. When would he even have time to carry on with Beverly? He wouldn't, especially not with baseball. Beverly's goal in life since the seventh grade seemed to have been to make Josie miserable. What better way to make her miserable than to cast doubt in Josie's mind about her relationship with Ray?

"You're right," Josie said. "I'm sorry for doubting you. It was just… a bad day."

The door to the office swung open and Beverly emerged, alone, still sobbing uncontrollably. Josie wasn't sure she had stopped since the stairwell. Beverly pressed a tissue to her face. Turning her head, she took one look at them and ran off down the hall.

"She's acting weird," Josie told Ray.

He laughed. "Who cares how Beverly Urban is acting? She pushed you down the damn steps."

Josie looked at her watch. "Ray, you're late for practice. Coach is going to kill you."

He squeezed her. "You're more important than some baseball practice."

Josie extricated herself and stood. "We're talking about the state championship, Ray. You have to get out there. Let's go. I'll run in and let my grandmother know we're headed to the field."

Ray waited as she went back inside the office, interrupting an awkward meeting among the principal, Beverly's mom, and her grandmother. Once she told her grandmother where she was headed, she went back out to the hallway. Ray jumped up and took her hand, leading her away. Josie looked over her shoulder but there was no sign of Beverly.

CHAPTER ELEVEN

"We need to talk to Plummer again," Josie said as they made their way from the morgue back to the car.

"Yes," Gretchen agreed. "That's a good place to start."

Gretchen used their Mobile Data Terminal to look up his home address in Quail Hollow Estates. Josie drove, her mind reeling with what had happened to Beverly. The girl had been a thorn in Josie's side for years. She had been cruel at times, dangerous at others. It had been a relief when she didn't return to Denton East in senior year, but now Josie saw her in a completely different light. Her mother had been experiencing financial difficulty. She knew this from the rumors at school and now from Plummer's file. Beverly had been seventeen years old and pregnant. Who was the father? Had Vera known? Had anyone known? Josie tried to bring more memories of Beverly into focus, but most of them were scattered and indistinct. High school seemed like a hundred years ago—like someone else's life.

"Would you look at this," Gretchen mused as they pulled up to the entrance of Quail Hollow Estates. "Protestors."

On either side of the sign announcing the development's name stood a handful of people in rain ponchos and beneath umbrellas holding crude signs that read: *Quail Hollow = Thieves and Criminals!*, *Charleston is a Mayor, not a dictator!*, *Dutton is a crook!*, and *Return Emergency Supplies!* One person had a sign that said both *Dutton for Mayor* and *Charleston for Mayor* with both candidates' names crossed out in angry red marker. The crowd surged forward when Josie turned in. She waved to the closest protestor and the woman stopped. She turned back to the people behind her and waved them off. "It's Detective Quinn," she told them. The rest of the protestors greeted her eagerly before letting her and Gretchen pass by.

"No wonder the Chief is having a conniption," Gretchen said. "The flooding is bad enough, but this is turning into a full-scale scandal."

They wound through the streets of the Estates. Twice they had to detour where roads had been blocked off due to the moat overflowing its banks and encroaching on the newer construction. Finally, they came to one of the original lanes where the homes were older, more stately, and set further back from the street. Calvin Plummer lived in a large, Tudor-style house surrounded by pink azalea bushes. Josie eased into the driveway behind a small Subaru with a dent in the back driver-side door.

Gretchen remarked, "I would have expected a lawyer living in Quail Hollow to be driving something a little fancier."

"That's not his," Josie said. "It's the secretary's. I saw it parked on the street when we left his office. She's lucky it didn't wash away."

Gretchen fake gagged. "I have a feeling this visit is going to make me feel even ickier than when we went to his office."

The large wooden door boasted a huge iron knocker with a lion's face on it. Josie lifted the ring and brought it down against the door several times. After a long moment, the door swung open and Tammy stood before them, now dressed in tight jeans and a form-fitting T-shirt. She looked even younger in casual clothes.

"We need to speak with Mr. Plummer," Gretchen told her.

Wordlessly, Tammy led them through an ornately decorated foyer to a large kitchen. White marble tile complemented the eggshell-colored cabinets, each one accented with elaborate molding and gleaming silver handles. The countertops were all granite, the color of white sand. Even the appliances were white. At the island table, Calvin Plummer sat in khaki pants and a polo shirt, a magazine in one hand and a fork in the other. He swirled pasta onto his fork and shoveled it into his mouth, leaning over the plate so the sauce dripping down his chin didn't get on his shirt. A half-eaten plateful lay across the table from him. Tammy took up her position there, digging back into her meal as if Josie and Gretchen weren't there.

Plummer looked up. "Didn't think I'd see you two again. What's going on?"

Josie said, "We've positively identified the murder victim found beneath the foundation of your property on Hempstead."

He put his fork and magazine down, wiped his mouth with a napkin, and sat back in his chair. His face was impassive. "*Murder victim?*"

"Yes," Josie said.

"How did it happen?"

"She was shot in the head," Gretchen told him. "Her name was Beverly Urban. She was seventeen. We believe she was a tenant of yours."

Tammy watched with wide eyes, her fork poised over her own plate.

Plummer scratched his chin. "Urban. She was the daughter, right? I rented to her mom. What was her name?"

"Vera," Josie filled in.

He nodded. "Yep, that's it. I rented to her for a while. Single mom. Nice lady but the last year she was there, she was late with the rent. I started eviction proceedings and then one night she up and left. Took all her stuff with her."

Josie and Gretchen exchanged a quizzical look. Gretchen took out her notebook and started jotting down notes. "She took all her personal things?"

"Most of them. She left behind a few knick-knacks. All the furniture. I figured she was taking off because she owed rent. I sold the furniture and used the security deposit to make repairs. Never heard from her again."

Gretchen asked, "What kind of repairs?"

He shrugged. "I don't really remember. I always had to have someone come in and paint the place between tenants."

Josie asked, "Was there any work being done to the basement?"

"I really couldn't tell you. Listen, I've got six rental properties, my office, and this big old place. We're talking about sixteen years ago. I'm sure there were repairs on Hempstead over the years, but I don't remember them all. I can tell you this though: I needed permits for anything I did to those rental properties. You should check with the City Codes office."

"We will," Gretchen said. "You didn't keep your own records of repairs made to your rental properties?"

"For taxes maybe," he said. "But not that far back."

Josie asked, "What about Beverly? Do you remember her?"

"I'm sorry to say, no. Not really. I don't think I ever met the kid. I just know Vera had one. She was required to list other residents on her lease. Plus, she always made a big deal out of being a single mother. Couldn't have a conversation with her where she didn't mention it."

"Are you aware of Vera ever having any men living or staying with her?" Gretchen asked.

"No," Plummer sighed. "Listen, I don't get to know my tenants, okay? They mail in their checks and call me if a pipe breaks. Then I call a contractor and pay them to make repairs. That's it. I don't see these people. I don't socialize with them."

"Got it," Josie said. "Do you have a list of contractors you use regularly?"

"Sure. Tammy can email a list of them to you. You have an email address?"

Gretchen jotted it down and handed it to Tammy.

"One last thing," Josie asked. "Do you own any firearms?"

He lowered his head, a smile on his face. "Of course," he said. "You think I might have killed this kid." He stood up and started walking out of the room, beckoning them along. "Come on," he called.

They followed him down a series of hallways to a study filled with shiny wooden bookcases and a behemoth of a desk. Along one wall was a gun cabinet and behind its glass, Josie counted three rifles and one shotgun. None were nine-millimeter. Gretchen studied them and wrote down their models. Plummer said, "I used to hunt. A long, long time ago. Never actually got anything, but I've had these guns ever since."

"No pistols or revolvers?" Josie asked. "For home or self-defense?"

"None," Plummer answered.

It would be easy enough to check with the State Police or FBI to find out whether he was lying or not. "Thank you for your time, Mr. Plummer," Josie said. "We look forward to receiving that list of contractors from your…"

"Secretary," he answered without missing a beat.

They thanked him and made their way back to the car. The rain had diminished to a light drizzle, for which Josie was grateful. It had to stop sometime, didn't it? As they pulled away, Gretchen made a face of disgust. "A guy like that? With a thing for young women?" she said. "There's no way he didn't notice Beverly Urban, as attractive as she was."

"Unless he's telling the truth that he never met her," Josie argued as they cruised out of Quail Hollow, waving goodbye to the gaggle of protestors. "He doesn't seem like the type to be bothered with lowly tenants, unless their rent is past due."

"True," Gretchen said. "Still, I don't think we can rule him out completely."

"Put him on the list then," Josie said. *With Ray*, she added silently.

Gretchen took out her phone. "It's late," she said. "We still have to wait for the list of contractors from Tammy the Secretary, and the City Codes office is closed. I don't know about you, but I'm exhausted. Should we call it a day?"

"Sure," Josie said. "I'm going to take my yearbook home, though, and see if I can put together a list of Beverly's closest friends."

CHAPTER TWELVE

The downstairs windows of Josie's house were alight. Inside, the dogs greeted her in a frenzy. The house was redolent with delicious smells coming from the kitchen. On the couch, little Harris snoozed in a pair of Spiderman pajamas. From the kitchen, Misty called out, "Josie, is that you?"

"Yeah," Josie replied, squatting to pet both dogs. Pepper lost interest after a moment, but Trout stayed, pushing his fat little body into Josie's hands.

"I'm making a roast," Misty said. "I hope you didn't eat." She poked her head out of the kitchen, a hopeful look on her face. "Did you bring anyone with you? I made a lot of food."

Josie smiled. "No, sorry. But Noah's car is out front. Isn't he here?"

"In the shower," Misty replied, disappearing back into the kitchen. "We'll eat in a half hour!"

Josie trudged up the steps with Trout racing anxiously behind her. She found Noah in their bedroom; a towel slung low across his hips, chest bare, toweling his thick brown hair dry with another towel. Sometimes, they got so caught up in their day-to-day lives, she forgot to admire him. She leaned against the closed door and studied the muscular lines of his body, her eyes landing on a circle of puckered flesh in his right shoulder, the sight of it bringing back a wave of guilt. She'd shot him once. He'd forgiven her, but she'd probably never forgive herself.

"Hey," he said, tossing the towel he was using to dry his hair onto the bed. His brown locks stuck up in every direction. Josie walked over and smoothed them down, away from his face. He rested his palms on her forearms and smiled at her. "I saw you on the news today."

She raised a brow. "I thought you were on emergency calls all day. You still found time to watch television?"

He pulled her in for a hug. She rested her cheek against his warm flesh. He said, "Mett and I stopped in at the station after we were finished and found out about it from a couple of patrol guys. It was easy enough to find the clip on the WYEP website. I'm glad you're okay."

She pulled back and looked into his face, glad that he didn't lecture her for doing something dangerous. "Did you hear about the press liaison the Mayor sent over?"

"I met her actually. She came in trailing the Chief after some meeting with the Mayor, just as cheery as could be. He went into his office and slammed the door in her face."

Josie shook her head. "I guess the meeting went well."

"Looks like we're stuck with her. Mett seems pretty happy about it though."

"What does that mean?"

"What do you think it means? I think he's got a crush on her. Either that or he was trying to make her feel really comfortable."

"When's the last time Mett tried to make someone comfortable? He's all about doing the job and that's it."

"Not today," Noah said. He let go of her. "Today he was all about this woman. Anyway, tell me about the body."

As he got dressed, Josie sat on the bed and ran through everything she and Gretchen had discovered that day. Noah listened without comment.

Josie said, "You were, what, two years behind me in high school?"

"Three," Noah said.

"Do you remember Beverly?"

"No, I'm sorry. I wouldn't have been in Denton East when she was a junior."

"Right," Josie said.

"I remember you and Ray, though."

Josie stared at him. Noah hadn't been on her radar at all until he joined Denton's police force only a few years after she and Ray had.

Noah sat beside her and took one of her hands. "I know you don't remember me from high school," he said. "I was a freshman when you two were seniors. I wouldn't expect you to remember anyone in the freshman class."

"But you remember me," Josie said.

Color rose to his cheeks. "Josie, come on, you've always known that I had a crush on you."

Her eyes widened. "I thought that started when you joined Denton PD."

He shook his head. "No. I knew who you were in high school. You were very beautiful then, just as you are now, and smart and…"

"And what?"

He laughed. "And you never took shit from anyone."

They sat in silence for a long moment. Josie said, "I didn't know. You remember Ray?"

"Of course," Noah answered. "I was jealous of him. I spent a lot of years being jealous of that guy."

Misty called from downstairs, interrupting them. Noah patted Josie's leg. "Listen, whatever you find out about Ray during this case, everything is going to be fine. Okay?"

Josie nodded, although somewhere deep in her core, she wasn't sure that was true. Thoughts and memories from high school played in the back of her mind all through dinner. If Noah, Misty, or Harris found her to be distracted, they didn't say anything. After dinner, she curled up on the couch with Trout snuggled against her and flipped through her yearbook while Noah chased a giggling Harris around the first floor, playing a game of tag.

Beverly hadn't had many friends. It didn't take long for Josie to find her two best friends in the yearbook: Kelly Ogden and Lana

Rosetti. Both had been in Josie's homeroom. Lana had had eighth period chemistry with Josie in junior year. They were Beverly's crew—her "cronies" Josie's grandmother, Lisette, had called them. Beverly was the leader, and like a three-headed snake, the trio wreaked havoc on the other girls in school. Kelly had been almost as mean as Beverly, never questioning orders, but Lana—if Josie remembered correctly—was kinder and more sensitive, often at odds with Beverly.

Josie remembered how once, at the beginning of junior year, Lana had been cast out for not agreeing to take part in a cruel joke. Beverly had wanted her to forge a note in the handwriting of the most popular, good-looking boy in their class and give it to a girl who was frequently made fun of for being overweight, asking her to homecoming. Luckily, because of Lana's resistance, the plan hadn't been carried out. The rest of the class had only found out about it after Beverly and Kelly had turned on Lana for not going through with it. They stopped talking to her and told everyone in the school that she had wet herself on a roller coaster ride at the beach over the summer. Humiliated, Lana sat alone and dejected in the cafeteria for two weeks. Then, as if by magic, she'd been taken back into the fold. Even then, Josie hadn't understood how Lana continued to be friends with them when they spent their time coming up with ways to torture their most vulnerable classmates. Especially since whenever Lana didn't go along with their schemes, they punished her.

Josie found her laptop on the coffee table beneath a pile of Harris's toys and opened it, pulling up Facebook to search for the two women. Kelly Ogden's profile picture showed a woman who looked much older than her early thirties, her brown hair pulled back into a tight ponytail and already graying at the roots. Her account was not private, but there weren't many photos or posts. Josie was able to glean that she had a teenage daughter and worked at a local supermarket. Lana's page had much stricter privacy settings, but her profile photo showed her, a man, and a small blond boy on a beach somewhere. All three were smiling. Lana looked like something out of a magazine, long blonde hair flowing in the wind, tanned skin, her blue eyes bright. Josie closed out Facebook and logged into one of the police databases, finding Kelly's address in town immediately. Lana's list of addresses was long, but her most current address was in Denton.

Josie didn't relish having to talk with either woman. She was content to leave her memories of high school in the past, but there was little choice now. Someone had murdered her high school bully, and it was her job to find that person and put him or her away.

The sound of two cell phones ringing at once startled her. Noah and Harris paused in the foyer. Noah took his phone from his back jeans pocket. "It's Mettner," he said.

Josie picked hers up from the coffee table. "I've got the Chief," she said.

Noah sighed. "This can't be good."

He swiped to answer the call and Josie did the same on her own phone. Chief Chitwood barked into her ear. "Quinn. I need someone down at the shopping district in South Denton. We got looters. Lots of 'em. Patrol rounded them up, but they need to be processed."

"I thought South Denton was under two feet of water," she said.

"Apparently, looters don't mind all that," Chitwood said.

He hung up. Josie looked at Noah, who had just hung up with Mettner. "I'll go," he said. "Mett's already on his way there."

Josie thought about arguing, but she was exhausted. She smiled at him. "I'll take the next call."

CHAPTER THIRTEEN

Noah slipped into bed beside Josie sometime in the middle of the night. Trout, who had taken Noah's spot in his absence, groaned as Noah nudged him. He stood up and went to Josie's feet, circling and dropping back down, his furry back soft and warm against her shins. She opened her eyes and could just make out Noah's form in the dim light cast by the green numbers on their alarm clocks. "How was it?" she asked.

"Sad," he told her. "The liquor store, the Spur Mobile store, that little clothing boutique, the pharmacy, all cleaned out. Everything gone except for the bookstore. Guess criminals don't read."

"That sucks," Josie replied. "Did you get them all?"

"Five of them," he told her. "They'll probably be released in the next two days once they're arraigned. Most of them were East Bridgers displaced by the flooding."

There were two bridges in Denton, one in the south and one to the east. The area beneath the eastern bridge had long been a gathering place for the city's homeless and drug trade.

Josie felt sleep pulling her back under and let her eyes drift closed. Noah touched her cheek. "Josie?"

She opened her eyes once more, blinking to bring him into focus. "Get some sleep," she told him. "It's after three. We have to be back at the station in a few hours."

"I just—" he began, but the sound of Josie's cell phone trilling stopped them. She rolled toward her nightstand and looked at it. "It's dispatch," she said.

Flicking on her lamp, Josie snatched the phone up and swiped answer. "Quinn."

"Detective Quinn?" said a male voice. "It's Officer Hiller. Sorry to bother you so late. We've got a woman on the line who wants to talk to you directly."

"Are you kidding me?" she said. "It's the middle of the night. You couldn't take a message?"

There was a beat of silence. Then, "I thought you'd want to talk to her. She knew the name of the Hempstead victim."

Josie sat up. Trout poked his head up from the foot of the bed, his ears perfect steeples. Noah patted the bedcovers next to him and Trout scampered over, settling against Noah's stomach. Josie asked, "What exactly did she say?"

"She called in and said that she needed to talk to Detective Josie Quinn about the Beverly Urban murder."

Josie's hand tightened around the phone. Beverly Urban's name hadn't been released to the press, nor had the fact that she was a homicide victim. The only people who knew her name and manner of death were Dr. Feist, members of Josie's team, and Calvin Plummer and his secretary. It couldn't be Tammy calling, could it?

"Did she give her name?" Josie asked. She glanced back at Noah, but his eyelids were heavy. He'd be asleep in moments.

"She would only give us the name Alice. That's it."

Josie stood up and padded quietly out to the hall and downstairs to the kitchen. "Put her through and text me the number she called from in case we get disconnected."

"You got it, boss."

The light over the sink had been left on in case Misty or Harris got up during the night. As she waited to be connected to Alice, Josie looked around, amazed at how clean Misty kept the kitchen. She wanted a drink of water but didn't want to disturb the orderliness. Instead, she leaned a hip against the counter and waited. There was a delay and then a change in the quality of the silence. Finally, a female voice said, "Hello? Detective Quinn?"

Too old to be Tammy, Josie thought. Unless she was somehow disguising her voice. A smoker, judging by the scratchiness. "This is Josie Quinn. What can I do for you, Alice? You have some information about the body we recovered from under the house on Hempstead?"

Hesitation. Then, "Y-yes. I do."

"What kind of information?" Josie asked.

"I know what happened to that girl," said Alice.

Josie listened for any background noise, but there was nothing. "What do you mean?"

"I know she was murdered. I know who did it."

It wouldn't be the first time that the department had received a call from someone looking for a bit of attention who claimed to have information about a crime. Josie needed to know that Alice was genuine. "How did Beverly die?"

"I can't talk to you on the phone about this," Alice said. "We need to meet."

Josie said, "Alice, I get a lot of phone calls. A lot of tips. I'm just trying to figure out whether you're telling the truth or not."

More hesitation. "She was shot in the head, okay?"

A chill rippled over Josie's body. "Okay, Alice. I think you're right. We need to meet."

"I can meet with you in private. Only you. No one else," Alice said hurriedly.

"Good," Josie said. "How about tomorrow at the police station in Denton? Do you know where that is?"

"I can't meet you there. It's not safe."

"Alice, I can assure you that there is no safer place in this city than the police station. I'll be there at nine a.m. You'll have to come in through the back. I can wait for you outside if you'd like, in the parking lot."

Alice's voice lowered to a whisper. "If you think the police station is safe, you're not as smart as I thought."

Before Josie could respond, the line went dead. Josie found the text from dispatch with the number and tried calling it back. It rang seven times before going to voicemail, but the outgoing message was an automated voice that read off the number she'd just called and told her to leave a message. "Alice," Josie said after the beep. "This is Josie Quinn. It's extremely important that you call me back. I need to talk to you. Please call me at this number as soon as you can. I'll meet you wherever you'd like." Josie rattled off her number and hung up.

She waited ten minutes but there was no return call. There was no way she was going back to sleep now. Questions whirled through her mind. Who was Alice? How did she know about Beverly's murder? Why had she kept it a secret for sixteen years? Had *she* murdered Beverly?

Josie went upstairs to get dressed.

CHAPTER FOURTEEN

Although two news vans sat in the municipal parking lot, no reporters waited near the entrance to the stationhouse. The rain was still coming down in a light drizzle. Josie was able to slip inside under the cover of darkness unnoticed. She checked in with the night desk sergeant and went up to her desk. She searched various databases, but the number that Alice had called from was a prepaid burner phone. Josie wrote up a warrant that would allow her to contact the major cellular networks and attempt to locate Alice's phone. Even burner phones had to use existing cellular networks to make calls. If Josie could figure out which network the number was using, she would be able to triangulate the phone's location. It would only bring her within a few miles, and she might not get the information for a few days, depending on the speed of the network's legal department, but it was better than nothing. She'd wait until regular working hours to ask a judge to sign it.

She tried calling Alice again but got only the voicemail. Next, she went through Calvin Plummer's files and her high school yearbook but found no one named Alice. Her eyes burned with fatigue as daylight crept through the windows. Rain spattered against the glass and Josie suppressed a groan. It seemed as though the rain would never end. The flooding was reaching doomsday proportions, and the river hadn't even crested yet. She heard the stairwell door swing open and a moment later, a steaming cup of coffee and a box of baked goods appeared in front of her.

Noah said, "The pastries are from Misty. You didn't even leave me a note. Everything okay?"

Josie sipped the coffee gratefully and leaned back in her chair. Noah took a seat across from her at his own desk. She told him about the call.

"Why didn't you wake me up?" he said.

"Then you wouldn't have had any sleep at all. Besides, it's a dead end right now. Unless she calls back."

Gretchen and Mettner banged through the stairwell door, both shaking water from their hair. They attacked Misty's box of goodies and settled in at their desks, ready to catch up. Gretchen booted up her computer, checked her email, and started printing documents out. Before Josie could brief them on the Beverly Urban case or the mysterious female night caller, Amber arrived, dressed in another form-fitting skirt and blouse, this time in darker tones. Instead of a briefcase, she carried a cup-holder filled with paper coffee cups. She set them down on Mettner's desk. "Hi, everyone," she said with a smile. "I thought you might need these." Her face fell as she saw the cup in Josie's hand, but she quickly covered it with a smile. "Now you'll have two," she told Josie, setting a cup in front of her. "Detective Quinn," she said. "Detective Mettner told me you like your coffee with two sugars and lots of half and half."

"Mett," Josie said. "We just call him Mett. Thank you."

Josie sipped the cup Noah had brought her as she watched Amber hand out the rest of them, each one made to the person's liking as per Mett's instructions.

Mettner said, "I told her we usually like Komorrah's, but they're flooded now."

Gamely, Noah said, "This was very thoughtful. Thank you."

When she had finished dispensing the drinks, Amber pulled a chair over from one of the unoccupied desks. She produced a tablet with keyboard which she opened on her lap. Then she looked at them expectantly.

Gretchen said, "Miss Watts, you'll be joining us for all of our briefings from now on?"

Amber smiled. "Please, call me Amber. Well, not every briefing but I thought for now, to get myself acclimated, I'd sit in on as many as I can. This will give me an idea of what types of cases you're working on and any press issues you might be up against."

Josie wanted to tell her that they'd handled the press just fine as long as she'd been with the department, but it was obvious that in spite of the Chief's protests, Amber was there to stay. When no one spoke, Amber said, "Look, detectives, I'm not the Mayor's plant, okay?"

"No one said that," Mettner told her.

Josie, Gretchen, and Noah all swiveled their heads to stare at him. Noticing their looks, he said, "What? You guys think she's a plant from the Mayor? Really?"

"It's okay," Amber said. "Really. Listen, I can't change the fact that the Mayor hired me, but I am here to do a job and that is to handle all press matters so that all of you can do your jobs. That's what I'm here to do, and if it makes you feel any better, I report to your Chief, not the Mayor."

No one spoke.

After a tense moment, Mettner said, "Come on, guys. We might as well make the most of this situation. We've got work to do."

Gretchen said, "What happens if Mayor Charleston doesn't get re-elected? Do you lose your job?"

Amber waved a hand dismissively. "Oh, the election is months away. I'm not worried about that now."

"But the primary is in a couple of weeks," Noah pointed out. "The other party doesn't have a candidate, which means either Charleston or Dutton will run unopposed for Mayor in November. You'll know in two weeks who your boss is going to be next year."

Josie said, "Dutton's running on a campaign to cut spending. He's made Charleston out as though she's gone buck wild with the city's budget."

Amber stared at them, a genial smile frozen stiffly on her face. An awkward moment passed. Then she let out a breath and said,

"Well, I can't worry about that right now. I have a job to do for as long as I'm here, so if you wouldn't mind…"

Reluctantly, they began their morning briefing on the Beverly Urban case. Gretchen ran down everything they'd learned the day before. Josie talked about having tracked down Beverly's two best school friends; the call from Alice; her search for the name in the Urban materials; and the warrants she had prepared for the cellular networks. Then Gretchen passed around a list of contractors that Plummer's secretary had emailed over that morning.

Noah skimmed over it. "Here," he said. "Newton Basement Waterproofing. I'd talk to them first."

"That's what I was thinking," Gretchen said. "But I'd still like to dig up the permits from the City Codes office."

"I'll go," Noah said.

Mettner said, "I'm supposed to be at the command post today. I can have someone take me over to Hempstead and see if it's still underwater. If it's not, I can poke around; see if I can find any clues."

"Look for the house downstream too," Josie told him. "See if you can find anything there."

"On it," Mettner said. He stood, picked up his coffee cup, and smiled at Amber. "I'll see you later."

Noah said, "I'll head over to the City Codes office. That's probably going to take a few hours. This way you two can start talking to people while I do that."

Amber clicked away on her tablet as Josie picked up several documents Gretchen had printed out that morning, looking for known relatives of Vera Urban. "There's a brother here," Josie said.

"Yeah," Gretchen answered. "I looked him up. He lives in Georgia. Not married. He's a chemical engineer. Looks like he's ten years older than her."

"Let's give him a call."

CHAPTER FIFTEEN

Josie picked up the phone and set it to speaker so they could both hear. She dialed Vera's brother's number. After six rings, a man's voice answered.

"Mr. Floyd Urban?" Josie asked.

"Who is this?"

Josie identified herself and Gretchen and told him why they were calling. For a long moment there was only dead air. Then he said, "You said my niece was murdered? I hate to tell you this, officers, but I don't have a niece."

Gretchen said, "You have a sister though, correct?"

"Well, yeah, but I haven't talked to her in decades. We're… how do you say? … Estranged."

"Why is that?" Josie asked.

"I don't really have time for this," Floyd told them.

Josie said, "Okay, well what we can do is contact the police in your area and have them bring you in for an interview at your convenience. Would that work better?"

The sound of a heavy sigh filtered through the line. Then Floyd said, "Our mother died when Vera was very young, but our father passed when Vera was just out of high school. He didn't have much, but she wanted it all. The house, the car, whatever was in his bank accounts. Said she needed it. Said I had been out of the house for ten years and was already established. When I insisted on getting my half of the estate, she tried to pass off a forged will, saying our dad had written it before he died, cutting me out and leaving her everything."

"How did you know it was forged?" Gretchen asked.

"My sister was eighteen at the time, and believe me, she was never a genius. I just knew. As soon as I threatened to get lawyers involved, she backed down. We split the estate down the middle and never spoke again."

"Not even once?" Josie asked. "Not even through social media? No calls for major life events?"

"Let me put it to you this way, officer, I didn't even invite her to my wedding. My kids are grown now and have no idea she even exists. I really didn't want someone like that in their lives anyway."

"Someone like that," Josie echoed. "Vera was just a kid."

Floyd laughed bitterly. "You sound like my father. She was old enough to know right from wrong. Listen, she wasn't a murderer or anything, sure, but she was conniving, and she had a problem with lying. The estate business was the final straw."

Gretchen said, "You had no idea that Vera ever had a child?"

"No, I'm sorry, I didn't."

"You haven't heard from or spoken with or been in any contact with Vera since she was eighteen years old?" Josie asked.

"That's right."

"Mr. Urban, do you know anyone named Alice?" Josie asked.

"No."

"Do you know if Vera knew anyone by that name?"

"No, I don't. I told you, we've never had a relationship. Listen, I really can't help you."

Gretchen said, "The medical examiner is going to be releasing Beverly Urban's body soon. They usually ask the next of kin to make the arrangements."

Bitter laughter erupted from the receiver. "I am not the next of kin."

Josie said, "I'm afraid you are, Mr. Urban."

"This kid of Vera's didn't have a father?" he asked.

"There's none listed on the birth certificate," Gretchen said.

He laughed again. "Yeah, that sounds exactly right. Well, you've got your work cut out for you, don't you? Find her father because I'm not paying for her funeral."

With that, he hung up.

Josie looked at Gretchen. "I have a feeling Vera was lucky that he stopped speaking to her all those years ago."

Shaking her head, Gretchen said, "I think you're right." She jotted down some notes in her notebook. "Well, that doesn't get us anywhere at all."

"We've got to find someone who knew Vera," Josie said. "Maybe old co-workers or friends?"

Gretchen suggested, "Maybe Beverly's friends would know where her mother worked or who her friends were."

"Worth a try," Josie said.

Chief Chitwood's voice boomed across the room. "Detectives," he said, striding out of his office. Ignoring Amber, he asked, "What have you got for me?"

They briefed him and he listened, the creases in his craggy face deepening with each detail. When they finished, he said, "Let's have a press conference."

Amber's head shot up from her tablet. "Chief," she said. "Are you sure that's a good idea this early on in the investigation?"

"Watts," he barked. "It's ultimately my decision when to have press conferences. If I tell my detectives to notify the press of what's going on, that's what they'll do."

Amber said, "This is a cold case, sir. There's no urgency—"

Chitwood cut her off, pointing a finger in her direction. "You don't think putting a murderer behind bars is urgent, Watts?"

Amber put a hand up. "That's not what I said. I only meant to say that it might be prudent to get more information before we take this public."

Josie cleared her throat. "Chief," she said. "I think what Miss Watts is getting at is that once we make the details of the case public, anyone who might know something about Beverly Urban's murder and the whereabouts of her mother may disappear or withhold information they might otherwise have told us. This Alice person—what if she runs once we release Beverly's name to the public?"

One of his bushy eyebrows kinked, a rogue gray hair like steel wool jutting out. "Quinn, in my office. Now."

With a sigh, Josie followed him inside his office, closing the door behind her. He paced in front of his desk, keeping his voice low. She expected him to reprimand her for disagreeing with him in front of the new press liaison but instead he said, "Listen, Quinn, I need these protestors over at Quail Hollow off my back. I have to give the public something else to gnaw on. What better than this? A murder case. For the love of all that's holy, I can't even speak freely in my own stationhouse anymore."

"Sir, I wasn't suggesting that we don't do a press conference, just that we limit what we tell the press. If this Alice woman is a real lead, I don't want to lose her. You can work out what to release and what to hold back. Just don't release Beverly's name yet. Make Amber do the conference. That's why she's here, isn't it?"

He nodded. "I need something to keep her busy until this Quail Hollow thing is resolved. If the Mayor thinks sending a spy is going to stop me from bringing the full force of the law down on her and her cronies, she's got another think coming."

Josie said, "Release some vague details today. We found the body of a seventeen-year-old girl under the house on Hempstead. We're working to identify her and determine how long she may have been buried there. The medical examiner has confirmed that the manner of death was homicide. Tomorrow, we send Amber out there with a little more."

His head bobbed along with her words. "Yeah," he said. "I can give her a tip line to handle. Ask people to call in. Good work,

Quinn. You take Palmer—get those warrants signed and run down some leads. Now, get out of my office and send Miss Watts in here. I'll settle this with her. Then I've got to go handle some more of this Quail Hollow horseshit before a riot breaks out."

Josie went back to her desk and told Amber that the Chief wanted to see her. She stood up, smoothed her skirt, plastered a smile across her face, and strode into the Chief's office.

"What was that about?" Gretchen asked.

Josie waited for the Chief's door to close before she relayed the conversation to Gretchen.

"Wow," said Gretchen. "There may be an unforeseen advantage to having a press liaison."

"Really?" Josie asked. "What's that?"

"He might be on our side more often now."

Josie's cell phone buzzed several times. She punched in her passcode and studied the text messages from Noah. "We've got a lead," she said. "Looks like there were some major plumbing issues at the house on Hempstead while Vera and Beverly were living there. One of the load-bearing walls got rotted. That work was handled by Zurzola Contracting."

Gretchen wheeled her chair over to her desktop computer and started typing. "Looks like they closed in 2007." She picked up a printout of the email she'd received from Tammy and studied it. "They're not even on this list. Does it say anything about who did the plumbing work?"

"Yes," Josie said. "You don't have to look it up, the plumber is dead."

"Great," Gretchen sighed. "We're really on a roll here."

"Hold on," Josie said, scrolling through the texts and PDF documents Noah had sent over. "Look up Newton Basement Waterproofing, the one Noah mentioned earlier. Around that same time, they applied for a permit to underpin the basement. If the plumbing issue was that large that they needed to dig up some or all of the basement, maybe Plummer decided to go ahead and have the whole basement lowered at the same time."

Gretchen's hands flew across her keyboard. A smile lit her face. "We're in luck. They're still in business—and their office is not in one of the flood zones!"

CHAPTER SIXTEEN

After taking care of the warrants, they headed to Newton Basement Waterproofing. The rain had stopped, but the clouds overhead were thick and gray. They showed no signs of clearing. Josie longed for the sight of blue skies and sunshine. The gloomy weather did nothing to help her mood. She turned briefly to Gretchen. "You find out anything about this company?"

"Looks like it's family owned," she told Josie. "Been around forty years. Father passed it to his son. Current owner is George Newton. He is in his forties. They have a staff of ten."

Josie skirted around the flooded portion of the city, taking a circuitous route until she reached North Denton, which was a more sparsely populated and mountainous part of the city. Newton Basement Waterproofing was housed in a flat-roofed cinderblock building with a large parking lot. Two pickup trucks sat in front of the building, their beds filled with equipment. Josie and Gretchen parked next to them and made their way inside. A ding sounded overhead as they opened the front door and stepped in. A few chairs sat unoccupied to their left. Directly in front of them was a tall, unmanned desk. Brochures were spaced in neat piles across its surface. From a doorway behind the desk, a male voice called, "Be right there!"

They waited five minutes and finally, a ruddy-faced man with short brown hair emerged from the doorway. He wore dirty jeans and a black T-shirt with white lettering that said, *Newton Basement Waterproofing. Since 1980.* "What can I do for you?" he asked.

Josie and Gretchen were getting their credentials out when he pointed at Josie and said, "Hey, I know you. You're that detective."

Josie handed him her credentials. "Yes, Detective Josie Quinn."

He gave Gretchen's ID a passing glance, his attention focused on Josie. "What can I help you with?"

Josie said, "I don't know if you've had a chance to watch the news in the last twenty-four hours, but we recovered human remains from beneath the foundation of a home on Hempstead Road."

He grimaced. "Oh yeah, I saw it on the news. It was a body, huh?"

"Yes, unfortunately. It was the body of a girl who lived in the house between 1997 and 2004. She had been buried beneath the foundation. We pulled city permits to see if anyone had worked on the basement of that house, and we found that your company applied for a permit for underpinning in 2004."

His face clouded with confusion. "You think I had something to do with this?"

Gretchen said, "Mr. Newton, is it?"

"Yeah," he said. "George."

"Right now, we're just trying to establish when and how the body came to be under the house. Do you remember working on Hempstead?"

His eyes were wide. "No. I mean if we applied for a permit, then I'm sure we did the work, but I don't personally remember it."

"Were you working here back then?" Josie asked.

"Oh yeah," he answered. "I wasn't in charge or anything, but I worked for my pops for a long time before he handed over the company. I was on the crews. He sent us to places and we did the jobs."

On her phone, Josie pulled up the PDF document Noah had sent her and showed it to him. He patted his collar and then searched the underside of the desk until he came up with a pair of reading glasses. "You mind?" he asked, reaching for her phone.

"Not at all," Josie told him, handing her phone over.

He studied the document for several minutes before saying, "Looks like my dad filed for the permit on this one. This is his signature. They had some pretty extensive plumbing and sewage problems. We had to tear up the whole basement and lower it, re-pour the foundation."

Gretchen asked, "Is your dad still around?"

"No, I'm sorry. He passed last year."

Josie said, "I'm so sorry to hear that. Do you have any records of your own from this job?"

George shook his head. "We only keep records going back seven years. I'm sorry."

"Do you know anyone who might have been on the crew who did the job on Hempstead?" Josie persisted.

"I couldn't tell you," he admitted. "I was probably on the crew. You've got to understand, we work hundreds of jobs a year and this is going back, jeez, almost twenty years."

Josie took her phone back and pulled up the last existing driver's license photo for Vera Urban to show him. "Do you remember her?"

He rubbed his chin. "She looks familiar."

Gretchen used her own phone to show him Beverly's yearbook photo. "How about her?"

He stared at the photo. "Oh, her," he said. "Yeah, I remember her. She was a real pain in the ass, that one."

Josie felt a tug of excitement at her core. "Why do you say that?"

"I remember this job now. Look, I don't remember a lot of jobs. Like I said, we do hundreds every year. Can't remember them all. It's the ones that are a pain in the ass that stick in your mind, you know?"

"Yes," Gretchen and Josie said in unison.

"Her mom was sick or something. Disabled. I don't know. She had a hard time getting around. We never saw her. She was up in a bedroom all the time. But this girl was there to let us into the house in the morning and then she'd come home from school and hang around. We couldn't get a damn thing done. She had a thing for one of our guys."

"Which guy?" Gretchen asked.

"I don't remember his name. He was only with us a couple of months. My dad hired him. We tried to train him, but he wasn't interested in learning the work. He just wanted the money to put up his nose."

"He had a drug problem?" Josie asked.

"Big time. Like I said, he lasted like two months and then one time, the day after payday, he was a no-call, no-show for his shift. Never heard from him again and then saw in the local paper he overdosed."

"So he is deceased," Josie said. Another dead end. "What did Beverly want with him?"

He shrugged. "I don't know. I didn't have time to spy on them. We had to get the job done. But whenever she was there, he'd be off in another room with her or outside with her, their heads together."

"You don't remember anything else about him?" Josie asked.

George took a long moment to think it over, rubbing his chin again; his eyes squinted as if the act of calling up the memories was strenuous. Finally, he said, "Name began with an A. Andrew, Ambrose, something like that."

Gretchen took out her notebook and jotted the names down. "How old was he then? Do you remember?"

"Probably my age, so back then he would have been in his mid to late twenties."

Josie asked, "Do you know if he saw Beverly outside of work?"

"No, sorry. I wasn't friends with the guy. Only reason I remember him is 'cause he was such a bad hire, and I wanted my dad to get rid of him. It was bad enough he was slacking off on the job. Then he was flirting with a high school girl? That's not cool. I didn't like him."

"Do you know, Mr. Newton, if that gentleman owned any firearms?" Josie asked.

"I don't think so, but I couldn't say for sure."

"How about you?" Gretchen asked. "Do you own any firearms?"

"No, not me," he answered.

"How long did the job take?" Josie asked, before he could ask why they were so concerned with whether or not he owned guns.

He shrugged. "I don't remember specifically. Probably the same amount of time they always do. Coupla months."

"Were there any interruptions to the job?" Gretchen asked. "That you remember now? Anything unusual?"

He looked from Gretchen to Josie and back. "You think someone buried this girl under the foundation while we were in the middle of the job? And we didn't notice?"

They said nothing.

Again, he gave them the grimace that indicated he was searching his memories. "A couple of times we had to stop because they were having plumbing work done, if I remember correctly, and we didn't work weekends. There was some time at the end of the job that the house was empty. My dad had to get the key from the landlord, I think. Back then, we just figured the mom and daughter were on vacation or something. We just wanted to finish the job. That's all I remember. I mean, I guess it's possible someone could have put her in there while we were in the middle of the job if they did it at the right time and left everything looking the way we left it." He shuddered. "That's a terrible thing. I'd hate to think we poured concrete over that girl and didn't even know it."

Josie took out a business card and handed it to him, telling him to give them a call if he remembered anything else he thought they should know. He took it slowly, suddenly looking dumbfounded and very distressed.

Gretchen said, "Mr. Newton? You okay? Is there something else?"

He shook his head and Josie thought she saw his eyes glistening. "It's just—who would do something like that? Something so awful?"

Josie said, "That's what we're going to find out."

CHAPTER SEVENTEEN

It was nearing lunch time so they got takeout which they ate in the car before heading to Kelly Ogden's address. As Josie drove, Gretchen sent a text to Noah asking him to check into the firearm ownership of Calvin Plummer and George Newton to confirm they were both telling the truth. She also asked him to see if he could find a death certificate or obituary for a man in his mid-twenties whose name started with A during the summer of 2004.

"So, possible suspects: we've got the landlord," Josie said. "Ray, George Newton, and now this guy Beverly was flirting with on Newton's work crew."

Gretchen said, "The list is getting longer with each person we talk to."

"It doesn't help that half of our list is dead," Josie said.

They pulled up in front of a crumbling five-story apartment building in a run-down part of Denton that had somehow escaped the flooding thus far. They found Ogden's apartment easily enough but after ringing the bell and knocking for several minutes, there was no answer. Since Josie had figured out from perusing her Facebook page that she now worked at one of the local supermarkets, they headed there, where they found her working checkout in lane seven. She passed people through her line with a blank-faced efficiency, only talking to customers to tell them how much their bill was and to ask if they had any coupons. As in her profile photo, her brown hair was pulled back in a tight ponytail. In person, she looked much older than her thirty-three years.

Gretchen left Josie just inside the store while she went in search of the manager. Fifteen minutes later, Kelly led them sullenly out to the parking lot, around to the side of the building. A light mist had begun to fall from the heavy clouds overhead. Beneath a small overhang, a lone ash tray stood among the weeds on the cracked asphalt. Kelly took a long drag from her cigarette and wrapped one arm across her chest like a shield. "I don't know nothing about that looting last night. I know you got my brother, but I wasn't there. I was home sleeping, minding my business. I got a job. I don't need to steal stuff. My brother, you know, he got into the drugs, or whatever. I don't do drugs. The looting and all that wasn't even his idea. He started running with that old dude, what's his name? He got arrested last night too, you know. You should talk to him, not me."

Josie and Gretchen stared at her.

Josie said, "We're not here about any of that."

Kelly thrust her cigarette into the air. "Zeke!" she exclaimed. "That's his name."

Josie's heart went into overdrive for a few seconds, before settling back down. Quietly, to Gretchen, she said, "Zeke was arrested last night for looting?"

Gretchen frowned. "I don't know, boss. Noah and Mett handled it."

Why hadn't Noah told her? Or perhaps he had tried to tell her, but she'd gotten the call from Alice and hadn't had a chance to speak privately with him since. Did it matter? she wondered. No, she decided. Nothing that Larry Ezekiel Fox did mattered to her. She cleared all thoughts of him from her mind and focused on Kelly.

Gretchen said, "Kelly, we're here to talk to you about Beverly Urban."

Kelly stared at her for a long moment. She took a final drag of her cigarette, tossed it onto the ground, and stepped on it. Then she took out another cigarette and lit it. After a deep inhale, she said, "Beverly Urban. I haven't thought about her since high school."

"You were good friends," Josie said.

Kelly straightened her shoulders and with some pride, said, "I was her best friend."

Gretchen asked, "When is the last time you spoke to her?"

Kelly's chin dropped to her chest. She sucked in some more smoke and let it back out. "Why don't you ask me when *she* last spoke to me? We were best friends and then one day she just stopped calling and stopped coming around."

"You didn't think to check on her?" Josie asked.

Kelly's brow furrowed. "Check on her? Like what? In case she was sick? She wasn't sick. I went to her house and she was gone. Her and her mom. They took off. Didn't tell anyone. Just left."

"You didn't find that unusual or suspicious?" Gretchen asked.

"Nah… they said they were going to have to leave. They were broke as hell. No way were they getting out of moving. I just didn't think they'd leave without saying goodbye or that Beverly wouldn't ever call me again. But it was probably her mom. She had a real bug up her ass."

Josie said, "About what?"

Kelly laughed. "You think I don't remember you? You were there. *About what.* Please. You knew what Beverly was like. Always getting into trouble."

"I wasn't friends with her. I need to know what kind of trouble she was in before she left."

For the first time, Kelly seemed to realize the significance of two police officers coming to her place of employment to discuss a friend she'd neither seen nor heard from in sixteen years. "Hey, wait a minute," she said, pointing her cigarette at Josie. "What's going on here? Did Beverly do something?"

"No," Gretchen said. "She didn't do anything. I'm afraid she's dead, Kelly."

"Oh shit!" Kelly said. She walked in a small circle, as if she couldn't contain her shock. "Oh shit, she was in that tarp, wasn't she? On the TV? She was under the house? She was, like, murdered?"

"Yes," Josie said. "We're trying to figure out what happened to her and who might have killed her. Besides you and Lana Rosetti, was there anyone else she hung around with regularly?"

Kelly shook her head but then she said, "No, we were her best friends."

"Did Beverly use drugs?" Josie asked.

"No, no drugs. She just had her men, you know?"

"Men?" Gretchen prodded.

Kelly rolled her eyes. "That's what she called them. I don't even know if they were real. Beverly liked to talk. Thought she was hot shit. I mean, she kind of was. She could get any guy, really, but she also liked to tell stories, exaggerate. Whenever she had a crush on a guy, she'd act like they were seeing each other, even if they weren't."

Josie said, "Do you remember the names of any of these men?"

"She never told us their names. That's why I'm saying it was hard to know if they were real or not. She talked about them all the time, but we never saw any of them or met any of them."

"What did she tell you about them?" Gretchen asked, pen poised over her notepad. "Particularly in the months leading up to the last time you spoke with her."

Kelly tapped ash onto the concrete. "She would tell us, like, what they said to her, like how much they complimented her and stuff and what they were like."

Josie asked, "Was she having sex with any of them?"

Kelly rolled her eyes. "She claimed they all wanted to have sex with her, but I don't know if she really was. Like I said, Beverly was a lot of talk. Most of what she said—about anything—was bullshit."

But Josie knew not everything Beverly had intimated was bullshit since she'd been five months pregnant when she was murdered.

"How many men are we talking about?" Gretchen asked.

"Like, four," Kelly answered. "I guess she might have really been sleeping with one of them, 'cause he had a tattoo she always talked about. Like it made him badass or something. Everyone's got tattoos. But we were young and dumb then. Dating a guy with a tattoo was a big deal."

"What kind of tattoo?" Gretchen asked.

Kelly shrugged and flicked some ash onto the ground. The light mist was turning into steady rain. "Don't remember. It was big, though, I think."

Josie said, "Where on his body? Did she say?"

Kelly took a few seconds to consider this. "I don't really know. I don't remember."

Gretchen said, "But you remember she talked about four different guys."

"Yeah. One of them was, um…" She stared at Josie and bit her bottom lip.

"Ray Quinn," Josie answered. "She was seeing him?"

Kelly said, "She told us she was, like, behind your back, but I don't think it was true. Every time I ever saw her try to talk to him, he never gave her the time of day."

And yet, Beverly had been wearing his treasured jacket when she was murdered.

"What about the others?" Gretchen asked, moving the conversation away from Ray.

"She said they were older. Ray was the only high school guy she said she was interested in. One guy was doing work at her house or something."

That tracked with what George Newton had told them. Josie asked, "If she never told you their names, what did she call them when she talked about them?"

"She had nicknames for them."

Josie asked, "Do you remember what they were?"

Kelly shook her head. She took one last puff from her second cigarette and tossed the butt aside. "Nah, I don't remember after all this time. Sorry."

"Was there one she was more serious about than the others?" Gretchen asked.

"I don't know if there was one she liked more than the others," Kelly said. "But there was one who lost interest in her, and she was pissed."

"Any idea who that might have been?" Josie asked.

"No, sorry."

Josie said, "What about Beverly's father? Did she ever mention him? Did she know who he was?"

"She didn't know who he was, and all her mom would ever tell her was that her dad didn't want to be involved. Beverly didn't believe her, but I think that was just because she didn't really want to believe that her own dad would want nothing to do with her."

It was a sad detail of Beverly's life, and Josie wondered what Vera Urban had been thinking when she had told daughter that. Josie wondered if there would have been a kinder way to explain Beverly's father's absence to her. Perhaps there wasn't, without lying.

"What can you tell us about her mother?" Josie said. "Vera?"

"She was, like, disabled."

"In what way?" Gretchen asked.

"She had a bad disc in her back. Had to take a ton of Percocet and oxycodones to do the simplest thing."

"Was it from an accident or something?" Josie asked.

Kelly pulled out her crushed pack of cigarettes and shook another one out, lighting it. The rain pattered on the aluminum overhang. "It was a fight."

Gretchen and Josie looked at one another. Josie knew Gretchen was thinking about the criminal record they'd found for Vera. A couple of speeding tickets and a dismissed charge for writing a bad check. Nothing violent.

"It wasn't, like, at a bar or anything," Kelly said, as if fights only happened in bars. "Her and Beverly got into a fight. They were always fighting. Beverly's mom could be a real bitch. In middle school they got into a real doozy, and Beverly pushed her down the stairs."

Josie said, "Beverly pushed her mother down the stairs?"

Kelly laughed, blowing a stream of smoke into Josie's face. "That surprise you?"

"No, I guess not. I just assumed she only took out her anger on people she didn't like."

"What makes you think she liked old Vera? I'm telling you, Vera was a pain in the ass. Wouldn't let Beverly do a damn thing. They never got along."

"Do you know why?" Gretchen asked.

"Are you listening at all? 'Cause Vera was a bitch!"

"Okay," Josie said. "Kelly, we have some other questions about Vera. You said she was disabled with a bad back. Do you know if she worked before that?"

"Oh yeah, she was a hairdresser. She stopped after Beverly knocked her down the steps. She had to. Couldn't stand all day, she said. She had surgery on her back, but it just got worse."

"Did Vera have a boyfriend?" Gretchen asked.

"No, she never did. Beverly used to tell her she needed to get laid and she should get a boyfriend and then Vera would say no man would have her because she had a rotten teenage daughter."

Again, Josie felt a stab of sympathy for Beverly even though she hadn't been able to muster any when they were in school together. Then again, Josie had had no idea what Beverly's home life was like back then.

Josie said, "Just one last question, Kelly. Did Beverly ever mention anything to you about being pregnant?"

Her eyes widened. "No. Never. You think she was pregnant?"

"We really can't discuss it," Gretchen said. "How about any friends of either Beverly's or Vera's named Alice? Do you remember anyone named Alice?"

Kelly shook her head. "No. Doesn't ring a bell."

Josie asked, "When is the last time you spoke with Lana Rosetti?"

"Not since high school," Kelly answered.

Gretchen handed Kelly a business card. "You've been very helpful. Call us if you remember anything else."

CHAPTER EIGHTEEN

2004

The air was abuzz with energy and excitement. People milled around the outside of the baseball field. The bleachers were already full. Some Denton residents had brought their own folding chairs and set them down wherever they could find a place. The sun had begun to sag, but the heat and humidity hadn't let up. Josie held her long black hair off her neck for a moment, reveling in the feel of the air on her nape. She waited at the chain-link fence along the first-base line where Denton East players' friends and families gathered before the start of each game to wish the players luck. Bodies pressed in behind her, but she held firm. Lisette was standing in the long concession line.

A roar went up from the crowd as the players ran onto the field. Josie knew Ray immediately from his loping run. He turned his head and winked at her before taking his place on the mound. He and the catcher warmed up while the other players ran around the field and threw balls back and forth, getting ready for the championship game. Josie let her hair down and put her hands over the top of the fence. A film of sweat covered her bare arms and legs. Around her, people shouted encouragement to the players. Several minutes later, the team broke to let their opponents come out and warm up. Tapping his glove against his leg, Ray sauntered over to Josie. He looked the picture of confidence, but she could tell by the way his eyes shifted all around that he was nervous.

She leaned in for a kiss when he reached the fence. "Don't be nervous," she told him. "You're going to do great."

He tucked his glove under his armpit and used one hand to smooth her hair out of her face. "You think so, Jo?"

Josie grinned. "I know so. This is going to be your best game. Wait and see."

"I hope you're right."

They kissed again until someone nearby hollered, "Get a room!" Then the coach came onto the field with a group of men dressed business-casual in collared shirts and trousers and called for the team. Ray looked over his shoulder. "Shit," he said. "I gotta go. We gotta take pictures with the sponsors before the game starts."

Josie reached up and straightened his ball cap. "I'd wish you luck, but you won't need it. See you after."

She watched him jog off, her heart stuttering in her chest. God, she hoped they won. Ray had been enjoying the baseball season so much, it had lifted him out of the depression he sometimes fell into. He'd worked hard, too, and she hoped she was right about all that hard work paying off. At home plate, the team lined up and knelt with the coach and four local businessmen standing behind them. Josie recognized the founder of their local coffee shop, Komorrah's Koffee, with his wispy white hair and stooped shoulders. Josie had heard he would retire soon and turn the business over to his daughter. Then there was the owner of the pizza shop just outside the university campus. Josie put him in his fifties. He had greasy blond hair and a moustache that looked as though it was struggling to grow in. He looked as though he ate as many pizzas as he sold. There were two other men who looked to be in their mid-to-late thirties. One was tall and lanky with thick, wavy brown hair and a thin pair of glasses that kept sliding down his nose. She was pretty sure he was the owner of a local software company that had had a lot of success recently, although she couldn't remember his name. The last guy was average height, tanned and toned, with brown hair cut close to his head, spikey and gelled on the top, like he was trying to appear younger than he actually was. She didn't know his name or remember which business he owned, but she'd seen him on television a few times. Something about remodeling the historic downtown theater.

The click and flash of cameras behind her drew Josie's attention. She turned away from the field to see several people holding up cameras. Josie muscled her way through the siege of people. They closed in on the fence the moment she stepped away, shouting at players and snapping photos. It took several minutes to find Lisette along the side of the bleachers, sitting in a lawn chair along the third base line. A matching chair sat beside her, its seat overflowing with food she'd bought from the concessions. "There you are," Lisette said. "Better sit before someone else tries to take this seat."

She pawed through the food she had bought, which would have been enough to feed the two of them for a week, let alone for a single game. There were four hot dogs, a half dozen bags of chips, French fries slathered in catsup, and some brownies.

Josie said, "Gram, this is too much."

Lisette shook her head. "Ray will be hungry after the game. We'll give whatever we don't finish to him. Oh no. I forgot to get napkins. Would you be a dear and run over to the concession stand? Grab a handful."

With only a few more minutes to game time, people were flocking toward their seats, jostling for space anywhere they could find it. Josie went around the back of the bleachers where it was just grass littered with food wrappers terminating at a taller chain-link fence. Beyond the fence was a parking lot and beside that, a wooded area. People still streamed in through the narrow entrance from the parking lot, and she had to fight her way to the concession stand, nearly falling on her ass when a wall ran directly into her. Not a wall, she realized, as strong hands gripped her upper arms, but a man. She looked up into the face of one of the sponsors. Tanned and toned. "I'm sorry," he said, smiling down at her with wide lips and straight white teeth. He might have been sexy if he hadn't held onto her for a beat too long and if his thumb hadn't brushed lightly over the side of her breast while he did it.

Pulling away from him, Josie put her chin down and tried to pass him. "It's fine," she said. People flowed around them without a glance.

He touched her shoulder, stopping her in place. "Do I know you?"

Josie hitched a thumb over her shoulder. "The pitcher is my boyfriend," she said. "You've probably seen me with him."

His smile had become conspiratorial, as though they were sharing a secret of some kind. "That kid is good," he said. "On the field."

Josie felt her cheeks pinken. "I have to—"

Before she could finish her sentence, something behind her caught his eye. Relief flooded through her as he said, "It was nice meeting you," before he stepped around her and went on his way. Josie didn't look back. She made a mental note to put him on her list of pervy men.

The concession stand was still packed, and several patrons yelled at her when she tried to cut the line to grab a handful of napkins. Tapping one foot against the worn dirt path in front of the stand, she dutifully waited ten minutes for the napkins. She rushed back, this time taking the long way around the outfield, hoping to avoid Mr. Tanned and Toned. And gross, she thought. Still there was a crowd near the bathrooms. If she didn't get back to her seat soon, she'd miss the national anthem. Poor Lisette would think she'd been abducted. As she strode past the line for the ladies' room, a player from the opposing team came running past, weaving through bodies as he went. He bumped her shoulder, spinning her and knocking the napkins from her grasp. Josie swore under her breath and squatted, gathering the napkins in her hand. Someone standing in the line yelled after the kid, "Watch it, jerk!"

Clutching the mess of napkins to her chest, Josie moved on. The announcer came on, welcoming everyone and asking them to stand for the national anthem. Before she turned toward the third base line, someone stumbled from behind the ladies' room building and directly into her path.

"Hey," Josie said. "Watch out."

Beverly Urban stood in front of her, eyes wide like a deer in headlights. Her thick curls were mussed.

"Shit," Josie said.

But no sneer slid across Beverly's face. No cutting words came from her mouth. She simply stared at Josie, as though she were looking through her. The first strains of the national anthem played over the speaker system. Pink splotches covered Beverly's neck. In one hand, she clutched something. A piece of white fabric. Without thinking, Josie said, "You okay?"

As if snapping out of a daze, Beverly's eyes narrowed. She stuffed her fist into her skirt pocket. "Get away from me," she snarled.

With a roll of her eyes, Josie took a wide step around her. "My pleasure," she said without looking back.

CHAPTER NINETEEN

The address they had for Lana Rosetti was on the western side of Denton in a neighborhood of single homes with ample acreage around them. The lawns were beautifully landscaped, although waterlogged as the rain continued to fall at a steady pace. So far, only part of the area had been flooded. Josie and Gretchen followed several detours until they came to Lana Rosetti's home, relieved to see it was out of the flood zone. A sign on the front lawn said: *Rosetti Psychology.*

"She's a psychologist?" Gretchen asked.

"Guess so," Josie said as they got out of the vehicle and walked up the driveway. Five steps led to a landing in front of the dark-red front door. On either side were potted plants. Josie rang the doorbell and they waited. A few moments later, a woman answered. She closely resembled Lana Rosetti but was too old to possibly be her. Her thin frame was draped in an ankle-length floral print dress. Wavy blonde hair fell to her shoulders. Bright blue eyes looked over a pair of glasses as she studied the two detectives. "Can I help you?"

They showed her their credentials. Josie said, "Mrs. Rosetti? Lana's mother?"

"Yes, that's me. You can call me Paige. Are you looking for Lana?"

Gretchen said, "We'd like to talk to her if we could. Is she here, by any chance?"

Paige studied both of them for a long moment. "May I ask what this is about?"

"Of course," Josie said. "We're investigating the death of one of her high school friends. We were hoping to talk to her about anything she remembers from that time period that could help us in our investigation."

"Oh dear," Paige said. "Maybe you should come in."

They followed her through an airy foyer with light hardwood floors into a kitchen which was dominated by an oversized rustic wood table at its center. A laptop stood open on one side of it. Paige glanced over her shoulder at Josie. "You went to high school with my daughter, didn't you?"

"I did," Josie said. "But we weren't friends."

Paige motioned to the mismatched wooden chairs tucked beneath the table. "Please sit," she told them. "Can I get you anything? Water? Coffee?"

They both declined. Gretchen said, "Is Lana here?"

Paige smiled. "No, but I've got a video call scheduled with her in seventeen minutes, if you'd like to wait around."

Josie said, "We'd much rather meet with her if that's possible."

Paige laughed, taking a seat in front of the laptop. "Oh, I'm afraid that's not possible. My daughter and her family are halfway across the globe. The only time I get to see or talk to them are these prescheduled video calls and half the time they fall through. The infrastructure where they are isn't the best."

"Where is she?" Gretchen asked.

"Burundi," Paige answered. "It's in Africa. Lana and her husband work with Doctors Without Borders. My grandson is there with them."

Josie said, "Maybe we will have some coffee."

Paige laughed. "Good choice."

She brewed a pot of coffee as they waited for Lana to come online. "You said this was about a high school friend?"

"Beverly Urban," Gretchen said. "Her remains were recently found here in Denton. It appears she was murdered just after her junior year of high school ended."

Paige said, "Oh how sad. That's terrible."

"Do you remember Beverly?" Josie asked.

"I do. I remember that her relationship with Lana could be rocky at times. I thought she must not have a good home life because she often acted out. She was very attention-seeking and my Lana, back then, was too nice for her own good."

"Did you know Beverly's mom?" Josie asked. "Or ever have occasion to talk to her?"

Paige set mugs and spoons in front of them, along with a bowl of sugar and a small carton of milk. As they each prepared their coffee, she took a moment to think about it and then shook her head. "No. I didn't. I thought about it sometimes. Beverly could be cruel toward Lana, but then they always worked it out. Then Beverly moved away, and it was no longer an issue."

A ding sounded from Paige's laptop. Josie and Gretchen sipped their coffee and waited while Paige and Lana connected and chatted briefly. Then Paige explained that the police were there and why. They heard Lana's voice. "Oh my God. Poor Beverly. They're there right now? I'll talk to them."

Josie and Gretchen stood and crammed into the frame behind Paige. They could see themselves in a small box on the top right-hand corner of the screen. Lana appeared in a box that filled the center of the screen. Her curly blonde hair was tied back in a messy ponytail. Her skin was sunburned, peeling along her nose. She wore a faded gray Doctors Without Borders T-shirt. It looked as though she was inside a drab green tent. Josie made introductions. It took longer than expected as every so often, the screen froze and their words were lost. Josie felt frustration mount inside her, but she stayed calm and focused. Finally, they got to their questions.

Gretchen said, "Lana, we understand you were good friends with Beverly. We have reports that she wasn't seen by anyone close to her after your junior year of high school ended. Was that the last time you talked with her?"

"The last time I talked to her was about a week after school ended. We hung out at my house. She slept over. She went home in the morning, and I never heard from her again."

Josie asked, "Did you go to her house? Call around? Try to find out where she went?"

"Of course," Lana said. "No one was there. No one else had seen her. We knew she was moving so I just assumed that's what happened. They moved away."

The screen went haywire for a moment. Where Lana had been was just a mess of lines. They waited as it snapped back. Gretchen said, "We spoke with Kelly Ogden earlier today. She told us that there were several males that Beverly was interested in at the end of your junior year in high school."

"That's right," Lana said.

Josie jumped in. "Kelly said there were four. Does that sound right to you?"

"Yes."

"Was one of them Ray Quinn?"

"Yes."

"Do you remember me?"

Lana leaned in, her eyes and forehead taking up most of the picture. "Yes, I remember you. Honestly, I don't know that anything was going on between her and Ray. She said there was, but I'm not sure. I didn't really believe it. I think she wanted something to happen with Ray, but he wasn't interested."

Gretchen asked, "Was one of the guys she liked a man who was doing construction work at her house?"

Lana sat back in her chair and scratched at the loose skin on her nose. "Yes. I do remember that. He was older. She really liked him. He did seem interested in her. I was at her house once when they were flirting. I don't remember his name though."

"Do you know who the other two men were?" Josie asked.

"No. Beverly was secretive about them. That's why Kelly and I weren't sure how much of what she was telling us was true. I can tell you this, though. She was only sleeping with one of the guys she was into. She made it sound like she was some kind of irresistible seductress, as though men couldn't control themselves around her, but she was actually only intimate with one guy. That's what she told me anyway. I'm not sure which guy that was, but I do know he had a tattoo." Lana laughed. "For some reason, she thought a guy with a tattoo was so... grown-up. Sexy."

Gretchen said, "Yeah, that's what Kelly told us. Do you know kind of tattoo this guy had?"

Lana smoothed a wayward piece of hair out of her eyes. "Oh, I think it was—" The sound cut out and onscreen, Lana's visage froze, twisting as lines burst across it.

"Oh boy," Paige said. "I don't know how much longer we'll be able to talk to her. Just wait a minute. She'll come back, hopefully."

After a long moment, Lana came back on. They asked her about the tattoo again. "Don't quote me on this, but I'm pretty sure it was a skull. I don't know where on his body, though."

Gretchen had her notepad out, jotting down this new detail.

"Lana, was Beverly into drugs at all?" Josie asked.

Lana shook her head. "No. I never saw her using any."

"Do you have any idea who might have killed her?"

"Oh God, no. I'm so sorry. I don't. I know she was seeing an older guy and she fought with her mom like crazy, but I can't imagine anyone killing her. Oh but—" She broke off and Josie thought the connection had been interrupted again, but Lana was just taking a moment to think. Almost to herself, she said, "I guess it really doesn't matter now. In fact, if she was killed right after school ended, you've probably already found out on autopsy. Beverly was pregnant."

"Yes," Josie said, surprised that Beverly had shared that with Lana but not Kelly. By all appearances in high school, Kelly had been closer to Beverly. Then again, Josie realized, Kelly was more of a minion. She had done whatever Beverly told her to do. Her function wasn't to provide counsel or comfort. Lana had obviously been the more sensitive of the two friends, refusing to carry out Beverly's crueler ploys. "That was confirmed on autopsy. Do you know who the father was?"

Lana frowned. "I'm afraid not. But as I said, it could only have been one of the men. That's actually how I found out she was only intimate with one person. When she told me about the pregnancy, I asked her if she knew whose it was and that's when she admitted to me she wasn't as active as she made herself out to be."

"Did she tell you any of their names? Other than Ray's?" Josie asked.

"No."

"Kelly said she had nicknames for them? Do you remember any of them?"

"No, I don't. It was such a long time ago. I'm really sorry. I wish I could. I'll give it some more thought, but… I mean, that was high school."

"I understand," Josie said. "What about someone named Alice? Did you guys know anyone by that name? Did Vera have any friends named Alice?"

"No, not that I remember," said Lana.

The screen blipped again, Lana disappearing once more and a strange metallic clang sounding from the speakers. Paige's fingers moved the mouse, clicking several times to try to get Lana back. They heard her voice before her face popped back up. "Vera knew."

Josie felt a chill on the back of her neck. "Vera knew? Her mother knew about the men?"

Multi-colored lines filled the screen. A sound like "Yes" came through.

Gretchen leaned toward the screen and loudly asked, "Did Vera know their names?"

"Yes."

For a long moment, there was nothing but blackness where Lana had been. Then she was onscreen again. Josie let out a breath she hadn't realized she'd been holding. Lana said, "Sorry. The connection isn't great."

Josie asked, "Did Vera know she was pregnant?"

"Yes, Vera knew about the pregnancy. Vera knew who the father was, evidently, although I'm not sure how 'cause Beverly wouldn't even tell me or Kelly. I don't even think she told Kelly she was pregnant. But she and Vera fought horribly about the pregnancy."

Gretchen said, "Would you say Vera was abusive?"

Lana's brow furrowed. "It's hard to say. I don't think she meant to be. I think they just had a very strained relationship."

Josie asked, "Do you think Vera could have killed Beverly?"

The screen twisted again into a kaleidoscope of broken digital images. They heard one word from Lana before the connection went down altogether. "Maybe."

CHAPTER TWENTY

Paige invited them back in a few days for Lana's next scheduled video call. She gave them Lana's email address but warned that Lana rarely had time to respond to emails. Back at the station house, Josie and Gretchen got takeout and sat at their desks with Noah, who had returned from the City Codes office. Amber was nowhere to be found, although her tablet still sat at one of the empty desks. Josie and Gretchen filled Noah in on their interviews with Kelly and Lana.

He finished off his cheeseburger and wiped his hands on a napkin. "Are you thinking that Vera killed her own daughter, buried her, and took off?"

Josie munched on a French fry, thinking it over. Then she went to her computer and pulled up a copy of Vera's driver's license again. "Here it says Vera was five foot five. Dr. Feist believes whoever shot Beverly was at least six feet tall. Based on the bullet's entry wound and both Beverly and Vera's heights, it seems unlikely. But Vera has been off the radar for sixteen years now. So either she went into hiding—and if she *did* murder her own kid, that might have caused her to go into hiding—or whoever killed Beverly killed her as well. I'm leaning toward Vera also having been murdered, though."

"Why's that?" Gretchen asked.

"Because if she was in as bad physical shape as George Newton, Kelly, and Lana said she was, I can't see her burying Beverly's body under the basement."

"Good point," Noah said. "But she could have had help."

"From who?" Gretchen said. "Vera didn't have a boyfriend. It doesn't even seem like she had any friends."

"That we know of," Josie pointed out. "We don't know enough about Vera. We really need to track down some people who knew her."

"We need to find out where she was working before she hurt her back. It had to be a local salon."

Josie's cell phone rang. When she looked at the number, her heart jumped into her throat. "It's Alice," she said, swiping answer. The room went silent, all eyes on her.

"Detective Quinn?" Alice said. "Is this you?"

"Yes, Alice. It's me. I'm glad you called. We really need to talk."

"Yes, we do."

Josie looked at Gretchen and Noah who nodded at her to keep going. "I can meet with you somewhere private, but I need to bring a colleague with me. Surely, you understand that. It's for everyone's safety."

"Who? Who would you bring?"

Josie thought about what Alice had said about the police station not being safe. She didn't believe for an instant that anyone on her team was corrupt, but obviously Alice had concerns. They could discuss those when they met. "Detective Gretchen Palmer," Josie said. "She came here a few years ago from Philadelphia."

There was a long silence. Then Alice said, "Fine. Bring her. But only her. You understand?"

"Yes," Josie said. "I understand. Where do you want to meet?"

"There's a Stop-N-Go by the interstate. You know it?"

"Yeah, I know it," Josie said. "Meet you in the parking lot? Half hour?"

"Not the parking lot," Alice replied. "Behind the Stop-N-Go."

"Behind the— Alice, there's nothing back there but trees and grass. It just drops off to the interstate."

"Then no one will see us," she said. "No one will think to look for us there. Don't tell anyone you're going to meet me. Do you understand? No one. If I see anyone besides two of you—anyone at all—I'm leaving. You got it?"

"Yes," Josie said. "I understand."

"I'll see you in a half hour," Alice said and hung up.

Josie pocketed her phone and looked at Gretchen. "Let's go."

In the parking lot, reporters huddled beneath umbrellas, rushing at them, shouting more questions. Like broken records, Josie and Gretchen said, "No comment" a half dozen times until they got out of the fray. The rain had slowed marginally. With so many roads barricaded, it took twenty minutes to go only a few miles to the Stop-N-Go. The gas station/mini-market sat atop a small hill just off the exit ramp from Interstate 80. Josie chose a spot in the parking lot, and they walked slowly around the back of the building. The other patrons were running to and from their cars, rain hoods pulled low over their faces, hurrying to get out of the rain. No one noticed Josie and Gretchen. The rain beat a steady rhythm on their raincoats. Josie smelled the dumpster before it came into view. It was flush against the back wall of the building, its green paint chipped, and its black plastic lid propped open. There was just enough asphalt for the trash truck to get back there and collect the refuse from the dumpster. Beyond that, as Josie had pointed out to Alice, was roughly an acre and a half of grass dotted with trees. The land terminated in a drop-off that overlooked the ribbon of route 80 below.

Their boots made sucking sounds in the grass as they walked toward the trees. "I don't see anyone," Gretchen said quietly.

"Let's wait," Josie said. They found a spot beneath a large, leafy maple tree and waited. In the distance, the interstate stretched out before them. Eastward, the Susquehanna was a thick brown smudge where it passed beneath the highway about a mile away. Red brake lights blinked periodically as cars approached the overpass.

"Shit," Josie muttered. "Look at that. I think the river might be overtaking the interstate."

Gretchen wiped rain from her eyes and squinted in the direction of the river. "There's a creek that runs parallel to the interstate on the other side, isn't there?"

"Yeah," Josie answered. "That overpass is going to be underwater in the next hour."

She took out her phone and called dispatch to ask them to call the emergency management department and the state police. As she spoke, she felt a thickness in her throat and tears welling behind her eyes. What was happening to her town? How much longer was this going to last? What would be left? She had spent her whole life in Denton. She'd graduated high school here. Gotten married here. Served on the police force for years. She had sacrificed so much for this city—literally bled for it on more than one occasion. It was hers and it was decimated. Turning away from Gretchen, she took in a shuddering breath and tried to focus on giving the dispatch officer instructions. For the first and only time since the flooding had started, Josie was grateful for the rain. Hopefully, Gretchen wouldn't be able to tell she was becoming emotional.

Ten minutes later, the brake lights were a steady glow as the water sloshed over the barrier and onto the overpass. There was no sign of Alice. Josie dialed her number, but she didn't answer.

"What do you think?" Gretchen asked. "She get spooked?"

Josie rubbed her temples, trying to keep the headache forming behind her eyes from getting worse and any errant tears from leaking out. "I don't know. Maybe this was just a test. Maybe she can see us, but we can't see her. She wanted to make sure we would come alone."

They took a slow walk back to the Stop-N-Go, eyes searching all around for any woman sitting in a vehicle or standing beneath a tree. Across from the Stop-N-Go on one corner was simply a grassy knoll beside the entrance ramp to the interstate. The other two corners held a bank, which was closed, and a modest ranch-style home. From where they stood, Josie didn't see anyone who might be Alice.

"Let's go," Josie said.

As they got into the car, the long wail of the emergency siren sounded again in the distance.

CHAPTER TWENTY-ONE

At the stationhouse there was a reprieve: the press was gone. Josie and Gretchen tromped up to the second floor where Mettner sat at his desk. His brown hair was in disarray, and his clothes looked wet. "Hey, boss," he said.

"Where are the reporters?" Josie asked.

"Amber is giving a press conference over at the command post," he explained. "Hey, I've got something." From the floor, he picked up a cardboard box and set it on his desk.

"What's this?" Josie asked as she came around to peer into it.

Mettner used both hands to slick his hair away from his face. "Hempstead is still under water. Nothing to see there. It will probably be another day or two before the water recedes. But I did locate the wreckage of Mrs. Bassett's house." He pointed to the box. "Those are some of her personal belongings. I grabbed whatever I could safely gather. Maybe when Emergency Management is able to do more of a clean-up, they can get further into the house and find more."

Josie stared at the contents: a few framed photographs, a small jewelry box, a couple of pairs of shoes, and several items of clothing. "Mett, this is great. I'm sure she'll be thrilled. We just have to figure out where Emergency Services placed her, and we can get this stuff to her."

Gretchen reached into the box and started taking items out. "Let's see if we can get some of this dried out."

They laid each possession out on paper towels on one of the empty desks. Mettner found a box fan in third floor storage, and they used that to speed up the drying process. Then he went out on a few more emergency calls while Gretchen tried to track down which salon Vera Urban had worked at nearly twenty years earlier. Josie took on the task of tracking down Mrs. Bassett, who—as it turned out—had been placed at Rockview Ridge, Denton's only skilled nursing facility, where Josie's grandmother, Lisette Matson, lived.

Josie stood and began gathering up Evelyn Bassett's now-dry possessions. "I'll take these over. I can talk with my grandmother while I'm there. She would remember Vera Urban. Maybe she'll have something useful for us."

Rockview Ridge sat on the outskirts of Denton, high atop a rock-strewn hill. Josie's eighty-three-year-old grandmother had been a resident there for nearly a decade. As Lisette grew older, her arthritis had made it more and more difficult for her to live on her own, so Josie and Ray had brought her to live with them. They'd taken care of her for as long as they could but after several falls when she was home alone, they'd had no choice but to find her a new home in an assisted living facility. It was one of Josie's greatest sources of guilt, that she couldn't keep Lisette home with her, but she knew Lisette was well taken care of at Rockview, and Josie had Lisette over to her house whenever time allowed.

Josie delivered Mrs. Bassett's personal items to the front desk and waited while the receptionist looked up her room number. Josie was intimately familiar with the layout of the facility. She delivered Mrs. Bassett's things to her in her room and helped her place some of the framed photographs on her dresser and windowsill before going off to find Lisette. As usual, Lisette was in the community cafeteria, sitting at a table, shuffling a deck of cards. Across from her sat a man—with dark hair and broad shoulders. Curious, she picked up her pace, striding over to the table only to discover the man was Hayes.

Josie stared at him.

Lisette said, "Josie, how lovely to see you."

She pulled her gaze away from Hayes to look at her grandmother. Her smile was strained, the lines around her blue eyes crinkled. "Gram," Josie said. "What's going on?"

Lisette pointed toward Hayes. "Nothing new. This is a friend of mine, Sawyer."

Josie said, "Sawyer?"

"That's my first name," he said.

"You're friends?"

"Josie," said Lisette.

Sawyer stood, a tight smile on his face. "I'll go," he said. "Mrs. Matson, it was great to see you."

Josie watched him walk off and then took his seat. Lisette raised a brow. "Well, that wasn't very polite, was it?"

"I'm sorry," Josie said. "We had a disagreement yesterday during a rescue. I don't much care for him, and I don't think he likes me at all."

Lisette's eyes dropped to the table. She shuffled her deck of cards and began laying them out for a game of Solitaire. "I'm sorry to hear that."

"How do you know him?" Josie asked.

Lisette began turning over cards. "We've had quite the influx of new residents with all the flooding. Sawyer has brought a lot of people in. We got to talking, is all."

Josie studied her for a long moment. Lisette wouldn't look at her. Josie had the distinct feeling there was something her grandmother wasn't telling her, but she couldn't imagine what it might be. Unless Lisette was truly disappointed that Josie hadn't given Sawyer Hayes a better reception. She knew Lisette's life at Rockview Ridge could be lonely. Who was Josie to deny her friendships? Josie reached over and touched Lisette's hand. "I'm sorry, Gram. I was impolite. I promise the next time I see Sawyer I'll make more of an effort."

Lisette looked up at her briefly before going back to her game. "I would appreciate that."

Josie let a moment pass, watching Lisette's gnarled hands mow through a game of Solitaire and begin shuffling again. Finally, she looked up at Josie. "Shall we play Kings in a Corner?"

Josie nodded. Lisette finished shuffling and dealt the cards. "I see on television you've got a homicide on your hands. A young girl?"

"Yes."

"So," Lisette said as they began playing in earnest, each of them on automatic pilot. They'd been playing Kings in a Corner since Josie was ten years old. "With everything going on in this city plus a murder, I know you're not here on a social call."

Josie leaned in toward Lisette. "The body we found? It was Beverly Urban."

Shock loosened the lines of Lisette's face. She bowed her head, her gray curls bouncing. "Oh dear."

"She was murdered, Gram. Shot in the head and buried beneath her house. Everyone thought she had just moved away. As far as we can tell, her mother disappeared around the same time. We can't find any record of Vera existing after the end of Beverly's junior year of high school."

Lisette shook her head. "It's a tragedy. That poor girl. I know you two didn't get along. Believe me, I had half a mind to throttle her myself when you were in school, but I always had the sense that she was struggling with something at home."

"That's why I'm here," Josie told her. "I know you had to meet with Vera on several occasions when Beverly and I…"

"Got into fights? Vandalized each other's lockers? Each other's cars?"

"I only vandalized her locker and car because she did it to me—and she spray-painted foul words on my stuff. All I did was break the lock on her locker and toilet paper her car."

Lisette regarded her with a raised brow, but Josie could see a small smile on her lips. "How about the time that Beverly pushed you down the steps at school and so you punched her in the face? She had a black eye. You were both nearly suspended. You both should have been suspended, really. I wore the principal down."

"She could have killed me," Josie said. "It's never okay to push someone down the steps."

"Is it okay to punch people in the face?"

"Okay, I was a hothead. Is that what you want to hear?"

Lisette laughed. "I'm giving you a hard time, Josie. You were a teenager, raging with hormones, and you were still trying to process all the abuse you'd endured before you came to live with me. I still think you would have benefitted from therapy, but you refused."

The game finished, Lisette victorious. Josie took the cards and shuffled them for another round. "I didn't need therapy."

"Pah!" Lisette said, laughing. "You need therapy right now."

Josie bristled but said nothing. She knew Lisette would not budge on this issue. "My point is, Gram, that you met and spoke with Vera many times. I need to know anything you can tell me about her."

"Well, let's see," Lisette began as Josie dealt the cards for their second game. "What I remember most is that Vera had barely any control over Beverly. I was essentially a single mother raising a hotheaded teenager, just like her, and I handled it just fine. Vera was… a mess. Weary, as though she was at the end of her rope with Beverly. Then again, she was pretty strung out on painkillers most of the time. At least when you two were in high school."

"We've been told that she had an accident."

"Yes," Lisette said. "She mentioned that at one of the meetings with the principal, about how her back was bad and her surgery had failed, and that being called to school so often was a trial for her. She used to complain about having to get a ride. She didn't drive, evidently—or she couldn't, because of her back."

"Who drove her to school? Do you know?"

Lisette shook her head. "Some guy. I only saw him a couple of times. He never got out of the car. Just dropped her off and picked her up."

"What kind of car?"

Lisette smiled. "A blue one. That's all I know, dear. Sorry. It was a very long time ago."

"That's okay," Josie said. "Vera referred to him as her friend, not her boyfriend?"

"Yes," Lisette said. "I don't think they were romantically involved. At the meetings, she never talked about anyone besides herself and Beverly. I don't think there was a male in their lives. She always talked about how she had to 'get' a ride, like it was a major inconvenience. She talked a lot about her back issues, but she never said anything about having someone around to help her."

"Do you think she was as badly injured as she said?"

Lisette thought about it a moment. "She was definitely injured, no question there, but she seemed to get around just fine whenever I saw her. Vera's problem was with drugs, not pain."

"What makes you say that?"

Lisette sighed, meeting Josie's gaze head-on. "Josie, I had had enough experience with a drug addict to know the signs."

"Right," Josie said. When Josie was three weeks old, one of the women who cleaned her parents' house had set the place on fire and kidnapped Josie. Josie's biological parents hadn't been home that day. They'd left their babies with a nanny. At first it seemed that only Josie's twin, Trinity, survived. Everyone in Josie's biological family believed that Josie had perished in the fire. In reality, her abductor, Lila, had brought her to Denton, and in an attempt to get back together with her old flame, Eli Matson, Lisette's son, she had passed Josie off as their baby. She'd told Eli that during the year they'd been broken up, she'd given birth to Josie and that Josie was his. Eli raised Josie as his own daughter until his death, which came when Josie was only six years old. Lila had descended into an abyss of drugs and violence after that, finally abandoning Josie to Lisette's custody when Josie got to high school.

"Do you think that Vera was violent toward Beverly?" Josie asked.

"I don't know, dear. I doubt it. Vera was frustrated and worn down and seemed mostly concerned with staying home and feeding her habit. You know there was one meeting where we waited and waited for Vera to appear. It was me and the principal. After an hour, Beverly showed up. She said that Vera had taken too many oxycodones and passed out. It was terribly embarrassing for her. That was the first time I had an inkling that Beverly was really struggling at home."

"Wow," Josie said. "I had no idea."

"Of course you didn't. You were a kid."

"Did you know Vera before the accident?"

"I met her a few times. She was quite vibrant and lovely. We had a good laugh over you girls. She was less worn down then, although she was having far more serious problems with Beverly's behavior than I was with yours."

"In what way?" Josie asked.

"She told me that at home Beverly was very disrespectful, that she was afraid that Beverly hated her. I told her that all young girls go through that phase, but she said it was something more than that."

"Did she ever mention Beverly's father?"

"Only to say he wasn't in the picture and that he hadn't ever been."

"Do you remember either Beverly or Vera ever mentioning anyone named Alice?"

"No, I don't. I'm sorry."

"Gram, by any chance do you know where Vera worked before her accident? We were told she was a hairdresser."

"Oh yes, she was," Lisette replied. "Before the accident, she was always so well dressed and put-together. Someone at her salon did her hair regularly. She always looked wonderful. Then after the accident, she became a different person."

"Do you remember what salon she worked for?"

Lisette pursed her lips, eyes squinting as she thought about it. "I don't remember the name. It was a very fancy place. Over on May-grove Street near the college, between the—oh dear, the businesses have changed after all this time. I think now there's a Starbucks on one side and a cell phone store on the other side. I believe the salon is still there, but it's changed hands since Vera worked there. It's called something completely different now, I'm sure."

Josie felt a small thrill of excitement. A lead. She couldn't recall the name of the salon Lisette referred to, but she'd driven past it plenty of times. What was more, if it was near the college, it was definitely not flooded. If it had always been a salon, then there was a chance that someone who still worked there would remember Vera. A slim chance, but she'd take it.

They finished the game and Josie stood to leave, walking around to give Lisette a hug and kiss. As she pulled away from her grandmother, Lisette gripped her and held her close. Into Josie's ear, she said, "You know how much I love you, right?"

Josie felt Lisette's curls tickling her cheek. "Of course, Gram. I love you too."

"You're mine and I'm yours, Josie. No matter what. Nothing in the world can change that. Don't ever forget it."

Josie's heart skipped a beat and then stuttered back to life. She pulled back and looked into Lisette's face. "You okay, Gram? Is there something you want to tell me?"

Lisette smiled and put a hand to Josie's cheek. "I just did."

Josie held her eyes for a moment longer. Her throat felt dry. "You're not dying, are you?"

Lisette laughed and relinquished Josie. "No, certainly not. There's nothing to worry about, dear. Now, I know you have to get back to work. I'll see you soon."

CHAPTER TWENTY-TWO

Lisette's strange words swam through Josie's mind on a loop as she drove through Denton, searching for the salon Lisette had mentioned. It was in a strip mall with large glass storefronts. The sign outside read *Envy*. Josie knew it hadn't always been called Envy, but she couldn't remember the name of the salon before it had changed over. She parked in the lot and walked in, immediately assailed by the smell of chemicals. The inside of the salon looked like something out of a magazine. The waiting room was filled with cushioned chairs, small tables covered in magazines, and even a table with complimentary snacks and drinks. Music played softly. Behind the receptionist's counter was a large room with ten styling chairs on each side and a hair-washing station at the back. Three of the chairs were occupied. Stylists, dressed all in black, flitted about, sweeping, mixing hair dye, and chatting up the clients.

Josie waited at the counter until someone called out, "Be right with you!"

A few minutes later, a door to the right of the reception area opened and a woman in her sixties walked in. She seemed to float in her long black cotton dress, her smile wide and welcoming. Dangling gold earrings clashed against her short silver hair, cut in a chic pixie style.

"What's your name?" she asked Josie, moving over to the reception desk and clicking away on the computer.

"Oh, I'm not here for an appointment," Josie said. She introduced herself and gave the woman her credentials.

She smiled as she handed them back. "What can I do for you, Detective Quinn?"

"I was wondering if you or anyone else employed here worked here before this place was called Envy?"

The woman nodded and placed a well-manicured hand on her chest. "I'm the owner. I was the owner back when it was called 'Bliss'. Actually, I was a co-owner of Bliss. I bought my partner out about ten years ago and rebranded. I'm Sara Venuto, by the way."

"Nice to meet you," Josie said. "I'm here to find out anything you could tell me about a former employee. Vera Urban."

Sara's smile faltered as she thought about it. "Vera Urban…"

Josie took out her phone and pulled up the driver's license photo of Vera they had found. She showed it to Sara.

"Oh my goodness, yes!" Sara exclaimed. "Vera. We called her V. Wow. I haven't thought about her in ages. Is she—" She broke off, the lines of her face deepening, sadness turning the corners of her mouth downward. Her voice lowered. "If you're here asking about her, I assume it's not good news."

Josie pocketed her phone. "I'm afraid it's not. You may have seen the news about the body found recently on Hempstead."

"I'm sorry, I didn't. I haven't been watching the news much lately. It's been very sad to watch our little city decimated by the flooding. There's only so much coverage I can take before I feel like I'll have a nervous breakdown."

"I understand," Josie said. "The house where Vera used to live with her daughter washed away yesterday. Under the foundation we found Beverly's body."

Sara gasped and braced herself against the desk, finally drawing the attention of the room behind her. "My God," she said. Glancing behind her, she gave the stylists a wave, and they carried on with their work. She turned back to Josie. "Why don't we go into my office?"

She led Josie through the door she'd emerged from into a small office painted in gray tones with a simple desk and some filing cabinets. A guest chair sat before the desk and Sara motioned Josie to sit. Then she dragged her own chair around so there was no barrier between the two of them. Her face was still distraught as she sat down, hugged her middle, and leaned in toward Josie. "Please," she said. "Tell me."

"Beverly Urban was murdered. We haven't been able to locate Vera."

"I would love to help you, Detective, but Vera hasn't worked here in almost twenty years, maybe longer," Sara explained.

"I realize that," Josie said. "The thing is, Vera has disappeared. In fact, we believe she disappeared many years ago. What we're trying to do now is piece her life together and find people who knew her, who could tell us anything about her life before she went missing. Anything we find out might help us locate her or move the investigation into Beverly's murder forward."

"Oh, wow, that's really strange and terrible. Do you think—do you think she's dead too?"

"We really can't say at this point, Ms. Venuto."

"Oh, Sara, please. I understand. Well, let me think. Vera was with us for a long time, you know. I had started the business with my partner. We'd been open a few years when I brought Vera on. Back then, as I told you, we were called Bliss. My idea was to provide an experience. We didn't just cut or style hair. I wanted our clients to feel like this was a safe haven where they could come and vent all their problems and be pampered. I wanted it to be… bliss!"

She laughed but it was cut short, her eyes filling with tears. "My God, I just can't believe this. Poor Vera and Beverly. She just loved that little girl. I remember we threw her a baby shower right here—the staff and the clients. Her clients adored her. It was right before she went on bedrest, thank goodness. She went on bedrest very early. But we made sure she had everything she needed before that. Then we didn't see her for months. She went and stayed with her brother until Beverly came."

"Her brother?" Josie said. "Floyd?"

"Oh, I don't remember his name. I just know she had an older brother—"

"Who lived in Georgia," Josie said.

"I don't know where he lived. Vera just told us he would take care of her while she was on bedrest. The next time we saw her, she had that beautiful little baby."

Josie asked, "Did Vera ever talk about Beverly's father?"

"No, not that I recall. She just said he didn't want to be involved. But she was over the moon to be a mother. Beverly was so sweet."

Sara's face fell as if she'd remembered something disturbing.

Josie said, "Until she wasn't."

"I don't want to say—look, it was hard on Vera being a single mother. Children can be very difficult, especially when they get to be a bit older, eleven or twelve. Right before puberty."

"Beverly had behavioral issues," Josie filled in.

"Yes," Sara said, an air of resignation around her. "Please believe me, I don't mean to speak ill of the dead."

"I'm only looking for facts," Josie told her. "Regardless of any issues that Beverly may have had in her short lifetime, my job is to find who killed her and put that person away for a very long time."

Sara smiled sadly. "Vera had her tested, professionally. By both a psychiatrist and a psychologist. She was… wild. Disrespectful. It started when she turned eleven or twelve, I think. I'm really not sure. I remember it though because Vera was so distressed. She came in here day after day, often crying, saying to the other girls, 'what happened to my sweet baby girl?' The other women who had children would laugh and tell her that this was just a phase, but privately Vera told me it was more than that. Beverly was… destructive. She broke things around the house, flew into rages. I think that Vera was afraid of her—and I suppose rightly so, because they had an argument, and Beverly pushed her down the steps."

Josie nodded. "I'm aware of that incident."

"It was an accident. It really was. I went over there a few times afterward to help out. Beverly was genuinely contrite."

"Did Vera ever tell you what the results of the psychiatric or psychological consultations were?" Josie asked.

"No. Only that Beverly suffered from low self-esteem, low impulse control, and depression. They talked about medicating her, but Vera was strongly against it. Things between them settled a bit after Vera's accident."

"Vera quit after that?" Josie asked.

"I kept her on as long as I could, first part-time and then whenever she could pick up a shift, but it became too much for her. I would have kept her on forever if I could. She was very talented and very personable. Her clients were devastated when she quit. Some of them had become extremely close with her. I believe they were friends outside of the salon."

"After she quit," Josie said, "did Vera keep in touch? Maintain friendships here?"

"Oh sure," Sara replied. "But they fell off over the years until we stopped hearing from her at all."

"What about her clients?" Josie said.

"Well, I wouldn't know. They kept coming here, but I didn't hear any of them discuss her."

"Do you remember if any of her clients were named Alice? Or co-workers, maybe?"

"No. I don't remember having any Alices."

"I realize you don't keep records that far back, but do you remember any of the names of any of her old clients? The ones who were very friendly with her?"

Sara shook her head. "I know I don't have records going that far back."

Josie said, "How about your other employees? Do you have any current employees who worked here when Vera was here?"

"I do have two girls—women—I could ask them. Or you could. They're not on till later this evening. I'm not sure either of them would remember more than I do."

"If you could ask them about Vera's clients, that would be very helpful," Josie said.

Sara clapped her hands together. "You know what I do have! Photo albums! Before cell phone cameras and social media, we used to take photos of our clients and keep them in albums for new clients to peruse. I could have the other two girls go through some of our old photo albums together and come up with a list of Vera's clients. It won't be a complete list, but it would be something."

Josie smiled. "I would be very grateful if you could do that. Perhaps you could even pull some of the pictures as well?"

"Certainly," Sara answered. "I'll let you know as soon as we have something."

Josie fished in her pocket for a business card as her cell phone rang. She took it out and swiped answer without looking at the number. "Quinn."

There was a breath and then, "Detective? It's Alice."

Josie's fingers brushed over a business card in her jacket pocket. She handed it to Sara and pointed to her cell number. "Call me at this number," she said. "I'll let myself out." Striding out to the parking lot with the phone pressed to her ear, she said, "Alice? You there?"

"I'm here."

"What happened today? We went to the place you suggested. You weren't there."

"I couldn't. I couldn't get there. It wasn't safe."

"Wasn't safe?" Josie said, ducking into her car to get out of the rain. "Alice, are you in danger? Is someone trying to hurt you? If that's the case, I can meet you somewhere right now, take you into protective custody until we get things ironed out."

They didn't actually have any facilities designated for protective custody at Denton PD, but if Josie could get this woman to come in, she'd work something out with the Chief and her team to make sure that Alice was out of harm's way.

"I can't. I really can't. It's… delicate. I can explain but it has to be in person."

Josie said, "Tell me where you are, and I'll come get you right now. No one has to know. No one will see us."

"No," Alice said. "If we do this, it has to be on my terms. Early tomorrow. In the morning. Seven a.m. You know that road that runs parallel to the interstate? There's a few buildings there. A motel, a warehouse, an abandoned bowling alley?"

"Lockwood," Josie said. "Lockwood Road. Alice, that's partially flooded. That area of the interstate beside it flooded earlier today. We watched from the Stop-N-Go. It's not safe."

"It's not all flooded," Alice insisted. "Behind the abandoned bowling alley. We'll meet there. No one will look for me there."

No one would look for anyone there, Josie thought. That whole strip was like a graveyard. "Alice, it's too dangerous to be that close to one of the flood zones. I think we should pick another place."

Alice made a noise of frustration. "Seven a.m. behind the abandoned bowling alley on Lockwood. This is the last time I'm putting myself out there. You come or you don't, but tomorrow at seven-fifteen, I'm gone, and you'll never hear from me again."

The next thing Josie heard was dead air.

CHAPTER TWENTY-THREE

It was nearing dinnertime when Josie got back to the stationhouse. The first thing she did was call the police department in the Georgia district where Floyd Urban lived. She explained that they had a murder and a missing woman on their hands and that in 1987 that missing woman, Vera Urban, claimed to have stayed with her brother while on bedrest. She asked them if they could interview Floyd as well as members of his family, and possibly neighbors as it looked as though he'd lived in the same house for over thirty years, to see if anyone remembered seeing Vera there. Next, she emailed them Vera's old driver's license photo. Josie had a feeling it was a dead end and that Vera had simply lied about going to be with her brother while on bedrest, but it would be irresponsible not to have a closer look at Floyd Urban.

Once that was finished, Josie met with Gretchen and Noah. Mettner was still out on emergency flood calls. Amber sat at one of the empty desks, typing away at her tiny laptop. She didn't acknowledge them, but Josie was sure she was listening to everything they said. Noah waved a document in the air. "I found your construction worker. The one who worked for George Newton's basement waterproofing company?"

He handed the pages to Josie. As she skimmed them, Gretchen wheeled her chair over so she could see as well. There was an obituary and a death certificate. Noah said, "His name was Ambrose McNeil. As you can see there, he had a history of arrests for drug possession and intent to sell. He was convicted of possession of heroin—four grams—and spent two years in prison before coming to work for Newton."

Josie pointed to a line on the death certificate. "He died of a heroin overdose."

Gretchen said, "And he was only twenty-seven."

"Yes," Noah agreed. "He overdosed within a year of the work on the Hempstead Road house being completed."

Josie asked, "Did you check with the state police and FBI to see if Ambrose owned any firearms?"

Noah pushed a few things around his desk before coming up with another stack of pages. "I did. Actually, while I was doing that, I took the list you two had made of people whose firearms purchase history you wanted to check and got everyone."

"That's great," Gretchen said. "What did you get?"

He read off the list before handing it to them to peruse on their own. "Ambrose McNeil owned one pistol, a .45 ACP. There are no records of George Newton ever having purchased firearms. Calvin Plummer owns three hunting rifles, one purchased in 1986, one purchased in 1999, and one purchased in 2003. He also owns a shotgun which he purchased in 2001."

Josie took the pages from him and studied them herself. "No nine millimeters."

"None that were legally purchased," Noah said.

"True," Gretchen said. "Any one of them could have obtained a nine-millimeter pistol illegally and there would be no record of it."

"But for now," Josie said, "we've got no proof that any of those people owned a gun the same caliber as the one that killed Beverly."

"Unfortunately," Noah agreed. "I also checked to see if Vera ever purchased a firearm. Found nothing."

"What about Ambrose McNeil's inmate records? Can we get those? Check and see if he had tattoos?"

"Already did," Gretchen said. "He's listed as having several tattoos but nothing described as a skull or skulls."

Josie plopped into her chair and slouched down. Fatigue weighed down every inch of her body. She closed her eyes for a moment, trying to still the whirling thoughts and brimming frustration inside. Gretchen said, "You okay, boss?"

Josie's eyes snapped open. "I'm fine. I do have a couple of leads."

Gretchen and Noah stared at her expectantly. She told them about the salon and then started to tell them about the call from Alice, but the sight of Amber behind them stopped her. Alice kept saying that it wasn't safe to meet at the police department. She was obviously worried about being followed. She hadn't trusted Josie and Gretchen to come to the meet alone that morning. Under normal circumstances, Josie could be absolutely certain that no one on the police force was a threat to Alice—or anyone else—but the circumstances were not normal. In fact, the only difference in the last two days was the addition of Amber to the staff.

"What did she say?" Noah asked. "Will she meet again?"

"Yes. She'll meet with us. Tomorrow," Josie said. "But I've got to wait for her to call back with the place and time."

She'd tell Gretchen the real details of the call later. For now, if Alice was that paranoid about the police, Josie had to take that concern seriously.

Before either Gretchen or Noah could ask any more questions, the stairwell door flew open and Officer Hummel walked in, carrying a document in one hand and a paper bag in the other. He walked over to the desks. Ignoring Amber, he placed a fingerprint report in front of Josie.

"Boss," he said. "This is the report from the prints we were able to get from the tarp and the duct tape. We got multiple unidentified prints from the tarps."

Her heart gave an excited little patter, which quickly died as she looked over the report.

"As well as Vera's prints and Ambrose McNeil's prints on the tarps—"

"But not on the tape," Hummel finished for her.

Noah said, "Did you get any prints from the tape?"

"One print that was still usable," Hummel said. "But it didn't get a hit on AFIS. So whoever left that print has never been arrested or charged with a crime."

Gretchen noted, "The tarps were probably hanging up in the house or laid out to cover something if there was ongoing work happening. I'm not surprised that some of the prints were from Vera or this Ambrose guy. I think the print on the tape is the killer's though."

"Which does us no good now," Noah complained. "We don't have a match."

"But we'll get one," Josie said. She smiled at Hummel. "Thank you. Great work."

Hummel nodded. "I also had a look at the inside sleeve of the jacket, and it was torn and resewn just as suspected. Also, there was this." He reached into the paper bag and pulled out an old piece of paper encased in plastic. He held it out for them to see. "This was in one of the jacket pockets."

Josie said, "It's a receipt from the Wellspring Clinic."

"What's that?" Noah asked.

"It was a doctors' office geared toward low-income people," Josie said. "Or people who didn't have insurance—or didn't have good insurance. They charged on a sliding scale based on your family income. I was a patient there until I left for college. It used to be in central Denton, in the historic district, but it closed years ago."

"Makes sense that Beverly would go there," Gretchen said, "from what we know about her and Vera's financial situation. What else does the receipt say?"

The print on it had faded. Even with her reading glasses, Gretchen had to squint to see it. "Looks like she was charged for an exam of some kind."

Noah said, "We can use the copier to darken that up, you know."

Hummel gave it to Noah. "I wanted you to see this before we dust it for prints so wear gloves and be very careful."

"You got it," Noah said.

From where she sat several feet away, Josie noticed Amber watching them with interest, her fingers frozen over the keyboard. They watched Noah don gloves, remove the receipt from the bag, place it face down on the copier glass, and then punch some buttons. A few moments later, he had darkened copies of the receipt for each of them. Josie looked at the date. May 28, 2004. Only a few weeks before school had ended that year. "There's no possible way to get records from this visit," Josie said. "Wellspring is gone and even if it wasn't, medical providers aren't required to keep records this far back."

Noah said, "Hummel, was there anything else in the pockets of the jacket or her jeans?"

Hummel shrugged. "Couple of dollars, a lip gloss. That was it."

Gretchen sighed. "So until we meet with Alice or get the list of clients from Vera's old employer—assuming they are able to compile one at all—we've really got no leads."

No one responded.

From the other side of the room, Amber cleared her throat. "Maybe now is the time to release Beverly's identity. We could ask the public for help in locating Vera as well. The Chief mentioned to me the possibility of rolling out a tip line since this case is quite old. I've already laid the groundwork during the press conference earlier today. All I would have to do is release a statement with some photos. The press will run with it on broadcasts and social media. I'm happy to answer the tip line."

Josie looked at Noah and then Gretchen and saw from their expressions that neither of them had any objections. Josie said, "If you get the Chief's approval, it's fine with us."

Gretchen said, "Come on, Watts. I'll go with you to talk to him. We need to work out what information we want to tell the public and what we want to hold back."

Josie and Noah watched them walk into the Chief's office. They waited a long moment, expecting to hear the Chief holler, but there were only the sounds of hushed voices and the tap of Amber's fingers over her tablet keyboard.

Noah said, "You ready to go home? Misty said she's making paella. Patrick's supposed to come over too. Bringing his new girlfriend, I hear."

Josie smiled. She hadn't seen her younger brother in a few weeks. He was a student at Denton University. Josie usually enticed him into coming over to visit by offering the use of her washer and dryer. Also, he had told her he was dating someone, but she hadn't yet met the woman. "That sounds wonderful," she said. "But I need to talk to Gretchen before I leave. You go ahead. I'll meet you there."

With no one else in the room, Noah walked over, leaned down, and kissed her. "Don't be long."

Gretchen and Amber emerged from the Chief's office a few minutes later. Amber sat down at one of the desks and started typing away. "I'll have this statement ready for your review in a few minutes, Detective Palmer," she said.

Gretchen gave her the thumbs-up and headed to the stairwell door. Josie followed her, waiting till they were in the stairwell and the door was closed to tell her about the plan to meet Alice the next morning.

Gretchen looked around the cramped stairwell. "You don't want Amber to know?"

"Just humor me, okay?" Josie responded. "Alice doesn't think this is a safe place to meet. The only thing different around here is our new press liaison."

"But she has no connection to anyone here. How could she be dangerous to our mystery woman?" Gretchen asked.

"She has connections to the Mayor who has connections to city council. Maybe it's not the police that Alice is worried about. Maybe it's someone else. Someone higher up."

Gretchen pursed her lips as she considered this. "Seems like a stretch, but there's no harm in keeping this from Amber, so she won't hear it from me."

Josie thanked her and headed home.

Dinner was fabulous, as always, and with Patrick and his new girlfriend, Brenna, there, Harris had new adults to regale with stories of the bugs he had seen outside; his grandmother's false teeth; and the exploits of Pepper and Trout. Josie laughed when everyone else did, but her mind was on the case. After dinner, Patrick and Brenna returned to campus and the rest of them went into the living room and watched the local news, which ran the spot about Beverly and Vera Urban as their top story. Josie sat on the couch with Trout on one side and Misty's dog, Pepper, on the other.

From his spot on the floor where he was putting together a Duplo Lego set with Harris, Noah laughed. "The Chief must be thrilled. For the first time in a week, the top story isn't Quail Hollow."

Josie listened as the anchor read off the scant details that Denton PD had offered: the identity of the victim recovered during the flooding on Hempstead had been verified as Beverly Urban; confirmation that Beverly had been murdered; the fact that Beverly had been a former student at Denton East High back in 2004, and that her mother, Vera Urban, could not be located. The tip line flashed across the screen, and then the newscast moved on to the next story.

"You think we'll get any calls?" Noah asked.

"No," Josie answered. "No way is Alice calling the press. No one else in the world noticed that Vera and Beverly hadn't simply moved away. It's like they had no one in their lives."

"Except a killer," Noah said.

"And whoever Beverly's baby belonged to," Josie added.

CHAPTER TWENTY-FOUR

2004

Downtown Denton was crowded on a Saturday morning. Josie parked her grandmother's car in one of the public parking lots and took a stroll down Aymar Avenue. The day was gorgeous with perfect blue skies, sunshine, and a light, cool breeze that tickled her bare arms. It was supposed to get hotter later in the day, but at noon it was still pleasant. Until she was almost to the construction site and heard the noises: men shouting, the ear-shattering metallic pounding of a hydraulic hammer, the hum of loaders, the squeal of drills, the roar of excavators, and the clang of their diggers as they scraped away earth and rock. Outside the six-story structure that was being built on the corner of Aymar and Stockton, a tall temporary chain-link fence had been erected along the sidewalk. Someone had affixed bright orange safety netting over it to alert anyone walking past that the area was potentially unsafe. Josie found the gate that Ray had told her about, which had several metal signs on it warning anyone not working on the site to stay out. On the other side sat a man in an orange helmet and vest, perched on a concrete barrier reading a magazine.

"Hey," Josie called to him. He didn't look up. "Hey," she said again. "I'm looking for Ray Quinn."

Without looking at her, the man pulled a walkie-talkie from his belt and squeezed a button. "I need Quinn," he barked. "Girlfriend's out here."

He went back to reading his magazine while Josie waited for Ray to appear. Five minutes later, he emerged, wearing his coveralls and a white tank top stained light brown with dirt. Sweat glistened along his arms and gave his face a sheen. He waited till they were out of sight of the gatekeeper before giving her a quick kiss.

"How much time do you have?" Josie asked.

"Half hour," Ray said. "Let's walk down to the other corner. There's an ice cream place."

"Only a half hour?" Josie asked. "Ray!"

He slid his hand into hers as they walked. "I'll see you tonight. After work."

"No, you won't," Josie said. "You'll be asleep right after dinner. Ray, this job is too much."

"I just have to get used to it. It's a long day out in the heat. Jo, it's only on the weekends."

She tugged at his hand, pulling him closer to her. "The weekends are the only time I get to see you. How long are you going to be working this job?"

"School is almost out, Jo. Then I'll be able to work during the week."

"I thought we were going to lifeguard together at the community center this summer," she said. "Like last summer. We'd see each other every day."

Ray let go of her hand and slung his arm around her shoulders, pulling her tight to his side. Sweat soaked into her linen dress, but she didn't push him away. "I make more at this job, Jo."

They came to an intersection, stopping at the *Do Not Walk* sign. Josie's gaze dropped to her feet. "Since when do you need to make more than you did last summer? Is something wrong? Is everything okay with your mom?"

"Oh, Jo," Ray sighed. He pulled her out of the way of other pedestrians as the sign changed to *Walk*. They stood on the curb together and Ray turned her to face him. "I was going to surprise you, but the real reason I took this job is for you."

Josie looked into his eyes. "For me? I'd rather see you. Next year we both leave for college. I want to take advantage of the time we have now."

He pulled her into him, wrapping his arms around her, locking hands across her lower back. Now the front of her dress would be soaked, but she didn't care. "Remember how you said you wanted to go to the beach?"

"Ray! What are you saying?"

"If I work this job for two months, I'll have enough to take you to the beach for a whole week and enough to put away for college and help my mom with bills. I was going to surprise you with the trip at the end of the summer. I already talked to your grandmother. She's going to help me plan the vacation."

Josie couldn't stop the grin from spreading across her face. She pulled him in closer, her cheek against his damp neck. "Ray!" she squealed. "I can't believe it! A whole week? Are you sure?"

"Yes. I already worked it out with your Gram, and my mom said it was fine too. It's going to be so much fun. A little getaway before senior year starts."

Josie practically skipped through the intersection when the light changed again, the *Walk* sign blinking on. She held tightly to Ray's hand, feeling a sense of euphoria she almost never experienced. Up until she turned fourteen and went to live with Lisette, her life had been filled with trauma and abuse. Any vacation was out of the question. She was lucky if she ate on a daily basis. Once her grandmother got custody of her, she'd tried to provide Josie with as many fun adventures as possible. It was Lisette who had first taken Josie on a trip to the beach the summer after her freshman year. Josie had instantly fallen in love with the small seaside town of Ocean City, New Jersey, and the ocean. Lisette had managed to take her back there for a few overnight trips, but she had always wanted to spend a whole week there. Now it was within reach, and she'd be going with Ray. She felt like she was floating.

"This place is good," Ray said, stopping in front of a glass storefront that said *Jessie Mae's Ice Cream*.

He could have suggested ground glass in that moment, and Josie would have agreed. Inside the quaint little shop, the air was frigid. Tiny tables for two lined the walls. A countertop extended almost into the center of the room. On either side of it were glass cases with various flavors of ice cream inside them. They stepped up to where a sign said: *Order Here*. Josie tore her eyes away from Ray to order and immediately, the rush of happiness she'd felt outside drained from her feet into the tile beneath her.

Beverly scowled at her from behind the cash register. A small hat in the shape of a cherry was pinned to the top of her head. Her luscious brown curls were pulled back into a ponytail. Her uniform was a pastel pink halter top beneath a set of white overalls. Even with the silly hat, she looked gorgeous. Womanly. Sensuous, even.

Ray seemed not to notice. Or maybe he did, and he was just pretending not to. His eyes were glued to the menu above Beverly's head. Did he come here a lot? Had he known Beverly worked here? They didn't acknowledge each other. Josie smoothed her now wrinkled linen dress, feeling self-conscious. "Ray," she whispered in his ear. "Maybe we should go somewhere else."

Before he could answer, Beverly turned away from them and shouted to a co-worker cleaning an ice cream machine behind her. "Morgan, you have a customer. I'm going on break."

Without another look, she sauntered into the back of the shop.

CHAPTER TWENTY-FIVE

The next morning, Josie woke at five a.m. to the sound of thunder cracking and rain pounding the roof. Trout had inserted himself between her and Noah in bed. He shivered and whimpered. Josie reached over to stroke his silky back and felt Noah's hand already resting there. "He doesn't like the boomers," Noah said softly.

"I know," Josie said. Her fingers crawled up to the downy area behind his ears and stroked it gently. The three of them lay there, Josie and Noah cocooning Trout until the thunder and lightning passed and it was time for Josie to get ready to meet Gretchen.

Gretchen was waiting in her own car in the parking lot of the Stop-N-Go. When Josie pulled up, she got out of her car and hopped into Josie's passenger seat. They turned out of the parking lot and down Lockwood Drive. There had been a break in the rain, but the sky hadn't cleared. Josie thought of Trout trembling beneath her touch and of the city being swallowed up by the floods a little more each day. A feeling of dread clawed at her, so intense it was almost physical, like darkness closing in on the edges of her peripheral vision.

The road was little-used, with nothing much to offer besides forest on one side and mostly abandoned businesses on the other—save for one of the seediest motels in the city, which was somehow still in operation. Road crews didn't spend much time maintaining this portion of Lockwood Drive. The asphalt was cracked and rutted. The yellow lines splitting the lanes had long ago faded to what looked like confetti loosely thrown down the center of the road. Josie maneuvered around several potholes. From the Stop-N-Go, Lockwood ran downhill, running parallel with the interstate for several miles. Except now, in the distance, large plastic orange barriers stretched across the highway where the flooding had risen. A huge white sign with black letters announced *Road Closed*.

Alice had been right. The bowling alley was the last building on the road before the flood zone started. Josie pulled into the parking lot, tires crunching over gravel and broken pavement, and parked behind the building. The weedy, litter-strewn lot behind the old building was empty. A broken-down fence separated it from a strip of land that ran along the concrete barriers of the interstate beyond. They got out and looked around, but there was no one in view.

"Should we go into the building?" Gretchen asked.

"No," Josie said. "She said behind the bowling alley, not inside. Besides, this place has been empty for years. I'm not sure the structure is safe."

To their right, about a half mile up the hill, was the back of the Patio Motel. Beyond that, the land abutting the interstate rose until it became the steep drop-off where they had stood the day before, behind the Stop-N-Go. To their left, about twenty yards of pocked land lay between them and the brown water of the Susquehanna, which had overtaken this area of Lockwood Drive when it flooded the interstate overpass. The fence that was supposed to separate the lots from the interstate had fallen into the water. Ten yards beyond that sat the portion of the interstate just before the flooded overpass. The State Police had erected concrete barriers across the lanes of the highway, and traffic had been diverted around the closure and through the city. Everything but the river was still and quiet, its current moving swiftly.

"I don't think she's coming," Gretchen said.

Raindrops splattered around them. "Not again," Josie said. She took out her phone. "I'm going to call her."

This time, Alice picked up immediately. Josie said, "Alice, we're at the meeting place. Where are you?"

"I see you," she whispered.

Josie spun around, searching the surroundings. "Where are you? If you can see us, just come out. There's no one else here."

"You don't know that. I'm waiting to see if you were followed."

"I think we'd know if we were followed," Josie told her.

Gretchen turned slowly in a circle, looking around. She pointed uphill toward the Patio Motel. Josie started to walk with her toward it but then Alice said, "Don't leave. Just a few more minutes to make sure no one followed you. That's all I'm asking."

Josie stopped. She looked at Gretchen and pointed behind them. They turned and walked back toward the flooded area. "Alice, you really need to tell us what's going on. If you're this concerned for your safety, I think you need to let us bring you in."

Silence.

"Alice?"

"I think I hear something," she said.

Josie pulled the phone from her ear, and she and Gretchen strained to listen for the sounds of tires over asphalt or footsteps, but there was nothing. Gretchen gestured toward the interstate and mouthed, *I think she's there.*

Josie followed her movement, eyes landing on the concrete barriers set in place so that drivers wouldn't go directly into the flood. There was still some area of dry interstate behind them before the water flowed up and over the overpass. It wasn't the safest hiding spot, but it would give Alice a clear view of the rears of all the buildings leading up the hill without being seen, and no one would look for her on the closed interstate.

Josie nodded to Gretchen and slowly, they began walking in that direction. Alice started to speak, but her words were lost when another call beeped in on Josie's phone. She pulled it away from her ear and looked at the screen. Noah. Whatever he was calling for, it could wait. She swiped *decline* and sent him to voicemail. "What was that, Alice?"

Gretchen's cell phone rang. "Noah," she said as she looked at the screen. She, too, sent the call to voicemail. As they climbed over the guardrail and stepped onto the highway, a woman emerged from behind the barricades. A cell phone was pressed to her ear. She pulled it away, pressed the screen, and put it in her jacket pocket. Her raincoat was dark blue and beneath that she wore a pair of black jeans and white sneakers. She was rail thin with long, dark hair that had obviously been dyed, but Josie recognized her features at once.

"Vera?"

The woman stopped and raised both hands. "Stop. This was a mistake."

Gretchen said, "No, it wasn't a mistake. Whatever is going on, we can help you."

Josie's phone buzzed again with a call. Noah. She put her phone into her own jacket pocket and let it go to voicemail again. From where they stood, so close to the river, the sound of the current was even louder. Behind the barricades, it looked as though the water was flowing more quickly. Rain continued to splatter them, growing steadier by the moment. With every drop, Josie felt her heart sink even more. It would mean more flooding, more flash floods, more damage. But right now, she had to focus on Vera Urban.

Josie said, "Vera, you wouldn't be here if you believed this was a mistake. You took a risk to meet us, didn't you?"

The woman nodded. With the rain beading on her face, Josie wasn't sure if she was crying or not, but her features twisted and a sob erupted from her throat. Then the concussive boom of a gunshot rang out and a dark red splotch bloomed across Vera's stomach. She stumbled backward, hands reaching for something, face slack with shock, and fell.

Immediately, Josie ran toward her. Gretchen's gun was already out and up as she panned it around them. Another shot shattered the air and a few feet away, a chunk of concrete burst from one of the barriers. "It's coming from the building," Gretchen shouted.

Flat on her back, Vera's mouth worked like a fish out of water. "The—they—the—"

"Get her on the other side of the barricades," Gretchen said, standing in front of them, gun pointed toward the bowling alley. Her right eye zeroed in on the iron sights of her Glock, but she didn't take a shot. Josie moved around to the top of Vera's head and hooked her arms under her armpits, dragging her behind one of the large concrete beasts. Gretchen followed and the two of them knelt down, pushing Vera as close to the barrier as they could so she wasn't exposed. Another shot sailed over their heads.

"Put pressure on that," Gretchen said, turning back toward the bowling alley, her gun ready. Another shot boomed, and they heard it hit the other side of the barrier. Josie's ears rang. She took off her raincoat and bunched it up, pressing it to Vera's abdomen.

Josie heard the familiar ringtone of Gretchen's phone. Shouting to be heard over the aftershocks of the gunshots and the steady rumble of the river at their backs, Gretchen said, "It's in my pocket. It's gotta be Noah. Take it. We need units now."

Josie kept one hand on Vera's abdomen while the other plunged into Gretchen's jacket pocket and pulled out the phone. She used her thumb to swipe *answer* but with the rain coming down, it took three tries on the slicked screen. "Noah," she cried.

Vera's hand gripped Josie's shoulder. Her mouth worked again. Josie put her free ear down toward Vera's face, trying to hear what she was saying. "Ple—please—"

In her other ear, Noah said, "Josie. Are you still on Lockwood? I'm on my way to you now. The railroad levee broke. With the thunderstorms overnight, it was too much. There's going to be a big surge downriver. You should get out of there."

The crack of another gunshot caused Vera to buck beneath Josie's hand. Noah was saying something, but Josie couldn't make it out. The rain fell harder. She felt something against her ankles and looked back to see that the surge Noah warned about was already happening. The water had been ten yards away only moments ago, and now it was at their feet. Panic squeezed at Josie's heart. She had to stay calm. Focused. Noah was on the way.

"We're pinned down," she shouted into her phone, trying to be heard over the roar of the river. "Someone is shooting at us."

"What? What the hell?"

"You need to call in extra units right now, and we need an ambulance right away. Do not approach alone and make sure you've got your vests on," Josie told him. "We're on the interstate. On the eastbound side behind the concrete barriers before the overpass. Vera—Alice—is wounded. Gunshot to the abdomen. She's alive but I don't know for how long."

"Jesus, Josie—"

"Listen to me. Gretchen thinks the shooter is up near the bowling alley. Either inside the building or near it. I'm going to hang up. Call in extra units and approach with caution."

As she put Gretchen's phone into her pocket, she heard a siren in the distance. Her heart leapt at the thought that backup was so close, but then she realized it was just the fire company's emergency siren. The river was about to ravage the city again, and Josie and Gretchen were in its maw, being shot at while trying to keep a wounded woman alive.

CHAPTER TWENTY-SIX

Gretchen retreated and pressed her back against the barrier, gun still at the ready. "There's nowhere for us to go," she said. Water now lifted Vera from her place on the ground. Josie slipped an arm beneath her head to keep her from dropping beneath the surface. "We're about to go downriver whether we like it or not," she warned.

"We can't leave this position," Gretchen said. "If we come out from behind the barriers, we're sitting ducks. We can't do it."

Vera's face was deathly white now, her mouth closed and her eyelids hooded. "I don't think we can move her," Josie said. Water swirled powerfully around her shins. "But we're about to get swept away."

She tried to keep pressure on the wound and keep Vera's head out of the water, but it was a losing battle. Blood trickled from beneath her raincoat. "I haven't heard a shot for a while," Josie said. "Maybe they left. We should move her to the other side. Onto the highway, away from the water."

Gretchen shook her head. "We can't. If you're wrong—"

Another shot boomed. They felt it slice the air just over their heads. Josie threw herself down over Vera, hugging the woman to her. She felt Gretchen's hand on her shoulder. Her voice trembled when she said, "Boss, look."

Josie turned her head, looking upriver to see the water level rising rapidly. They had only moments before a rush of churning, brown river swept them away. Noah and the rest of the cavalry would never make it in time to stop the shooter and come for them. It took a split second for Josie to make the decision. "Hold her," she told Gretchen, lifting Vera toward her. Gretchen kept her gun pointed skyward and slipped her other arm under Vera's lolling head. Josie stood, keeping her upper body bent so she couldn't be seen over the top of the barrier, and pulled off her boots, tossing them into the water. Then she unzipped her jeans, peeling them off. Gretchen looked at her with wide eyes. "Boss, I don't think this is the time—"

"Watch," Josie shouted at her. The water was knee level now. She tied the pant-legs together. Holding the waist of the jeans, she flapped them, trapping air inside the legs. As fast as she could, she bunched and tied off the waist area. The pant-legs were fat with air. Josie said, "Help me," as she tried to slip Vera's head between them. Gretchen helped work Vera's head through the inflated pant-legs so that the jeans acted as a flotation device. Then she let herself fall back into the rising water. A moment later, her boots bobbed to the surface and floated away. Then came her jeans. Josie kept one hand on Vera while Gretchen tied her own pant-legs together. She couldn't get the air into the top, so she took hold of Vera while Josie did it.

The water lifted them, carrying them away. Gretchen slipped her head through her floating pants and reached for Josie's hand. But Josie and Vera were already on the current, rocketing downriver. Josie struggled to keep proper hold on Vera. The woman's body was completely limp. Water surged over Josie's head, and she spluttered as her mouth broke the surface. Again, she felt a squeezing in her chest. *Calm,* said a voice. *Stay calm.* But there was no staying calm. A scream ripped from her throat as she turned onto her back and pulled Vera onto her stomach. The makeshift flotation device wasn't enough for them both. Josie's head kept sinking below the surface. Her lungs burned.

She concentrated on trying to keep her arms wrapped around Vera. Water poured over her head, into her lungs. Flailing, she broke the surface again, and her body hacked so hard trying to expel the water that pain pierced her upper back. Then the water surged over her again. Her eyes were open but all she saw was darkness. The black abyss of the angry, voracious river. It was swallowing her whole. She couldn't stop it. She couldn't stop anything. Not the river. Not Vera's death. Not her demons or the tears that came even now in her last moments as she sank.

The darkness can't hurt you, Jo.

It was Ray's voice, one of the last things he had said to her. She heard it as clearly as if he were talking into her ear. But that was impossible because she was underwater, clinging to a dying woman who was still bobbing along the surface of the river only by virtue of Josie's pants. There was some kind of shift in the current, as though they'd passed through an eddy or something. Their bodies spun sideways and Josie's head broke water again. She coughed, trying to get the water out of her lungs. Vera's head flopped against Josie's shoulder. Josie willed her legs to work, to paddle, to keep herself afloat. In her periphery, she saw a large branch shoot past them. Trees. She had to get to the shore or close enough to any trees overtaken in the flooding to grab onto them. They'd never make it following the current. Emergency responders wouldn't find them before Josie tired out and drowned.

Her legs kicked as she craned her neck, trying to find any sign of land. Finally, to her right, a grove of trees came into view ahead. Every muscle in her body burned with the effort of paddling sideways with Vera hooked onto one of her arms. They barreled past the trees before Josie could reach them. A grunt of frustration escaped her. It was getting harder to take in breath, to stay afloat, to hold on. But she was closer to the edge of the water than she had been. She sent up a silent plea to any higher power that might be listening, and a moment later she was rewarded by another smattering of trees, these with more spindly trunks but grouped closer together. She reached out her free hand as the current carried them past. Her palm slapped against the trunk and slid off. The same thing happened with the next tree. The water was moving too fast. With every ounce of energy she had left, she kicked again, thrashing her body into a turn and bracing herself for impact.

Her back slammed into the next nearest tree trunk and then her body was crushed by Vera's weight. It nearly knocked the wind out of her, but luck was with them finally. Even as the current tried to slide them around the side of the trunk and back downriver, the tree branches extended down and stopped the water's progress. Josie reached her free hand up and grabbed onto the thickest branch she could find, holding the two of them in place. She squeezed her eyes shut and held on, feeling a small bit of relief.

When she heard screaming, her eyes snapped open. Hurtling toward them was Gretchen, inflated pants under her arms. She was either going to hit the tree trunk or fly right past them. Keeping hold of Vera, Josie shifted her position, trying to get closer to the trunk. With one arm looped around Vera and the other around the tree trunk, she extended her legs, letting them bob in the current. "Grab on!" she shouted to Gretchen.

As she neared, Gretchen reached out both hands toward Josie. They latched onto one of Josie's thighs and slid down.

"No!" Josie screamed.

Gretchen's grip tightened around Josie's ankle. For a second, Josie waited for her hands to loosen, for her to be swept past them, but Gretchen held so tightly that Josie could feel her skin bruising. With agonizing slowness, Gretchen used Josie's leg to pull herself closer to the trunk until she could wrap her arms around its girth. Josie's arms felt jelly-like. She didn't know how much longer she could hold on—to Vera and to the tree. Once she was sure that Gretchen wasn't going anywhere, she shifted Vera's weight and drew closer to Gretchen. "We have to climb," she said. "Up into the tree. There are some branches above that will hold us, at least until rescue comes. Help me with Vera. I've got to get her up there."

Gretchen's face was paler than Josie had ever seen it. Her lips were nearly blue. The air was warm, but the water was cool, and they'd been in it… how long? Josie had no idea. It seemed like an eternity. Days. Weeks. Gretchen took one arm from the trunk and turned Vera's face toward her own. Her fingers pressed into Vera's neck. "Boss," Gretchen said. "She's gone."

"No," Josie said.

Beneath the water, something banged against her legs. Debris. God knew what was in this water. Josie hated to think about it. She reached up to check Vera's pulse for herself, but she couldn't find it. Slapping Vera's cheek, she yelled, "Vera! Vera! Wake up!"

"She's gone," Gretchen repeated.

"No!" Josie insisted. More slaps. "Vera! Come on! Wake up!" Frantically, she looked around. She couldn't do CPR out here. There was no way to do compressions. She could try to inflate Vera's lungs, but there was no way to position her head and neck properly so that the air actually reached her lungs. "No," Josie sputtered. "No."

Gretchen reached across Vera and shook Josie's shoulder. "Boss, she's gone. There's nothing we can do for her now."

"Then what?" Josie shouted, spittle and rain and river water flying from her lips. "What now? We can't just—what do we do? Just let her go? Let her wash away? No!"

Gretchen's fingers dug into the muscles above Josie's shoulder blades. "We can tie her—tie her here to the tree using our pants. We climb up, wait for help. She might hold here long enough for rescue to come."

Josie looked at Vera's ashen face, felt her lifeless body against her side. Gretchen held tight to Josie, watching her with wide eyes, waiting. Beyond her, the river roared on. The peaked roof of a house came into view, someone's home—someone's life—floating past with glacial slowness that seemed at odds with the power of the water all around them. Something broke inside Josie. She felt it. Like the railroad levee. A dam bursting open. What was beyond it was unstoppable. Silent sobs wracked her body. The emotion flowed out of her so fast and so hard, like it was pummeling every soft place inside her on its way up and out, that she couldn't speak. Tears blurred her vision until Gretchen and Vera were hardly visible.

She wanted to tell Gretchen that she agreed they should tie Vera's body to the tree so they wouldn't lose her, but her throat wouldn't cooperate. All that came was the raging mass of emotions. A lifetime's worth, it seemed. Josie nodded through her tears. Up and down, up and down until she heard Gretchen say, "Okay, okay. You just hold onto her while I tie our pants together, okay? That's the only way they'll fit around the trunk and Vera."

More nodding. More sobbing. The world was a tear-soaked kaleidoscope of murky brown and death. A few minutes later, she heard Gretchen's voice again. "Boss, you're a stronger climber than me. I need you to go first. You find a spot and help pull me up."

Josie nodded.

"Boss? Josie? I need you to go. Climb."

Gretchen's hand wrapped around her wrist and placed her palm against the trunk of the tree. "Josie," she shouted. "Climb! I need you to climb." Gretchen shook her again and Josie's arms reached upward, finding two small branches to help pull herself upward. Gretchen said, "Climb, Jo, climb!"

Her body went onto automatic pilot. She was ten years old again, in the woods behind her trailer, hiding from her abusive mother. Lila never looked in the trees. Beneath her, Ray whisper-shouted, "Climb, Jo! Climb!"

She scrambled up into the tree, legs wrapping around the trunk and propelling her upward until she found a branch strong enough to hold both hers and Gretchen's weight for some time. Blinking the tears and rain out of her eyes, she looked down to see Gretchen struggling to inch up toward Josie. When she got close enough, Josie extended a hand and Gretchen took it, muscling her way up to where Josie perched. Breathless, they clung to one another and the tree. Below, Vera's body wrapped around the tree. Debris gathered at her back, hitting against her and then dislodging to be carried downriver. Josie watched as a tangled mass of mayoral candidate signs floated past.

CHAPTER TWENTY-SEVEN

In a twist of irony that Josie cared not to examine too closely, Sawyer Hayes was in one of the rescue boats that finally located them. The other boat, piloted and tended by city swiftwater rescue crew members Josie didn't know by name, collected Vera and carried her off—to the morgue, Josie assumed. Sawyer helped Gretchen and then Josie down into the other boat. He averted his eyes from their naked legs but once they were fitted with life vests and tethered to the inside of the vessel, he flipped open a pouch in his vest and took out a small silver package with a blue wrapper. Josie recognized it immediately as an emergency Mylar blanket. It seemed like hours ago that her mind had disconnected from her body. Around the time her teeth started chattering. In reality, she had no idea how long they'd been in the tree. Sawyer took the blanket out and unfolded it, using two hands to shake it loose. As the boat operator steered them away from the trees and back to safety, Sawyer covered them with it, tucking its edges beneath them with care.

"Thank you," Gretchen said.

Sawyer gave them a thumbs-up. Josie tried to smile. She wasn't sure if her face worked or not, but he smiled back at her. She closed her eyes and let her head fall onto Gretchen's shoulder.

The next hour was a blur. The rest of the city park had been swallowed up by the additional flooding, so a new boat ramp had been built closer to the command post. They were herded from the boat launch directly into the back of an ambulance where they were seated along the soft vinyl bench inside and wrapped in more blankets. At the hospital, they were put in the same curtained area, each assigned to a gurney. A nurse handed Josie a hospital gown and then dug one out of the linen cart for Gretchen. "You gals put these on. I'll be right back."

"I'm fine," Josie said. "I just need pants… and a ride home."

The nurse laughed. Gretchen was already dropping her wet jacket and shirt onto the nearby tray table and slipping into the gown. "Honey," the nurse said to Josie, "your lips are blue, you're soaked to the bone, and you've got a nasty laceration on your leg there."

Josie looked down at her legs, for the first time noticing the large gash on the outside of her right thigh. "Shit," she muttered.

The nurse patted the gurney. "How about some warm blankets? How's that sound?"

Josie couldn't argue with that.

Gretchen said, "Hell, yes."

Two hours later, Josie dozed beneath three heated blankets. There were eight stitches in her thigh, and her hair was finally dry. Beside her, Gretchen slept deeply, her breath long and even, and her eyelids twitching periodically. Josie didn't know how she could sleep so soundly. Every time Josie closed her eyes, she saw Vera's lifeless body in the river.

The Chief's voice startled them both fully awake. From somewhere on the other side of the curtain, he said, "Where are my detectives?"

A second later, the curtain scraped back and the Chief, Noah, and Mettner rushed in. Noah came straight to Josie's side, touching her face, her hair, her arms, and finally taking one of her hands. He leaned in close, studying her eyes. "You okay?"

She wasn't. She was as far from okay as she could remember being in a very long time. She nodded anyway.

"You scared the hell out of me," he said softly. "I thought you were gone."

She gave his hand a light squeeze. "I'm sorry."

"I just—I—" He broke off and Josie thought she saw tears in his eyes. He let go of her hand, straightened and turned away from her for a moment. He was trying to maintain his composure, she realized.

"I really am sorry, Noah," she croaked.

Turning back, he swooped in to kiss her. "Don't be. I'm just glad you're here."

Chief said, "Quinn and Palmer, you two are to stay out of the water until further notice. Jesus. What a day. You get shot at and swept away. What do you think this is? Some kind of action movie?"

Mettner, who stood between their gurneys, frowned at the Chief. "It's not their fault, you know."

The Chief pointed a finger at Mett. "Don't tell me what I know, son. I almost lost my two best detectives today."

Mettner chuckled. "Gee, thanks."

"Shut up, Mett."

Noah perched on the side of Josie's bed and from the side of his mouth, mumbled, "I guess this is what it's like when he's genuinely upset."

Gretchen pulled her blankets up to just under her chin and said, "Did you get the shooter?"

Mettner shook his head. "No. Sorry. By the time we got there, no one else was around. We did find shell casings next to the bowling alley. Nine millimeter. But we didn't see anyone driving away when we arrived."

Noah said, "We pulled security footage from the Stop-N-Go and the bank across the street to see if we could see any vehicles coming up from that direction, but neither camera views reached the street."

"Of course," Josie said.

The Chief said, "Hummel collected the shells. We'll see if he can pull prints."

"Speaking of prints," Mettner said. "We did confirm that the woman you met with was Vera Urban. Dr. Feist is working on the autopsy now."

Noah asked, "Did she tell you anything before…"

"Someone started shooting at us?" Gretchen filled in. "No. We recognized her right away and she got skittish. The next thing we knew, she was bleeding out from a gunshot wound to the stomach and then the river took us. Good thinking, using our pants as flotation devices, boss."

Josie nodded, afraid to speak as emotion welled inside her again. She thought she'd gotten it all out or, at the very least, that she would be too spent to muster more but there it was, causing a lump in her throat and a tremble in her lower lip she hoped no one noticed.

"That's why you two are pant-less?" Chitwood said.

"How did you know we were pant-less?" Gretchen asked.

Noah said, "When we called to make sure you were both here safely, the nurse told us to bring pants."

Josie found her voice. "Yet I don't see any pants."

Noah, Mettner, and the Chief looked at one another. The Chief said, "Where the hell would I get pants from?"

Noah laughed, breaking the tension in the room. "I'll take care of it."

Gretchen said, "Before you go, I think we need to talk about the fact that Vera Urban has been alive for the last sixteen years."

"Not only that," Josie added, "but she knew that her daughter had been murdered, and she knew how it happened. I think she knew who did it. I think that's why she wanted to meet. To tell us."

"But why come forward now?" Mettner asked.

Noah said, "Because now the rest of the world knows that Beverly was murdered. Now the police are looking for the murderer."

Mettner said, "What the hell has she been doing for sixteen years?"

Gretchen said, "Hiding, obviously. She hasn't had a utility in her name, she hasn't filed a tax return; there hasn't even been a cell phone in her name. Who doesn't have a cell phone these days?"

Josie said, "She had to have assumed some other identity. Alice. Unless that was just a name she gave us."

Noah said, "The landlord told you two that all of hers and Beverly's personal things were gone from the house on Hempstead, right? She had to have taken them with her. She wanted it to look like they simply moved away. She's known all along who killed her daughter. The question now is, who has she been hiding from?"

Gretchen snaked a hand out from under her blanket and pushed it through her spiked hair. "The same person who killed Vera this morning."

The Chief said, "Who would want to kill Beverly? What would make Vera go into hiding instead of reporting her own daughter's murder?"

An image of Vera's face flashed across Josie's mind—her mouth trying to make words as she bled out behind the concrete barrier on the empty interstate—begging Josie to save her. She'd been trying to say the word "please." Josie hadn't been able to save her. Hadn't even been able to help her. What was she hiding? What did she know? Who would kill her to keep it a secret?

"I don't know," Josie said. "But I think the first thing we should do is try and track Vera's movements."

"How do we do that?" Mettner asked.

"She had to come from somewhere," Josie said. "No one has seen her for sixteen years. Beverly's body is found and a couple of days later, she's here in town?"

Noah said, "Right. She wouldn't have been living in Denton for the past sixteen years.

But she's been off the grid, for lack of a better expression, for all this time. Or rather, living under an assumed identity: Alice. Somehow, Alice got here, and she obviously spent the night here, based on her calls to Josie."

Gretchen nodded. "If she was trying to keep a low profile, she wouldn't want a hotel with security cameras."

Josie said, "Maybe she was staying at the Patio Motel. It's the seediest place in town and it happens to be between the two places she chose to meet us—the Stop-N-Go and the abandoned bowling alley."

Mettner said, "I'll have someone go by the parking lot and run all the plates there."

Josie said, "I want to talk to the manager. She must have left some things in her room."

The Chief raised a brow. "You almost got killed today, Quinn. Twice. You're taking the day off."

"Chief—" Josie protested but he held up a hand to silence her.

"We'll get a warrant written up for you to take to the Patio first thing in the morning. I've already got two patrol cars sitting out there, 'cause the flooding is damn near in the Patio's parking lot now. It'll keep. I can't spare Fraley or Mettner right now anyway. I need all bodies over at the command post."

Relieved, Josie let her head sink into the pillow. Noah gave her hand a warm squeeze.

The Chief added, "Fraley, get these two some damn pants so they can go home and rest."

CHAPTER TWENTY-EIGHT

Rest didn't come easy. Each time Josie moved, her leg throbbed. Whenever she began to drift off, she saw Vera's face—her last attempt at words—and heard the gunshots, then the wail of the emergency siren. The only other thought in her head as she lay on her couch and tried to sleep, was of Wild Turkey. She thirsted for it in a way she hadn't in a very long time. She could practically taste it, feel it burn its way down her gullet into her stomach where it would sit all warm and tingly and help blot out her heart-sick thoughts for a while.

Except she didn't have Wild Turkey in her home anymore. They had no alcohol. Only coffee, some green tea concoction that Misty made, and apple juice for Harris. She wished Misty and Harris were there, but Misty was at work and Harris was with Ray's mom for the day. Noah was at work. She thought about calling her sister, Trinity, in New York City, but her phone had been destroyed. She'd need a new one. Beside her, Trout whined, as if sensing her inner turmoil. Pepper sat across the room on the armchair, unperturbed. Josie stood and looked out front where her vehicle sat in the driveway. Someone on the team had retrieved it from Lockwood for her. The keys were on a table in the foyer. She could just run over to the nearest liquor store. It was late afternoon, the store would still be open. Plus, it wasn't in the flood zone.

Without even realizing it, she picked up the keys. But she didn't have her ID. Her wallet and credentials had been soaked in the river. Noah had laid everything on the kitchen table to dry out. Josie turned away from the front door to go get her ID, but the doorbell rang.

Trout and Pepper jumped up from their spots and ran to the door, barking furiously until Josie opened the door and saw Gretchen and Dr. Feist standing on her doorstep. Gretchen was freshly showered and dry in a pair of jeans and a white tank top under a light sweater. Dr. Feist wore khakis and a blue button-down blouse, her silver-blonde hair loose around her shoulders. A small laptop was tucked beneath her arm. Gretchen thrust a box of pizza into Josie's hands. "I was going to call," she said. "But we've got no phones."

Josie stepped aside and let them in. They congregated in the living room, eating the pizza right from the box. Josie sat on the couch with Dr. Feist beside her. Gretchen disappeared momentarily and returned with napkins and three bottles of water, which she set on the coffee table next to the pizza and Dr. Feist's laptop. "I couldn't stay at home. Too antsy." She sat cross-legged on the floor facing them.

Dr. Feist wiped a splotch of sauce from the corner of her mouth with a napkin and said, "She showed up at the morgue asking if I'd finished Vera's autopsy."

Josie laughed but it came out sounding nervous. She should have been the one showing up unannounced at the morgue looking for information about Vera Urban. Instead, all she could think about was Wild Turkey. If Gretchen noticed anything off, she didn't point it out. Instead, she said, "Then I thought you would want to hear whatever Dr. Feist had to say, so I convinced her to come over here with me."

"And we figured you'd be starving," Dr. Feist added. "So here we are."

Somehow, Josie didn't feel hungry at all, but she took a slice of pizza anyway. "Thank you," she said. "What can you tell us about Vera Urban?"

The doctor opened her laptop, clicked a few times, and then began to read off some of her findings. "I estimate her age to be between fifty and sixty."

"That tracks," Josie said. "She was fifty-eight."

Dr. Feist nodded. "The cause of death was the gunshot wound to her abdomen. Her lungs weighed more than expected and when I opened her up, they were somewhat overinflated, indicating that she had taken in some water before she died, but based on the damage in her abdominal cavity, I believe she died before she had a chance to drown."

Josie put her half-finished pizza back into the box and leaned back into the couch. Trout jumped up and crawled into her lap, whining. Absently, she stroked the back of his neck. Gretchen said, "We did everything we could, boss."

"Did we?" Josie asked. "We should have brought some kind of backup. Going there alone was stupid."

Gretchen said, "To meet one person with information about a sixteen-year-old murder? There was nothing to indicate we needed to bring in an army to meet with Vera Urban. We didn't even know it was her when we went there. We only knew we were meeting a woman named Alice."

"She told us—she told me—that it wasn't safe, and I didn't take her seriously enough. She was right, and now she's dead."

"That's not your fault," Gretchen told her.

Dr. Feist said, "Josie, if it helps, I don't believe she would have survived long enough to make it to the hospital. Even if you had been able to move her to safety and wait for an ambulance, she would have died before she made it to the ER, and Denton Memorial is not a trauma center."

Josie shook her head, fighting tears. "I should never have put any of us in a position where someone was shooting at us—she was shot because of me."

"She was shot because she's mixed up in something she shouldn't be," Gretchen argued. "She knew her daughter was murdered, and she hid that for sixteen years, boss. If she didn't get shot before our eyes, she might have been killed some other way at some other time by whoever was after her."

Silence descended over the room as the full weight of the violence of Vera Urban's death and the gravity of what she'd been hiding from set in. Then Dr. Feist cleared her throat and said, "There were some other incidental findings you might be interested in: her liver was extremely diseased, either from long-term alcohol use or some other underlying condition."

"Opiates," Josie supplied. "We believe she was addicted to opiates."

Dr. Feist nodded. "That would certainly do it. Also, in her lower back I found evidence of an old lumbar surgery. A tri-level lumbar fusion."

"Yes," Gretchen said. "Several people who knew her reported she had had back surgery."

"Lastly, she had a bicornuate uterus."

Gretchen's pizza slice froze halfway to her mouth.

Josie said, "What is that?"

"Vera Urban's uterus was heart-shaped. Bicornuate uterus is a congenital defect. I'll spare you the scientific details. Basically, the uterus forms with two separate cavities. A deep indentation forms at the top of the uterus, essentially splitting it in the middle. It can be surgically corrected these days—and perhaps even when Vera Urban was a young woman—but hers was not corrected. It doesn't affect fertility, but it makes it very difficult to carry a baby to term."

"But we know she had a baby," Josie said. "Was there dorsal pitting on her pubic bone?"

Dr. Feist said, "No, but not every woman develops scarring in her pubic bone after childbirth. I've seen plenty of women who have given birth without parturition scarring on autopsy. I usually only use that as an indicator that a woman *has* given birth."

Josie said, "Meaning if it's there, then she likely had a baby."

"Right. But its absence is not an indicator that the woman never gave birth. As I said, Vera's condition wouldn't have prevented her from having a baby; it just made the odds of a successful pregnancy much lower. She was very lucky to have carried Beverly to term."

Gretchen said, "That might explain why she was on bedrest for so long and why she had to deliver at Geisinger and not here in Denton."

The weight of the Urban women's tragedy hung heavy on Josie's shoulders. Poor Vera. According to her former boss, she'd badly wanted a baby and had been thrilled when Beverly came along even though the father wasn't in the picture. But somewhere along the line, things had gone wrong. Beverly had developed behavioral issues. Josie knew firsthand how Beverly's penchant for acting out could cause not just emotional drama but physical harm. What had Beverly and Vera gotten themselves into that was so dangerous it had ended up with Beverly pregnant and murdered at seventeen years old and Vera forced into hiding for almost two decades? What had Vera been hiding from? Where had she been all these years? Who had killed her and why?

Josie said, "She was worried that someone had followed *us* when we went to meet her—not that someone was following *her*. In fact, the whole reason that she wanted to meet in private in an out-of-the-way place was because she didn't think the police station was safe."

"Who is left in the Denton PD that would have been involved in Beverly's murder sixteen years ago?" Dr. Feist asked. "I thought you cleaned house five years ago after the missing girls' case."

Gretchen said, "Amber Watts."

For Dr. Feist's benefit, Josie shared her suspicions about their new press liaison.

"How old is this woman?" Dr. Feist asked.

Gretchen said, "Young. She would have been in elementary school when Beverly was murdered."

"Not necessarily her," Josie said. "Mayor Charleston. Amber knew we were going to meet the mysterious Alice this morning, but she didn't know where. She could have told the Mayor."

"So you think she is a spy?" Gretchen asked.

"I don't know. But someone knew we were going to meet Vera Urban. Someone wanted her dead. Someone shot her so she couldn't tell us what she knew."

"I know Mayor Charleston is well versed in lying and covering things up," Dr. Feist said. "She's not that well liked here anymore, with this Quail Hollow thing—although Kurt Dutton is involved in that, too, I believe—but I'm not sure she's capable of murder."

"Me either," Josie conceded. "But maybe she's not directly involved in whatever is going on here. I'm just saying that it's a pretty odd coincidence that Amber gets hired by the Mayor this week, and shows up right after we recover a body from beneath the house on Hempstead. She's been at all the briefings, and knew we were going to meet someone who knew what happened to Beverly, and suddenly we're getting shot at and Vera Urban is dead. Maybe I'm reading too much into things, but what's the alternative?"

"That someone's been following Vera Urban this whole time— since she returned to Denton from wherever she's been—and she just didn't realize it," Gretchen said.

Josie gestured to Dr. Feist's open laptop. "Do you mind?"

She pushed it across the coffee table to Josie. Then she and Gretchen sat on either side of Josie on the couch, peering at the computer screen as Josie did an extensive background check on Amber Watts, finding nothing amiss and no red flags. "The ad," Josie mumbled. "The Chief wanted me to see if the Mayor put the ad up for a press liaison several months ago. Amber says that was when she answered it." Sure enough, Josie found the ad posted on several job search sites two months earlier.

Dr. Feist sighed. "Looks like your Amber/Mayor Charleston lead is a dead end."

Gretchen said, "Let's just focus on Vera for now. Hopefully we'll find something that leads to her killer—and Beverly's as well."

CHAPTER TWENTY-NINE

There was no opportunity to sneak off to the liquor store for the rest of the evening. Misty and Harris showed up before Gretchen and Dr. Feist left and shortly after that, Noah came home. Josie went through the motions, passing the rest of the night in a daze and giving an unconvincing, "I'm fine" every time Misty or Noah asked if she was all right. Sleep eluded her, especially given the pain in her leg, which ibuprofen did little to relieve. The moment the gray of morning began filtering through their bedroom windows, she got up, showered, and took Trout for a run. She stopped at the Spur Mobile store to get a new phone before picking up Gretchen in the parking lot of the stationhouse.

Warrants ready, they headed to the Patio Motel. It had been around as long as Josie could remember, a scar on the community. The city police made more drug and prostitution arrests there than anywhere else in the area. It was a sagging, two-story building with eight rooms on each floor. Most of the room numbers were now marked in Sharpie on the doors. Beat-up vehicles sat in the parking spaces just out front of the rooms. Josie knew from asking Noah the evening before that none of the vehicles found in the lot were registered to anyone named Alice. However Vera had gotten to Denton, she hadn't driven a vehicle of her own.

Between the parking lot and the tiny motel office was an in-ground pool that had long been filled with garbage. At one point, someone had attempted to grow a small garden at one end of the pool, but now all that was left was a bright red tulip jutting out of soil littered with broken glass and fast food wrappers.

A sullen woman with black hair and narrowed eyes greeted them at the motel office. Even with a warrant, it took a great deal of negotiating for her to admit to them that a woman matching Vera Urban's description had, in fact, checked in two days before. Vera hadn't given the Patio staff any name, and the Patio staff hadn't asked for it. That wasn't how things worked at the Patio Motel. Its only appeal was its protection of the guests' anonymity. Only after Josie and Gretchen outlined the penalties for not complying with a search warrant and assured the woman that Vera Urban was deceased did she agree to show them to her room. "Take her stuff," she told them after unlocking room two. "I need this room if she ain't coming back."

Like all the rooms at the Patio, the one Vera Urban had occupied was small, dated, and stank of cigarettes, stale body odor, and spoiled food. A full-sized bed took up most of the room. Its ratty floral comforter was undisturbed. Across from it, a television sat on top of a small, nicked dresser. Near the window just inside the door was an orange armchair with stains on its cushions. The room looked unoccupied.

Josie stepped past the bed and into the bathroom, which was a glorified closet, the toilet and sink practically touching. No tub, only a shower with a rusted out drain and mildewed shower curtain. Still, there was no evidence that anyone was staying in the room. Gretchen was poking around beneath the bed when Josie emerged. "There's nothing here," Gretchen told her.

"There has to be something," Josie insisted. "She had to bring at least a change of clothes."

She walked back over to the chair and studied it. Pulling a pair of gloves from her jacket pocket, Josie snapped them on and lifted the seat cushion. "Here," she said, lifting a small blue backpack into the air. Gretchen, too, snapped on gloves and they emptied the backpack onto the bed. There were some undergarments, two pairs of jeans, two shirts, a nightshirt featuring several cartoon cats that read "Cat Nap", a hairbrush, several make-up items, and some toiletries. Josie lined up a toothbrush and tube of toothpaste, deodorant, and some small bottles of shampoo and conditioner.

Gretchen said, "There's no wallet or phone."

"Right," Josie agreed. "We know she had her phone with her yesterday, and if she had a wallet, that was probably with her too. It's in the river now."

"What's that?" Gretchen said, pointing to a small, orange plastic bottle.

Josie turned it over, a small thrill of excitement running through her like an electric shock. "A prescription pill bottle," she said. "For a woman named Alice Adams. Looks like it's for lorazepam."

"Ativan," Gretchen said. "It's an anti-anxiety drug. Does it list a pharmacy and doctor on the bottle?"

Josie took out her phone and snapped some photos of the label. Then she Googled the pharmacy. "It's a locally-owned shop in Colbert."

Gretchen said, "That's about ninety minutes from here."

"We'll need warrants," Josie said. "For the pharmacy records and then for whatever address we find for this Alice Adams. We'll need to call the local PD there too and let them know what we're doing."

"Let's go," Gretchen said.

CHAPTER THIRTY

At the stationhouse, Gretchen prepared the warrants while Josie called the Colbert PD to coordinate efforts. Within a half hour, Josie was informed that the address that Alice Adams had been residing at was a rental. The Colbert officer gave her the name and phone number of the landlord. He offered to pay the landlord a visit and explain what was going on to pave the way for Josie and Gretchen to execute their search warrant at Alice's apartment later that day, if possible. "Now we just have to wait for a return call," she told Gretchen.

Amber, who had been sitting several desks away the entire time, walked over. "I was hoping you could bring me up to speed on all the developments," she said. "Seems like a lot has happened since yesterday. I know that 'Alice' was really Vera Urban and now she's dead—the Chief told me that—but that's all he would say. He wouldn't give me any details. But I heard some of the patrol officers talking about a shoot-out. They said you and Gretchen were there. They said Vera Urban was shot. Can you tell me what happened? Did she have any information for you?"

Gretchen said, "No one else told you anything? The Chief? Lieutenant Fraley? Mett?"

"I haven't had a chance to talk with anyone. Everyone's so busy."

Josie looked up and met her eyes. "How about the Mayor? Have you had a chance to talk with her?"

"No, I— Why would I need to talk with the Mayor?"

Josie went back to typing up a report on her computer. After several awkward moments, Amber plunged in again. "I just have a few questions."

Josie pushed her chair away from her desk and headed for the stairwell. The stitches in her leg tugged with each step. Amber followed, calling out questions, holding her tablet in one hand and tapping away at it with her other hand as she followed Josie from the great room to the break room. Josie gave monosyllabic answers whenever possible or referred Amber to the Chief. She was more focused on getting coffee than telling Amber a damn thing. She poured herself a mug and went to the refrigerator for the half and half, but Amber stepped in front of her, blocking Josie's way. "Detective Quinn," she said, her trademark smile replaced by a look so earnest it bordered on desperation. "If I'm going to do my job, I need to know what you know."

Josie said, "Please move."

Amber straightened her posture, standing at least two inches taller than Josie in her four-inch heels. "What is your problem with me?" she blurted out.

Josie squeezed the bridge of her nose between her thumb and forefinger. She could feel a headache forming behind her eyes. Folding her arms across her chest, she met Amber's eyes. "Look, I really don't have time for this, and you're standing between me and the half and half. If you want to get along well here, you won't do that."

Amber's chin jutted out stubbornly as she glared at Josie. Her lips formed a straight line, and her blue eyes blinked frenetically, giving away her nervousness. Josie couldn't help it. She laughed. Amber deflated before her, slinking away from the refrigerator in defeat. "Just a minute," Josie said before she left the room. Amber stopped in the doorway.

Retrieving the half and half, Josie returned to the table in the center of the room and fixed her coffee. "I understand you have a job to do, but the fact is that the Mayor put you here."

"I told you," Amber groused. "I'm not the Mayor's plant."

Josie sipped her hot coffee, relishing the taste of it. There was no point in confronting Amber with her suspicions. If Amber was in league with the Mayor, she'd never admit it. If Amber was completely innocent and had been inadvertently feeding the Mayor information, she certainly couldn't control what the Mayor did with that information. Josie said, "You liaise with the Mayor's office. That makes you not trustworthy at this particular time. Between the Quail Hollow scandal and—" she stopped herself from saying the words "Vera's murder," instead concluding, "It's a problem. So yes, we're playing things a little close to our vests on this one."

Amber sighed loudly and tugged at her hair. "What am I supposed to do?"

"I can't answer that," Josie told her. Mug in hand, she walked to the door. Amber didn't move. "All I can say," Josie added, "is that trust is earned."

She slid past the small gap between Amber and the doorframe, brushing up against her. Before she could return to the stairwell, the desk sergeant, Dan Lamay, came shuffling down the first-floor hallway. "Boss," he called. "There's something—"

Josie held a hand up to silence him until she heard Amber cross the hall behind her and go back upstairs. "Okay," she said. "What is it, Dan?"

"The Mayor is here to see you. She's in the lobby right now."

"She's here to see me, specifically?"

"Yeah, she says she wants to speak with you and only you."

"Put her in the conference room down here, would you? I've got to run upstairs and let Gretchen know where I am, and I'll be back to talk to her."

A few minutes later, Josie took her half-finished mug of coffee to the conference room where Mayor Tara Charleston waited. She paced along one side of the large table, a cell phone pressed to her ear. Her skirt suit was a muted teal, and her long legs were accentuated by a pair of six-inch heels. Her hair was chin-length and smartly styled, her face perfectly made-up, covering almost all of her wrinkles. As she barked instructions to someone on the phone about an upcoming city council meeting, Josie stood on the other side of the table, sipping her coffee.

Tara hung up and tossed her phone onto the table with a clatter. She blew out a long sigh and put her hands on the back of the nearest chair. "Detective Quinn," she said.

Josie said nothing.

Tara strode across the room and closed the door. Josie's heart raced a little. The last time she had been truly alone with Tara Charleston, the Mayor had asked her to do something illegal and when Josie refused, she had threatened Josie's job.

Tara returned to her position across the table from Josie and narrowed her brown eyes, her gaze bearing down on Josie. "I need to get ahead of something here."

Josie held up a hand and said, "If this is about Quail Hollow, you have to talk to the Chief. It's not my place to—"

"Stop," Tara commanded. "It's not about Quail Hollow. It's about Vera Urban."

"Vera Urban?" Vera's identity hadn't yet been released to the press. The only people who knew that she had been murdered the day before were the police.

Tara put a hand on her hip. "I've asked Amber to keep me apprised of what's going on over here."

But Amber wasn't the Mayor's plant, Josie thought ruefully.

Tara kept talking. "I know Vera Urban was killed yesterday in some very unusual circumstances."

"She was shot," Josie said pointedly.

"Yes, and before that she was evidently missing for sixteen years, isn't that right?"

Josie didn't answer.

"Detective Quinn, I know you. I know how deep you'll dig on this case, so I am heading you off at the pass. I knew Vera."

Josie felt a tickle of discomfort. The Mayor had a reputation for aggressively protecting her own interests, often crossing lines to do so. "What are you saying?" Josie asked. "That in the course of my investigation, you think we would need to talk?"

Tara gave an exasperated sigh. "Yes, that's what I'm saying. Here I am, telling you I knew Vera, but it was a very, very long time ago. She was my stylist at a salon called Bliss. I'm talking twenty years ago, at least. When her daughter was small, even before that. That's why I wanted to talk to you before you come at me with everything you've got. You'll find out I knew her and think I'm hiding something."

"Are you hiding something?" Josie asked.

Tara smiled but it didn't reach her eyes. "Of course not."

"But now you're going to ask me to keep it quiet that you knew the murdered mother of a murdered teenage girl."

Tara rolled her eyes. "I'm not asking you to keep it quiet, I'm asking you not to broadcast it. It's irrelevant. Vera was my hairstylist, for Pete's sake."

Josie narrowed her eyes. "Sara Venuto told me that many of Vera's clients were friends with her outside of the salon. Would you count yourself among that group?"

"You've already been to the salon?"

Josie smiled. "Not my first time solving a murder case. Yes, I've been to the salon."

Tara waved a hand in the air. "Whatever. It doesn't matter. I was friendly with her outside of the salon on occasion. I wouldn't call us friends but back then, I was the young wife of a surgeon with no ambition of my own, no job, and nothing to do all day. I was bored. I had money. My parents left me a trust fund. I was the one who put my husband through medical school but with him on a surgical residency, I was alone ninety percent of the time. I had Vera over a couple of times for a glass of wine and a chat. That was all."

"How about when Vera got pregnant? Do you remember that?"

"Very vaguely, yes."

"Sara Venuto says several of Vera's clients threw her a baby shower. Were you in that group?"

"No, I was not. Like I said, we were friendly, not friends."

"What do you remember about Vera?" Josie asked.

Tara placed a manicured hand on the table and leaned forward. "Nothing except what I just told you. She was my stylist. We had a glass of wine once or twice. She had a daughter named Beverly. That's all."

"You had Vera over to your house when you had your glasses of wine?" Josie asked.

"Yes."

"Had you ever been to her home, either before she moved into the house on Hempstead Road or after?"

"Of course not."

"When is the last time you were in contact with Vera?"

"Detective Quinn, it was so long ago that I couldn't even tell you. Decades."

"Where were you yesterday morning at seven a.m.?"

"Oh please. You can't really think— I was in my office in City Hall, meeting with my campaign manager and some aides. At least a half dozen people can confirm that."

Josie appraised her, wondering exactly what it was that Tara was trying to hide. There had to be something. Otherwise, she wouldn't have come to the police station and demanded to see Josie alone. "You know I've got to tell my team about this, right?"

Tara sighed. "I don't see any reason to tell anyone. I've just told you everything I know, and all of it is completely irrelevant to a murder case that took place in 2004."

"What about a murder case that took place yesterday?" Josie asked.

"Still irrelevant. By the time Beverly was killed, I hadn't spoken to Vera in nearly ten years. Really, Detective. I know we've had our… issues over the years, but I would appreciate your discretion in this matter."

"My discretion?" Josie laughed. "You're joking, right? You've been trying to get rid of me from day one. What is your angle here? Are you trying to protect yourself or are you trying to set me up for something?"

Tara glared at her.

Slowly, Josie picked up her coffee cup and took a long sip, never taking her eyes from Tara. She placed the cup back on the table and said, "Mayor Charleston, you know how these investigations work. You should also know me to some degree by now. Under no circumstances am I keeping secrets from my team. There is no amount of influence you can exert to make me dishonest."

"Don't be so dramatic, Detective Quinn. I'm not asking you to be dishonest. I'm simply saying that any investigation into me so far as it relates to Vera Urban is a dead end. I'm asking you to treat it as such."

"The fact that you're asking me to treat it as such is the very thing that makes me think you have something to hide. Why don't you just tell me what it is that you don't want people finding out?"

A tense moment unfolded between them. With each second that passed, Tara's face grew ruddier. Josie waited her out, content to let the silence in the room build the pressure. "Fine," Tara spat, finally. "If you must know, Vera was a drug dealer. Okay? Are you happy now?"

Josie leaned in with interest. "What are you talking about?"

"What did I just say? Vera Urban dealt drugs. I found out what she was doing, and I distanced myself from her, okay? I never took anything from her or bought anything from her."

"What kinds of drugs was she dealing?" Josie asked.

"Painkillers. Sometimes marijuana but almost always painkillers."

"Where did she get them?"

Tara threw her arms in the air. "How the hell should I know? Wherever dealers get their drugs."

"Okay, okay," Josie said, raising her hands to indicate for Tara to calm down. "How do you know she was a drug dealer?"

"Because I saw her sell drugs to the other clients at the salon. You have to understand, back then I was newly married to a surgeon. A doctor. Do you understand? I couldn't be associated with someone who was selling prescription drugs to people!"

"Because they might think your husband had a hand in supplying her with them," Josie filled in.

"Yes," Tara said. She sighed and pulled out the chair before her, flopping into it.

Josie said, "Why wouldn't you just lead with that?"

Tara let out a long breath. "Because I know you don't trust me."

"Was your husband helping to supply Vera with prescription drugs?"

"Of course not."

"I had to ask. Where else did she sell them or was it just in the salon?"

Tara sighed. "I don't know. I think mostly at social events—I think some of her clients invited her to their houses to hang out not because they wanted to spend time with her but because they were buying painkillers from her. I never purchased any from her. I just… knew about it."

Josie said, "We can keep this out of the press as long as neither you nor your husband had anything to do with Beverly or Vera's murders. That's the only thing that I can promise you. I have to tell my team. As long as everything you've told me is the truth, then you've got nothing to worry about."

Tara raised a brow. "Your Chief isn't exactly my biggest fan right now. How do I know he's not going to use this as leverage to get the upper hand in the Quail Hollow situation?"

Josie rolled her eyes. "I can't speak to that. That is between you and the Chief. My job is to find whoever killed Vera and Beverly and bring them to justice. That's it."

"So you won't help me with the Chief?"

Josie laughed. She walked to the door and pulled it open. Before she left, she looked over her shoulder and said, "You're the one who hired him."

CHAPTER THIRTY-ONE

2004

Josie had only been sitting on one of the hard metal chairs in the Wellspring Clinic's waiting room for ten minutes, and her ass already ached. Really, if they were going to make patients wait so long for their appointments, they ought to have more comfortable chairs. What was taking so long anyway? she wondered. She was the only person in the waiting room. Just as the thought crossed her mind, the front door swung open.

They'd better not see this person before me, Josie thought. She was only there for a physical for her lifeguard job. She'd be in and out of there in fifteen minutes.

Beverly Urban stepped through the door. Josie stared at her, open-mouthed. It was bad luck, pure and simple. Josie looked away from Beverly and picked up a magazine, spreading the pages and pretending to read. A few seconds later, the door swooshed again. She looked up. Beverly was gone.

Josie turned her head and looked out the window, watching Beverly run across the street. She ran along the safety fence in front of the construction site where Ray worked. He was over there now. Josie was going to try to see him after her appointment. What the hell was Beverly doing? Maybe she was just walking past it.

But she wasn't. She stopped at the entry gate where Josie had picked Ray up only a couple of weeks earlier. Josie watched as she had a conversation with the man behind the fence.

"Matson? Josie Matson?" a voice behind her called.

Josie turned to see the nurse standing in the doorway to that led to the exam rooms, holding a chart. She turned back to the window. Beverly was still talking to the guy.

"I'm sorry," Josie said. "I have to go."

"Do you want to reschedule?" the woman asked, but Josie was already out the door.

She walked a few paces down from the clinic where someone had parked a large truck. She could see Beverly from behind it, but Beverly wouldn't be able to spot her very easily. After a few minutes, Beverly waved at the man behind the fence and started walking back in the direction of the ice cream shop where she worked. Josie edged around the truck and as soon as there was an opening in traffic, darted across the street.

She followed Beverly down the block. What had she been talking to the gatekeeper about? Why had she waved to him so familiarly? Like they were old friends. But how could they be old friends unless Beverly was a frequent visitor to the site?

Josie was only a few feet behind Beverly. Was she headed back to work? The corner was coming up. Josie would find out soon enough. Except that she didn't cross the street to go to the ice cream shop. She stopped in front of the old theater, which was under construction according to the news. Or rather, it was being "revitalized." Josie hung back a few feet to see what she would do. Beverly hesitated in front of the reflective glass of the door, fluffing her hair and unbuttoning the top button of her shirt. As she reached for the door handle, a woman pushed through from the other side. The door hit Beverly full-on, knocking her to the ground. The woman, clad in form-fitting black clothes—long sleeves and pants even in the heat—started to apologize. Huge sunglasses rested on her face, making her look like some kind of bug. She lifted them up and peered down at Beverly. "I'm so sorry," she was saying. "I didn't even see you. Are you—"

She stopped mid-sentence, staring down at Beverly as if the girl had just transformed into a three-headed snake before her eyes. Josie took a step forward, getting close enough to see yellow bruising around both the woman's eyes just before she flipped her sunglasses back down. Straightening her posture, she flipped her long brown locks and stepped over Beverly, striding away from the scene with her head held high.

From the ground, Beverly turned her head and watched the woman walk off. She spotted Josie standing on the sidewalk. They locked eyes for the second time that day. The moment stretched out until Josie felt she had to say something.

"Are you okay?"

Beverly stood up, brushing off her rear. "Just leave me alone," she spat. Instead of going into the theater, she went in the opposite direction, jogging across the street toward the ice cream shop. She didn't wait for the light and a car beeped as it swerved around her. The driver rolled down his window and yelled something unintelligible at her.

Beverly kept running.

CHAPTER THIRTY-TWO

"A drug dealer?" Gretchen said. "That's interesting."

Josie said, "We'll have to get some corroboration if we can."

They sat at their desks in the great room waiting to hear from the landlord of the property Vera Urban, posing as Alice Adams, had rented from in Colbert. It was a little after ten a.m. Noah had come in and then been sent right back out on calls with Emergency Services. The rain had finally let up—it hadn't fallen all morning—but they had yet to see sunshine. Mettner was over near the copier helping Amber to work the machine. Josie watched out of the corner of her eye as Amber's hand slid from Mettner's forearm to his shoulder. She laughed at something he said, and he blushed.

Gretchen said, "Think about the way Beverly was killed. Execution-style. Then you've got Vera's murder. Also similar to the way some drug-related gangs handle things."

"You think we should be looking at the drug angle rather than the father of Beverly's baby angle?" Josie asked as she rifled through her desk looking for ibuprofen. Lucky for her, the bottle had two tablets left in it, which she swallowed dry. "We can't be sure they were murdered by the same person."

Gretchen shrugged and ran a hand through her short hair. "I think we should explore every angle. You're right, we can't be sure of anything, but Vera was hiding from someone and that someone killed her to shut her up."

Josie's cell phone rang. Hoping it was Colbert PD, she hit *answer* without looking at the number.

"Detective Quinn?" said a female voice. "This is Sara Venuto. We spoke yesterday. I've got a few things for you."

"That's great news," Josie told her. "I've got my colleague with me today. We can come over now if that's convenient."

Gretchen drove to Envy. Sara waited inside at the reception. The styling area was packed with clients and stylists working. No one gave them so much as a passing glance. Sara beckoned them to her office. On her desk, several photographs were spread out, along with a piece of copy paper with a handwritten list of names on it.

Sara said, "I talked to a couple of the girls who worked here with Vera. Among the three of us, we came up with a handful of names. I'm not sure it's helpful, but we did find pictures in our old salon photo albums."

Gretchen slipped on her reading glasses and leaned over the list. To Josie she said, "Our lovely mayor is on this list."

Sara said, "Oh yes, she was quite young then. None of us would have expected her to go into politics."

Josie studied the photographs. There were about a half dozen showing Vera beaming proudly beside a client in a chair, showing off their freshly cut or dyed and styled hair. Josie recognized a young Tara Charleston in one of them.

Sara said. "If you look on the back, we tried to identify each client by name."

Josie turned one of them over. It read: *Marisol.* Another read: *Connie P?* She used her phone to take a photo of the front of each picture and then the back where the client's name had been written. Once she finished with those photos, she moved on to another stack. She fingered a photograph of Vera Urban standing in what looked like the reception area of the salon—although decorated quite differently—surrounded by other women, some of them the clients in the other pictures. Vera was smiling widely and held a paper plate overflowing with bows and ribbons onto her head. She wore a black, shapeless dress and with her other hand, she splayed her fingers across her belly. Not cradling it, Josie thought, as most pregnant women seemed to do. This was more of a protective gesture.

"That was the baby shower I told you about," Sara said. "I was only able to find a few of those."

Josie riffled through them. Vera in a cushioned chair, surrounded by pink balloons and large gifts, gazing at a stroller that had been pushed in front of her. Vera, holding up various gifts. In one photo, she held up a baby monitor in one hand and a card in the other. The card was spread open. Josie leaned in and saw that it said, *Sorry I couldn't be there. Love, Marisol.* More photos followed. Vera in her chair of honor, surrounded by several smiling women, each of them holding up onesies that said *Cutie.* One of them was Tara Charleston. Clearly, Tara had lied about not attending the baby shower. Josie had the distinct feeling that Tara and Vera had been much closer than Tara let on.

"Sara," Josie said, as she snapped pictures of the baby shower photographs. "Was there ever any indication that Vera might be into drugs?"

Sara laughed, "Oh no. Not Vera."

Gretchen said, "Maybe she wasn't doing any drugs, but did you ever notice whether or not she gave out or sold drugs to any of the clients?"

Sara looked stunned. She put a hand to her chest. "Do you think I would ever allow something like that?"

"We have to ask," Josie said. "The women who helped you with the list, do you think we could speak with them? Are they here?"

Sara's face had gone from smiling and helpful to stricken and pale. Quickly, Gretchen said, "We're only asking because of the way that Beverly was killed. It had some markings of a drug-related homicide. Beverly was a minor. To our knowledge, the only significant adult in her life was Vera. We have to explore all possibilities."

Silently, Sara nodded, some of the color returning to her face. "I'll go get them," she mumbled.

Josie and Gretchen waited till all three women were in the room before breaking the news that Vera had been killed the day before. All of them were visibly upset. Gretchen fielded their questions expertly with what scant information they were allowed to disclose while Josie fought back another wave of grief over the events of the day before. Then Josie and Gretchen spent some time with the two stylists who remembered Vera. Neither of them recalled her either selling drugs to clients or using drugs herself—even when asked out of Sara's presence.

Josie and Gretchen took the list and photos back to the station house to track down as many of the former clients as they could. The list wasn't long. There were only seven names, and they were not all complete. Sara Venuto and her staff had only been able to provide last names for some of the women and for others, only the first initial of their last name. They were names from thirty years earlier, anyway. Josie knew there was the possibility that some of the women would have changed their names now, due to marriage or divorce. She and Gretchen ordered lunch and tried to track down the women on the list. Two of them were deceased. One of them now lived in California and another in Texas. Josie spoke with both of them by telephone. Their stories were the same. They vaguely remembered Vera, spoke kindly of her, and said they hadn't had any contact with her since she left the salon after her injury. Neither remembered her selling or using drugs.

There were three names left: one was Mayor Tara Charleston. Josie crossed her off. Then there was a woman named Marisol and another named Connie P. Marisol was a fairly uncommon name. It only took Josie about a half hour to locate Marisol Dutton, wife of city councilman and mayoral candidate, Kurt Dutton. The Duttons' close neighbors—also residents of the original development before it became Quail Hollow—were Joseph and Constance Prather. Connie P. Josie brought up Constance Prather's driver's license photo and compared it to the picture of Connie P. taken at Vera's baby shower. It was a match.

There was still no word from Colbert PD. There was plenty of daylight left. "Gretchen," Josie said, "finish your lunch fast. I found Vera's other clients."

CHAPTER THIRTY-THREE

They returned to Quail Hollow with Josie at the wheel. This time there was no rain and even more protestors out front. Across from them, on the other side of the drive leading into the Estates, was a handful of people that Josie quickly surmised were Quail Hollow residents. They stood in a cluster and shouted at the protestors; "Leave us alone!" and "Go away!" One woman yelled, "These are our homes! Go back to your own!" A man in his forties hollered, "Mind your own damn business." The protestors retaliated with indignant accusations.

Gretchen said, "Maybe we should call the Chief? Or have someone from patrol come out here to monitor this?"

Josie pulled just inside the gates and parked. "See if you can get a patrol unit," she said. "I think I saw Connie Prather in that group. Let's go talk to her."

As they walked back toward the feuding groups, a slight hush came over the protestors. Josie heard her own name whispered and gave them a wave. She and Gretchen made their way over to the Quail Hollow residents. Grateful that the throbbing in her thigh had receded to a dull ache, Josie picked up her pace. She zeroed in on a woman in her late fifties wearing a charcoal-colored sweater beneath a puffy pink vest, stretchy blank pants, and Uggs. In her hand was a leash that led to a small white dog who stood idly, looking utterly unimpressed by everything going on around him.

"Constance Prather?" Josie asked.

The woman raised a brow. "I know you're not here to arrest me. I had nothing to do with 'diverting' or 'stealing' resources. I'm just here to help get rid of these people. They won't give us a moment of peace. Honestly, I've lived here thirty-five years and we've never had any trouble like this. You want to talk to someone about your precious emergency resources, talk to Marisol Dutton. Her husband is the one trying to iron this all out with your Chief." Without giving Josie or Gretchen a second to speak, Prather turned slightly and looked behind her. "Marisol," she shouted. "Mar!"

Josie recognized the woman walking toward them from the photo of her and Vera at the salon, as well as photos of her in the press in recent months standing dutifully beside her husband during campaign events. Marisol was shorter than Prather, her brown hair streaked with gray and styled in waves to her shoulders. Her pale skin was thick with make-up. She also wore a pair of black stretchy pants, as well as knee-high boots. She clutched the lapels of a lavender sweater and pulled them across her ample bosom. "What's going on?" she asked as she joined them.

Josie opened her mouth to speak, but Prather started talking again. "These are cops. You can't tell? They're cops. You need to talk to them about the supplies."

Marisol glared at Prather. "You're kidding me right now, right, Connie?" She turned back to Josie and Gretchen and extended a hand, which they each shook. "I don't know anything about the supplies, honestly, but you can talk to my husband. As I'm sure you know, he's a candidate for Mayor."

"We're aware," Gretchen said.

Connie put in, "He's also a real estate developer. He's the one who had the bright idea to expand this place and call it Quail Hollow Estates." She waved a hand around them. "I don't know why he would mess with a perfectly good neighborhood, but he couldn't leave it alone. Had to make it fancier. Now look. We've got a moat that's flooding the back half of the properties and protestors."

"Jesus, Connie," Marisol snapped. "Shut it." Turning back to Josie and Gretchen, she said, "He's at his office. I can give you the address if you'd like."

Josie took out her credentials and held them out for both women to study. "We're actually not here about that."

The two women looked puzzled. Marisol gave a weak smile. "What, then?"

Gretchen said, "We need to talk to both of you about Vera Urban."

Prather said, "Vera who?"

Marisol lightly slapped her shoulder. "Please, Connie. 'Vera who?' Don't you remember? It was on the news last night."

Connie said, "Oh, she was the one you found in the flood, all wrapped up in a tarp."

"No," Josie said. "That was her daughter, Beverly."

"Oh, right," said Connie.

Marisol shook her head. "I can't believe you don't remember! It's so tragic."

Josie and Gretchen looked at one another, silently agreeing to hold back the news of Vera's murder for now. Some of the other residents had stopped engaging with the protestors and begun drifting closer to them. Connie said, "Mind if we talk about this somewhere else?"

Marisol said, "Come back to my house. It's the closest."

The four of them walked along the tree-lined lanes of Quail Hollow until they came to the section where the original homeowners lived. Marisol Dutton lived only a block over from Calvin Plummer in a large, stately brick home. It was silent as a tomb when they entered. Single file, they followed Marisol through a large tile foyer into her kitchen. Connie scooped up her small dog and carried it in her arms. To one side of the kitchen was a solarium that looked out onto a deck. The sliding glass doors were closed but beyond, Josie could see the Duttons' large yard and trees beyond that. A small table sat near the doors with four chairs, one for each of them.

Wordlessly, Connie took a seat at the table. Josie and Gretchen followed. One of the panes of glass near the table had been broken. Someone had sloppily taped a plastic bag over it. Fragments of glass rested on the floor beneath it. Marisol saw them staring at it and said, "Kurt broke it. He hasn't called to have it fixed yet."

From the refrigerator, Marisol pulled a bottle of red wine. She poured a glass, then held out the bottle in their direction. "Anyone?"

Gretchen said, "We're working, Mrs. Dutton."

She shrugged. "Suit yourself. Connie?"

With a scowl, Connie replied, "You know I don't drink, Marisol."

Marisol rolled her eyes and sauntered over, languidly taking a seat of her own. "Oh right. Forever the addict."

Two spots of color rose in Connie's cheeks. "I'm an alcoholic, Mar. That's not something that goes away."

Marisol raised her glass and took a sip of wine. The sleeve of her sweater slid down, and Josie saw a series of purple bruises along the inside of her wrist. "Whatever. I don't want to argue right now." She turned to Josie and Gretchen. "Why are you here to ask us about Vera Urban?"

Josie said, "We understand that you were both clients of hers when she worked at one of the local salons. Back when it was called Bliss. We were wondering what you could tell us about her?"

Connie's lips pressed into a thin line. "God, that was… what? Thirty years ago? Something like that? I don't remember that much."

With a mischievous grin, Marisol swished the wine around in her glass and said, "Because she was drunk."

Connie's jaw tightened. "Dammit, Marisol! This is why I never—" She stood up, pressing her little dog against her chest. "I'm leaving."

Marisol shook her head. "Calm down, Connie. Honestly. You're too high-strung. Sit." She turned to Josie. "We were Vera's clients. But that was a long, long time ago. We were all in our twenties, married to successful, powerful men. Bored out of our skulls. Weren't we, Connie?"

Slowly, Connie sat back down, loosening her grip on her dog. "Speak for yourself."

Marisol laughed. "Please. You were just as bored as the rest of us."

"The rest of you?" Josie asked.

Marisol said, "Well there was a group of us, Vera's clients, we became friendly. It was Connie, myself, Tara—" she leaned in toward Josie and Gretchen and in a stage whisper said, "The Mayor." Leaning back, she said, "Who else, Connie?"

Connie's back was ramrod straight. "I-I don't know. How would we know Vera's clients?"

"I'm talking about our WORMM club."

"WORMM club?" Gretchen echoed.

"That's with two 'm's," Marisol explained. "It's an acronym. Wives of Rich Missing Men. WORMM."

Connie's eyes flitted to the dog in her lap. She stroked its head. "Our husbands all traveled. That's why we called them 'missing men.' You forgot Whitney."

Marisol snapped her fingers. "Whitney! Yes. She didn't live around here, but she did join us for some of our parties."

Gretchen took out her notepad and flipped a few pages. She found the list of names they'd gotten from Sara Venuto. Whitney was one of the women on the list they'd discovered to be deceased.

Josie said, "What kinds of parties?"

Connie said, "Oh, they really weren't parties."

Marisol said, "Sure they were."

"A handful of us sat around drinking and complaining about our husbands," Connie said. "That is not a party."

Marisol gave a shrug as if to say "whatever."

Gretchen asked, "Was Vera Urban ever at any of these parties?"

"She was," Connie said.

Josie looked back and forth between the two women. "Mrs. Prather," she said. "What is it that you and your husband do?"

"She doesn't do anything," Marisol teased. "Her husband is the CEO of a software company."

Connie bristled. "I have a job." She turned toward Josie and Gretchen. "I'm the head of the Prather Foundation. We give out scholarships to female college students who want to major in STEAM—that's Science, Technology, Engineering, Art, and Math."

"That sounds wonderful," Josie said.

Connie smiled, a true smile for once. "My oldest daughter is an epidemiologist, and my youngest is a computer network architect," she said proudly.

"You must be very proud of them," Gretchen put in. She turned to Marisol. "We know what your husband does, but what about you?"

She sighed and gulped down the rest of the wine. "I am Kurt Dutton's beautiful, dutiful wife. I sit around all day looking good and coming up with inventive ways to spend his money. That's what I do. That's what Connie used to do before she became the alcohol police."

Connie glared.

Josie tried to bring the conversation back to Vera. "The two of you as well as Mayor Charleston and this Whitney—you were all well-off, you all had busy husbands, and spent a lot of time together and you invited Vera? Your stylist?"

Connie swallowed. "Yes. Vera was a friend."

Marisol slammed her wine glass onto the table, eyes flashing. "Oh for goodness' sake, Connie. Just tell them. What does it even matter now?"

Connie's eyes widened but she didn't speak.

Marisol looked at Josie and Gretchen. Laughing, she said, "Vera was our drug dealer."

"Mar!" Connie exclaimed.

"Oh please," Marisol said. "What? You think they're going to arrest us for buying pills from some hair stylist thirty years ago? Come on."

"Your husband is running for Mayor, Marisol!"

"And if he doesn't get elected, it will be good news for everyone," Marisol said with a laugh. She picked up her wine glass to sip again, realized it was empty, and set it back down.

Gretchen said, "We've already heard from some other sources that Vera supplied painkillers to many of her clients. We're not here to arrest anyone or get anyone into trouble. We're just trying to find out as much about Vera as we can. We've been unable to locate anyone who knew her well at the time that her daughter was killed."

Marisol said, "Yeah, well, after she had her daughter, we all grew apart. Stopped hanging out. Didn't really keep in touch. Connie left first, didn't you, Con?"

Connie nodded. Her eyes were on the table. "I had to. My daughter—" She broke off, eyes now on Josie and Gretchen, pleading. "I started it, okay? I didn't mean to. It wasn't like we were all hanging out trying to score drugs. With my first daughter, they messed up the epidural. The labor was excruciating, and I had pain in my back and down my leg for months afterward. The doctors didn't believe me. Vera said she knew someone she could get oxycodone from."

"Someone like who?" Josie asked.

Connie squeezed her dog close. "I don't know. Like an ex or a friend or something. Anyway, she got them for me, and they helped. I was so grateful to her. She even came over a few times when my husband was out of town and helped me with my daughter. She always wanted a baby, you know. She was hoping to meet someone, get married, and then have a baby, but it just didn't work out that way."

Josie said, "So you two became close, then."

Connie nodded. "I already knew Marisol and Tara. They both live nearby. A few times I had them over, and Vera was already here. Eventually, we just became this little group. We'd get together— sometimes at my house, sometimes here or at Tara's—and hang out."

Marisol took her wine glass and walked back to the fridge to refill it. "We hung out and we drank," she clarified. "And eventually, Vera was getting the rest of us pills, and sometimes pot, and sometimes—"

Connie lowered her gaze. "Stop, Mar."

"Why? Does it matter now?"

When Connie didn't answer, Marisol said, "Cocaine. That was Whitney's thing. But she had a heart condition. Those two didn't go together. She was coked up for years before her heart gave out."

Josie said, "We're aware that Whitney is deceased. It was Vera supplying her with the cocaine the entire time?"

Marisol said, "Not the entire time. Just at first."

Gretchen looked at her notes. "Whitney died in 1998." For Josie's benefit, she said, "Beverly would have been ten."

"Right," Josie said. "Vera continued to sell painkillers and other drugs after her daughter was born?"

Connie said, "I'm not entirely sure."

"Why is that?" Gretchen asked.

Connie cleared her throat. "I, uh, I had an incident. It was before Vera got pregnant. I got so high on painkillers that I fell asleep. I was home alone with my oldest daughter. She was very young. I passed out for hours. Twelve, to be exact. My husband came home, found me unconscious on the couch and our daughter upstairs in her crib, wet and covered in filth, starving and crying." Tears spilled down her cheeks. "Oh God, it was horrible. That was the end. The end of all of it. The drinking, the pills. I was so ashamed."

For this she got another eye-roll from Marisol. "Oh please. You make it sound so dramatic. Your daughter was fine!"

Connie's eyes flashed as she glowered at Marisol. "You don't know what it's like. You never had kids. You don't understand how it feels to know your baby was suffering for all those hours, crying for you, and you didn't feed or change or comfort her because you were wasted."

Marisol snapped, "I went to rehab, too, Con."

Gretchen held up a hand. "Ladies, please. Slow down. Connie, after the incident with your daughter, what happened?"

Connie shifted the dog in her lap, shooting Marisol one last dirty look before answering. "I went into a thirty-day inpatient rehab program. My mother came and cared for my daughter. My husband didn't travel during that time or for the month after that. I haven't touched anything since."

Josie said, "You stopped going to parties with Vera and the girls as well?"

"I had to. The point of those parties was to drink and get high. Plus, I had a baby at home depending on me and a husband who supported me through rehab. I couldn't let them down."

"But you still maintained contact with Vera?" Gretchen asked.

"Well, Vera was the best stylist I ever had," Connie explained. "She was a friend, I guess. I just didn't see her outside of the salon anymore."

"You were at her baby shower," Josie said.

"Well, yeah. Like we said, Vera always wanted a baby. I was happy for her. It wasn't planned, and it didn't take the form she always wanted: marriage and then a baby, but she was thrilled. I did visit her a few times when Beverly was an infant. She was exhausted, as all new mothers are, and a little overwhelmed."

Josie said, "We understand that Vera went onto bedrest early. Did either of you see her while she was on bedrest?"

"No," Connie said. "She went to stay with her brother."

Josie suspected this was a lie. A lie Vera had told to people who were supposed to be close friends. She would know for sure once she heard back from the police in Georgia with respect to their investigation into Floyd Urban.

Connie went on, "I saw her a few times after she came home with Beverly but after that, we drifted apart. Marisol stayed in touch with her, though."

Marisol said, "You're wrong. You stayed in touch with her longer than I did."

Gretchen said, "I didn't see you in the photos from Vera's baby shower, Marisol."

"I was in rehab then." She laughed humorlessly. "We were all in rehab at one point or another. Except Tara, I suppose."

"And Whitney," Connie added.

Marisol put her wine glass down and folded her arms across her chest. "I don't have a big dramatic story to tell. I just realized that I was taking so many pills that I was sleeping more hours a day than I was awake. I put on a ton of weight. I wasn't myself. When my husband came home from traveling, it was a struggle to stay awake to spend any time with him. He was worried. He said he didn't even recognize me. I think he was more worried that I was depressed than anything else. He didn't even know about the pills. I had to come clean. I told him about everything—how I was bored while he was away, and I'd been getting together with the girls for drinks, which turned into us trying some pills and then me taking them on my own when I wasn't with the girls. The whole spiral. We talked about it and decided I would go into rehab."

Connie blurted, "Is that what you call it? That was a lot of rehab for someone who's on her second glass of wine in the middle of the day."

Marisol waved a dismissive hand at Connie and sipped her wine again. To Josie and Gretchen she said, "She's just jealous that I got to really go away for rehab. I didn't have kids so I went to a swanky place in Colorado."

"Money well spent, obviously," Connie spat.

"Oh please," Marisol said. "I had a problem with pills, not with alcohol."

Again, Josie tried to bring the conversation back to Vera. "So after you returned from Colorado, Marisol, did you see Vera?"

"Of course. I wanted to see her sweet baby girl. I knew how excited she was about being a mom. I didn't understand it myself—I never wanted children—but I knew how she felt. I went to see them a few times. But then we lost touch."

"You didn't continue to see Vera at the salon?" Josie asked.

"No," Marisol said. "My husband felt it best I make a clean break from all of my old habits. To him, the salon was the scene of the crime, as it were. So, I went to another one. Eventually, Vera and I fell out of touch. Life went on."

"Did Whitney continue to see Vera?" Gretchen asked.

Connie said, "Probably, but I'm not sure. Whitney didn't live around here, so we never saw her."

Marisol added, "I couldn't tell you for sure."

"Did Vera ever tell either of you who Beverly's father was?" Josie asked.

Connie shook her head.

Marisol said, "No. She just said he didn't want to be involved. I got the feeling it was a one-night stand sort of thing."

"Did the two of you stay friends?" Gretchen asked.

The two women looked at one another. Connie said, "We stayed *neighbors*."

Marisol raised her glass of wine. "I didn't have children. When you don't have children and your friend does, you have nothing in common anymore."

"We could have stayed close," Connie said.

"Let me clarify that," Marisol said. "I don't *like* children."

"These parties you had," Josie asked. "Was it always just you ladies? Did anyone else ever attend?"

"No," Connie answered. "Just the girls."

"Do you know the names of anyone else Vera associated with or was close to? Any other friends, or perhaps the person who supplied the drugs to her?"

"No," Marisol said. "That was part of the deal. We didn't want to know. She just always had everything when we wanted it."

Josie turned to Connie. "You said you went to Vera's home to help her out when Beverly was small. Was there ever anyone else there?"

Connie shook her head. "No. Just Vera. But she was happy. Overwhelmed and sleep-deprived, yes, like all new mothers, but so happy."

"We just have one last question," Gretchen said. "Where were you two yesterday morning? Say, around seven a.m.?"

Marisol and Connie looked at one another and laughed. "At seven in the morning?" Marisol said. "We were home, probably still in bed. I know I was."

"I was awake," Connie said. "But yes, I was home."

"Your husbands can verify this?" Josie asked.

"Well, sure," Marisol said. "Mine can. What about Joe, Conn? Was he home?"

"He doesn't leave for the office until eight-thirty," Connie answered. "So yes, he can verify that I was home. Why are you asking this?"

Gretchen stood up and handed each woman a business card. "Just standard police questions. Thank you for your time. Call us if you think of anything."

Marisol stared at them, as if she was going to ask for more of an explanation, but then she clamped her mouth shut.

Josie stood as well. "We'll let ourselves out."

CHAPTER THIRTY-FOUR

"All right," Gretchen said, once they were in the car headed back to the station. "Let's go over what we know."

Josie eased out of the Quail Hollow entrance, waving to the protestors and to the patrol unit now stationed between them and the residents. "Do we know anything? Really?"

Gretchen laughed. "It always seems like we don't until we do." She took out her notebook and flipped through some pages. "Vera Urban was a stylist at this upscale salon, Bliss."

"A very good stylist," Josie said.

"Yes," Gretchen said. "Her clients, boss, and co-workers have agreed on that."

"She was single," Josie added. "If she had any significant boyfriends, no one remembers their names."

"Right. She started peddling painkillers to her clients at the salon, unbeknownst to her boss and co-workers."

"It seems like that started with Connie Prather. She starts getting them for her. They strike up a friendship. Vera starts getting invited to things. Starts providing more drugs for more women."

"But keeping it within a pretty small circle," Gretchen said. "But no one knows who was supplying her with these painkillers. Is there any chance that Mayor Charleston's husband was supplying them? He's a surgeon, right?"

"He is," Josie agreed. "I asked the Mayor about that and of course, she denied it. I don't trust her. I don't trust her husband. He's cheated on her in the past, which means he has no problem lying, but I'm not sure he would put his career in jeopardy that way. He would only have been a resident back then. Besides that, Vera also supplied pot and cocaine. She couldn't have gotten those from a surgeon."

"True," Gretchen said. "We can check him out, but we're not looking at him as the supplier. Also, if Marisol Dutton knew that Tara's husband had supplied drugs to Vera Urban as a resident, don't you think she'd tell her husband so he could use it against Tara in the campaign?"

"No," Josie said. "I don't think Marisol would want any of that exposed because of her own part in it. It would be terrible for Tara and her husband, but it would also make the Duttons look bad. Did you happen to see the bruises on Marisol's wrist?"

"No," Gretchen said. "I didn't pick up on that. You think Kurt Dutton abuses his wife?"

"I can't say for sure, but the bruises were suspicious. Anyway, we can probably rule out Tara's surgeon husband as Vera's drug supplier, which brings us back to someone in the local drug trade, most likely."

"Connie said it was either Vera's ex or a friend who was supplying her with stuff. So if that person had access to several different types of drugs then yes, he was probably known in the local drug trade. Okay, we've got Vera getting drugs from an unknown person, selling them to these rich housewives at parties at their houses while their husbands are away," Gretchen went on.

"The Mayor claims she begged out of these parties early on," Josie said. "Leaving Whitney, Connie, and Marisol although Connie and Marisol's accounts dispute that."

"Right," Gretchen said. "At the very least, we know the Mayor didn't stop going to these parties as early as she claims she did. But let's say eventually her attendance drops off. Whitney dies. Connie and Marisol both go into rehab."

Josie went on, "Vera had Beverly. The parties stopped. The women all fell out of touch although Vera continued working at the salon until Beverly was thirteen."

"Beverly and Vera had a fight. Beverly pushed Vera down the steps, injuring Vera's back badly enough for her to need surgery—"

"And go on painkillers," Josie finished.

"If she was taking as many painkillers as your grandmother implied she was—enough for her to pass out when she was supposed to be at a meeting with the principal—then she wasn't getting them from a doctor," Gretchen said.

"She found someone to buy them from illegally."

"Or she already knew someone who could supply them," Gretchen argued.

"Exactly."

"If she was spending a lot of money on painkillers from an illegal source, that might explain the issues with her making her rent."

"True," Josie agreed. "Her addiction gets worse. She's broke. Beverly's having behavioral problems. Beverly gets pregnant. Vera finds out."

"Their relationship was already strained," Gretchen said. "I'm sure news of the pregnancy didn't help."

"I agree. But now we've got a blind spot. A period of time in their lives where we have no idea what happened. The next thing that we can gather is that someone killed Beverly and buried her beneath their house."

"Right," Gretchen said. "Vera goes into hiding—whether she was involved in the murder or just a witness, we can't say at this point—but she disappeared off the face of the earth."

"There was no one in their lives to even notice they were gone," Josie said. "Don't you think that's strange?"

She looked over long enough to see Gretchen shrug.

"You don't think it's odd?" Josie pressed.

Gretchen flipped her notebook closed, eyes focused on the outskirts of the city flying past them. "I don't think it's that odd. When I moved here, other than my work colleagues, no one would have known if I went missing."

"Not true," Josie said. "Your old partner from Philadelphia—he would have come looking for you when you didn't check in."

Gretchen smiled. "Guess so."

Josie said, "At the very least, Vera's drug dealer would have noticed. Or the guy my grandmother told me was giving Vera rides back and forth to school whenever Beverly got in trouble and she had to meet with the principal."

"They might be one and the same," Gretchen pointed out. "Her drug dealer and her only friend. For all we know, he's the one who killed them."

"Then we need to find him. And I know just who to ask."

CHAPTER THIRTY-FIVE

Noah stood next to his desk in the great room at the stationhouse, towel-drying his hair with an old sweatshirt. His jeans and Denton PD polo shirt were soaked. Mettner was nowhere to be found. The Chief's door was closed. At the desk that had now become hers by default, Amber sat with her small laptop, tapping away at the keys. Josie wondered what she was working on. She smiled at Josie and Gretchen as they entered. They didn't smile back.

Gretchen said, "Fraley, you know you can go home and get changed after emergency flood calls."

Noah grimaced. "I wasn't on a call. The water breached the sandbags out front, and we're still short the tube barrier we were supposed to have for around the building. Lamay and I got plastic barricades from Dalrymple Township and put them out. I don't know how well they'll hold up, but it's better than nothing."

Josie said, "We haven't had rain all day. Maybe the water will recede soon. Hey, you know those looters you picked up the other night? Are they still down in holding?"

Noah froze, the sweatshirt in both hands, his sandy hair sticking up every which way. "Uh, yeah. They are, but, uh—"

"I already know," Josie said, cutting him off. "I know Needle's down there."

Amber had stood up and now inched closer to them. "Who's Needle?"

Noah balled up the sweatshirt and put it on his chair. "This is a personal matter. Do you mind?"

Amber gave a wan smile. "Oh, sure, sorry."

Josie kept her eyes on Noah. "I know that's what you were trying to tell me the other night when you came home. It's okay. He's the person I need to talk to."

Noah came around the desks and stood within inches of her. Lowering his voice, he said, "You need to talk to Needle? What the hell for?"

Gretchen, too, walked over, inserting herself into their small circle. "It's about the Vera Urban case."

Noah looked at her. "You're kidding, right?"

"Afraid not," Gretchen replied.

Josie said, "He has information we need. He's been part of the Denton drug scene since before I was born. There's a very good chance he'll remember Vera Urban and maybe who was supplying her with the drugs she was peddling to her salon clients."

Noah said, "Send Gretchen. You don't need to talk to this guy."

Josie put a hand on her hip. "I don't?"

Gretchen said, "He's right, boss. I can talk to him myself."

Josie looked from Gretchen to Noah, thrust her chin forward and said, "I'm talking to him."

She turned to walk away, but Noah caught her hand. Quietly, he said, "You don't have to do the hard stuff all the time. The last twenty-four hours have been... difficult."

In the last twenty-four hours, Josie had watched biblical flooding swallow up her city; she'd been shot at; she'd been swept away; and she'd failed to save Vera Urban, the only solid lead they had in the Beverly Urban case. The culmination of those things had hollowed her out and pushed her to the brink of a mental breakdown, but she said, "Noah, it's fine. Besides, we have a history of sorts, Needle and I. He'll be more likely to tell me what we want to know than Gretchen. Trust me."

He let go. "Okay, but let me have him brought up to an interview room. You can butter him up with coffee and cigarettes."

"Fine," Josie said.

Twenty minutes later, Josie and Gretchen walked into one of the interview rooms on the second floor. A cloud of cigarette smoke hung in the air. Larry Ezekiel Fox, the man Josie had come to think of as "Needle" sat in a chair next to the metal table centered in the room. In front of him was a half-empty paper cup of black coffee and an ashtray that already contained two cigarette butts. Josie hadn't seen him in three years, but he looked like he had aged a full decade. He was in his mid-sixties, but a hard life of drug use, homelessness, and criminal enterprise had aged him well beyond that. His skin was tanned and wrinkled. He had unkempt, stringy gray hair and a long beard that yellowed at the edges. In Denton's holding cells, he'd been allowed to wear his own clothes which included a drab, olive green jacket that he'd owned for as long as Josie had known him. It was threadbare and faded now, worn over a black T-shirt, dirty jeans that had seen better days, and a pair of boots that were blackened with age and grime. He smelled as if he hadn't bathed since the last time she saw him.

He looked up and smiled at her. "JoJo," he said, using her childhood nickname. "I was wondering if you'd pay me a visit."

"Zeke," she greeted him, using the name he went by. Only Josie called him "Needle"—he didn't even know about the private nickname she had given him as a small child, knowing him only as the man who brought needles to the woman who had posed as her mother. As a child, Josie hadn't realized the needles were so that Lila could inject herself with drugs. She just knew this man came to their trailer often and as much as she didn't like him or his wares, the truth was that he'd saved Josie from terrible things as a child. Not all the terrible things that had happened to her—he'd stood by while Lila locked her in a closet for days, starved her, and otherwise abused her, but he had saved her from the worst that Lila had tried to do to her.

Josie was never sure if she should feel grateful to him for having improved her life with Lila even incrementally, or if she should be furious with him because he never stepped in and tried to have her removed from Lila's care. Then again, he had been Lila's drug dealer. That he noticed Josie at all and tried to help her was probably more than was warranted.

"Sit," Needle said, waving toward the other chairs in the room, as if he were hosting them in his living room and not in an interview room at the police headquarters.

Josie took the seat closest to him, trying not to grimace as her stitches pulled. Gretchen sat opposite, her notepad in hand, pen ready to go. "I'm not here for a social visit," Josie told him.

He took a long drag on his cigarette and blew the smoke upward, away from her. "I know that, JoJo. But it's good to get out of that cell. Never liked them cells much. Truth be told, I'd rather be out under the stars with nowhere to lay my head than in a cell."

Josie took out her phone and brought up a photo of Vera from her days at the salon, before Beverly was born. She slid it across to Needle. "Do you remember that woman?"

Needle put his cigarette in the ashtray and sipped his coffee as he studied it. "She dead?"

"Yes," Josie told him.

He looked up at her, smiling again, but this time she saw a familiar look in his pale gray eyes. A little bit of suspicion and a lot of hardness. "You tryin' to pin something on me, JoJo?"

Josie said, "That cell you hate so much? It's your alibi. I'm not trying to pin anything on you. I just need information. Her name was Vera. I went to high school with her daughter. She used to work at a salon here in Denton which is where she sold drugs to rich women. Painkillers, pot, that sort of thing."

He kept studying the photo. Josie reached over and swiped through several more photos. He eyed each one as if it were some kind of hieroglyph he was trying to decipher. Josie waited. When he didn't say anything, she picked up the pack of cigarettes that Noah had secured for the interview and shook a new one out, handing it to Needle.

He took it, lit up, inhaled, and on the exhale, said, "I remember her. No one's seen her in years though."

"How many years?" Gretchen asked.

"Lotta years."

Josie said, "What else can you tell me about her?"

He looked up from the phone and Josie took it back. "She wasn't in it heavy, not at first. The painkillers were a side hustle, to get extra money. You're right, sometimes she needed other things, but it was mostly painkillers. She had those rich bitch clients but there were only a few. She didn't need much. Not until she started taking them herself."

"She had an accident," Gretchen supplied. "Then she started taking painkillers."

Needle shrugged. "I don't know what all happened to her. She was around a lot looking for them for a lotta years, then she wasn't, then she was back, and it was like someone put her through a damn time machine. She couldn't hardly walk, didn't have no money, and all she wanted was more and more and more. Then one day—nothing. Figured she overdosed."

"Did she buy from you?" Josie asked.

He chuckled. "Come on, JoJo. I'm already in here for lootin'. You said you wasn't gonna pin nothing on me."

"I don't care if she was," Josie said. "I'm not charging you for drugs you sold to someone thirty years ago or sixteen years ago—someone who's dead. I need to know who supplied her. I need a name."

Needle sat back in his chair and puffed away at his cigarette. He stroked his beard. "A name," he said. "I might have a name for you."

"You do or you don't," Gretchen said.

His eyes darted in her direction and then landed back on Josie. "I do. But JoJo, you caught me at a bad time, you know? I'm in here. Tomorrow they'll be taking me over to central booking. Then I'll be in for a few months before all this gets straightened out."

Josie smiled at him. "Three meals a day, Zeke. You could do worse."

"Never had no trouble finding meals," he said.

Josie leaned in toward him. "What do you want?"

"You're a big shot now, JoJo. You could pull some strings for an old friend. Get me some reduced charges. Hell, maybe get me out of here completely."

She felt something harden inside her. "You're not an old friend, and I'm not pulling any strings for you. Give me the name. I'll make sure you're comfortable while you're here."

He sighed, put his cigarette out, and folded his arms across his chest. "Maybe we're not friends, JoJo," he said. "But you always were a smart kid. You know how the world works. I have something you want. You have something I want. Seems to me that's a fair trade."

Josie said, "I don't even know if the information you've got is of any use. What if the person I'm looking for is dead? Then what? You can't guarantee anything. I'm not making any deals with you. Either you give me a name or you don't."

"And if I don't?"

Josie smiled. "I'm a smart kid. I'll figure it out."

Needle narrowed his eyes at her. "Jojo—" he began, but his words were cut off by her new cell phone ringing on the table between them. Josie glanced at the screen, then back at Gretchen. "It's Colbert PD. Come on, let's go."

CHAPTER THIRTY-SIX

Ten minutes later, Josie and Gretchen were on the way to Colbert in Josie's vehicle. The landlord had been tracked down, and he was more than happy to help them. He said he'd meet them at Alice's address with keys and a copy of the lease she had signed. The emotional roller coaster of the past day seemed to slow with this news. It felt like they might have a real lead.

Gretchen said, "I think when we get back, you should talk to Needle again."

Josie's hands tightened on the steering wheel. "I'm not asking Needle who Vera's supplier was. I'm not doing him any favors."

"Boss," Gretchen said. "It's the fastest way to get the information."

"By asking the district attorney to go easy on him? Gretchen, he's a career criminal."

"Yes, he is, but he's also a non-violent offender. His rap sheet up until this past week was made up entirely of drug offenses."

"What are you saying?"

Gretchen sighed. "I'm saying that if you just talk to the DA and ask them to consider a reduced charge in exchange for information on a current murder case, and they agree to it, it's not like you're endangering the public—not in the sense that he might go out and assault or murder someone."

Josie took one hand from the steering wheel to wipe sweat from her brow, only to discover that it was trembling. Was this one of those times when she wasn't thinking clinically enough? she wondered. The road they were traveling down was blocked where flooding had inundated it. Josie pulled up to the "Road Closed" sign and stopped, her foot pressing hard against the brake. When she spoke, her voice shook. She stopped and tried again, attempting to steady it. "My whole life that man stood by and did nothing while terrible things happened to me. No, not happened to me—were *perpetrated* against me. Violent things. Unspeakable things. Yes, he intervened a couple of times when things were very bad, but he left me there. He left me there with—with a crazy woman. He gave her the drugs that made her… made her…" The words seemed to get hung up in her throat. A sob threatened, making her shoulders quake. Gretchen touched Josie's shoulder.

"Boss," she said softly. "It's okay."

Tears stung Josie's eyes. What the hell was wrong with her? Why was she crying all the time now? She understood her feelings about Vera Urban's death. She'd tried and failed to save the woman. That warranted tears, although even those tears were anathema to Josie's career-long professionalism. But she didn't cry over just anything like this. Certainly not over things that had happened decades ago. Things she couldn't change. She tried to push it all down the way she always did, but it wasn't working.

Gretchen reached between them and put the gear shift in park. "Let's take a minute," she suggested.

Josie shook her head. Her whole body quaked. She opened her mouth, willing the words "I'm fine" to come out but instead, different words came out, high and squeaky. "Lila tried to cut my face off! She tried to cut my face off. She was crazy, and he supplied her with everything she asked for, even when she didn't have any damn money, and it didn't matter to him or to anyone else what she did to me. He's not—he's not—"

"Boss."

"He's not a good person!"

Once the last words were out, Josie felt like she might crumble. She sank back into her seat, hands in her lap. Suddenly, she felt light, as though she weighed nothing. Everything around her began to spin. Gray crept in around the edges of her vision. Gretchen tapped her shoulder. "Boss," she said again. "Look at me."

Josie stared into her brown eyes.

"Focus on my voice," Gretchen said.

Josie nodded. That was easy. She listened as Gretchen spoke in a calm and even tone. Normal, matter-of-fact. Not pitying. Not sympathetic to the point of being saccharine. Not patronizing. "You don't have to do anything you don't want to do," said Gretchen. "We'll get around this. We'll find another way to get the name we need. You know where the usual suspects hang out. We'll go and talk to them. There might be someone else besides Needle who knows who Vera's supplier was."

The more Gretchen spoke, the clearer Josie's vision became. Her breathing returned to normal. The heaviness returned to her body. She could feel a flush creeping from her collar to the roots of her hair. She nodded. "Okay, yes," she said. "Yes. Let's do that."

Gretchen waited a few more moments for Josie's full composure to return.

Josie looked straight ahead. Then she whispered, "What just happened to me?"

Gretchen said, "You can only push trauma down for so long before it starts coming out in weird ways and at weird times."

"I thought I had dealt with it," Josie said.

Gretchen smiled. "By doing this job? No, not the same thing as dealing with it, processing it, moving on from it."

Josie knew Gretchen was just as intimately acquainted with trauma as she was. "What do you do?"

"Since everything came out a few years ago," Gretchen said, "I've been in therapy."

Nothing sounded quite so painful to Josie as therapy. Gretchen must have seen it in her face because she said, "I know you don't think it will help. A lot of people don't see the value in it, which is understandable, but it's helped me a lot. Anyway, what do you say we turn around and get back on the road? Check out Vera's apartment, see what we can turn up there?"

"Yes," Josie breathed. "That sounds good."

CHAPTER THIRTY-SEVEN

Colbert was a small town to the west of Denton, its quaint streets laid out in a grid pattern with all the necessary amenities and shopping at its center in old brick buildings that looked like they'd been built in the 1800s. The apartment that Vera Urban had been renting under the name Alice Adams was on the first floor of a duplex about five blocks from Colbert's main street. It was well kept but nondescript, just like the street it sat on. The landlord met them at the front door. After they made introductions, he handed them a copy of the lease. Josie studied it. It had been signed five years earlier. "It was always month-to-month," he told them. "She always paid cash, rarely complained. She was a model tenant, really. I'm sorry to hear what happened to her." He unlocked the front door and ushered them inside. "She said she didn't have any family. I guess that means all her stuff is… well, I'm not sure what I'll do with it so feel free to take anything you'd like. I'll wait outside."

The apartment was small but bright, airy, and clean. The living room held a couch and coffee table across from a small stand with a television and DVD player on it. Along one wall was a row of bookshelves. Half of them held DVDs and the other half held dog-eared, broken-spined paperback books. Beyond that was a kitchen/dining area fit for no more than two people. A hallway off the kitchen led to a bathroom and large bedroom.

Josie and Gretchen searched meticulously, finding few personal items other than some pieces of junk mail which were addressed to "Resident". The bathroom had a few more prescription bottles—painkillers, additional anti-anxiety drugs, and heartburn medication. In the bedroom were more well-used paperback books on the bedside table but again, nothing personal. No photos, no cards, not even home décor items like knick-knacks or wall hangings. It was obvious someone lived here, but the entire apartment seemed very impersonal. Almost like a hotel room.

A noise from the bedroom closet startled them. Gretchen's hand lingered over the Glock at her waist. At Josie's nod, she unsnapped her holster and drew her weapon, keeping the barrel toward the ground. Josie did the same. Gretchen moved to stand behind Josie, and together they approached the closet door. Heart thundering in her chest, Josie swung open the door and lifted her gun, trying to focus in on any potential threat. Before she could even process what she was seeing, Gretchen erupted into laughter behind her. Both women holstered their weapons and stared at the large striped orange cat doing its business in a litter box on the floor of the closet. A moment later, it sauntered out of the closet and meowed loudly. It went straight to Gretchen, rubbing its body against her legs. She reached down to pet it, and the cat arched its back at her touch.

Josie took in a couple of breaths, waiting for her heart rate to return to normal. "Looks like Vera—or Alice—wasn't living alone, after all."

Gretchen picked the cat up and talked softly to it. It purred in her arms. She held it away from her body before hugging it again. "It's a she," she told Josie. "No collar though. Let's hope Alice took her to a vet regularly. Maybe they'll know her name."

She placed the cat back onto the floor so she could help Josie explore the contents of the closet, but the cat stayed close, weaving in and out of Gretchen's legs. "She likes you," Josie noted. The closet took up almost an entire bedroom wall. There was a rack filled with clothing and then several shelves from floor to ceiling holding shoes, folded sweaters, and jeans as well as some plastic bins. Josie pulled one of them down and handed it to Gretchen before retrieving another. They set them on the bed and began going through them.

Gretchen said, "This looks like old medical bills for Alice Adams. Paid, paid—these are all paid. Looks like with cash. Oh, here's a bill for a vet. It says the cat's name is Poppy." She took a photo of it and kept going, mumbling, "A copy of her lease. Receipts from when she paid rent…"

Josie pawed through the other bin. "I've got photos."

Hundreds of photos had been piled into the bin. They seemed to span from Vera's own childhood through Beverly's birth and beyond. There were several pictures from Vera's baby shower similar to the ones that Sara Venuto had provided them with. Then there were photos of Beverly as an infant, sleeping in a swing, in her crib, and one or two of her cradled in Vera's arms.

"Wonder who took those?" Gretchen said, looking over Josie's shoulder.

"Here," Josie said. "Connie Prather."

She fingered another set of photos showing Connie holding baby Beverly. There was the occasional photo of some of Vera's co-workers with Beverly as well, taken both at the salon and at what looked like Vera's home. However, by the time Beverly was five or six—from what Josie could estimate—it was only Beverly in the photos. Dressed up for Halloween; blowing out candles on a birthday cake at a park surrounded by other small children; wearing a backpack on what Josie assumed was a first day of school: the photos captured all the small milestones and other hallmarks of a normal, American childhood. Milestones and hallmarks that Josie herself had never gotten to experience. Again, she wondered what had gone wrong between Beverly and Vera. Or maybe nothing had gone wrong. Maybe something had happened to Beverly sometime during her otherwise idyllic childhood to lead to her behavioral issues. Or was it chemical? Had she had some psychological condition or mental health issue that made her so volatile? Josie wondered if they'd ever know.

Poppy jumped up onto the bed, walking right across the photos that Josie had spread out, again headed directly for Gretchen. Josie laughed. "Tell your friend there she needs to wear gloves if she wants to handle evidence."

The photos went up through high school, although sometime around Beverly's adolescence they suddenly seemed to reduce in volume. Either Vera had taken fewer photos during that time or Beverly had refused to be photographed. Perhaps a combination. Or, Josie thought, after Vera's back injury, she simply wasn't up to taking photographs.

Josie went to the closet to retrieve another bin. Gretchen said, "It's strange that she kept these, don't you think? She went into hiding, changed her name, but kept all this evidence of her former life."

Josie set the next bin onto the bed. "True, but by all accounts, she genuinely loved her daughter. We still don't know what happened at the end of Beverly's life and how much involvement Vera had with it. We know that Vera knew she was pregnant, but we have no idea how Vera felt about Beverly by that time. Vera returned to Denton after Beverly's body was found. Why would she do that?"

Gretchen didn't answer. Josie lifted the lid of the bin and started pulling out items. There were yearbooks from Denton East High School. "I think these were Beverly's things," Josie said. There were some CDs from bands Josie had liked in high school, a few items of costume jewelry, and a handful of photos of Beverly with her best friends: Lana Rosetti and Kelly Ogden. There was a journal which gave Josie a jolt of hope until she opened it to find one unenthusiastic entry about how her "dumb mom" thought she should "write down her feelings" and then empty pages after that.

"Guess Beverly wasn't much for a diary," Gretchen sighed.

There were three paperback books, all of them well-used and dog-eared. One of them was *False Memory* by Dean Koontz. The other two were by V.C. Andrews, one titled *Ruby* and the other *Pearl in the Mist*. Josie remembered how the girls in her school loved to pass around the V.C. Andrews books, whispering about the scandalous stories within them. She opened *Ruby* and flipped through its pages. A photo fell out and fluttered to the bed. Gretchen picked it up as Josie fanned through the rest of the book to see if there was anything else pressed into it. There was nothing. She tossed the book back onto the bed and studied the photo. It was of a young man with blond hair. He wore a white T-shirt and jeans with a workbelt hung low around his waist. Something about the tension in his smile suggested he was uncomfortable being the object of the photo. Behind him was a wall with a blue tarp hung on it and next to that, a doorway that looked as though it led to a set of steps going downward. Josie said, "This is Ambrose, the guy from the basement waterproofing company that Beverly was flirting with."

Gretchen peered at it. "Yeah, that matches up with the driver's license photo we have of him."

"This must be the house on Hempstead." Josie pointed to the doorway. "He's on his way down to the basement to work."

"Yeah," Gretchen agreed. "And I'll bet that tarp is one of the tarps the killer used to wrap up Beverly." She took the photo from Josie and turned it over, but the back of it was blank.

Josie picked up *Pearl in the Mist* and shook its pages. Only an old bookmark fell out. She set it down and grabbed *False Memory*, flipping the pages. Three photographs fell out. One by one, Josie lined them up so they could study them. One photo was of Vera and a man standing in a kitchen, a sink and stove behind them. The photo had caught them in profile, facing one another. The man was thin and a head taller than Vera. He looked as though he was in his mid-thirties from what Josie could tell. He had short brown hair and light stubble covering what they could see of his face. It looked as though the picture had been taken from behind a doorway, as half the photo showed a close-up of wooden molding. Josie pointed to it. "She took this without them knowing."

Gretchen nodded. "You think this was Vera's drug dealer? Or her friend?"

"I don't know. Maybe. We really have no way of knowing when this was taken, but it's the only contact we can definitely establish between Vera and someone besides her co-workers and old clients."

They turned their attention to the next photo. Josie's breath caught in her throat as her late husband's face smiled up at her. It was Ray at sixteen years old in his baseball uniform. His cap was pushed up just a little, the way it used to get when he'd wipe the sweat from his forehead. He was leaning on a fence, his elbows hanging over it. Behind him, Denton East's baseball field was filled with other players, out-of-focus blobs against the green grass.

"It's creased," Gretchen said, pulling Josie from her memories of that time. She picked up the photo, and Josie saw where it had been folded. Gretchen turned the flap up and there was teenage Josie, only part of her face visible. She'd been standing on the opposite side of the fence to Ray, leaning in to give him a good luck kiss. There had been many games and many moments like this, Josie remembered. It had been an exciting season for the Denton East Blue Jays. Josie hadn't missed a single game. The players had always come to that section of the fence before each game to receive a last round of well-wishes from family and other students. There was always a crowd there. What Josie had never realized was that Beverly had been somewhere behind her in that crowd, taking a photo of Ray without either of them knowing. Or had Ray known? Had he seen Beverly take the photo? Had he let her? Had something been going on between them after all?

"Look at this one," Gretchen said, setting the photo of Josie and Ray back onto the bed and picking up the last one.

Josie shook her head slightly, trying to rid her mind of thoughts of Ray and Beverly so she could focus on the present. The photo was of a man lying in a bed. He was naked, on his side, facing away from the camera, and only his back from the shoulders down and a sliver of his hip had been captured. "Look," Josie said, pointing to his left shoulder blade. "That's a tattoo of a skull."

Gretchen leaned in, slipping on her reading glasses, and peered at the photo. "It sure is," she said softly. She pointed to another part of the photo where one of the man's hands reached back toward the camera, as though he was trying to shoo away the photographer. His hand was slightly out of focus, but Josie saw what Gretchen had picked up on.

"That's a wedding ring," she said to Gretchen.

"Yes."

"This is the guy she was seeing," Josie said. "The one she was actually intimate with. No wonder she didn't tell anyone about him. He was married."

They spent a few moments examining the picture again to see if there were any clues as to where it had been taken, but all they could glean from the background was that the man was in a bed with white sheets and it appeared to be daylight.

Gretchen snapped a photo of the picture with her phone. "Not just that but she was a minor."

"He would have faced criminal charges if they were caught."

"His reputation and marriage would be destroyed as well, assuming he had a reputation he wanted to keep."

"Right," Josie agreed. She sighed and looked back at the closet where only one small plastic bin remained. "We still have no idea who this guy was or how she met him."

Gretchen picked up the photo of Vera with the man in the kitchen. "Could it be this guy?"

Josie compared the two pictures but there was no way to tell. "I don't know. I can't even tell if he's wearing a wedding ring in this photo."

Gretchen walked over to the closet and took out the last bin, returning to the bed with it. Poppy immediately sauntered over and rubbed herself against Gretchen's arms, her tail flicking across the lid of the bin. Gingerly, Gretchen picked her up and set her on the floor. Seconds later, she hopped back up onto the bed, only this time she kept her distance, watching the two women with suspicion.

"Would you look at this?" Gretchen breathed as she pulled several items from the bin.

They were driver's licenses, Josie realized. Three of them, all with different names, all expired. Josie picked one up and ran a finger across the photo of Vera. She felt the slightest imperfection at the edge. "These are doctored," she said. "And not very well."

Gretchen picked up another and with some effort, managed to peel away the photo of Vera to reveal a completely different woman. "You're right," she said. "Not very good quality at all."

Josie took out her phone and snapped pictures of each one. "We'll look up these names when we get back to the stationhouse."

They started bagging the evidence they intended to remove. As they worked, Poppy meowed loudly from the head of the bed. Josie said, "I wonder when she ate last."

Gretchen said, "Let's take care of the cat and then we'll head back and see what we can come up with in terms of these doctored driver's licenses. Then we can try to track down the guy in the picture with Vera."

CHAPTER THIRTY-EIGHT

A half hour later, they were back in the car with Poppy in a carrier in Josie's back seat. The vet had supplied all the records without any questions but then suggested they take the cat to a nearby shelter. When they arrived, Josie parked and Gretchen went inside with Poppy. Fifteen minutes later, she came back out. With Poppy. "I can't leave her there," Gretchen told Josie.

It seemed Josie wasn't the only one experiencing an overload of emotions lately.

With Poppy settled in the backseat, they started back to Denton. Gretchen used the Mobile Data Terminal to look up Alice Adams as well as the other names they'd found on driver's licenses in Vera Urban's closet. "It looks as though Vera's modus operandi was to physically steal these other women's licenses and change the photo. All of these women reported their licenses stolen and had them replaced. All four of them lived more than an hour away from where Vera lived in Colbert, although we have no idea where she was living before she moved there."

Josie said, "Did Vera steal their identities as well? She didn't open credit cards in their names or anything like that? Bank accounts? Utilities?"

Gretchen jotted something down in her notebook. "No," she said. "There's no record of anything."

"But if she wanted to rent a room in certain establishments— even with cash—or even an apartment, she'd need identification," Josie pointed out.

"Don't most landlords require a credit check these days?" Gretchen asked.

"I believe they do but if I were Vera, and I were using stolen identities, I'd try to find someone who wasn't going to check my credit. Although, if the landlord did, and Alice Adams, for example, had good credit, that would only work in Vera's favor."

"True," Gretchen said. "And if the real Alice Adams wasn't monitoring her credit closely, she might not notice an inquiry. So you think she stole these driver's licenses and put her own photo on them just to get an apartment?"

"And also to go to the doctor. As long as she never went to collections for an overdue bill, the real Alice Adams would have no idea that she was seeing doctors or getting prescriptions in her name."

"That's insurance fraud," Gretchen said.

"Assuming she had insurance. You said the medical bills you found in her closet showed she'd paid them in cash."

"That's taking a big chance," Gretchen noted. "Not having insurance. If something catastrophic happened, she'd be in real trouble."

"True," Josie agreed. "But look at the way she was living. Speaking of cash, we don't even know how Alice survived. Where did she get her income? How was she paying for that apartment?"

Gretchen said, "She would also need identification to cash a check or a money order."

"Right," Josie said. "The landlord said she always paid cash, but she had to get it from somewhere."

Gretchen took out her phone. "I'm going to call the local PD and see if they'll interview some neighbors, ask around town, see if anyone spoke with her regularly or if she had some kind of under-the-table job."

A few minutes later, she hung up. "They'll get back to us," she told Josie. Turning in her seat, she reached into the footwell and riffled through some of the documents they'd brought with them until she came up with the lease. She flipped the pages and skimmed over it. "All the utilities were paid for by the landlord and included in the rent," she said. "Which means Alice Adams never needed to have any utilities in her name. Unless she needed cable, I guess."

Josie thought about the small apartment and what it hadn't contained. "There were hardly any electronics," she said. "No laptop. No tablets."

"There was a television though and a DVD player as well as all those DVDs."

"She didn't want her name on anything, and she couldn't afford to have the real Alice Adams figure out that she'd stolen her identity. She didn't want anyone tracking her down, but she's been surviving all these years somehow. She had to have had help from someone."

"We're missing something," Gretchen said. "Something big."

As they came into town, Rockview Ridge rose high above them on the right-hand side. Josie put her signal on and turned toward it. "You know what? Let's see if my grandmother recognizes the man in the photo with Vera. She saw Vera's 'friend' a few times."

A few minutes later, they pulled in. Poppy snoozed in her cage in the back. They left her there, certain that the cat would be safe in the car for a few minutes, and went inside. Josie's leg ached after having been in one position in the car for so long but she managed to keep up with Gretchen. The door to Lisette's room was open. She sat in her recliner staring out of the window, the sunlight making her silver curls gleam. She had a white shawl pulled around her shoulders—always cold even in her room, where Josie knew the thermostat was set to seventy-five. Her walker sat in front of her, between her bed and dresser. The rooms at Rockview were nice but very small. Josie knocked lightly on the doorframe to get Lisette's attention.

Lisette smiled. "Hello, dear. Gretchen. Come in. Or would you be more comfortable if we went to the cafeteria?"

Josie gave her grandmother a quick kiss and sat on the foot of the bed. Gretchen sat beside her. "Here is fine. We had a photo we wanted you to look at, if you wouldn't mind."

Gretchen took out her phone and found the photo. She handed the phone to Lisette.

Josie asked, "Is that the friend you saw picking up and dropping off Vera by any chance?"

Lisette studied the picture. "I do believe that's him, yes. It was a long time ago, but this looks like him." She gave the phone back to Gretchen. "I wish I knew his name. I'm sorry I can't be of more help."

"You are being of help, Gram," Josie told her.

Gretchen said, "Could you think back and see if you remember any other details about him? Any little thing could be of use. Maybe something else that Vera said about him? Did Beverly mention him at all the day Vera was passed out and she came to school instead?"

Lisette shook her head slowly. "No, no. Beverly never mentioned him. Not in front of me. I don't remember Vera ever saying anything about him except that he was the friend who gave her a ride. But, oh, wait!" She lifted a gnarled finger in the air. "He always wore this… uniform of sorts. I only ever saw him in the car, but he always wore the same shirt. A blue thing, very thick, sometimes dirty. It had a name tag sewn onto it, but I was never close enough to see it."

Josie sat up straighter. "What kind of uniform?"

Lisette lowered her hand and frowned. "I'm not sure, dear. What kinds of jobs require uniforms? What kind of establishment would have the name sewn onto the uniform?"

Gretchen started listing some. "Delivery drivers sometimes, bus drivers?"

Josie said, "Mechanics."

"Come to think of it," Lisette said. "That makes sense. Sometimes it was quite dirty. I'll bet he was a mechanic. I could be wrong, though. You have to remember this was such a long time ago. I really only remember these things because your ongoing feud with Beverly took up such a significant amount of time back then."

She winked at Josie and held out a hand, which Josie took and squeezed. "Gram," she said. "You've got one of the best memories of anyone I know! We'll look into it."

Before Lisette could reply, a nurse's aide came sailing into the room with a large vase of flowers. "Hello," she called from behind the lush, colorful arrangement. "Mrs. Matson! Delivery for you!"

She set the bouquet down on Lisette's dresser and beamed at them.

"My goodness!" Lisette exclaimed.

The aide tore off the card that was stapled to the plastic and handed it to Lisette before leaving them alone.

Gretchen stood and took a whiff of the flowers. "These are lovely, Lisette."

Smiling, Lisette struggled to get the card out of its tiny envelope. "They are, aren't they?"

"Need help?" Josie asked, wondering who would be sending her grandmother flowers. Did she have a suitor that Josie didn't know about? It wouldn't have been the first romance at Rockview Ridge.

Lisette handed her the envelope, and Josie easily removed the card. She read it once, her heart giving a double tap. Then she read it again, not understanding.

Lisette said, "Who are they from?"

Feeling something uncomfortable stir inside her, Josie handed the card back to Lisette who squinted at the words. They scrolled across the screen of Josie's mind on a loop, making her feel cold.

Lisette, thank you for being so kind and receptive to me. It is a great honor and a thrill to finally be in touch with you. Hope we get to spend much more time together. Love, Sawyer

What the hell was going on?

Lisette's smile faltered as she read. Reading the room, Gretchen said, "Boss, I'm going to check on Poppy. I'll meet you at the car?"

Josie nodded.

Gretchen pulled the door closed behind her as she left. Turning to Lisette, Josie said, "Gram, why is Sawyer Hayes sending you flowers?"

Lisette leaned forward and tucked the card into one of the pockets of the basket affixed to her walker. "Josie, I want you to stay calm."

Josie stood up, the agitation welling up inside too great for her to stay seated. Disturbing thoughts pinged around her mind like balls in a pinball machine. What was Sawyer Hayes after? It was one thing to run into her grandmother when he was at Rockview in his capacity as an emergency worker and strike up a conversation, but this was something else entirely. Was he trying to con her somehow? Was this Josie's fault? Did he think because of Josie's fame, Lisette might have something that he could trick her into giving over? Money? Some kind of inheritance? If that was the case, he was in for a rude awakening. Or worse—was he pursuing Lisette? He couldn't be. The age difference was—

Lisette's words cut into her morass of horrifying thoughts. "Josie! Look at me."

Josie realized she had started pacing. She stopped and met Lisette's eyes. "Gram, this seems a little inappropriate to me. You barely know this guy. This isn't right. It's a sweet thing for him to do, but what is he even talking about? Receptive? What does that mean?"

Lisette stood up, grabbing her walker and shuffling over to the foot of her bed to the spot Josie had just vacated. She sat down and patted the bed. "Please, Josie. Come sit."

Reluctantly, Josie lowered herself onto the bed. Their shoulders brushed against one another. Lisette found Josie's hand and took it, squeezing tightly. "There's something I need to tell you, dear."

Josie's heart began to thunder, the roar in her ears growing more deafening by the second. Why did she feel afraid? What could Lisette possibly have to tell her that had to do with Sawyer Hayes? If he was conning her or pursuing her, Josie could still stop it. She was a police officer. She'd come after him with the full weight of her department.

Lisette's bony fingers tightened around Josie's hand until it hurt. Lisette gave news the same way that Josie did—swiftly and without qualifiers. Josie had always thought of it as ripping off the Band-Aid. The sooner you got it over with, the sooner the person could process what they were about to learn.

Lisette said, "Sawyer is my grandson."

A perfect silence fell over the room. Everything became so still that even the dust motes floating in the shaft of light coming through the window seemed to freeze. The bustling noises of the rest of the facility outside of Lisette's door receded into nothingness. Surely, Josie had heard her wrong.

"What did you say, Gram?"

Lisette took a deep breath. On the exhale, she repeated, "Sawyer is my grandson."

Josie started counting off seconds in her head, trying to maintain her composure. He was running a con. That son of a bitch. *One, two, three.* She sprung up from her seat, tearing her hand out of Lisette's grasp, pacing frenetically in the tiny room. "Gram, I don't know what he told you, but he obviously thinks he can get something out of you. Some grand inheritance or something. This is a con. He's a con artist. I knew there was something I didn't like about this guy. Listen to me, I want you to stop all contact with him until I sort this out. I'll talk to the front desk and tell them he's not to come in here any longer."

"Josie," Lisette said. "Sawyer *is* my grandson."

Josie pointed to her own chest. "I'm your grandchild. Me. Just me. Sawyer Hayes is a complete stranger."

Lisette stood, pushing her walker out of the way. Using the bed to hold onto, she made her way to her nightstand and opened the drawer. She pulled out a sheaf of papers and brought them to Josie. "This is real, Josie."

Trying to calm the tsunami of anxiety about to overtake her, Josie took the pages and studied them. She was looking at a DNA report of some kind. It was from one of those sites where you sent in your DNA sample via saliva, and they analyzed your ancestral origins and also, if you chose to participate, they would put you into a database with other people and match you with family members you might not know you had. According to the report, Sawyer Hayes shared twenty point six percent DNA amounting to thirty-eight segments with Lisette Matson. *Life Lineage predicts that Lisette Matson is your grandmother*, concluded the report.

Josie's hands shook. She placed the report onto the bed. "When did you do this? When did you submit your DNA? Who—who helped you? Was it him?"

Lisette reached for Josie's arm, but Josie tore it away. "It was several weeks ago, dear and yes, Sawyer helped me. He came to me a couple of months ago—"

"So he lied the other day when he said that he ran into you here!" Josie said, realizing quickly that her voice had risen to a shout.

"Josie, please," Lisette said. "Stay calm. I'll explain everything."

"This isn't real," Josie said, pointing to the report. "This is a con. He did this to trick you. I don't know what he wants or what he thinks he's going to get from you but it's a lie. All of it is a lie. Gram, you're vulnerable."

At this, Lisette wobbled and grabbed her walker to steady herself. "Don't talk to me like that, young lady. I'm not some old, doddering fool. I've still got my mind. I think I can figure out what's real and what's not." She pointed to the pages. "This is real. I took the test. I had one of the nurses here help me log into the site myself so I could make sure he wouldn't bring me doctored results. I knew you would react badly to this, which is why I didn't tell you right away."

"How long have you known?"

Lisette sighed. "The results only came back about a week ago."

"When were you going to tell me?"

Lisette threw her hands in the air. "I don't know, okay, Josie? Soon. But not while you're working a big case or while you're consumed with the flooding going on in this town. I was going to tell you. How could I not?"

Josie felt her legs weaken. She sat back on the edge of the bed. Lisette joined her. Neither of them spoke for a long moment. When Josie was sure she could speak without letting a sob escape, she said, "How is this possible?"

Lisette smoothed the fabric of her slacks over her thighs, looking at the floor. "I don't know if you remember me telling you this a few years ago but your dad—my Eli—he dated Lila Jensen for a long time before you came along."

"I remember," Josie whispered. "You didn't like her. You were happy when they broke up."

Lisette nodded.

If only that had been the end of it. If only Lila had stayed away forever. Eli would still be alive. Lisette would be whole. Josie would never have met either Eli or Lisette, but they would have had good lives. Lisette would never have had to bear the horrific burden of losing a child. But instead, Lila had gone to live somewhere a couple of hours away from Denton. She'd gotten a job with a housecleaning service and gone to work at the home of Shannon and Christian Payne. They were both successful in their careers—she as a chemist for Quarmark Pharmaceutical and he as the head of marketing for the same company. They'd just had twin daughters. When Shannon realized that Lila had been stealing her jewelry, she reported it to Lila's boss, leading to Lila's firing. At that point, in her early twenties, Lila was already mentally ill as well as sociopathic, with likely more than one personality disorder. In retaliation, she'd burned the Paynes' house to the ground and as the fire raged, she stole one of the three-week-old twin girls, leaving the other to be rescued.

That baby had been Josie.

The Paynes believed their daughter perished in the fire, but in reality, Lila had taken her and returned to Denton after a year away from Eli Matson. She'd brought infant Josie to Eli and told him that she was his daughter—that Lila had stayed away for the entire pregnancy and beyond, but that she couldn't keep his child a secret from him any longer. Eli hadn't had any reason to doubt her. There were no DNA tests back then, no way to prove paternity, not that it had ever crossed Eli's mind. He'd taken Josie in as his own and loved her more than anything in the entire world until his death.

Josie said, "You also told me that Dad was seeing someone else after Lila left. It was her, wasn't it?"

Lisette nodded. "Sawyer's mother. Her name was Deirdre Hayes. They'd only gone on a few dates, but they really liked one another. When Lila came back to Denton with you and told Eli that you were his daughter, he broke things off with her. He wanted you. He was so happy to be your father. He wanted to try to make it work with Lila. Give you a real family. He didn't know then that that would be impossible."

"Sawyer's mother—why didn't she ever tell anyone? Did she even tell Dad?"

"His mother passed on last year. Cancer. Before she died, she told him the truth about his father. All his life he believed his dad was dead—which was true, I suppose. You two are about the same age, so Eli died when he was about six as well. She wanted him to know the truth before she died. She went to tell Eli that she was pregnant and instead, she met Lila."

"Lila threatened her," Josie said. "Because Lila didn't let anyone get in the way of what she wanted, and back then, she wanted Eli."

"Yes," Lisette breathed. "Evidently it was enough for her to never contact Eli again. Then he was gone."

"And she wasn't about to mess with Lila," Josie said.

"Yes."

Josie put her face in her hands. "My God."

After a few moments, Lisette slid her arm around Josie's shoulder and pulled her close. "Josie, this changes nothing between us, do you understand? You're still my granddaughter. You always will be. It's just that Sawyer—well, his whole life he's never known the truth, and I am the last of the family he has on his father's side."

Josie stood up, still feeling shaky. "Gram," she said. "You know that I would never stand in the way of you and Sawyer. If this is real, and he's really your grandson, then of course, I—it's okay. I—"

She couldn't finish the sentence.

"Josie," Lisette said, reaching for her.

Josie backed away. Tears threatened again, and she wondered once more what was happening to her. Her hands went up in front of her, in a defensive posture. "I just—I just need time," she told Lisette. "Time to—"

To what? she wondered. What did this mean? She was no blood relation to Lisette. They'd been through so much, and it had always been them against the world. For a long time, Ray had been part of their small group. But most of the time it was just Josie and Lisette. Now there was someone else. A stranger with more right to Lisette's affection than Josie.

She couldn't breathe. It took momentous effort to force her body into motion. She went over and kissed Lisette's cheek. "We'll talk soon," she choked out. "I have to work."

Before her grandmother could protest, Josie left the room, the scent of flowers following her.

CHAPTER THIRTY-NINE

In the car, Gretchen waited, scrolling on her phone. Josie made it halfway there before she doubled over, her lungs on fire, a lump in her throat so thick she thought she would choke. A few seconds later, she heard a car door slam and then Gretchen hovered nearby. "Boss?"

Josie put a hand up to signal for Gretchen to give her a moment. But her breath wouldn't come. She felt Gretchen's hand on the nape of her neck. Slowly, she straightened. Gretchen kept her palm between Josie's shoulder blades and steered her toward the car. Gretchen took Josie's keys from her jacket pocket and then deposited her into the passenger's seat. She went around and got into the driver's seat. Firing the car up, she said, "I'm not going to ask. I don't need to know unless you want me to know."

"Thank you," Josie managed.

"I'm going to talk now," Gretchen told her.

Josie nodded.

Gretchen pulled away, navigating the streets of Denton that were free from flooding while she spoke. "The police department from the town in Georgia where Floyd Urban lives called the station while we were out and left a message. I just got off the phone with them. As far as they can tell, Floyd Urban's story checks out. They questioned several people in his life. No one even knew he had a sister. No neighbors remember ever seeing her there and one of his neighbors lived next door to him from the day he bought his house."

"Floyd was telling the truth, then," Josie said. "Vera lied about going to stay with him on bedrest while she was pregnant with Beverly."

"It appears that way. Listen, it's very late. I'm going to drive to the stationhouse so you can drop me and Poppy off at my car. I think you should go home. Eat, sleep. Tomorrow, we'll meet back at work and check and see which auto mechanic shops were open thirty or more years ago. It's a pretty slim lead, but we can try to track down Vera's friend and see if he knows anything that will help us find the killer—or killers."

Josie nodded.

"Will you be okay to drive home or should I call Noah?"

Josie shook her head. "No. Please don't. I'll be fine."

Josie had no memory of driving home but when she stepped through her front door, she was immediately rushed by two jumping dogs and one very excited toddler. "JoJo!" Harris said, throwing his little arms around her legs. She scooped him up and smelled his blond hair while he chatted away about everything he had seen and done that day: the dogs fighting over a tennis ball; the latest episode of *Paw Patrol*; the trip he and Misty had taken to the command post to drop off baked goods; the cookies Misty wouldn't let him have for breakfast. The list went on, seemingly endless, and Josie couldn't help but smile as she always did at his innocence and unbridled excitement about everything. Josie carried him into the kitchen where Misty was preparing dinner. She was using pots and pans that Josie hadn't even known they owned.

From her place at the stove, she smiled at Josie. "Harris," she said. "Give JoJo a few minutes to get settled in."

"Settled in to what?" Harris asked.

Josie laughed. "It's fine," she said, taking a seat at the kitchen table and holding Harris in her lap as he prattled on.

When he tired of telling her every minute detail of his day, he hopped down and chased after Trout and Pepper. Misty said, "Noah called me."

Josie took out her cell phone and logged in to find five missed calls from Noah.

Misty said, "Lisette called him. He's stuck at work, and he couldn't reach you."

Josie massaged her temples. "What is this? Some kind of network you guys have? Has anyone else been notified that my grandmother has a long-lost grandson, and she's worried that I might lose my shit?"

Misty shrugged. "You've lost your shit before. This is a whole lot to take in."

She turned off the burners on the stove and sat down across from Josie, focusing all of her attention on Josie's face. Her blue eyes bore into Josie, making her feel like she was the only person on the planet. Squirming in her chair, she waited for the barrage of pitying questions, but they didn't come. Misty said, "Did you check this guy out?"

Josie resisted the urge to come around the table and hug Misty. "Not yet."

"Don't you think we should get that over with at least?"

Josie laughed. "You know me very well."

"I'll get the laptop."

Josie downed more ibuprofen and spent the next hour searching the internet and every database she had access to for Deirdre and Sawyer Hayes. Everything checked out. There was an obituary for Deirdre from the year before. From what Josie could gather, she'd moved the two of them out of Denton shortly after Sawyer was born. Josie wondered what, exactly, Lila had said to Deirdre that had made her feel she had to not just stay out of Lila's way but leave town altogether? They'd lived for a long time in Williamsport. Sawyer had gone to college at Penn State, then hopped around the state a bit before settling just outside Denton a few years earlier and taking the EMS job in nearby Dalrymple Township.

"There's nothing here," Josie told Misty as she placed a plate heaped high with steak and steamed vegetables in front of her.

"You mean there's nothing suspicious."

"Right."

Josie heard the rapid *clickety-clack* of dog feet on the tile of the foyer. A moment later, Harris hollered excitedly, "Noah!"

A few minutes later, after properly greeting child and dogs, Noah entered the kitchen. He looked around and went straight for the stove to make himself a plate. "Misty," he said. "Josie and I have been talking, and we'd like you to move in full-time."

Misty laughed. "You know, my cooking's not that good. But thank you."

Around a mouthful of food, Josie said, "Trust me, your cooking is the best."

Noah sat down at the table with a plate of food and dug in. "Or maybe it's that Josie's cooking is just that terrible."

Josie said, "I'd get mad but he's actually right about that. Plus, his cooking is only passable."

Noah chuckled. "And I would get mad about that but it's true."

They ate in silence. Misty went in search of Harris so he could join them. Noah put his fork down and regarded Josie. "Are we going to talk about it?"

She said nothing.

"Josie," he said. He left the questions unspoken. He knew that if he asked her if she was okay, she'd say she was fine. She was always fine. But he wasn't going to leave it alone. Not until she said something. He never left her alone with anything. Sometimes it was maddening, but she understood that he was trying to tell her something. He was going to be there for her whether she liked it or not.

She said, "I'm still in a little bit of shock."

"I can imagine," he said. "Lisette wanted me to tell you that this doesn't change anything."

But of course it did, Josie thought. *It changes everything*, she wanted to shout at him, but she didn't. What she wanted more than anything was for this conversation to be over. By now, she knew there was only one way to accomplish that. She mustered a smile for Noah and said, "I just need some time, okay?"

He smiled back and nodded. "You got it."

That night, sleep was even harder to come by than the night before. Her mind was so full, it felt like it might explode. Her thoughts swirled with questions about Lisette and her new grandson, Sawyer, and the Urban case. Beverly, Vera, the WORMM club, the Mayor, Ray. Had Vera really been some kind of upscale drug dealer, peddling painkillers to rich women? What else was the Mayor not telling Josie? What did Ray have to do with any of it and how had Beverly gotten his jacket? Why had Vera hidden all these years if she knew exactly who killed her own child? Who killed her? Was it the same person who killed Beverly? Was all of it drug-related or was there something else in play?

She was up and out of bed before anyone else in the house woke. She left Noah a note and went to work. Surprisingly, Gretchen sat at her desk in the great room, typing away at her keyboard. When Josie plopped into her desk chair, Gretchen pushed a paper coffee cup across to her.

Josie said, "Have I told you how much I treasure our friendship?"

Gretchen chuckled. "One of the guys working the holding cells yesterday left an envelope on your desk."

Josie found it on top of a pile of paperwork. Her name was on the front. She turned it over and slid a finger under the seal to open it. "How was your first night with Poppy?"

Gretchen put a hand through her hair. "She doesn't sleep either, so I think we'll get along just fine."

Inside the envelope was a blank piece of printer paper. It smelled like cigarette smoke. Josie unfolded it and read it. The handwriting was surprisingly neat.

Jojo: the name is Silas. That's all I got. – Z

Josie felt something go out of her. Some kind of tension she'd been holding onto for so long, she couldn't remember when it first started. Maybe when she was a child. She had no idea why Needle had chosen to help her now when there was absolutely nothing in it for him, but the act brought all kinds of feelings to the surface. She pushed them back down and showed Gretchen the note. Within ten minutes, they had a driver's license photo, rap sheet, and background check on one Silas Murphy, age fifty-five. Although he was much older in his driver's license photo, it was definitely the same man they had seen in the photo they'd found in Beverly's possessions, of Vera standing in her kitchen talking with a man.

His employment history showed that he'd worked at several local auto repair shops and from what they could see, he'd gotten married in 2000. They didn't have divorce records, so it wasn't clear how long he'd been married or if he was still married, but he was definitely the friend they'd been searching for.

Josie did more searching. "He has never legally purchased a firearm."

"He wouldn't be able to," Gretchen said. "Not with his rap sheet. The prison inmate records show he's done time for possession on several occasions and—check this out—he has a large tattoo on his back. Under description it says: skull."

Adrenaline surged through Josie's veins. "Let's go find him."

CHAPTER FORTY

Silas Murphy's apartment was in a six-story building in West Denton. The area was flooded, with a couple of inches of water in the streets, but the level wasn't high enough to reach people's homes. Now that the rain had stopped, patrol units had let traffic back into the area. Josie parked out front of Silas's building. It had seen better days. Its brick face crumbled in several areas. Where the brick had worn away near the windows, birds had burrowed inside the walls. A set of double glass doors were centered on the first floor of the building. One of them had been broken and boarded up with plywood and duct tape. Inside was a small room filled with dented metal mailboxes, each one bearing an apartment number. Silas's number was 612, which meant he was on the sixth floor.

Gretchen looked around. "There's no elevator."

Josie shook her head. "Figures."

Josie led the way, trudging up six flights of stairs, trying to ignore the pain in her leg. She was glad for all the early morning jogs she, Noah, and Trout took. Even though she was in good shape, she felt beads of perspiration along her hairline. The stagnant air in the stairwell was hot and cloying. By the time they reached the sixth floor, sweat ran down the sides of Gretchen's face. The hallway was at least twenty degrees cooler. Josie and Gretchen took a moment to suck in the air before they searched out Apartment 612.

Josie pounded on the door. There was no answer. They waited a few minutes, knocked again and waited. They turned when they heard the sound of the stairwell door creaking behind them. Silas

Murphy stood there in a black T-shirt and jeans, a white plastic takeout bag in one hand and a set of keys in the other.

Gretchen said, "Silas Murphy."

He dropped the bag and his keys and took off, banging through the stairwell door. Josie pushed past Gretchen and ran after him. She was faster and in better shape, even though the stitches in her thigh ached with the exertion. As she got to the stairwell, she heard his footsteps pounding down, down, down. Josie tore after him, jumping down as many steps to each landing as she safely could.

As she reached the lobby, she saw the double doors flap closed. She was gaining on him. Bursting outside, she saw him run across the street, his footfalls splashing up water. He slipped into an alley between two buildings—one condemned and the other a mirror image of his apartment house. Josie sprinted after him, running down the alley, catching a flash of his shirt before he turned left, behind the condemned building. Josie emerged into a lot flanked by high concrete walls on two sides. A dumpster lay tipped over in a two-foot puddle of murk where the floodwaters had collected with nowhere to recede to. Silas dashed across the lot toward the dumpster and jumped on top of it. He was going to scale the wall, Josie realized.

"Stop," she yelled. "Police!"

His sneakers slipped on the surface of the dumpster, and he fell on all fours. Scrambling to his feet, he reached up and tried to grab the top of the wall. It was too high.

"Stop," Josie said again. "Stop right there! Police!"

He jumped up, trying to reach the edge again as Josie waded through water so grimy, dirty, and greasy that it was black with a rainbow oil slick running across it. There was no time to be concerned about what was soaking through her pants into her skin and her fresh stitches. Hopping onto the dumpster, she rushed at Silas, slamming into him from behind and knocking the wind out of him. He fell forward and she stayed on him, flipping him onto his stomach and applying zip ties to his wrists.

"Get off me," he wheezed when he caught his breath. "I ain't done nothing!"

Gretchen appeared from the alley, huffing and pale. Josie jumped down from the dumpster and dragged Silas through the water to where Gretchen stood, leaning against the wall of the building. Josie shoved Silas forward and he stopped, turning back toward her, his dark eyes flashing. "Are you crazy? I didn't do nothing. Take this shit off me."

Gretchen said, "If you didn't do anything, why'd you run?"

He stood in the mouth of the alleyway facing them. "I don't trust cops, that's why."

Josie sighed. "I've seen your rap sheet, Mr. Murphy. You ought to know that the quickest way to get in trouble with the cops is to run. I don't really believe you when you tell me you haven't done anything."

Under his breath, he let out a stream of curses. Then he said, "You arresting me then or what?"

Gretchen said, "That depends on whether you answer our questions or not."

He sneered. "That depends on what the questions are."

Josie said, "We need to talk to you about Vera Urban."

"Oh Christ. That? All right, all right. Yeah, I saw that stuff on the news about her kid. But look, I haven't seen Vera in damn near twenty years. She was on me every day for this and that, owed me a lot of money, and then one day she skipped town without a word."

"Did you look for her?" Gretchen asked.

"Of course," he said. "Never found her."

"You said she owed you money," Josie said. "What was that for?"

His face changed as he realized his slip. Josie could tell by the way his eyes went up toward the sky that he was trying to come up with a good lie. Josie said, "You don't have to make anything up. We're not here about your drug dealing."

"I don't deal drugs."

Josie knew he was lying but, for the moment, it didn't matter. They needed information from him about the past. "Silas," she said. "We don't care about that. We need to know about Vera Urban."

Gretchen said, "Where were you two mornings ago?"

His gaze snapped toward her. "What?"

"Two mornings ago," Gretchen repeated. "About seven a.m. Where were you?"

"Why?"

"Why do you think?" Josie asked.

"I don't know what the hell happened or what you're trying to pin on me, but I was at home asleep."

Josie said, "Can anyone corroborate that?"

"Shit," he said. "My dog, okay? He can corroborate it. Why are you asking me this stuff?"

"Tell us again the last time you saw Vera Urban," Gretchen said.

"I don't know. Like, almost twenty years ago. It was—it was the year that the Jays won the state championship."

Josie and Gretchen exchanged a look. Josie said, "You mean the Denton East Blue Jays?"

"Yeah," Silas said. "Everyone in the city was following it. You don't remember?"

Gretchen said, "I'm not from here."

Silas shook his head. "Well, it was a big deal. We don't have professional sports teams. People were into it, you know? Anyway, it was around then; that was the last time I saw her."

"How long had you known Vera?" Josie asked.

"I don't know. My whole life, practically. We went to school together. She was a few years ahead of me, but we just knew each other, from, like, around."

Josie said, "Silas, we looked at your rap sheet before we came here. We know you've been in and out of prison your entire life for drug offenses. So I'm going to ask you again—and we're not interested in arresting you—did you supply Vera Urban with drugs?"

"You can't arrest me," he said. "This is, like, off the record."

"We're not journalists, Silas," Gretchen told him. "But just as Detective Quinn said, we're not interested in any drug-related crimes you might have committed decades ago. We just want information from you."

"Fine," he said. "I might have helped Vera get some drugs back in the day." He turned slightly and shook his bound hands. "Will you take these off now?"

Ignoring his plea, Josie asked, "What kinds of drugs?"

"Pills," he said. "That was all she wanted. It wasn't even for her, just so you know. Vera wasn't like that. I mean, not then."

"Who were the pills for?" Gretchen asked.

"She worked at this hair place, you know? She had all these rich bitch clients. They were taking them like candy. Vera was in tight with them. She liked being a part of their little group, I think. So yeah, I helped her out."

"That was it?" Josie prodded.

She let the uncomfortable silence play out until Silas became agitated, one of his feet tapping against the broken pavement. "All right, fine," he said. "One of them liked pot and there was another one who got hooked on cocaine—and I mean *hooked*. She would do anything."

Josie said, "How do you know that? Wasn't Vera the one supplying them with the drugs?"

His eyes widened as he realized he had said too much yet again. "Shit," he repeated.

Gretchen said, "You met these women? Vera's clients?"

"Listen," he said. "I didn't do anything wrong. These women, you gotta understand, they were bored. Bored rich bitches."

"Vera invited you to their parties?" Josie asked.

"Not at first, but then one night they were partying, and they needed more so Vera called me up. I went over to one of their fancy-ass houses, and they wouldn't let me leave."

"Wouldn't let you leave?" Gretchen echoed.

"They were all over me. Their husbands were rich assholes, out traveling and playing golf or whatever rich assholes do. Everything that happened—they wanted it. They asked for it."

"It was consensual?" Josie said.

"Yeah, consensual."

"What exactly was consensual, Silas?" Gretchen said.

"Oh come on. You gonna make me say it? You know what. The sex, okay?"

"You had an affair with one of them?" Josie asked.

He laughed. "An affair? No. It wasn't like that. They just wanted a boy-toy."

"They?" Josie prompted. "How many women were there, Silas? Did you sleep with them all?"

"Sort of."

Josie said, "You 'sort of' had sexual relationships with all of them?"

"A couple of them flirted with me but then when things started to get… heated, they backed out."

"Do you remember the names of the women you actually had encounters with?" Gretchen asked.

"That was a long time ago, okay?"

"What about Vera?" Josie asked. "Did you ever have sex with her?"

"That was a huge mistake," he said. "I should have known. She was always hung up on me, you know? We were together a couple of times, and then I had to put a stop to it. She was getting clingy and jealous. I had to stay away from that. She wanted a relationship and shit. She wanted to get married. I wasn't into it."

"But you got married eventually, didn't you?" Gretchen asked. "In 2000?"

He rolled his eyes. "That was a mistake, okay? Lasted a coupla years and then I kicked that bitch to the curb."

"You got divorced?"

"Yeah, she took care of it. All I had to do was sign some papers."

Josie said, "We understand there were four women who were regularly at these parties with Vera and her wealthy friends. Do you remember their names?"

"Like I said, I don't remember no names. That was like, thirty years ago."

"But you remember four women?" Gretchen asked.

"Yeah. Four."

"Of those four, you slept with how many? Two?" Josie said.

"I guess, yeah. I mean, not at the same time. They didn't know about each other. I don't think. Unless they talked to each other behind my back."

Was this what Mayor Charleston was hiding? Josie wondered. A thirty-year-old tryst with a local drug dealer while she was married? "You know that one of those women became the Mayor of Denton?" Josie said.

"I thought that was her, yeah," he replied.

"Did you sleep with her?"

Color crept into his cheeks. "I don't want to say," he told them. "I don't actually remember. We got hot and heavy this one night, but I don't remember what happened. I was pretty drunk at most of those things."

Josie said, "Did you ever try to use this information against the Mayor in any way?"

He raised a brow. "Like what way? Like blackmail? It's not like I have proof. I'm not even sure what happened. It would just be my word against hers and she's the Mayor."

But Josie knew that wasn't the way Tara Charleston handled things. Silas Murphy was a loose end, and Tara would have tied him up one way or another.

"She never came to you? Offered to help you in some way in exchange for you pretending that you'd never met her? Never partied with her? That you definitely never hooked up with her?"

He said nothing.

Josie looked at Gretchen. "You have his rap sheet on your phone, by any chance?"

"Sure thing, boss," Gretchen said. She took a moment to pull it up. Silas stared at them in confusion. For a moment, thoughts of Lisette and Sawyer Hayes crowded Josie's mind, but she pushed them away. Finally, Gretchen handed her the phone.

Josie scrolled down the list. "Silas, you've got a lot of charges here that were nolle prossed."

"So I got charges dropped, so what?" he said.

"Not dropped," Josie told him. "Nolle prossed. That means the prosecutor chose not to prosecute you. It doesn't mean they were dropped. You could still be tried for them."

"Wait, what? No, no. They were dropped. That's what she said. They'd be dropped. Gone."

"She?" Josie asked, handing Gretchen's phone back. "So the Mayor has helped you?"

"Oh come on, man," Silas complained, groaning. "Why are you doing this to me? So what? The Mayor put in a good word for me now and then with the prosecutor. I agreed that nothing ever happened between us and that it was unnecessary for me to ever bring it up. I don't even know why you care. You know, it wasn't like we were doing terrible things. Me, Vera, the Mayor, their friends? We were all just having a good time. We were all young—like in our early twenties—and high and drunk. We'd party together. People party when they're young like that. Sometimes I'd end up in a bedroom with one of them. Things happened. It wasn't a big deal."

"For how long?" Gretchen asked. "How long did things happen?"

"I don't know. Till one of them had to go into rehab. I was at a couple more parties after that and that was it. Vera stopped doing it. The cocaine lady, I saw her for a while longer. She stopped going through Vera and came to me directly. That lasted a lotta years but then she died."

"We're aware of that," Josie said. "So you were providing drugs for these 'parties' that your friend Vera was having for a select number of her salon clients. You attended those parties and eventually ended up engaging in a sexual relationship with some of these women. Then one of them went into rehab and the parties stopped happening. But you maintained your relationship with Vera."

"Well, yeah. We were friends. I didn't really see her after the parties stopped. Then she got pregnant. I hardly saw her at all after that."

Josie thought of the photo that Beverly had taken. "Never again?"

"It was a long time, okay? Her kid was like, grown up and shit by the time she started coming around again. She hurt her back and she needed stuff, so I helped her."

"You helped her by getting her painkillers."

"I helped her with her pain," he corrected.

"Were there other things you helped her with?" Gretchen asked.

"Like what?"

"You tell us," Josie said.

"I don't know. I guess. I gave her rides and stuff. Sometimes I picked up some groceries or cigarettes for her. That kind of thing. She was in real bad shape, and her kid was all over the place. Vera had a hard time controlling her. She was something else."

"Beverly," Josie said. "How well did you know her?"

"Not that well." He noticed them staring at him intently and added, "I ain't no pervert, so don't even think that. She was grown up but too young for me. Plus, she was Vera's kid, you know? I don't mess with shit like that."

"You sure about that?" Gretchen asked. "Because we've got evidence that Beverly was fixated on you."

"That wasn't my problem. That kid was wild. She wasn't really interested in me, anyway. She was trying to piss Vera off. I never gave her anything to work with."

"What does that mean?" Josie asked.

He blew out a loud breath. "It means that she flirted with me every chance she got but only when Vera was around to see it. I made sure to shut her down every time. I tried telling Vera that she only did it when Vera was there, that it was fake, to get a rise out of Vera, but she didn't believe me. That kid wouldn't give me the time of day if her mom wasn't there to witness it. She wanted to make Vera jealous. No way was I getting in the middle of that. I didn't need that crap, and like I told you, I'm not a perv. I don't mess with young girls. That ain't right."

"You never had sexual contact with Beverly Urban?"

"Of course not! Even if I wanted to—which I didn't—Vera would have kicked my ass."

"Did Vera ever talk about Beverly's father?" Josie asked.

"Not at first. But then right before she did her disappearing act, she tried to tell me that the kid was mine. Crazy, right?"

Josie said, "Was she your daughter?"

He gave her an incredulous look. "Of course not. Vera and I were together a few times, but I never got her pregnant."

"How do you know?" Gretchen asked.

"'Cause I know, okay? I can count."

"You remember precisely when the last time you were with Vera in a sexual way was?" Josie asked.

"No, no. I just know it couldn't have been me, okay? I don't remember dates and stuff. Just that at the time when she told me, I knew it couldn't be me."

Josie said, "Would you be willing to give a DNA test?"

"Does it hurt?"

"No. It would be a simple cheek swab."

"Sure, whatever. I don't care."

Gretchen took out her notebook and pen. She flipped to a clean page and jotted down some notes. "Great. We'll have a couple of officers from our evidence response team come by your place and do the test. Try not to run from them."

"Does that mean you're going to let me go?"

Ignoring his question, Gretchen asked, "Do you know if Beverly was involved with anyone? A male?"

"Hell if I know. Look, I know you gotta do your job, ask all these questions and stuff, but I don't know what you want from me. Me and Vera were friends. I dealt her some drugs over the years. When she was at the salon and going to these drug parties. Then I didn't see her for a long time. She got in touch after she had back surgery. I kept her out of pain as much as I could. I helped her because we were friends, even though she was behind in paying me. Then one day she was gone. Never saw her again."

"Do you have any idea where she might have gone? Was there anyone who might have helped her move away? Anyone you can think of who might have offered her financial help?" Josie asked.

Again, Silas laughed. "Financial help? Vera owed everyone money. She had a real problem by that time. I always thought that was why she left. I thought she took her kid and found some place to lay low."

"Did she have other friends that you know of?" Gretchen asked. "Besides you?"

He shook his head. "No. She was private. The last time I saw her, her only real friend was Percocet. So are you gonna let me go or what?"

Josie said, "That depends. Would you be willing to let us see the tattoo on your back?"

He let out a sigh of frustration. "You bitches want anything else? A lock of my hair or something? Shit. Fine. You want a look at the goods, go ahead."

Josie turned him around and she and Gretchen lifted his T-shirt, pulling it up to his neck. Gretchen said, "That's not a skull."

Silas said, "Whaddaya mean it's not a skull? It's a coyote skull. Took weeks to get that shit."

Josie could see why. The coyote skull took up his entire upper back. Silas Murphy was definitely not the married man they were looking for.

"Let him go," Josie said, feeling defeated.

CHAPTER FORTY-ONE

"Do you think he's telling the truth?" Gretchen asked as she drove them back to the stationhouse.

Josie checked her jeans for blood. The gash on her leg was aflame. She was convinced the stitches had popped, but no blood soaked through. Regardless, the filthy water could introduce infection into her leg. She needed to get it clean as soon as possible. The pain and worry over the possibility of infection were only momentary distractions from thoughts of her grandmother and Sawyer Hayes. She'd managed to evade them while they were questioning Silas Murphy, but the moment they got into the car, the thoughts came roaring back. "What's that?" Josie asked.

"Silas," Gretchen said. "Do you think he's telling the truth? About not being involved with Beverly and about not having seen Vera in all these years?"

"Actually, I do," Josie said. "He's pretty easy to crack. Aside from the fact that he ran, he gave up his secrets a little too easily."

"Well," Gretchen said. "He's not the brightest bulb on the tree."

Josie laughed. "He's pretty guileless."

"Or pretending to be guileless to fool us into thinking he's not a threat of any kind. He has no alibi for when Vera was killed."

"True," Josie agreed. "But we've got no evidence that would connect him to Vera's murder. I don't see what reason he'd have to kill her."

Gretchen said, "Unless he killed Beverly and Vera saw it and she's been flying under the radar all this time because of that. His rap sheet lists him as six foot one. Definitely tall enough from what Dr. Feist said—although ballistic testing would be needed to confirm something like that."

"I don't see the motive there, though," Josie said. "Silas is the kind of person who is only ever worried about his next payday or his next smoke or his next drink. He's like Needle in that way. They don't think long-term. They try to stay off people's radars as much as possible unless those people want to buy drugs from them. Violence isn't really in their wheelhouse. Not that they could never be violent, but given Silas's history and that interview, I just don't see him killing Beverly or Vera."

Josie panned the municipal parking lot as they pulled in. It was filled with news vans from WYEP. A crowd of reporters much larger than the one that had assembled the day Beverly's body was recovered stood before the back door. Across from the news vans were two patrol cars, lights flashing. Chief Chitwood and Amber stood in front of the first car. The Chief looked smug and triumphant, whereas Amber looked terrified.

"Come on," Josie said as Gretchen squeezed the vehicle into the nearest parking space. "Let's see what's going on."

The reporters didn't even register them as they walked toward the Chief. Uniformed officers emerged from the cars and began unloading their prisoners from the back seats.

"Sweet baby Jesus," Gretchen muttered under her breath as the Mayor and her husband were taken from the back of the first car in handcuffs. Connie Prather followed, also cuffed. From the backseat of the second car, the officers brought out Marisol Dutton and two men, one of whom Josie recognized as Kurt Dutton. She had only seen him in campaign photos around town, but the Dutton Enterprises insignia on his navy polo shirt left no doubt. All of them were lined up in single file. The Chief began marching them inside. As the Mayor passed Amber, she glared. "Did you know about this? Did you know? If I find out you knew about this and didn't tell me, you're fired."

"Shut it, Charleston," the Chief said over his shoulder. "You're not firing her. You wanted a press liaison so now we have a press liaison. Watts! Handle the press!"

He left Amber behind, standing before a gaggle of reporters. Josie and Gretchen slipped past her and into the building where the Chief was directing the women into one holding cell and the men into another. All of them except Connie Prather were shouting, demanding phone calls and attorneys and hollering about how the Chief had no right to arrest them.

Chief Chitwood stood before the two cells, holding his hands up until he had complete silence. "I know what your damn rights are. You'll each get a phone call so you can have your attorneys down here. You just wait until we get you booked in here."

"This is outrageous," Tara Charleston shouted, her voice full of venom. "You're done in this town, Chitwood."

"Save it," the Chief told her. "I'm not interested."

Kurt Dutton stepped forward, wrapping his hands around the bars. When he spoke, his voice was calm and reasonable. "Chief," he said. "I understand you're trying to make a point here, and you've made it. What can we do to resolve this without having to involve our attorneys?"

Tara said, "Kurt, didn't you see the press out there? It's too late to not involve our attorneys! If nothing else, we should sue him for defamation of character."

Tara's husband, who sat on one of the benches in the men's cell dressed in surgical scrubs, said in a weary voice, "Tar, just stop, okay? Let Kurt handle this."

The third man, a stocky guy with thinning blond hair dressed in a suit, stepped up to the bars. He called out, "Conn? You okay?"

Connie Prather spoke for the first time since they'd entered the station. "I'm fine, Joe," she said tightly.

Her husband, Josie realized. Mr. Prather turned his attention to the Chief. "I'm interested in hearing your answer, Chief. What can we do to avoid taking this any further?"

The Chief raised a brow. "I've been fighting with you people for days. Now you're ready to talk? Now I have your attention?"

Kurt Dutton's expression was conciliatory. "Look, Chief, I apologize. Perhaps some of the city's supplies were… misappropriated."

The Chief snorted.

Kurt went on. "We owe you an apology for making your job more difficult."

Josie said, "You could have cost this city lives by taking resources meant for other areas."

The Chief didn't shush her. Instead, he looked at his prisoners, bushy brows raised, as if waiting for one of them to give an explanation. Connie Prather came to the front of the women's cell and said, "What we did was wrong, okay? Is that what you want to hear?"

"No," the Chief said. "What I want to hear is that you'll return every last thing you took from Emergency Services."

Tara's husband said, "What if they return it? Kurt?"

Dutton glanced back at the surgeon, looking uncomfortable at being called out specifically. Turning his attention back to the Chief, he said, "Take us back to Quail Hollow, and your officers can supervise the return of every last resource. It won't happen again, and we can forget this whole thing."

The Chief studied him for a moment. Josie sidled up to him and without moving her lips, spoke low enough so that only he could hear her. "We need to talk to the wives about the Urban matter."

"Fine," the Chief said to Dutton. "But just you three. Patrol will take you back to Quail Hollow. Once everything is returned, you can collect your wives. I'm going to ask Emergency Services to patrol around the back of your development until all this is over to make sure you're not sneaking supplies over there."

Protests erupted from both cells. Chitwood shouted, "I'm not done!" and they fell silent.

"You'll also be cited."

Tara said, "You've got to be joking."

Prather said, "For what?"

The Chief said, "I'll think of something! You're not getting off scot-free, you got that?"

"No deal," Tara said. "Forget it."

Chitwood shrugged. "Okay, we'll do it your way. We'll book you all in, and you can call your attorneys one at a time." He walked away, Josie and Gretchen following. The patrol officers went to the desk. One of them started booting up the computer. Everyone in the cells began shouting at once. The noise rose to a deafening crescendo before Chitwood stopped. He looked over his shoulder. Josie glanced back as well. Tara's face was hot pink with fury. Kurt Dutton said, "We'll pay any fines you deem necessary. Please. We'd much rather do it your way."

Josie could see from the way Tara's lips pressed into a thin line that it was killing her not to be in control of the situation, but she kept silent. After a long, drawn-out moment, Chitwood nodded at the patrol officers. "Get these guys back over to Quail Hollow."

An audible sigh of relief sounded from the back of both cells. Chitwood went back upstairs. Josie and Gretchen lingered, waiting for the men to be escorted back out to the patrol cars. There was the whoosh of the door followed by the shouts of reporters and then silence as the door closed again. Josie checked her wet, dirty pants again but no blood had soaked through. Still, she'd have to clean her wound as soon as possible. Alone with the women, Josie and Gretchen took up position just outside of the cell. Tara remained at the front with her hands white-knuckling the bars. Connie and Marisol sat on the benches behind her, Connie hugging herself and rocking slightly, and Marisol slouched down, looking bored.

Josie said, "We spoke with an old friend of yours today. Silas Murphy."

Connie's head snapped up. Marisol looked over slowly, unsurprised. The pink of Tara's cheeks turned to dark red. Gretchen said, "It's interesting that none of you mentioned him when discussing Vera Urban and her drug habits—well, your drug habits."

"Silas Murphy is irrelevant," Tara snapped.

"Is he?" Josie said. "Or is the real reason none of you mentioned him was because you had sexual encounters with him while you were married?"

Now three sets of eyes widened and stared at them. After a long couple of seconds, Tara said, "Don't be absurd."

Connie turned toward Marisol. "Were you with him, Mar?"

Marisol wrinkled her nose. "Of course not. He was our drug dealer. I was bored with Kurt but not *that* bored."

Connie looked at her feet but not before Josie noticed her lower lip quiver. "What about you, Tara?"

Tara whipped around. "Oh Connie, for Pete's sake. What do you think?"

Connie looked up at her. "I don't know what to think. So tell me. Were you with Silas?"

"It was Whitney," Marisol said. "She had an affair with him. It went on for years. Until she died."

Connie wiped a tear away.

Marisol said, "Wait a minute. Were *you* with him, Con?"

They all stared at Connie Prather. She said, "Please don't tell my husband. It was only a few times. I was young and stupid. It was before my kids and before rehab. I'm a different person now. I have been for a long time. That was just a mistake."

Josie said, "Some people can let go of their mistakes. Others spend their lives trying to keep them secret. Wouldn't you say, Tara?"

Swearing under her breath, Tara turned back to Josie. "I wasn't with Silas Murphy, so just stop trying to pin that on me."

Gretchen said, "Are you sure you didn't have a sexual encounter with him?"

Giving an exasperated sigh, Tara threw her hands in the air. "No, I didn't. Was I attracted to him? Yes. We all were. Back then he was young and handsome and completely unlike our boring old husbands. He came to the parties and we treated him like he was some kind of god. It's no wonder he tried to sleep with all of us. He came on to me, yes, but I shut down his advances. But someone like him could easily lie about it. I was there at those parties, taking pills and drinking. I was afraid he would go around telling people he had slept with me. I knew he'd been making his way through the circle."

"Hey," Connie said. "That's not fair."

Marisol laughed. "It's not? Please. Stop acting like you're somehow better than the rest of us, Connie. We were all there. We all loved it. We loved the way we felt at those parties. We loved doing something *bad*." She said the word "bad" in a breathy tone of feigned excitement. "Some of us just took it too far."

"You mean me," Connie said. "I took it too far."

Marisol shrugged. "You, Whitney, Vera."

Again, Connie looked stricken. "Vera?"

Marisol rolled her eyes. "Oh come on, Connie. Really? You didn't know? Yes, Vera. She was in love with the guy."

Tara wrinkled her nose. "Vera never made good decisions."

"Oh and the rest of us did," Marisol said, laughing.

Tara said, "Well obviously. We're here and she's not."

"We haven't made great decisions either," Marisol said. "I don't know if you realized it or not but we're in jail."

Connie said, "We're in jail because of your husband!"

Marisol pointed at Tara. "It was her damn idea. She's the Mayor!"

Before a full-blown argument could take place, Josie raised her voice so she could be heard. "Vera Urban was murdered two days ago. The Mayor knows but it hasn't been made public yet."

Their silence was so complete, Josie could hear the wall clock over the officers' desk ticking. Then they started calling out questions. Before Josie could calm them again, her cell phone rang. It was Paige Rosetti. They were supposed to meet her in a half hour to take a video call from Lana again to see if she had anything useful to tell them that she might have thought of since their last chat.

"Excuse me," Josie said and walked away.

CHAPTER FORTY-TWO

Gretchen stayed behind to answer the wives' questions while Josie used the station bathroom and first aid kit to clean and dress her leg wound before driving to Paige Rosetti's house. Several areas of the city were still closed down, as the flood water was slow to recede, and she had to take several detours to get there. Alone in her car, she turned her radio up, trying to drown out the thoughts of Lisette and Sawyer crowding her mind again.

She was relieved to arrive at Paige's house. She tried to clear her mind as Paige led her into the kitchen again where two cups of coffee waited. She handed one to Josie and kept the other, taking a seat in front of the open laptop. Josie sat next to her and thanked her as she sipped the coffee. It was smooth and made to perfection. The knots in her shoulders loosened as they waited for Lana to come online. She felt a degree of comfort here, she realized, in this bright and airy space with Paige Rosetti.

A few minutes later they were staring at Lana onscreen. After she and Paige exchanged pleasantries, both women went silent, and Josie realized it was her turn to ask questions. Except she couldn't think of any. What was happening to her brain lately? "I'm sorry," she said. "Lana, was there anything else you remembered about Beverly that might be helpful?"

Lana shook her head. "I don't think so. I was thinking about it, and I don't know that I have any information. I just think, you know, Beverly wanted attention."

"That makes sense," Josie said. "It would explain a lot of her behavior."

Lana nodded. "Beverly felt like her mom didn't really want her. It started when we were in middle school after she heard her mom on the phone, talking about her. Beverly never knew who Vera was speaking with, but she said things like, 'this is not what I signed up for' and 'come get her because I can't handle her anymore.'"

Josie held her mug in both hands. "Did Beverly speculate as to who Vera might have been talking with?"

"Yes," said Lana. The screen blipped momentarily and then she came back into focus. "Beverly believed Vera was talking to her dad, but Vera would never talk about the call or tell Beverly anything about her dad. After that, Beverly was sad and angry."

"And her behavior got even worse," Josie said. She felt an acute ache in her chest. Poor Beverly had been a child entering one of the most difficult phases of growing up—being a pre-teen—when she'd overheard her mother telling someone she didn't want her anymore. Asking that someone to come get her. But no one had come for her. Certainly, no father figure. Instead, she had died a horrible death, buried alone beneath a house and forgotten. Her own mother knew about her horrible ending and hadn't even reported it. The ache in Josie's chest hardened into something else. Resolve. She didn't care what she had to do. She'd figure out who killed Beverly and make sure he or she was brought to justice.

Quietly, Paige said, "I think few things are worse than feeling unwanted, especially when you're a child."

"You're right," Josie said.

Lana spoke again. "Beverly hated Vera after that. Vera would never tell her the truth. Beverly did everything she could to make Vera tell her who her dad was but Vera refused."

"Did Beverly ever mention a man named Silas?" Josie asked.

"Not that I recall," Lana said. "Oh, I meant to tell you, I remembered that one of the last times I talked to Beverly she was worried and upset about something. I asked her what was going on. She said Vera had found out about everything; that she knew everything—like, about the baby and the father's identity. She said Vera was going to kill her. She couldn't figure out how Vera found out the father's identity. She said Vera didn't even know the guy. That's all I remember. Sorry."

Josie smiled. "No need to be sorry. You've been really helpful."

Paige and Lana chatted for a few more minutes while Josie finished her coffee. Paige walked her to the door. Before Josie could open it, Paige said, "I'm sorry we weren't more help."

"It's no problem," Josie said. "I actually enjoyed being here. It's been a tough few days. You and Lana are good company."

Paige said, "You don't have to leave, you know. You're welcome to stay. Talk, if you'd like. I'm a pretty good listener." With a laugh, she gestured toward the other side of her house where Josie knew her office was located.

"Oh," Josie said. "I don't—I'm not—therapy isn't really for me."

"It's usually the people who say that who could benefit from it the most, you know," Paige said, a warm smile on her face.

"I don't think it's appropriate," Josie said. "I went to high school with your daughter. I'm here about a case…"

Paige nodded. "Fair enough. But we could just talk. I'll go first. Sometimes I worry that Lana doesn't believe me when I tell her how proud I am of her because I am always so concerned about her safety and her health. I feel like a terrible mother. I am proud of her, but I wish she was here, closer to me, not half a world away in an underdeveloped country. It's selfish and yet, sometimes I can't help it. But I really am proud of what she's doing. I think she's amazing."

"Have you told her that?"

Paige laughed. "Of course. We've fought about it many times. I don't think she believes anything I say at this point. I've lost all credibility. Remember when you were a teenager and you would go through stages where nothing felt right? You felt awkward and maybe a little ugly, and your mom—"

"My grandmother," Josie corrected, her voice catching on the word.

Paige nodded. "Your grandmother. Maybe she told you that you were beautiful and perfect? Did you believe her?"

In fact, Lisette had used those very words on several occasions, as well as many others. Her favorite thing to tell Josie in those low teenage moments of self-esteem crisis was that Josie was "extraordinary."

"No," Josie said. "I didn't believe her for one second. But I'm glad she said it."

Paige nodded. She looked at the floor, smiling. Suddenly wanting to fill the silence, Josie said, "My grandmother gave me some news yesterday, and I'm not really handling it all that well. I don't want to talk about it because—" She broke off.

Paige said, "Because then you'll have to deal with it."

Josie nodded.

"Is she okay? Your grandmother?"

"Oh, yes," Josie answered. "It's not anything medical. Actually, for her, it's great news."

"But not for you?"

"I don't know. I guess it's not bad for me. It just changes things."

"In a bad way?" Paige asked.

Josie shrugged. "I don't know. I really don't know."

"Change is scary but it isn't always bad, you know," Paige told her.

It is if you get left out in the cold, said a voice in the back of Josie's mind. She didn't say it out loud. She didn't want to, but she felt she should tell Paige something true, something borne of her own vulnerability, since Paige had done so. Also, she felt comfortable with Paige. Perhaps it was because she didn't know every horrifying detail of Josie's past already. Right here, right now, in this moment, Josie was just a woman with an issue, not a damaged person whose childhood had been filled with unspeakable torture.

"I'm afraid I'll be… left behind," Josie said carefully. "It was always just me and my grandmother. Us against the world, sort of. There used to be Ray too."

"Your boyfriend from high school?" Paige asked. "I remember you discussing him with Lana the other day."

"Yes. After college we got married. Then he died. My grandmother and I have been through so much together, including his death. Now there's—" She stopped. She didn't even want to say it. It couldn't be real, could it? Had she imagined the entire conversation? Gretchen hadn't been there to overhear it. Was she in some kind of fever dream? No; Lisette had called Noah, warned him about the bombshell. Now he and Misty were waiting for some dramatic emotional reaction from her, and yet, she still couldn't believe it was really true. "Now someone has come forward and says that he's her grandson. No one knew about him. He didn't know about her either until recently."

Paige said, "That's wonderful that they could get to know one another."

"It is," Josie agreed. No matter what her own feelings were about the situation, she would never deny her grandmother happiness, especially not the happiness that came from finding a family member after having lost so many. Josie remembered her own joy at being reunited with her biological family. No matter how uncomfortable the situation made her or how territorial she felt over Lisette, this was and should be an exceptionally happy time for both Lisette and Sawyer. Josie knew this in her heart, and she knew that she needed to get past her own feelings. They didn't really matter. What mattered was Lisette and her happiness.

Paige said, "But you're worried that you'll no longer matter now that there's another grandchild in the picture?"

Josie laughed. "That sounds ridiculous. I'm sorry. This was a bad idea."

Paige touched her arm. "No, it's not ridiculous."

Josie pulled away. "It is. I'm a grown woman. This is just silly. I can't be worried that someone else is going to take my place with my grandmother. I'm not a five-year-old." She went to the door and twisted the knob, pulling the door open.

"Josie," Paige said, her voice firmer. "No one is suggesting you're a five-year-old. I think it's a valid concern that your dynamic with your grandmother might change now. In fact, it *will* change, but that doesn't have to be a bad thing."

Josie stepped through the door. "I'm sorry. I shouldn't have—thanks for the coffee. I'm sorry. I've got to go."

CHAPTER FORTY-THREE

Back at the stationhouse, the holding cells were empty, and the team was gathered in the great room. Josie walked over to her desk. "I guess Chitwood let the wives out of holding?"

"Yeah," Noah said. "Things seem to have been smoothed over with the Quail Hollow people, although the Mayor is pretty pissed about everything being covered by the press. I'm sure she'll be up all night with her people trying to figure out a way to spin it. What did Lana Rosetti say?"

"Nothing that we can use," Josie said with a sigh.

Noah said, "Hummel couldn't pull prints from the casings found at the abandoned bowling alley, but he's sending them on to the state police lab for ballistics testing."

"Which could take weeks," Josie complained. "If not months, and even then, it will only tell us if the same gun killed both Beverly and Vera. It doesn't get us any closer to finding out the identity of the killer. I'm not sure where to go from here."

"You ran DNA on Beverly and the baby, right?" Noah asked. "Something might come of that."

"Only if the father's DNA is in the system. If it doesn't, we're right back to where we are now. All we know is that the father of Beverly's baby was a married man with a skull tattoo on his back."

Noah said, "If he was married, then we need to be looking at adult men Beverly was exposed to—I'd start with teachers. Do you remember if she had a job in high school?"

"Great point," Josie said. "She worked at this ice cream place on Aymar Avenue, but it closed ages ago. There's something else there now."

Josie fished her yearbook out from under a stack of paperwork on her desk. "I'll make a list of teachers who were on the faculty at Denton East when Beverly and I went there."

As she paged through the yearbook, she winnowed out the male teachers who were single at the time. That left five teachers. All of them still lived in the area and two of them still worked at the high school. Josie started making calls and interviewing them. Most of them didn't remember Beverly and had only been reminded of her when her murder was featured on the news. All of them had alibis for Vera's murder.

More dead ends. Josie started going through all the reports, paperwork and photos that had amassed in the Beverly and Vera Urban files, hoping she might find some clue they'd overlooked.

Gretchen took a call from the Colbert Police Department. They had interviewed the neighbors of Alice Adams as well as several local establishments. Although many people in town knew of her, no one was close to her. No business would admit to hiring her on a cash basis. It was another dead end.

"We're missing something," Josie said, echoing one of their earlier conversations. "What the hell is it?"

Before Gretchen could answer, Hummel emerged from the stairwell with a sheaf of papers in his hands. "Hey, boss," he said, walking over and handing them to Josie. "More reports. Mostly to do with the clothing that Beverly and Vera Urban were wearing at the times of their deaths. We also processed everything you found in Vera Urban's motel room for prints and DNA. No prints other than Vera's. I'm sorry we don't have more for you."

"It's okay," Josie said. "This case is just one dead end after another." She flipped through the reports, a familiar name catching her eye. "What's this?" she asked, pointing to it.

Hummel leaned over her shoulder. "That's from the receipt we found in Beverly's jacket pocket from the Wellspring Clinic.

There were some unidentified prints, most likely hers, and then Ray's prints as well."

Josie stared at Ray's name in black and white on the report. Her heart hammered in her chest. She choked out a "thank you" so that Hummel would leave. She felt three sets of eyes on her: Gretchen, Noah, and Mettner, all staring.

It didn't matter, she told herself. It wasn't important. So what if Ray's prints were on the receipt from the clinic that Beverly had gone to shortly before her death? Maybe they had been involved. Maybe they'd had a relationship behind Josie's back. Maybe Ray was the father of Beverly's baby. That would explain why she was wearing his jacket. Lana had said Beverly was only intimate with one man, but Beverly could have been lying to Lana. Josie still didn't believe Ray killed Beverly, and he certainly could not have killed Vera. Something much larger was at work in the case. Something that had nothing to do with Ray. It was ancient history, anyway, she thought. Both Beverly and Ray were gone. Anything that might have happened between them no longer mattered. The only thing that mattered was finding who killed Beverly and Vera and putting them away so they wouldn't hurt anyone ever again.

So why did Josie feel as though her heart was about to burst out of her chest?

She placed the report onto the desk and said, "I've got to use the bathroom."

Then she walked into the stairwell, down the steps, and out into the parking lot. She barely registered the reporters. Their shouts were drowned out by the rush of blood in her ears. Without even realizing it, she got into her car and began to drive. Her cell phone chirped, but she ignored it. She came out of her daze when she found herself parked in front of the nearest liquor store which, mercifully, had escaped the flood zone. Her feet carried her out of the car and into the store. Some part of her fought to be heard.

The part that had been buried beneath the avalanche of emotion as a result of Lisette's news, the guilt over Vera's death, the terror of having nearly drowned when they were swept downriver, and the possibility that Ray had lied to her, back when they were both still innocent and in love.

Her hand closed around the neck of a bottle of Wild Turkey.

Don't do it, said the muffled voice.

Just one sip, said the voice that was now firmly in control of her body. The voice of panic, loud and unpleasant, driving away reason, wanting only to soothe the demons that now swirled around the periphery of her consciousness. Demons that had been there since childhood. She thought she'd pushed them down, exorcised them. They didn't *matter*. But they were here.

"Cash or credit?" said a male voice.

Josie looked up at a young cashier placing the bottle of Wild Turkey into a bag. "No," she said.

He gave her a lopsided smile. "Well, those are the only two ways to pay, so…"

"I'm sorry," Josie said. "I—I have to go."

She went back to the car, trying to slow her pounding heart, and peeled out of the parking lot. She didn't realize where she was headed until she was already through the gates of the cemetery. After parking, she picked her way between the headstones to Ray's grave. Following his death, she had come there often, but she hadn't been there in months. A bouquet of flowers lay limply at the stone's base. Most likely from Misty, Josie thought. Misty visited religiously. The ground was damp from weeks of unrelenting rain, but Josie sat down anyway, crossing her legs. She wasn't sure why she had come. After five minutes, she realized she didn't feel any better.

"It doesn't matter," she muttered at the headstone through gritted teeth.

She needed to focus on her job. Letting things like Lisette's news and silly high school mistakes that her dead husband may have made in the past interfere with her present-day life was a huge problem. What was happening to her?

She heard Gretchen's voice in her head. *You can only push trauma down for so long before it starts coming out in weird ways and at weird times.*

Closing her eyes, she took in several deep breaths. She would calm herself down, get control. Then she would take all these strange, cumbersome feelings threatening to overtake her and push them down as far as they would go into some black hole in her mind. She would move on. Go back to work.

"Josie."

Noah's voice startled her. She jumped to her feet, swiping at the back of her jeans, brushing off dirt and grass. He stood several feet away, hands jammed into the pockets of his khaki pants.

She said, "What are you doing here?"

He stepped closer until there was only a foot between them. "You didn't come back. I was worried."

"How did you know where to find me?"

He shrugged. "You come here when something has really gotten to you, especially when it's something from your past. Since you just saw Ray's name on that fingerprint report, that made it a little easier to guess where you'd gone, but to be honest, with what's going on with Lisette, I would have bet on you being here regardless."

"I'm fine," she said. "I'm ready to go back to work." She hated that her voice quavered.

"Let's get it out in the open before you go back to work," he said. "It's just you, me, and Ray here. Say whatever it is you need to say and then we'll go back."

She wanted to punch him. "Why do I always have to say things?"

He smiled. "That's how talking works. Seriously, it might help."

"It's not going to help."

"Fair enough," he said. "Then just say things to hear yourself talk."

In spite of the tension knotting her shoulder blades, Josie laughed. Then it turned into a strangled cry. She clamped a hand over her mouth. When she was certain she wasn't going to sob, she took her hand away. "I don't know what's wrong with me lately. I'm so emotional. Everything is just getting to me."

"It's been a horrific week, Josie. Our city is damn near destroyed. You found a dead body. You got shot at. You almost died in the river with Vera Urban. Add Lisette's news to that and it's a lot to adjust to."

"But Gram's news doesn't matter," Josie said. "Even finding Ray's stupid fingerprints on that receipt and his jacket on Beverly's body doesn't matter."

Noah raised a brow. "How does it not matter?"

"None of that should affect me or my work."

"But it is, and maybe that's okay. Maybe it's okay for you to have a period of time where you need to mentally process big, difficult things like a normal person."

"I'm not normal," she muttered.

"Because of all the messed-up things that happened to you?" Noah asked.

"Not just that," Josie said. "Because I should be hunting down Beverly Urban's murderer right now and instead, I'm in the goddamn graveyard where my ex-husband is buried because when we were in high school he might have cheated on me and gotten Beverly pregnant. Who cares?" She threw her arms in the air and began pacing.

"You do," Noah said. "So let's go there. What if Ray was seeing Beverly behind your back? What if they were sleeping together, and he got her pregnant? How does that make you feel?"

Josie paused long enough to roll her eyes. "What? Did you take a crash course in psychology or something? Are you serious right now? How does it make me *feel?*"

When he didn't respond, staring at her in a way that made it clear he expected an answer, she said, "It makes me feel like shit. It makes me feel sad and alone and like my whole life was a lie."

"Your whole life?" he coaxed.

She shook her head as though that could clear it. "Noah, nothing about my life was what it seemed. My mother wasn't really my mother. My dad wasn't really my dad. He didn't really kill himself. My grandmother wasn't really my grandmother. My goddamn name wasn't even Josie. Don't you get it? The only thing that was real, that was true, that was consistent in my life was Ray. Since I was nine years old he was..." She searched for words, for the right metaphors. "My—my anchor. My—this is so stupid—"

"He was your constant," Noah filled in.

"Yes," Josie said, feeling a rush of relief that he understood. "He was the one person who knew everything that had happened to me and loved me anyway. Even my grandmother never knew all the things that Lila did to me. Ray was there through it all. He kept me sane, he kept me focused. He made me feel like I was worth something. I know that he turned out to be a drunk and a liar and a dishonorable person, but I'm talking about Ray the *boy* that I loved in school, not Ray the man I married. Ray was my foundation, Noah. If it was all a lie, if even back then he wasn't who he pretended to be, what does that say about me?"

"Nothing," Noah said. "It says nothing about you."

Tears stung the backs of her eyes. She fought to hold them back. "You're wrong," she argued. "If the one person who loved me when I was at my worst didn't really love me—if he was a liar, then what does that mean? How can I be—how can I be—" She couldn't finish.

Noah stepped closer to her and put his hands on her shoulders. "Josie," he said. "You were a child."

"But if everything I thought about the best parts of my childhood were a lie, what does that mean? If the foundation of my life—or the one thing left of it, Ray—was a lie, then what does that mean for me? Who the hell am I?"

"You're Josie Quinn," Noah said simply. "And that doesn't depend on Ray or Lisette or your biological family or me or anyone. That foundation you're talking about? It wasn't Ray. Foundations are built, Josie. They're built up over time. Ray helped you lay that foundation just like your grandmother did by being a positive, loving, stable force when everything around you was completely fucked up. The foundation you're talking about—that's all you."

"How do you know that? How do you—how can you love me? You don't even know who I am. I don't even know who I am!"

He smiled again. One of his hands tilted her chin up toward him. "I know exactly who you are. Everyone who loves you knows who you are. You're the woman who shot me, trying to save a teenage girl who desperately needed help."

She looked away from him. "I wish you wouldn't bring that up. I still feel guilty about that."

"Don't," he said, cupping her cheek to bring her gaze back to him. "You're the woman who is now best friends with Ray's girlfriend—a woman you used to hate. You're Harris's Aunt JoJo. You're the woman who saved a baby from drowning in a river, who jumped into a burning car to try to save a man because he was the only person who knew where two missing persons were. You're the woman who solved my mother's murder. You're the woman who delivered a baby in the back of your car in a damn thunderstorm. You run toward the danger, Josie. Every time. You never hesitate. What does that make you? I know what it makes you to me, but only you can say what it makes you to yourself. My point is that nothing you find out about the past, no matter how terrible, can change any of that."

She sank into his arms, pressing her face against his chest. Inhaling his familiar scent immediately sent her heart rate back down to a normal range. "Thank you," she mumbled. "But I still wish I could know for sure about Ray and Beverly."

Noah pressed a kiss into her scalp. After a few moments, he said, "You know, we could ask Misty for a DNA sample from Harris. Well, I guess if we're going to start asking people for DNA samples then we could just go directly to Mrs. Quinn. You think she'd give us one to compare against the DNA profile of Beverly's baby?"

"Probably," Josie said. "But maybe I'm just being… I don't know. I never would have believed that Ray slept with Beverly. Back then he was so good. He was still kind of innocent. We were deeply in love in the kind of crazy hormonal way that only teenagers can be. We had all these stupid plans. The summer before senior year we were going to take this road trip, drive to the beach and spend a week there. We had a list of places we were going to visit between here and there. It was so silly, and we were completely broke. But Ray wanted to make it happen for me, and he did. He spent that entire summer working construction. He was a day laborer for this general contractor. I barely saw him at all. He'd have to be on the job site at six in the morning and by the time he was finished, he'd be so tired. They were building that office building—oh my God."

She pulled away from him. Noah looked at her, confused. "What is it?"

"Good God," she said. "I know what we're missing. I know why Beverly had Ray's jacket and why his prints were on the Wellspring receipt."

CHAPTER FORTY-FOUR

2004

Ray and Josie stood outside the construction site. The structure had walls and windows now, resembling a building instead of some kind of Erector set. The noise from inside was still steady but less deafening. Josie swiped the sweat from her upper lip and squinted at Ray, wishing she'd brought her sunglasses. While she was wishing for things, she wished they were somewhere with air conditioning. The July heat was sweltering. She had no idea how he worked in it all day long.

"Ray," she said. "How much longer?"

He checked his watch. "Not long. He said he'd be here to check out the site around noon today."

"You don't know that he's really going to show up. These rich office people say all kinds of things they don't mean. This is a waste of time."

"No it's not," Ray insisted. "I'm telling you, this guy is really nice. He was one of the team sponsors last year. He was at the big game. Don't you remember us having to take all those pictures?"

"Yeah, but I didn't meet those guys," Josie said.

"It doesn't matter," Ray said. "I told him all about you. He was the one who told me to bring you around. He has some foundation or something, and all they do is give out scholarships to girls. I'm sorry. Young women."

"That's it?" Josie said. "You just have to be a female?"

Ray gave a half shrug and adjusted the tool belt slung around his waist. "I mean, I guess you have to be studying a certain field. Like science or whatever. Technology. Computers."

"I'm going into criminal justice, Ray. That's none of those things."

"Come on, Jo. Just talk to the guy. Even if you don't qualify, it's worth a try."

Two large droplets of sweat raced down Josie's back before soaking into her shirt. "Ten minutes," she said. "Then I'll be so sweaty he won't even want to shake my hand."

Ray pulled his hardhat down so it shaded his eyes and looked down the street. "There," he said. "There he is!"

Two men walked from the direction of the old theater. They both wore suits even in the intense summer heat. As they drew closer, Josie recognized them from the championship game. One wore glasses and the other was the man she'd run into. The one on her list. Tanned and Toned. She was about to tell Ray she wasn't comfortable with this, but Ray was already walking up to them, hand extended. The man with glasses shook it. "Hello, Ray."

"Mr. Prather," he said. "Nice to see you."

CHAPTER FORTY-FIVE

Noah followed Josie to the City Codes office. Having been there recently, he was able to help her find what she was looking for relatively quickly. Still, it took over an hour. Josie spent that time on her phone, locating the other pieces she needed to present her theory to the team. Back at the stationhouse, Gretchen, Mettner, and the Chief waited. In the corner, Amber lurked.

Everyone was seated at their desks except the Chief who stood behind Josie, arms folded over his thin chest. "What've you got, Quinn?"

Across her desk, Josie spread a map of Denton's central business district which she'd gotten from the City Codes office. She pointed to Aymar Avenue, which was a few blocks from where they stood and still underwater. "Here," she said. "On this corner of Aymar is the Denton Theater Ensemble Playhouse. It's been a fixture here since before I was a kid."

"So?" Chitwood said.

"You're not from here so you won't know the background," Josie said. "It's a historic building. It used to be run by various theater companies. Then they ran out of money. Eventually the college took it over. Now it just features student performers and guest speakers." Josie pointed across the street from the playhouse. "There," she said. "It's a pizza shop now, but it used to be the ice cream shop where Beverly Urban worked in the fall of 2003 and spring of 2004, which was mine, Ray's, and Beverly's junior year of high school. The theater was being remodeled that same year."

"I'm listening," Chitwood said.

She ran her finger down the line that represented Aymar Avenue. "Here," Josie said. "This is the corner of Aymar and Stockton. This is an office building. One of the businesses it houses is Joe Prather's software company. The Prather Foundation is also located there. Construction on this building started six months after the theater remodel, in the spring of our junior year. Ray worked on the site as a laborer during the summer between our junior and senior years. And over here," she pointed to another square directly across from the office building, "was the Wellspring Clinic."

Chitwood had gone from looking frustrated to looking bored.

Gretchen said, "Beverly worked within a block of the clinic and the construction site where Ray was working the summer she was killed."

Mettner added, "And you've got the Prathers moving in after this office building was built. That seems a little coincidental."

"Not really," Josie said. "Guess who orchestrated and supervised the remodel of the theater and the building of that office complex?"

They all stared at her.

"Dutton Enterprises," Josie said. "I looked it up. It's all there in the permits and land records. Kurt Dutton has always been in commercial real estate development. The Duttons have been friends and neighbors of the Prathers for decades, so of course they rented out space to them."

Noah held up a sheaf of papers he had printed out before the meeting started. "Then there's this."

Everyone crowded around him. He held up the page for them all to see. It was an article from the *Denton Tribune* dated September 3, 2003. The headline read: *Dutton Enterprises to Revitalize Historic City Theater.*

Chitwood said, "Just give us the highlights, Fraley."

Noah read quickly and then summarized it for the others: "Basically, the theater changed hands several times during the one hundred fifteen years it's been in Denton. Dutton Enterprises bought it for a song. Kurt promised to restore it and worked with the City Council to have it added to the city's historic registry. He wanted to do a full remodel, which would take about a year, and bring it back to its 'former glory.' Then at the end of the article, he says, 'I'm going to be personally on site here every day until the project is finished. It's an honor to be a part of a project so dear to this city.'"

Once he finished reading the article's highlights, Noah said, "There's a photo here too."

Josie squinted at it as he held it out for everyone to see. There stood Kurt Dutton and several other town officials in front of the then-dilapidated theater, grinning. Dutton cut a handsome figure, just as she remembered when they had met behind the bleachers at the championship game. He looked vastly different now that he was in his sixties. Josie hadn't realized that the present-day mayoral candidate who had negotiated so smoothly with the Chief from behind bars was the same man who had groped her at the championship baseball game.

Gretchen said, "So, during Beverly Urban's junior year of high school, she worked at the ice cream stand which was right across the street from the theater where Kurt Dutton was personally overseeing a remodel."

"Right," Josie said.

Gretchen went on, "And the summer after your junior year, Ray was working at a site across from the Wellspring Clinic where Beverly went, probably to confirm her pregnancy."

"Yes," Josie said. "I think that's how she got his jacket and how his prints got on her receipt. Ray must have seen her there or coming from there. She was probably upset. Ray could never help himself when it came to vulnerable women being upset. He'd spent his entire childhood trying to comfort his mother every time his father beat her up. Then when his father finally left, Ray was fiercely protective of her."

"But Ray was fiercely protective of you as well," Noah pointed out. "And Beverly was your enemy."

"I know," Josie agreed. "But if he'd seen Beverly coming out of the clinic upset, he would have helped her or tried to comfort her. I know he would."

Gretchen said, "Ray sees her, goes to her, comforts her. Gives her his jacket. That's why he never told the truth about what happened to it. He couldn't get it back from her because she was buried in it. Like everyone else in your high school class, he figured she just moved away and took the jacket with her."

Josie nodded. "And Ray knew how much she liked him. He wouldn't have been surprised that she left town with his beloved jacket. He definitely would not have told me what happened at the time because he would have known I'd go ballistic back then."

Mettner said, "All right, we've got the Ray connection sorted out. It makes sense, and if we're wrong, we'll know it from the baby's DNA test. If we're right, Ray definitely didn't kill her. What's the final piece?"

"Kurt Dutton," Josie said. "He and Beverly were having an affair. He was the father of her baby. That would have been problematic for a number of reasons, including the fact that Vera had a prior connection to Dutton's wife."

Chitwood said, "How did you get from Beverly working across the street from Dutton to him fathering her child?"

"From this," Josie said. She laid another piece of paper on the desk for all of them to see. It was a color photograph pulled from Marisol Dutton's Facebook page. The post had been made nearly ten years ago, but that didn't matter. The picture told them everything they needed to know. In it, Kurt Dutton stood on a beach staring out at a sunset. A drink rested in his hand. His head was turned back toward the camera, a smile on his face. On his left shoulder was a skull tattoo. Marisol had captioned it simply: *Paradise*. Josie placed the photo they'd found among Beverly's things beside it for comparison.

Mettner gave a low whistle. "Damn."

"All right," Chitwood said. "We have a solid link between Beverly and Kurt Dutton. I think a defense lawyer's gonna argue that in Beverly's photo you can't see the guy's face so we can't prove it was Dutton, but we'll let the lawyers sort that out at trial."

"What about Vera?" Gretchen asked. "Where does she fit into all this?"

Noah said, "Maybe she saw him kill Beverly? She disappears because she's afraid he'll kill her, too, and then when Beverly's body is found, she comes back to Denton and he actually does kill her."

Gretchen shook her head. "I don't think that makes complete sense. If Vera saw the murder, why wouldn't she just report it? We're talking about her kid here."

Noah said, "Dutton was rich and powerful and, at that time, he was running for City Council."

Gretchen said, "But he wasn't cartel powerful or federal government powerful. She could have turned him in easily. I think we're still missing something. Besides, he's got an alibi for the morning Vera was shot. After we met with Connie and Marisol, I made some calls to confirm their alibis. Both were home with their husbands."

Mettner said, "Maybe Marisol lied for her husband."

Josie said, "Or maybe she slept late that morning and never knew he was gone. What if she'd been drinking heavily the night before? Passed out? It's possible he could have snuck out and back in before she even woke up. We're onto something now. It's a start. We also checked Dutton's firearm purchase records. He has owned a nine millimeter pistol since 2000."

Chief Chitwood said, "You've got enough to bring him in and talk to him. Do it. Tomorrow. Schedule him to come in. Two of you stay here to question him while the other two serve the warrant at his home for the gun. We'll go from there."

CHAPTER FORTY-SIX

The next morning, Josie and Noah waited in her car just outside the entrance to Quail Hollow Estates. Gone were the protestors and the residents opposing them. Josie sipped her coffee while Noah looked at his phone. "Dutton was due at the stationhouse ten minutes ago."

"He's running late," Josie said.

They had driven past the Dutton residence upon their arrival at Quail Hollow and seen both Dutton vehicles in the driveway. Then they'd taken up position outside of the development so they'd know exactly when he left. But he never emerged.

Josie's cell phone chirped with a text message. She looked at it. "Gretchen," she told Noah. "Dutton's attorney is there waiting for him. He's called Dutton's cell phone but didn't get an answer."

Noah grimaced. "You want to go in or wait a few more minutes?"

"Let's give it ten more minutes," Josie said. "Then we'll knock."

The ten minutes passed slowly. Gretchen texted once more to let them know Dutton's attorney had tried again, unsuccessfully, to reach Dutton. Still there was no sign of Dutton's vehicle leaving the development.

Josie put the car in drive, a sinking feeling in her stomach, and headed toward the Dutton residence. She parked on the street and together, she and Noah approached the house. They knocked on the door but there was no answer. They rang the doorbell. Nothing.

"I don't like this," Josie said.

"We can't go in without cause," Noah said.

Josie took out her phone and fired off a text to Gretchen. "I'm going to ask her to make sure attempts to contact both the husband and the wife have been made. Wait here, I'm going to see if any of the neighbors are home. Maybe one of them has a key."

Noah stood at the front door, alternately knocking and ringing the doorbell to no avail while Josie went door to door along the street. Of the six houses she went to, three of the neighbors either weren't home or didn't answer. Two didn't have keys. The last neighbor was Connie Prather. She answered the door in jeans and a fitted T-shirt that said *Mama Bear* on it. In her arms was her tiny dog.

"Mrs. Prather," Josie said. "By any chance do you have a key to the Duttons' home?"

"What's going on?"

"Mr. Dutton was supposed to meet his attorney at the police station this morning, and he didn't show up. Both vehicles are there, but we're not able to get in touch with Marisol or her husband."

"Oh," Connie said. "I don't—well, I might have one from a long time ago. I don't know if it would still work, but I can—"

"Could you get it for us?" Josie asked, cutting her short.

"Um, sure, I guess. Wait here."

Josie could see Noah's outline on the Duttons' front steps from where she stood. It took Connie thirteen minutes to find the key. She left her dog in the house and walked to the Duttons' with Josie. "This is so strange," Connie said. "Maybe they just didn't want to pay the fines."

Josie was deciding whether or not to tell Connie that Dutton wasn't going to the police station to work out the fines the Chief had levied against him for the supplies Quail Hollow had taken illegally, when a concussive boom shook the air around them. Both women froze. Josie looked toward the Dutton house where Noah was already kicking the front door. Josie left Connie behind and ran toward Noah, unsnapping her holster as she ran. By the time Josie reached him, the door had broken away from its frame. Noah took out his pistol and pushed inside. Behind him, Josie was ready, gun in hand, following him as he cleared each room on the first floor. Finding no one, he pointed toward the ceiling and Josie nodded. She let Noah lead as they padded up the steps.

Behind the second door in the upstairs hall, Marisol slumped on the floor at the foot of a king-sized bed. Her hair was greasy and unkempt. Blood trickled from a split in her bottom lip. When she looked up at them, Josie saw that her nose had been smashed in, and her left eye was black and swollen.

"Gun," Josie said quietly to Noah.

"I see it," he said, advancing on Marisol. He pointed to the Glock on the floor beside her. "Mrs. Dutton, I need you to move away from the weapon."

Josie went in the opposite direction, where Kurt Dutton lay in a heap on the floor near a large walk-in closet. A gunshot wound in his chest pulsed blood. Josie checked him for weapons but saw none. Dropping to her knees, she took off her jacket and used it to put pressure on the wound. With one hand she felt for a pulse. It was weak and thready. "Noah," she said. "He's not going to make it. We need an ambulance now."

Noah had helped Marisol onto the side of the bed. He took out his phone and made the call.

"Marisol, what happened here?"

Noah and Josie looked toward the bedroom doorway where Connie stood, face pale, eyes wide, taking in the destruction in the large room. Overturned furniture, broken lamps, blood stains in the carpet.

Josie said, "Connie, stay where you are. Don't come any closer."

Connie seemed not to hear her, eyes still glued to Marisol, but she didn't step inside the room. "Mar?" she said.

Tears streamed down Marisol's face. She hugged her middle, flinching, and looked over at Josie. "Is he dead?"

"No," Josie said. "But he's lost a lot of blood."

"Ask him what he did," Marisol said.

Noah hung up his phone and put it back into his pocket. He holstered his weapon and went over to Marisol. "Are you wounded?" he asked.

"He hit me," Marisol replied. "He came after me. He was crazy."

"No gunshot wounds, though," Noah said.

She shook her head. "I shot him," she said.

Connie gasped and covered her mouth with one hand.

"I shouldn't say that," Marisol said. "I know. I should wait for an attorney. You don't know what he did. Ask him what he did."

Josie looked at Noah and gave a slight shake of the head. Beneath her hands, the life was bleeding out of Kurt Dutton. He was barely breathing. There was no way he could hold a conversation.

Noah said, "He's not in a position to talk right now, Mrs. Dutton. Why don't you and I go downstairs and wait—"

Marisol sprang off the bed only to flinch, the movement obviously causing her pain. She put her right hand over the left side of her rib cage. "He's a monster. He killed them both. Vera and Beverly—and Beverly's baby. Did you know that he knocked Beverly up before he killed her?"

Noah said, "Mrs. Dutton, you're in shock right now. We can take a statement once you've been checked out by a medic."

He reached for her arm, but she swatted him away. "I saw her once, you know. She came to the theater to see him, but I was there that day. I never forgot that. He told me last night that he had to go to the police station today. I asked him why, and he said it was about the city flood supplies. But then he called our lawyer, and I knew he was lying. All night I asked him what was really going on until he hit me. I asked him if it had to do with Beverly Urban's body being found. He told me. He admitted it. He killed her all those years ago, and he killed Vera because she wouldn't keep his secret any longer. She was going to tell the police the truth."

Connie gasped again but said nothing.

Marisol continued, "I asked him what the truth was, and he said that he and Beverly were having an affair. When she was in high school! I knew he was telling the truth because of the girls."

"Oh, Mar," Connie whispered.

"What girls?" Josie asked. She checked for Kurt's pulse again. It was barely there.

"My husband liked young girls," Marisol spat. "When we first got married, it was just college-aged girls. Interns. Unpaid interns. He'd hire them from Denton University and then romp around town with them. Like I wasn't going to find out."

Josie looked at Connie. "You knew about this?"

Connie nodded. "My husband saw him with college girls a few times. It was obvious that he was… involved with them, but they were adults, so we never said anything."

"But they weren't all adults," Marisol said. "Beverly Urban was sixteen when they started their affair. I asked him if that was why he killed her—because if anyone found out he was having a sexual relationship with a minor, it would have ruined his life. He would have faced prison. He said he never meant to kill her, only to scare her because she was pregnant with his baby, and she was threatening to keep it. She invited him to her house when she thought her mom was out and told him. They had a big fight about it. Vera showed up. Things got worse. He was going to pay her, pay them both, to take care of it, but Beverly refused. He said he took out his gun to scare her, to scare them both into doing what he wanted, but things got out of hand and he shot her."

Josie knew this to be a lie. There was no scenario that she could imagine in which Kurt Dutton had shot Beverly in the back of the head by accident or in the heat of the moment. From Dr. Feist's findings, Kurt would have had to be standing behind her, a few feet away, with her walking away from him when he pulled the trigger. But they were getting Dutton's confession second-hand.

Noah said, "Why didn't Vera go to the police?"

Marisol said, "I don't know. He said he offered to pay her as long as she disappeared and never talked about it. He told her if she ever went to the police, he would tell them how she dealt drugs to his wife and her friends for years. He would ruin her. I asked him why, if he'd already killed Beverly sixteen years ago, he didn't just kill Vera, too, and he said he wasn't thinking straight and hadn't meant to kill Beverly. Vera was so freaked out that she just did what he said. They made some kind of deal. I don't know what it was or how it worked—just that he paid her, and she kept quiet. But he said Vera came back after Beverly's body was found. She begged him to go to the police, explain it had been a mistake, and said she would go herself if he wouldn't. He couldn't risk it—especially not now, with the mayoral race going on—and so he killed her. He knew where she was staying so he followed her and killed her. I slept in that day. I just assumed he was here all that time, but he wasn't. I was his alibi and I didn't even know it. Then he said he would kill me too if I told. I tried to get to my phone, and he started to beat me."

Sirens sounded outside. Marisol collapsed onto the bed, weeping. Noah brushed past Connie and out of the room to meet the cavalry outside. Josie felt for Kurt Dutton's pulse again, but it was gone.

CHAPTER FORTY-SEVEN

Josie sat at her desk at the Denton PD stationhouse, flipping through pages of records recovered from Vera's apartment. She felt a presence behind her and looked over her shoulder to see Chief Chitwood lingering. "You still on that Urban thing, Quinn?"

"We never found evidence that Kurt Dutton was supporting Vera Urban financially. I asked Marisol's attorney if we could have the Duttons' financial records, and he said he'd look into it, which means I'm never going to see a single record."

Chitwood pulled over an empty chair from Gretchen's desk. He sat in it and leaned toward Josie. "Quinn," he said. "The case is closed. We have the wife's statement. The ballistics on Kurt Dutton's gun match up to the bullet found in Beverly's skull and to the shell casings found in the old bowling alley. It fits. Hummel couldn't pull any prints from the casings but the ballistics match and that's good enough for me."

"Chief, some things don't fit. Mostly Vera."

"You think someone else killed Vera?"

With a sigh, Josie leaned back in her chair. "No. I think he did kill her."

"Then what's the problem?"

Josie picked up a stack of pages on her desk and let them fall loosely back to the surface. "Vera was a loose end. He had no trouble killing her when she returned to town after being in hiding for sixteen years. Why didn't he just kill her right away? Why spend all that money supporting her? Money I can't account for, by the way."

"Quinn," Chitwood said. "Has it occurred to you that maybe he was having an affair with Vera?"

"No," Josie said. "Marisol said he liked younger women. Connie Prather confirmed that."

"Have you corroborated that? Talked to any young women Dutton had affairs with?"

"Well, no, but—"

"Quinn," Chitwood said. "Let it go."

"I think Marisol knew something," Josie blurted.

"Like what? You think she knew her husband knocked up a minor sixteen years ago, killed her, buried her, and paid her mother off for almost twenty years to keep quiet about it, and she just chose last week to confront him?"

"No," Josie said. "Not exactly. I don't know. I just think she knew something. I'm not sure if she knew something in a concrete way or if she knew it in the sense that something was always off, but she chose to ignore it and not ask questions because she liked her comfortable life and there was nothing particularly glaring in front of her face. Either way, she knows a lot more than she's told us."

Chitwood appraised her. He folded his hands over his stomach.

"Quinn, I've been at this a long time—"

"I know, I know. Since I was in diapers," Josie said with a groan. Immediately, she regretted it. She waited for Chitwood to leap out of his chair, point a crooked finger at her and berate her. But none of that happened. Instead, he laughed. Josie was so stunned she momentarily wondered if she had hallucinated. She looked around the room, devastated to find that none of her colleagues were there to witness it. They'd never believe her. Chitwood said, "Since the time you were in diapers, Quinn, I've had more cases than I can count that left me feeling uncomfortable after they wrapped up, like I had missed something even after I had my guy. Sometimes, that's just the way it is. Sometimes, Quinn, you have to live with the discomfort."

With that, he stood and walked away. Josie watched him go back to his office and close his door, wondering if that last item was about the Urban case or about her. When she tore her gaze away from his door, Gretchen was coming out of the stairwell with two coffees in hand, both from Komorrah's. In most areas of the city, the flooding had finally receded, and local businesses and residents were getting their lives back to normal. There were still problem areas which Emergency Services were monitoring and flood zones that were being patrolled regularly, but for the most part, pre-flood life had resumed. Misty had taken Harris and Pepper and gone home, leaving Josie and Noah strangely lonely and very hungry. Gretchen put one paper cup in front of Josie and went around to her own desk.

Josie peeled back the tab of the lid and let the smell of her favorite Komorrah's brew waft up to her nose. To Gretchen, she said, "You might be my soul mate."

Gretchen laughed. "Fraley will be sorry to hear that."

Mettner walked in, waving a sheaf of papers. "Boss," he said. "I just ran into Hummel. He gave me these DNA results from the Urban case. Apparently, Mayor Charleston pulled some strings to get them expedited. Another nail in Dutton's literal coffin just days before the primary. Guess we're stuck with her for another two years."

He handed her the reports. She flipped the pages. "Marisol was right. Kurt Dutton was the father of Beverly's baby, and Silas was Beverly's father. Vera was right when she told him he was the father."

"Think we should tell him?" Mettner asked.

Josie set the pages on her desk and sighed. "Do you think he'll reimburse the city for Beverly's funeral expenses?"

Gretchen gave a dry laugh.

Before anyone could say more, Amber came in through the stairwell. Her alabaster skin was flushed and she walked fast, almost as though someone was chasing her. "Detective Quinn," she said. "I have something for you."

She pulled a chair from one of the other desks and wheeled it over, plopping down next to Josie. From her pocket, she pulled a small flash drive and handed it to Josie.

"What is this?" Josie asked.

"Look at it," Amber said. Her breath came quickly, her chest heaving. "Please."

Josie plugged it into her computer and waited for the PC to recognize it.

Mettner came around to stand behind them. "Amber, what's going on?"

Amber looked at each of them and then said, "I was at the Mayor's office." She put up a hand. "I know, I know. You all think I'm some kind of plant. I'm really not. I just have to liaise with her office. That means communicating with her about things that might go out in the press. So I was over there waiting outside of her office and Connie Prather was waiting to see her."

"At City Hall?" Gretchen asked.

Amber nodded. "Connie went in before me. I didn't think anything of it at first, but then I heard them shouting at each other and I moved my chair closer. I heard them talking about what to do with the files now that Kurt was dead. Mayor Charleston said it was none of her business and she couldn't get involved, but Connie said it was her business because she was the Mayor. I couldn't hear what they were saying next—something about Marisol. Tara asked Connie why she didn't just take the files to the police, and Connie said she didn't want the police to find out, she just wanted Tara to handle it. Then someone else came into the waiting room, and I lost the rest of the conversation, but Connie Prather came storming out of there in tears. She had this flash drive clutched in her hand. Anyway, I followed her to the bathroom. She was in one of the stalls. She came out and put her bag down next to the sink.

She was crying and so when she saw me, she went back into the stall to compose herself. She left her bag right on the countertop. I reached right in and found the flash drive. She didn't see me."

"Wait a minute," Josie said. "You stole this? We can't look at this, Amber. That's not legal. Whatever's on here—"

"Please," Amber said. "Just look at it. It's important."

Mettner said, "Amber, why would you steal a flash drive from Connie Prather?"

She looked up at him, eyes wide. "No one believes that I'm on your side in this department. You all think I'm the Mayor's puppet. Now she's going to be in office even longer. I needed you all to trust me. Trust is earned, not given."

Josie tried not to flinch at the words as she opened the PDF files on the drive and perused them. "These are files from the Prather Foundation," she said. "Looks like scholarship applications."

She skimmed through more documents. "There are some emails here as well. It looks like Marisol Dutton chose a student every four or five years to get a scholarship from the Foundation."

Amber said, "Dutton Enterprises has been a huge donor to the Prather Foundation over the years."

Gretchen said, "That's not illegal. Neither is Marisol choosing the students. The Prather Foundation is private. They're not bound by the rules non-profits are subject to."

Josie scrolled through the applications more slowly. The names were familiar to her, but she couldn't place them. "How did Marisol even find these students and vet them? I thought her only job was to look pretty and spend Kurt's money."

Josie came to the last application and read the name. A cold shock ran through her.

Gretchen said, "What is it, boss?"

"Alice Adams," Josie said. "These applications—they're all names we found on the driver's licenses that Vera had been using."

"Which means what?" Mettner said.

Josie scrolled through more documents. "The Foundation was able to send its checks directly to students or to their parents rather than to the school. Like Gretchen said, private foundation, private rules. Every four to five years, Marisol Dutton would choose a young woman to receive ongoing checks from the Foundation from their freshman year through their graduation. Connie approved these applications and the checks went out."

"But not to the young women," Gretchen said. "To Vera. Posing as these women."

"Right," Josie said. "Kurt Dutton wasn't funding Vera all these years, Marisol was. She funneled it through Connie's foundation."

"Holy shit," said Mettner. "But why?"

"I have an idea," Josie said. "But we have to talk to Connie and Marisol. Unfortunately, because Amber stole these files, we can't use them. We'll need them to confess to some or all of this."

Amber bit her bottom lip and said, "How will you do that?"

"I don't know," Josie said. "But I think we should start by talking with Connie."

CHAPTER FORTY-EIGHT

Josie and Gretchen stood on Connie Prather's front stoop. They'd rung the doorbell several times and knocked but there was no answer. Gretchen said, "Maybe she's walking her dog?"

"Let's take a stroll," Josie suggested.

They were halfway down the next block when they passed Calvin Plummer's house. The attorney's Lexus LX was parked in the driveway, as was Tammy's Honda. As Josie passed, Tammy emerged from the house, headed toward her car. Josie waved at her. She waved back. "What are you doing here?"

"Looking for someone," Josie told her. "Connie Prather? She's got this little tiny dog. White fur. Looks like you could fit it in your purse."

Tammy pointed down the street, in the direction Josie and Gretchen were headed. "She walked down toward the flood area about a half hour ago."

"Is it still flooded?" Josie asked.

"Around the back of the development? Yeah. When you get to the end of this block, turn left. You'll see a big, unfinished house. Behind that is where the moat got absorbed into the larger flood area. It's still pretty bad back there. Just be careful. I don't know what she's doing down that way but a lot of people have been walking down there to look at the damage."

Josie thanked her and she and Gretchen followed her directions until they came to the house, standing tall and majestic but covered in Tyvek wrap that whipped in the wind, making a loud fluttering sound like that of a hundred huge flying insects. There was no sign of Connie and her dog, so they picked their way around the side of the house through mud and dirt to the backyard.

The deck at the back of the house was unfinished. Beyond it was at least an acre of water-logged land on a downward slope, leading to a grove of trees. Josie couldn't see much beyond the trees.

"You think she came back here?" Gretchen asked.

"I don't know," Josie said. "To walk her dog? Seems strange." They walked deeper into the yard.

"Is that water?" Gretchen stopped and pointed. "On the other side of those trees?"

Josie studied the property line until she saw a few flashes of muddy water. "I think that's the infamous moat."

They took a few more steps toward the trees. "Look," Gretchen said, pulling up short and barring Josie's progress with an arm. Looking at her feet, Josie saw that the grass gave way to a large muddy patch filled with concrete chunks. A backward glance revealed that they were about halfway between the house and the line of trees. "There used to be a wall here," Gretchen added. "This is where the yard ends."

"The wall broke down," Josie said. From where they stood, the neighboring houses were just visible. Each one had a solid barrier wall between their well-manicured lawns and the tree line which separated the properties from the moat.

Gretchen said, "What's on the other side of the moat back here?"

"One of the still-active flood zones. One of the tributaries coming from the river runs through the neighborhood next to Quail Hollow on this side. When it flooded, it ran over into the moat, which made that flood. It's all just one large flood zone now."

"The barrier wall at the back of this house either wasn't finished or it was too weak to withstand the moat overflowing, 'cause there's nothing left of it," Gretchen said. "There is no reason for Connie Prather or anyone else to be back here."

"Something's not right," Josie said. "Do you hear that?"

They paused and listened. The wind rustled the leaves of the trees and voices floated up from the direction of the moat.

"Let's go," Josie said. "Be careful."

As they began to negotiate the slippery, mud-covered field of uneven concrete pieces, Gretchen pointed to a series of footprints. Two sets, both mingled. "Step where they stepped. Maybe we won't fall."

Josie kept her arms outward for balance as she stepped from one block of misshapen stone to another. Gretchen put both hands on Josie's shoulders for support and slowly followed. The voices grew louder. Finally, the stones gave way to mud, veined with tree roots. Josie saw the moat now, about thirty yards ahead, beyond the trees, its brackish water churning. Beyond it was just more water.

She and Gretchen followed the voices through the trees until they became clearer. The mud sucked at their feet, making it difficult to move quickly. Each time their sneakers made a small popping sound, Josie expected the voices to stop, but they didn't. Finally, they came to the place where the trees ended. A narrow dirt ledge stood between the tree line and the moat. More tree roots reached their gnarled arms from the earth. There had obviously been a small landslide in the area at some point. Probably when the flooding overtook and destroyed the barrier wall above them. From where they stood, Josie estimated that it was a twelve-foot drop from the ledge into the water. They paused behind a large oak tree and craned their necks to find the source of the voices.

About twenty feet upstream, Josie saw Connie Prather first, standing close to the trees. Her tiny dog was clutched to her chest. Bright pink rubber boots adorned her feet. A matching raincoat completed the ensemble even though it was no longer raining. "Come back from the ledge, Mar. Really. You're scaring me."

Marisol stood about three feet away, as close to the ledge as she could get before the ground would just disintegrate beneath her. One of her black rubber boots nudged at a mud-covered tree root.

When she said nothing, Connie continued, "I don't know why we had to talk out here."

Marisol laughed but kept her back to Connie. "Because you're going to accuse me of something very bad, and I don't want to take the chance of anyone hearing it."

"I'm not accusing you of anything. I'm telling you that with everything that's come out about Kurt, there seem to be some… irregularities with your involvement in our foundation. I talked to Tara and she—"

Marisol whirled on her, eyes flashing. The swelling in her face had gone down but her skin was still various shades of purple and yellow from the faded bruising. "You talked to Tara? Are you out of your mind?"

Connie hugged her dog closer to her body and took a step back. "Tara didn't even want to hear it. She told me to go to the police."

Marisol seemed to calm down. Gone was the momentary flash of rage Josie had seen. In its place was a sardonic smile. "You want to go to the police because you let me choose a couple of students to give scholarships to for your foundation? Are you listening to yourself? Connie, I know your life is boring, maybe you're looking to liven things up a little, but leave me out of it. I had to kill my husband last week. I've been through enough."

"Then explain to me what you did with the applications?"

Marisol rolled her eyes. "I don't know what you're talking about, Con."

"It was your idea—to use my foundation."

"Use it for what?"

Connie's voice rose. "You know damn well what!" Her little dog gave a squeak and Connie placed it on the ground, its leash loosely tied around her wrist. "The girls that you supposedly 'selected' for scholarships—you were the one who filled out their applications. Four different applications, four different names, many similar answers and all with the same handwriting in the signature part—yours."

"You can't prove that," Marisol scoffed.

"I'm right, aren't I? You didn't select any girls. You made them up and filled out applications in their names and then you collected the money, didn't you? What was it for?"

Marisol didn't respond. Instead, she took another step back toward the ledge. Josie and Gretchen stepped out from behind the tree.

"She was supporting Vera Urban," Josie said.

Connie jumped at the sound of Josie's voice. Marisol looked up. Now that they were closer, Josie could see that her eyes were bloodshot. "Oh great," Marisol said. "Connie, did you do this? Call the cops?"

Connie shook her head. "No. I didn't call them."

"Then why are they here?" Marisol said, her voice rising to a near-shout. The scent of alcohol wafted toward Josie and Gretchen.

Josie took another step closer, Gretchen right behind her. To their right, water stretched for miles, several empty houses rising from the muck in the distance, their windows like sightless eyes.

"We came here to ask you a few questions," Gretchen said.

"Me?" Marisol asked. She took a small step backward and stumbled briefly before righting herself.

"Both of you," Josie said.

Marisol started to walk back into the trees. "I don't have to stay here for this bullshit."

She had just passed Connie when Josie called out, "You don't want to explain to your friend how you used her foundation to fund Vera Urban's life for the last sixteen years?"

Marisol stopped in her tracks. She glared past Connie at Josie. "You don't know what the hell you're talking about. All of you are crazy."

Josie looked at Connie. "If Marisol hadn't used the foundation, she wouldn't have been able to explain to her husband what she was spending so much money on every year. The names of the applicants? They were real women. Vera chose them. Stole their licenses. The Foundation mailed Vera checks in the names of her aliases for years and no one was the wiser. She used her doctored IDs to cash the checks at the banks they were drawn on—probably traveling to a branch far from wherever she was living so she wouldn't be remembered by anyone local."

Connie's head swiveled in Marisol's direction. At Connie's feet, her small dog whined. "Is this true, Mar? Why? Why would you do that?"

Marisol said nothing.

Josie continued, "Yeah, Mar, tell us, why did you need to support Vera all those years while she was in hiding? Why did she need to go into hiding in the first place?"

"You know why," Marisol said. "I told you."

Josie said, "After you shot Kurt you told us that Vera went into hiding because she witnessed Beverly's murder. She was there the night Kurt killed Beverly, wasn't she? What really happened?"

Marisol jammed both hands into the pockets of her black jacket. Slowly, she lifted her head to meet Josie's eyes. "I already told you this."

Gretchen said, "You told us a version of what happened. Now we want the truth."

Connie stared at her friend, stricken. "Mar, what are they talking about? You said Vera tried to stop Kurt and then—"

Marisol made a noise of frustration in her throat. Then she cut Connie off. "Vera didn't intervene. You think Vera could have stopped Kurt? She had a bad back. He had a foot and a half on her. He was terrifying. She hid. She came home, through the back door, and heard Kurt and Beverly arguing in the living room. Beverly wanted to keep the baby. She was going to expose him.

Kurt killed her in cold blood. Vera told me that Beverly said there was nothing he could say to convince her to get rid of the baby. Beverly told him to leave. She turned away from him—to walk away—and Kurt took a gun out of his pocket, aimed and fired. Vera saw the whole thing. As soon as Kurt shot Beverly, Vera ran and hid in the hall closet. She was terrified that he'd do the same to her if he found her there. You saw what he did to me. He could get bad, and I never knew if he was going to kill me or not. He didn't beat me often—only when I confronted him about his girls or when I talked about leaving—but when he did, it was very bad. He was a monster. Vera saw that side of him and she was afraid."

"Oh God, Marisol," Connie said. "But how do you know all this?"

"Because Vera told me."

Josie said, "Vera went to you instead of the police?"

"Why?" Gretchen asked.

"Kurt was my husband," Marisol said, as if it was the most obvious thing in the world. "Vera was my friend."

"But you hadn't seen Vera in sixteen years," Josie said. "By all accounts, Vera had never even met Kurt. It's not like he was there when you were having your parties. Vera had no loyalty to him. She didn't even have any reason to be afraid of him as long as she got out of the house without him realizing she had been there."

"He was a very powerful man," Marisol said.

"No," Gretchen put in. "Not that powerful. Vera was an eyewitness. All she had to do was get to a nearby phone and call the police. They would have caught him burying Beverly's body under the basement."

Josie said, "Vera came to you because of something else."

Connie looked from Marisol to Josie and Gretchen and back. "What are they talking about, Mar?"

"Shut up," Marisol snarled.

Josie kept going. "The only reason I can think of why Vera would come to you—after sixteen years—instead of the police, is because you both had something to hide. You were dependent on one another to hide it. You'd both be in big trouble if it came out."

"If *what* came out?" Connie asked, eyes darting back and forth.

Josie met Marisol's eyes. "You were Beverly's mother, not Vera."

Marisol sucked in a breath.

Connie flinched. "Is that true, Marisol? You had a *baby*?"

Marisol's face twisted in an ugly scowl. "Shut up!" She looked at Josie. "You can't prove that."

Josie shrugged. "I could if you submitted to a DNA test."

Connie said, "How did you—how could you possibly know that?"

"Marisol was in rehab while Vera was pregnant. In fact, she sent her a card apologizing for not being there. She said she was in rehab in Colorado for a year. Plenty of time to have a baby. Vera went on bedrest very early in her pregnancy and yet, no one knows who helped take care of her during that time. She told everyone that she'd gone to her brother's in Georgia but in fact, records show that she gave birth at Geisinger."

Gretchen said, "Also, Vera and her brother had been estranged for years. She'd never go to him, and she didn't. No. I think Marisol came here, back to Pennsylvania, before it was too late for her to travel, and she and Vera holed up in the Hempstead house until she went into labor."

Josie said, "Mrs. Dutton, how did you manage to get Vera's name on the birth certificate?"

Marisol didn't speak. Connie said, "Mar? Did you do this? You did all this?"

Glaring at her friend, Marisol said, "I'm not some idiot, Connie. I know you think I am, but I pulled this off for all these years, didn't I?" She looked at Josie and Gretchen. "I took Vera's driver's license and pretended to be her. That was the first time she doctored a driver's license. She put my picture on her license. No one knew either of us at Geisinger. No one asked questions. A few days later,

I went back to Colorado. I had been living in an apartment there by then. My husband had no idea. Nor did he care."

"He never knew you were pregnant," Josie said. "You didn't want him to know because you were having Silas Murphy's baby."

Connie let out a strangled cry. "You had his baby? Mar? Is that true?"

Ignoring Connie, Marisol gave a bitter laugh. "Yes, it's every husband's dream for his wife to give birth to a drug dealer's baby. Of course I couldn't bring that baby home, and I couldn't go through with... not having it."

"Did you ask Vera to take the baby or did she offer?" Josie asked.

"I don't know anymore," Marisol said. "It's all a blur. Vera wanted a baby desperately and my husband did not want children at all."

Connie's hands fell to her waist. The dog's leash slipped from her wrist, but she made no move to pick it up. She couldn't take her eyes off Marisol.

Gretchen asked, "Why not leave him?"

"Besides the fact that he would have actually killed me? Because I would have been broke. The money? It was all his. He brought it to the marriage, and he made more and more and more money. We had a prenuptial agreement. I had to be faithful and childless for twenty years before I'd be entitled to any marital property."

"Is that even legal?" Josie asked.

Connie's dog trotted off into the trees, sniffing around, its leash trailing behind it. Tears fell from Connie's eyes as she listened to her friend pour out decades-old secrets.

"I don't know," Marisol answered. "Why don't you ask eighteen-year-old Marisol? She was a smart girl. A girl who met a guy at a restaurant where she was waitressing, signed whatever he asked her to sign, stayed home like a good little wifey, cooking and remodeling while he went off looking for the next eighteen-year-old girl to satisfy his urges. Who sat in that big old house alone year after year while he traveled the world, sometimes for months at a time. Who got hit when she complained about it. The girl who thought all of that was just fantastic could probably tell you if that prenuptial agreement she didn't even read until she was twenty-five was legal."

"I'm sorry," Josie said.

Tears glistened in Marisol's eyes. "Vera was my friend. I know it sounds stupid, but she was a good friend to me. We cooked up this plan. We were stupid and young, and I was scared shitless. But I knew that if we pulled it off, Vera would take good care of the baby, and she did. She was a wonderful mother. Much better than I would have been. At least until Beverly got a little older and started to act out."

"Vera got frustrated and called you," Josie said. "She wanted you to take Beverly."

Connie took a step closer to Marisol, staring into her friend's face as though she were a complete stranger. "You did all of this?" she asked incredulously.

Ignoring her, Marisol sniffed and addressed Josie. "I don't know if she was serious about that or if she was just venting but yeah. I told her there was no way. We couldn't undo what we'd done. We couldn't just come clean. I offered her more money. I was able to funnel money to her for years until Beverly pushed her down the steps. Kurt gave me an allowance for spa treatments, clothes, getting my hair done, stuff like that. I cut back on a lot of things and gave the cash to Vera. Then she got hooked on pills and there was never enough money for her. She wouldn't leave me alone and then Kurt—fucking pervert Kurt—met Beverly across the street from that old theater. She worked at some pizza place or something."

"It was an ice cream shop," Josie said.

Marisol rolled her eyes. "Whatever. That was his MO though. He'd go to these shitty eating spots where college girls would be working and he'd pick them up, have a little fun with them and move on. Except Beverly wasn't a college kid."

"She looked like one," Josie said.

Marisol nodded. "Yeah. She did. Anyway, I found out about it. I knew about all his girls. I tried to keep tabs. I was waiting for a good blackmail opportunity, but it never seemed right."

Connie's hands shot out, pushing Marisol violently. Stumbling back, Marisol nearly went over the ledge. Her feet scrabbled to gain purchase, the mud disappearing beneath her in rapid fashion. Josie leapt toward her, falling onto her stomach, and grabbing both of Marisol's wrists. The stiches in her leg burned. "Help me," she shouted to Gretchen.

Gretchen knelt on the ground, trying to find a place on the ledge that wouldn't give way and reached over, helping Josie to pull Marisol back onto the ledge. Once she was safely back over, Marisol sat on her rear, chest heaving. She glared at Connie. "What is your problem?"

Connie pointed an accusing finger at her. "My problem? My problem is that you're a lying, conniving bitch with no backbone!"

"Oh piss off, Connie, with your perfect marriage and your perfect kids and your charitable foundation. You make me sick. Always judging everything."

Josie and Gretchen stood, brushing the mud from their jeans, positioning themselves closer to Connie in case she tried to knock Marisol into the water again. Josie tried to ignore the pain in her thigh.

Hysterical laughter bubbled up from Connie's throat. "Me? Judging you? You gave your kid up. You covered up her murder! You slept with Silas."

"You slept with Silas too."

Connie shook her head as if to shake off the accusation. "You did all this and then you used my foundation to keep up the lie. That could ruin our lives if it gets out!"

Marisol heaved herself to her feet. "You're the one talking about going to the police. Well, here we are! With the police."

"You're a criminal, Mar. You could have left Kurt decades ago. Instead, you let him take advantage of girl after girl. You let him beat you. You let him sleep with your own daughter!"

"I didn't *let* him beat me. Jeez, Connie. Here you go again, judging the rest of us through the lens of your perfect, easy life. You think it's a simple thing to divorce someone who has nearly killed you on more than one occasion? And for your information, I didn't *let* Kurt sleep with Beverly!" Marisol shouted. "It just happened, and I confronted him. I never told him who she was or how I even knew her. I just said I'd seen them together and that I'd followed her and found out she was a high school student. We had the fight to end all fights. He broke my wrist. I knew he wasn't going to stop seeing her and the whole thing was just too gross—"

Connie said, "So you drank until you forgot about it?"

"No, I asked Vera to intervene, to talk to Beverly."

"But Beverly was already furious with Vera, resentful," Josie cut in. "She thought Vera was hiding her father's identity from her."

"Well, she was," Marisol said. "But yeah, Beverly wasn't about to listen. Then she got pregnant. Vera and I were trying to figure out what to do. I knew that Kurt would not want that baby. He never wanted children. I knew it would end in disaster. We didn't know what to do and then he killed her. Vera ran off. She came to me. She was terrified and upset. A complete mess. She wanted to go to the police."

"But you convinced her not to."

"I couldn't risk it. What if my secret came out?"

"Vera had brought Beverly up as her own daughter," Josie said. "She just went along with it?"

"Not at first," Marisol said. "It took a lot of convincing to get her to go along with my plan, but she did. I told her that Kurt would kill us both if we tried going to the police—or if she went to the police without me, he'd bury her, literally and figuratively. I offered her a life of luxury. All she had to do was shut up, take my money, sit on her ass with her cat, and watch TV."

"Until Beverly's body was found."

Marisol said, "We never knew what he did with it. When Vera saw it on the news, she came back. She took an Uber or something. Showed up on my doorstep. I don't know what she was thinking."

"She was thinking that it was time to do the right thing."

"And Kurt killed her for it," Marisol said.

"No," Josie said. "He didn't. He had no idea she was even still alive. He never even knew she'd witnessed the murder. She didn't come to him and tell him she would finally come clean. She came to you, and she said she was going to talk. Tell the police everything. Every last detail."

Connie whimpered. "You killed Vera?"

Marisol turned back to her friend and stared at her for a long beat. From the corner of her eye, Josie saw Marisol's hands disappear into her jacket pockets again.

"Marisol, stop!" Gretchen cried, but it was too late.

Her right hand pulled a pistol from her pocket. Before she even pointed it at Connie, Josie had her own weapon unholstered and aimed at Marisol's chest. Gretchen stepped up beside Josie. She, too, had her weapon trained on Marisol.

"Stop," Josie told her. "Don't move."

Marisol took a single half-step toward Connie and pressed the barrel of the gun into Connie's forehead. Connie's voice was high and squeaky, almost incredulous, as if what was happening wasn't real. "Mar, stop! Do you even know how to use that thing?"

Marisol nudged Connie's head with the barrel of the gun. "I do. Guess who taught me? My loving husband. Ironic, isn't it? He wanted me to be able to defend myself at home while he was traveling. I hoped one day I'd be able to use it on him, and I did."

She'd also intended to kill Connie when she brought her out here, Josie realized.

When Marisol didn't lower the gun, Connie cried, "Mar, what are you doing?"

Gretchen said, "Marisol, calm down. Put your weapon down. There's no need for this."

Marisol rolled her eyes. "No need for this? You're the police. I just told you everything. You think I'm just going to let you slap some cuffs on me and march me to jail?"

Josie said, "You're outgunned."

Marisol laughed and needled Connie's skin with the gun barrel. "Oh really? You think one of you can shoot me before I kill Connie? Isn't that a whole thing with cops? Aren't you supposed to preserve life or something? I've got a hostage. Don't you have to negotiate with me?"

"We can talk," Josie told her. "But not like this."

A full-body shudder engulfed Connie's body. Her face was so pale it looked translucent. She said, "She's going to kill me. If she killed Vera and Kurt, she'll kill me."

Marisol didn't deny it.

In her periphery, Josie saw Gretchen inching closer to Connie. She tried to keep Marisol's attention on her. "Killing Kurt was a lot easier than killing Vera though, wasn't it?"

Marisol stared at Josie with narrowed eyes.

Gretchen stepped closer to Connie.

Josie kept talking. "Did Kurt lie for you? He was your alibi for Vera's murder. Did he know you had killed her?"

Marisol shook her head. "I told him I was going for a run that morning. He had no clue. Then someone from the police called to 'verify' my alibi. He said I was home because he assumed I'd just taken a jog right here in the neighborhood but when he got the call about coming to the station to talk about Beverly and Vera Urban, he knew something was up. That's what started our argument."

"The one that led to Kurt's death?" Josie asked.

"Yes. He beat me until I told him everything. I tried to tell him it was going to be okay because Vera was finally gone. I killed her so the whole thing would go away."

"How could you do it?" Connie whined. "How could you kill her?"

"Shut up!" Marisol hollered.

Connie blanched, shrinking back toward the tree, slouching down a little. Gretchen was almost on top of her, even though her gun was still pointed at Marisol. Josie felt a tiny wave of relief that for a moment, the barrel of the gun wasn't on Connie's head. Still, she whimpered. "Vera was your friend! How could you?"

"Friends keep secrets, Con," Marisol shot back. "Vera wasn't a true friend. After all I did for her, she wasn't going to keep my secrets. Just like you."

CHAPTER FORTY-NINE

Everything seemed to slow down, the seconds clicking coldly by, like the blinking of an eye. *Blink.* Marisol's finger depressed the trigger. *Blink.* The concussive boom of a gunshot shook the air around them. *Blink.* Gretchen lunged toward Connie. *Blink.* Josie fired at Marisol. *Blink.* Another crack blistered through the air. *Blink.* Gretchen and Connie went down hard on the ground. *Blink.* The world fell out from beneath them.

It took another blink for Josie to realize what had happened. She was falling. Then water engulfed her. Sludge and tree roots slid down onto her head. Her mouth opened, only to take in soil and thick, grimy water.

Landslide.

Her limbs fought to find the surface. She opened her eyes but there was only blackness all around her. The water was thick with dirt, making it nearly impossible to move through it or even to breathe. More weight fell onto her head. That has to be up, a voice in her head told her. The surface. She kicked and punched through the sludge. Something latched onto her hand and pulled. Striving toward it, she kicked harder. Finally, her head broke the surface. Hacking, she reached her fingers into her mouth and tried to clear it of the debris from the landslide. The dirt was gritty in her teeth. Clearing her eyes, she looked around. Neck-deep in the dirty water stood Connie.

"Thank you," Josie told her. Frantically, she panned the area. The entire ledge had fallen into the moat. The trees behind it were now horizontal, hanging above their heads.

"We have to get out of here," Josie told Connie. She took the woman's hand and together, they fought their way further out into the water where the muck dissipated and their limbs could move more freely. As they moved away from Quail Hollow and toward the adjacent neighborhood, the floodwater grew deeper and colder. On the tips of her toes, Josie could just keep her chin out of the water.

"Have you seen Gretchen?" Josie asked. "My colleague?"

Connie shook her head.

Josie looked around again. A loud, eerie creaking sound filled the air, and the trees slowly began to upend into the moat.

Where was Gretchen?

Please don't be dead, Josie prayed.

Josie turned as she heard splashing behind her. Marisol swam away from them, toward the houses in the distance. They were at least a mile away. Josie didn't know how strong a swimmer Marisol was, but she wasn't letting her get away.

"Stay here," Josie told Connie. "Look for my friend."

With long, even strokes, Josie swam after Marisol. "Stop!" Josie shouted.

Marisol paused when Josie was within a foot of her. She turned and flew at Josie. Josie tried to balance on her toes to keep her head above the water. Throwing her hands up, she attempted to block Marisol, but she slid her arms through Josie's and wrapped her fingers around Josie's throat, squeezing. Josie thrashed against her and fell backward into the water. Her fingers worked at Marisol's hands, trying to pry them loose as Marisol pushed her and held her beneath the water. Josie floundered until her feet found purchase and she tried to push up, to break the water's surface and find air, but Marisol held her firmly under the water. Josie's lungs burned. She abandoned her efforts to loosen Marisol's grip on her throat and instead threw her fists, trying to find some part of Marisol's body. When that didn't work, she went back to work on Marisol's death grip, scrabbling to find Marisol's fingers. She was beginning to black out when she felt a long fingernail. She snapped it back and Marisol's grip loosened just enough for Josie to push away.

Swatting Marisol's hands away, Josie's head punched up above the water and she gulped air. She got one deep inhale before Marisol was on her again, screaming, her hands grabbing at Josie's clothes, her arms, her throat, her hair. Josie wanted to punch her, to subdue her, but in the water, all of her training was useless. They thrashed and flopped, locked in battle with Marisol trying to hold Josie under the water long enough to kill her and Josie fighting to get air in her lungs long enough to fight Marisol off. How was this woman so strong?

Desperation, Josie thought. This was the pure adrenaline of a woman desperate to keep her secrets, to escape her past. Josie knew a thing or two about wanting to escape the past. With renewed vigor, her arms and legs surged, as she twisted out of Marisol's grip and landed a solid kick to her ribs. As Josie sucked in more air, she was dimly aware of noises around them. Someone shouting, and some other noise. A hum of some kind.

Josie paddled away from Marisol, taking the few precious seconds she had while Marisol recovered from the kick to her ribs. She needed to regroup. She'd always been a strong swimmer, but the tussle had taken a lot out of her. But again, Marisol's adrenaline drove her. She caught up with Josie and gripped one of her legs, pulling her back under the water. Josie kicked up and out of her grasp, breaking the surface again, coughing so violently that a devastating streak of pain seared across her chest. Then Marisol was pulling her back down beneath the water. She flailed again and her vision grayed.

Then, suddenly, she was free. She turned back to see Gretchen, a vision in mud, holding a fistful of Marisol's hair. Profound relief streaked through Josie's entire body. Marisol still thrashed, trying to get away from Gretchen. Josie drew closer to help Gretchen get her under control when something bumped against the back of her head. She turned to see the bright red of a rescue boat. Paddling in place, she wiped strands of her hair from her face. A hand reached down to her. "Come on," said a familiar voice.

Josie looked up to see Sawyer Hayes. When she didn't take his hand, he shook it at her. "Take my hand," he said. "Get in."

She let him pull her in and once on the floor of the boat, her body snapped in on itself, trying to expel the last of the dirt and water she'd breathed in. Through watery eyes, she saw Gretchen lose her grip on a wild Marisol Dutton. Marisol disappeared beneath the water. The boat operator was already getting close to Gretchen. Hayes lifted her into the boat. Beside Josie, Gretchen's body was racked with spasms as she, too, coughed and hacked. Finally, they both collapsed against the inside of the boat. Josie looked down to see a streak of blood soaking through her jeans. She'd definitely popped the stitches in her leg this time. Along the shoreline, where the trees had fallen, Connie held fast to a large branch. Beyond her, on firm land, her little dog ran back and forth, barking. The boat steered in Connie's direction and picked her up.

"Marisol," Josie gasped. "Where is she?"

Sawyer shook his head. "I don't know. She went under."

"We have to get her."

"I just watched her try to kill you."

"That doesn't matter," Josie said. "I—"

He held up a hand to silence her. He unsnapped his helmet, took it off and threw it onto the floor of the boat. "I know," he said. "You don't leave anyone behind. Dead or alive."

Then he jumped into the water.

CHAPTER FIFTY

Josie stood in front of Ray's headstone watching the cemetery staff prepare to lower Beverly Urban's coffin into the plot next to his. Glancing behind her, Josie lifted a hand and waved to the people assembled there. None of them were related to her but all of them were family. Noah, Lisette, Misty, Gretchen, Mettner, Chief Chitwood, and even Amber Watts had shown up—all to pay their respects to Beverly and Vera Urban. Once Sawyer had rescued Marisol from the moat, he'd revived her with CPR. She'd spent a few days in the hospital before turning herself in to police at the direction of her attorney. The details of the plea bargain she was after were still being worked out between her lawyer and the District Attorney but in the meantime, she'd agreed to pay all funeral arrangements for both Beverly and Vera. Josie had chosen the plots and luckily, there were two available right beside Ray.

Beverly would finally get what she wanted. In death she'd be with the boy she'd pined after for all of eternity. She'd have a proper burial and Josie would care for her grave just as she cared for Ray's. Vera had been buried an hour earlier and with both women being interred on the same day, only a few feet apart, Josie had chosen to have a small ceremony.

One of the workers gave a wave to indicate that the mourners should pay their final respects and the others stepped up beside Josie. Misty had brought flowers and she handed them out to each person. They each took a moment to place one on top of Beverly's coffin before walking off toward their vehicles. Josie and Noah hung back, watching as Gretchen and Chief Chitwood assisted Lisette and Mettner held Amber's elbow each time her heels sank into the grass.

Josie felt a tickle at the back of her neck. She turned and saw her twin sister, Trinity, several yards away. Unable to suppress her grin, Josie broke away from the funeral party and jogged over to her, throwing her arms around her sister.

"Whoa," Trinity said into Josie's hair. "I missed you too."

Josie let go and stepped back. They looked each other up and down. Trinity said, "Are we wearing the same little black dress?"

Josie laughed. "Looks that way. What are you doing here?"

Trinity linked her arm with Josie's. "I thought you needed me."

Josie raised a brow. "No, that's not it."

Now Trinity laughed. "Okay, that's not it. I have news. It looks like I'm going to get my own network show."

"Trinity, that's incredible! Congratulations, I'm so happy for you."

"We should celebrate," said Noah, walking up to them.

"He's right," Josie said. "Can you stay in town for a day or two?"

"To celebrate me?" Trinity asked. "Of course!"

She winked and headed off to say hello to Lisette.

Noah stepped up beside Josie and slid his hand into hers. They watched as Trinity was received by Lisette, Misty, and their colleagues like an old friend. Noah said, "Are you okay? Don't tell me you're fine. You always say that."

Josie smiled. "I'm working on it. It's better now that Trinity is here."

Noah leaned over and kissed her. "That's the first honest answer you've ever given to that question."

Josie watched Trinity and Gretchen help Lisette navigate her walker through the headstones. "Noah, how would you feel about inviting my grandmother and Sawyer to dinner?"

He bobbed his head, as if considering this. "Only if you can get Misty to cook."

She elbowed him. "I'm serious."

He smiled. "I think that would be a good start. The foundation of something new."

A LETTER FROM LISA

Thank you so much for choosing to read *Save Her Soul*. If you enjoyed it and want to keep up to date with all my latest releases, just sign up at the following link. Your email address will never be shared, and you can unsubscribe at any time.

www.bookouture.com/lisa-regan

I love hearing from readers. You can get in touch with me through any of the social media outlets below, including my website and Goodreads page. Also, if you are up for it, I'd really appreciate it if you'd leave a review and perhaps recommend *Save Her Soul* to other readers. Reviews and word-of-mouth recommendations go a long way in helping readers discover my books for the first time. As always, thank you so much for your support. It means the world to me. I can't wait to hear from you, and I hope to see you next time!

Thanks,
Lisa Regan

LisaReganCrimeAuthor

@LisalRegan

www.lisaregan.com

ACKNOWLEDGMENTS

I must thank my readers, first and foremost. Your passion for this series makes every word worth writing. You make this journey the most fun I've ever had in my life. I love writing Josie stories for you, and I hope you'll continue on her journey with me. Thank you, as always, to my husband Fred and daughter Morgan for your support and patience. Thank you for going so many hours without my attention while my head is in Denton. Thank you to my first readers: Dana Mason, Katie Mettner, Nancy S. Thompson, Maureen Downey, and Torese Hummel. Thank you to my Entrada readers. Thank you to Matty Dalrymple and Jane Kelly. This book would not have gotten written without our writing sprints and all of your brilliant suggestions! Thank you to Cindy Doty for your proofreading help! Thank you to all of the usual suspects for your unwavering support and love and for always spreading the word—you know who you are! I'd also like to thank all the fabulous bloggers and reviewers who continue to read and spread the word about Josie Quinn books. Your passion for this series is inspiring!

Thank you so very much to Sgt. Jason Jay, as always, for answering all my law-enforcement questions during a pandemic! You are truly an amazing human being. Thank you to Michelle Mordan for answering many of my questions related to emergency services. Thank you to my cousin, John Conlen, for all the swiftwater rescue information which was invaluable. Thank you to John Matz, Emergency Manager of Schuylkill County for spending your Saturday morning during a pandemic answering all of my questions. Your generosity astounds me!

Thank you to Noelle Holten, Kim Nash, and the entire team at Bookouture for making life feel normal while the world is in crisis and helping to keep my spirits up as well as all the behind-the-scenes publicist things you do so wonderfully well. Last but certainly not least, thank you to the incomparable Jessie Botterill for finding all the hidden gems in this book that I couldn't see. Thank you for pulling work out of me that I didn't think was possible—especially during a pandemic. You're an amazing editor and a wonderful human being, and I would not want to do this with anyone but you!